Perishing Waste

Perishing Waste

Ian Miller

RESOURCE *Publications* · Eugene, Oregon

PERISHING WASTE

Resource Publications
An Imprint of Wipf and Stock Publishers
199 W. 8th Ave., Suite 3
Eugene, OR 97401

www.wipfandstock.com

PAPERBACK ISBN: 978-1-6667-3723-3
HARDCOVER ISBN: 978-1-6667-9647-6
EBOOK ISBN: 978-1-6667-9648-3

03/23/22

This is a work of fiction. The events described are imaginary, the settings are fictitious and not intended to represent specific places or living persons.

Map by Sean Tromp (www.seantromp.myportfolio.com)

To Christine, my greatest encourager

Contents

Acknowledgements

Annelie Miller, Li Feng—linguistic advisors

Chris Deller—science advisor

Richard Freeman—tech advisor

Christine Miller, Ian Hunter, Chris Deller, Phil Miller—readers

Sean Tromp—artistic inspiration

New World
Colony, Zhinu

CRASHED
ALIEN
SPACESHIP

GRAVIMETRIC
DISCRIMINATOR

SUBSTATION

XIN BEIJING

3RD FLEET
BIVOUAC

BEIJING
CHONGSHENG

GUI DIFANG

1

Shrouds of Mystery

Y ENKO WAS SELDOM NERVOUS, but he was now. The holographic
image above his telecommunicator was none other than Zhou Li
Qiang, the Director of the Astronomical Union based in Xianggang.

"Professor Macpherson," the Director said, "we need your expertise
in the field of Space-Time Kinematics."

"My expertise?"

"Yes . . . Professor, what do you know of the Zhinu Project?"

The Zhinu Project. Yenko's pulse quickened at the mention of the
name.

"Only what everyone knows," Yenko replied honestly. "The New
World Colony captured my imagination as a boy. It's why I pursued the
study of Astrophysics. But I don't know anything of its recent history. It's
all classified. I've tried many times to investigate, but I've been blocked
on every attempt."

"If you are willing to help me, your attempts shall be blocked no
longer," Li Qiang assured. "I have a Low Orbiter on standby to bring you
to Xianggang."

"A Low Orbiter?" Yenko whispered. On standby? To bring him to
Xianggang? "I don't understand. Space-Time Kinematics?"

"I can tell you no more at this stage, Professor," the Director said. "Are you willing to help?"

"Help? Yes . . . Yes, of course! A Low Orbiter? I don't understand."

"It can be in Aidingbao to collect you before your afternoon is out."

Normally, Yenko would be upset by someone calling his city Aidingbao. Edinburgh was its name in the Scot Province. But there was no place for offence when talking to such a high ranking official. Especially when a Low Orbiter was set aside to fly him halfway across the world to Xianggang. And it would only be a few short hours before he would learn the answers to one of the greatest mysteries of his time.

Zhinu. The New World Colony.

———◄◦►———

Macpherson Yenko surveyed the conference room. Large, floor to ceiling windows looked out over an impressive courtyard garden, beyond which he could see the skyline of Beijing. Only three days after landing in Xianggang, he had found himself on another flight to the Zhongguo Xin Shijie capital. Secrecy had cloaked every meeting, shrouded every conversation. Government Agents were everywhere. On more than one occasion, he had wondered if there was an international crisis going on that the world at large was unaware of.

Signatures were demanded of him agreeing to lengthy non-disclosure agreements, swearing him to absolute silence. But for the hope of discovering what had become of the New World Colony on Zhinu, Yenko would have walked away without signing a thing. He was, when all was said and done, a citizen of the Scot Province, not the global Zhongwen superpower, and did not respect their dominance over the affairs and culture of so much of the world. Security debriefings, interrogations more like, did nothing to allay his growing sense of unease. And nothing much at all had been said of Zhinu.

Seated now at a large, polished oak table with thirty other men and women, Yenko knew he was about to get some answers. Answers that would explain why he was there and what this all had to do with Zhinu. Some of those about him, he knew personally, others only by sight from global news reports. There were several provincial leaders of both the Qin One World Dynasty and the India Unity Party, the two major world governments sitting together around the one table. Yenko recognized some of his academic contemporaries, leading engineers, and theoretical physicists. Six men were obviously military officials. From both nations.

All stood to their feet in respect as Zhou Li Qiang, the Director of the Astronomical Union, entered the room, escorted by a small entourage of assistants, and took the head of the table.

"Thank you for your attendance at this gathering," he began.

"Thank you for your attendance," Yenko repeated silently. Who would be audacious enough to reject the invitation? Given the military presence in the room, he suspected that it would have been impossible to turn it down even if someone had wanted to. But like him, Yenko knew that none of those around the table would forfeit the opportunity to learn, at long last, the reason for the silence that shrouded the Earth colony on Zhinu.

Li Qiang continued. "For different reasons, you all have a seat at this table today. Allow me to get right to the point. We are soon to launch a Third Fleet to the New World Colony." There was an audible, involuntary inhalation of air around the room. "But it will not be an easy venture. We are not at all sure of what is happening there. I have invited our leading Astrophysicist, Li Feng Mian, to give the background. The information you are about to learn has been withheld from the global media. I remind you all that you have signed comprehensive NDAs. What you hear today is classified Top Secret."

A demure woman, perhaps in her late thirties, immaculately dressed in a white blouse and black suit, stood to her feet. Studying the room, she nodded in acknowledgement of many of the faces. Yenko knew of her, though not personally; she was a respected figure amongst the astrophysics community.

Confidently, she began her address as a panoramic video of a reasonably sized city played on the wall behind her. Towers of ten stories or more dotted the inner business precinct. About the city, large rural tracts boasted plantations of orchards and extensive grain crops.

Yenko's heart raced in anticipation as he recognized the cityscape before him. It was the thriving heart of the Earth colony established on a planet circling the star, Zhinu, twenty-five light years away. In his undergraduate studies, he had taken part in collaborative studies with the university that had been established in Xin Beijing, the city that now panned in video form across the wall in front of him. Those studies had considerably advanced scientific understanding of Astrophysics, Space-Time Kinematics and Xeno-Biosphere Technologies.

"You are all familiar," Feng Mian began, "with the New World Colony, first settled in 2235. The video you are now seeing has been adapted from documentary footage taken in Shi Yue, 2347."

"October, 2347," Yenko wondered silently. Not long before the information blackout.

"It is one of the last communications received from the colony. We have heard nothing of them since then and for the best part of a decade, we have suppressed reports until we can determine what has happened and what the implications are, if any, to our future plans for the ongoing colonization of Zhinu and beyond. We have sent probe after probe, but all we can discover is that the city is slowly sliding into decay. What you are about to see is Xin Beijing as it is today."

A series of short video clips, taken from high altitude, told a shocking story of the New World Colony. The assembled gathering held its collective breath. Together, the videos spoke of a city lying in collapse, as if there had been a war or an earthquake or some other natural disaster. A deserted, decaying ruin, bit by bit being reclaimed by the surrounding landscape.

"No one walks its streets. There is no industry. We have witnessed life in the rural lands, but the farming communities do not have the technology of the city and we have no way of communicating with them. They are likely not even aware that our probes regularly spy on them from orbit.

"Five years ago, a joint taskforce was convened, drawing together senior political leaders from both global nations. Zhongguo Xin Shijie and Bhaarat Ekata sat side by side because the implications affect all.

"We must know what has happened. The population of Xin Beijing and its surrounding communities at the last census was 21,354. To the best of our estimations, fewer than fifteen hundred remain in three small farming settlements. They appear to go about their business, but never once have we observed them within the ruins of Xin Beijing.

"It is of international importance, and both Zhongguo and Bhaarat have put aside old tensions; they make little sense in the face of our need. As we speak, a third interstellar craft is being constructed in the Tiangong Space Station. It is only two years from completion, so now is the time to escalate preparation for the mission.

"This is no small news we are bringing to you. Preparations are well underway in assembling the Third Fleet that will join the survivors on Zhinu."

Those around the table sat in silence at the shocking realization. Something dreadful had happened to Zhinu and Earth's global leaders were mounting a Third Fleet to aid the outlying colony.

Li Qiang rose again to his feet. Bowing slightly, Li Feng Mian resumed hers.

"Those who are chosen," the Director began, "will need skills that may not have been required in previous missions. We do not know what dangers await them, so we intend to pick an army of one thousand from our best forces. We will need a large team of engineers, physicists, and medical experts. Yet, we may not send too many. The survivors on Zhinu will be hard pressed to sustain too great an increase in population without infrastructure support, particularly food production. Difficult decisions must be made.

"You have been especially selected for this initial meeting. Each of you are leaders in your respective spheres. Not all of you will be willing to make the journey to Zhinu, but each of you is being asked to search your heart. It will come at no small cost. For now, you are sworn to absolute secrecy. You may not converse with your loved ones yet.

"If you decide to accept the offer to join the expedition, you will resign your current occupation immediately. Training will be rigorous. There is much you will need to know that you currently do not. And you will all be trained in the martial arts and weaponry because we do not know what you will face.

"Effective as of right now, you are under lockdown. A communications dead zone has been established."

The woman sitting beside Yenko fingered her telecommunicator, checking reception. Noticing that he was watching her out of the corner of his eye, she tilted the screen almost imperceptibly to show him the truth of the Director's claim.

"There will be further debriefings tomorrow and the following day with plenty of opportunity for you to ask whatever questions you have. At the end of the week, you will be asked if you will commit to the mission. We do not intend to give you a long time to consider your response. The need of Zhinu is upon us.

"If you do not accept, you need not fear losing face. But you will necessarily commit to the secrecy of the project, no matter what. You are dismissed."

———◁◦▷———

Yenko was lost in thought. Two days of debriefings had not really answered his questions, despite the Director's assurance. Stepping from the main entrance of the conference building, he started down the marble stairs. A group of soldiers, dressed in black as if they were ready for military operations, made little attempt to clear a space for him to negotiate. It was not a comfortable encounter, but Yenko was used to the stares and suspicions cast upon him from outsiders.

Outsiders. That is how he saw them. But in truth, he was the outsider. His height at six foot four and red hair set him apart.

One soldier, in particular, seemed to deliberately make it difficult for Yenko to pass.

"*Yang guizi*," the soldier muttered, loud enough to provoke a response.

Yenko stopped and looked the man squarely in the eye. "If I was a devil," he replied confidently in his thick Scottish accent, "I would not have been asked to take part in this mission."

At the boldness of the reply, the soldier stood a little more alert, hoping for a physical confrontation, one that he knew he would have the upper hand in. "You were not their first choice," the soldier said. "This is no place for people like you. You don't belong."

Yenko was used to the taunts. In the past, he had taken the bait far too many times, and it had caused him an amount of grief. The court systems were not always impartial when it came to cases involving separatists. Apparently, there was no room for them in the modern world. But he was now in his mid-thirties. He had learned wisdom the hard way. Ignoring the jibe, he walked past the group.

It was true, though; he was not the mission leaders' first choice. That had become clear in the briefings. They needed an expert in the field of Space-Time Kinematics. Two other candidates had been considered in preference to him, but before the meetings could be called, one of them was arrested on corruption charges and faced legal proceedings that would likely go on for many years. The evidence of her guilt was compelling, and it was probable that she would face an extended time in prison. The other was a much younger scientist, an up-and-coming protégé, currently studying in Xianggang University. He was certainly brilliant, but Yenko had far greater credentials. From the gossip he had picked up over the last two days, there had been a considerable argument concerning the two of them. There were those on the selection committee who would rather a less qualified candidate than a decorated separatist. But in the end, he had been chosen, and that had led to the conversation a week ago with the Director of the Astronomical Union, Zhou Li Qiang.

He had not decided yet whether he was going to accept the challenge set before him. It would mean giving up all that he knew. His beloved Scotland. His friends.

He had no family ties, as such, to hold him back, however. When he was a small boy, a political uprising provoked a heavy-handed response from the ruling Zhongguo Xin Shijie regime. The little village in which he lived was made an example of for all those who would challenge the legitimacy of the largest of the two world powers. Yenko was orphaned in the conflict that followed.

Yet having no family only made the decision more complicated. Would it be an insult to his father's house if he left the Scot Province and took a place in the mission to Zhinu? But it was an honor that such a significant offer was being made to him. The Director had said that no one would lose face if they refused to go, but that was not strictly true for a separatist. His rejection of the invitation might be construed as the choice of a coward. He would be little better than a *diu lian*, one who had discarded his face.

Above everything else was one compelling vision. Zhinu. His boyhood dream of freedom, family, and peace. A new world. A new start. A new dream. He was being offered the chance to be a part of the one thing that had captivated his imagination for as long as he could remember.

There were many things that worried him, though.

The thought of cryostasis was not appealing. He knew that technology had made it a safe form of space travel, but he would be asleep for four decades. When he would finally awake, on approach to Zhinu, Earth would have moved on. He would no longer be a leader in his field. Of course, he was smart enough to bring himself up to speed with advancements in theory. Communication with Earth was quick, and he would have access to any scientific developments he had not taken part in. But there was an element of professional pride that he would have to sacrifice. He himself would not be part of those developments. By the time he woke up, they would be history.

And he did not much like the thought of trusting himself to the artificial intelligence of the interstellar spacecraft. There were so many things that could go wrong, and his life would be in the hands of micro-circuits and molecular memory algorithms. Part of his cultural identity as a separatist would be threatened by such an abandonment to technology.

On top of everything else, he would have to see out the rest of his days amongst the international community. It would be unlikely that many separatists would be offered a place in the mission, and less likely that they would be from the Scot Province.

A handful of Scots had been part of the First Fleet back in 2195. It was celebrated with mixed feeling amongst his people. Perhaps some of their descendants remained. This was of particular appeal, because Yenko's great, great, great granduncle, Robert Macpherson, had been a member of the brave explorers who boarded the *Zhinu Hope* on its perilous journey in and out of warped space-time.

Yenko wondered if he had relatives amongst the survivors of the New World Colony. Robert Macpherson. Back in those days, the Scottish tradition was for family names to be given last. That all eventually began to change following the global wars of the mid-twenty-second century which saw the birth of the two world governments that now governed humanity. Zhongguo, then known as China, ruled over the ancient nations of the Orient, North America, western Europe, Australia, and the Pacific. Most of the remaining world was taken over by Bhaarat, India. English remained as the global lingua franca, though many Chinese and Indian expressions had made their way into popular speech.

Night fell, but Yenko could not see Zhinu in the cloudy sky. His thoughts were of his family. Some of them may yet be up there, lost in the mysterious silence of the New World Colony. Robert Macpherson had married on Zhinu. Yenko knew that much, but he knew nothing of Robert's descendants, if indeed he had any. Perhaps family honor demanded that he join the mission and in so doing help uncover what had become of the Macpherson line. He would sleep on it.

———◄○►———

Around an artificial lake in the Training Complex, a group of thirty men and women ran in ordered ranks. Although they were decked out in the close-fitting leather uniforms of the Zhongguo army, they were not, for the most part, military. A solitary red head in the center of the group jogged comfortably along with the troop.

"Delta Squad, dismissed," shouted the woman at the front.

The training regime of the last two years had been nothing short of brutal. At first, Yenko had wondered whether he had made the right decision in accepting the offer of volunteering for the Zhinu Mission. Though he was never overweight, his life had been one of academic research and experimentation. But the program demanded a high level of personal physical fitness. No one knew what they would face when they arrived in Zhinu. All that was known was that Xin Beijing was in ruins. There had been a catastrophe, but what? Was there a present threat to the remaining inhabitants of Zhinu, those living in the remote farming communities, far from the decaying capital? What would this Third Fleet step into?

In the end, only twelve hundred men and women had been chosen to take part in the daring project. Half of these were professional, elite military personnel. The rest consisted chiefly of scientists, engineers, construction workers, and paramedics. These, however, had to train alongside the elite forces. It was a grueling two years of study and physical application.

Delta Squadron, Yenko's assigned detail, had fifteen military commanders attached to it. From the way they trained, Yenko thought they were more assassins than soldiers. They were deadly accurate with plasma weaponry, and frighteningly efficient in hand-to-hand combat. On the many occasions that he had to train alongside one of these, they did not pull any of their punches or well-placed kicks.

———◄◦►———

The first year of training had been the hardest and more than once, Yenko's position amongst the volunteer company was put into jeopardy . . .

"You fight well for a *yang guizi*," Commander Huang Li Jie reluctantly admitted as he and Yenko shaped up yet again for unarmed combat drill. "But you leave your lower ribs unguarded." And with that, he planted his heavy boot into Yenko's chest.

Involuntarily, Yenko's lungs expended their reserves as he dropped to his knees. Darkness followed as Li Jie aimed a second kick to the side of his head. When at last he came to his senses, he was once again in the infirmary of the base hospital. It was his third trip in as many months. The Commander seemed hellbent on ensuring the separatist would not be fit for travel on their mission.

Li Jie's targeting of him only served to settle Yenko's resolve, however. He had grown up on the streets of a city at war with the world about it. He had lost both parents and an older brother to those conflicts and had been hardened to bloody fights. It would take more than a Commander's boot and fist to keep him from his chosen path.

By the end of that first year, Yenko had found himself in the base hospital no fewer than seven times. The aggressive assaults and full body contact had a way of toughening him, however, and it effectively strengthened his defensive technique.

Squaring up against his training partner yet again, he held the disdaining stare with his own.

"You don't know when to give up, do you?" the Commander said.

"You overestimate your ability," Yenko replied and struck a roundhouse kick followed by a backhand fist to Li Jie's chin. It got past his defenses, and the Commander stepped back to reassess his strategy.

With a flurry of front snap kicks, the Commander forced Yenko back into a slow retreat. Feigning a front kick to the head, Li Jie spun about and planted the heel of his boot into Yenko's chest. The pain was overwhelming and Yenko staggered backwards. Wincing, he stood erect and braced himself for the second volley of punches and kicks.

A well-aimed punch took Yenko by surprise as it slammed just below his throat. He choked and gagged but did not drop his guard. And despite the staggering pain he was in, he retaliated with a rotating progression of kicks and punches. This time, the Commander was forced backward. But grabbing Yenko by the arm and shoulder, he used the momentum of his separatist opponent, and rolled backwards onto the ground, flipping Yenko casually above his head.

The Scot sprawled on his back as Li Jie pounced on him.

"You don't quit, do you?" the Commander said. "I think I'm beginning to like you, *yang guizi.*"

The following day began with what was to be a routine parachute drop in preparation against any unforeseen difficulties when landing on Zhinu. It proved to be a day that changed everything between the two men.

"Squadron Leaders, assemble your troops." The Commanding Officer, Mannat Ahuja, a Bhaarateey Commodore, was personally overseeing the day's training schedule and had called her leaders together for the morning debrief. "We do not know what we will face when we arrive at Zhinu. If an enemy is at large and is responsible for the destruction of the colony, we have seen nothing of them. But that does not mean they are not there. As soon as we enter orbit, we may come under attack ourselves. We must prepare for the possibility that our landing craft will be fired upon.

"Your troops have been trained in parachuting, and they will think that today is another routine drop. But it will not be. Your pilots will simulate an in-air catastrophe and your troops will be put to the test."

Large troop carriers conveyed eight squadrons each to fifteen thousand feet, where they were to open their rear cargo doors. The planes took off together and set out for different destinations, far from each other.

At twelve thousand feet, the pilot's voice yelled over the intercom of Yenko's plane.

"Troops, fasten restraints! I'm getting unusual instrument readings. Something's not right."

As one, the company ensured they were safely harnessed into their positions. Yenko looked about him. No one seemed concerned, but everyone was alert. Suddenly, the plane pitched and yawed. For a moment, Yenko was weightless and then slumped heavily into his seat and lurched from side to side.

The cargo door at the rear of the plane, designed to receive large military vehicles, crashed violently open as the plane pitched crazily to one side.

"Get out, she's going down!" the pilot screamed over the intercom. "I've lost all controls. Pilot ejecting." The sudden blast of air from the cockpit told of the pilot's escape as the plane reeled like a broken toy plummeting through the air.

Squadron Leaders barked their orders. "This is what we've trained for, people. Keep your heads. We're jumping earlier than expected. Go now!"

The exit was orderly enough amidst the wild pitching of the plane, but to Yenko, who fought to maintain his balance despite being hooked onto the belay line, it seemed to take forever. Squadron after squadron dived out of the open cargo door to safety. Crashes and the sound of metal ripping from the plane's fuselage fought with the noise of the engines for dominance as the troops took to freefall.

Delta Squadron was the last to jump, Yenko and his Zhongwen training partner, Li Jie, at the rear. They unhooked their restraining lines to make their exit. Almost at the same instant, the plane lurched violently to one side into a barrel roll. The last of the squadron stumbled into their dive. But Li Jie had been thrown backwards, hitting his head dangerously hard on an unforgiving internal structural support. Yenko saw the blood pouring over the Commander's face as the troop carrier spun about, and the man slid headfirst out the cargo hatch.

"Li Jie!" Yenko screamed and dived after him, the last to jump from the troop carrier.

The air was filled with the deployed parachutes of his company. Yenko searched the air below for signs that Huang had recovered. There, he saw the Commander tumbling recklessly, still unconscious. Li Jie was in trouble and falling to his death. High above now, the plane ceased its wild bucking and levelled off, circling round to make a routine landing.

The incongruity of the plane's sudden flight correction was noticed by many of the parachutists, but Yenko was intent on only one object, now plummeting toward the unforgiving earth. Yenko was new to skydiving, but he knew that he was the Commander's only hope. Using everything he had learned, he pencil-dropped, increasing in speed. Huang came closer.

It took some effort, but eventually Yenko was able to deploy the Commander's ripcord. The slumped body appeared to jerk upwards as its parachute filled with air. Yenko did the same with his own and kept as close as possible to assist when his partner landed.

Moments later, Yenko was throwing off his harness and running to where the Commander was descending, calling for medics as he did so. Li Jie's landing was not pretty, but it did not need to be; the Commander survived the fall, crashing heavily onto the ground.

That afternoon, Li Jie was released from hospital. He had suffered a severe concussion but would not remain under observation for more than two hours after he came to. He found Yenko at a bar having a drink with a half dozen of Delta Squadron's military members. They had a newfound respect for the Scot scientist after the story had circulated around the base.

"*Yang guizi*," Li Jie said, calling for a drink for himself, "I heard what you did."

Yenko studied the soldier. He was strong, confident, and no stranger to battle. If he was not such a racist, Yenko thought he could like him. Despite having been put into hospital so many times by him.

Li Jie took a long, slow draught from his glass, staring hard at the redhaired Scot as if he had never seen anyone like him before. At length, something seemed to snap within him. Exhaling loudly, he downed the rest of the drink, and pushed the glass towards the barkeeper, raising a finger to order another. Before the drink could be poured, however, he shook his head and raised two fingers. As these were placed before him, he pushed one towards Yenko.

"I cheated death today because of you, Macpherson," he said solemnly. "You've only been training a year, but already you're a better soldier than half the regular army."

All eyes were intent on the two men, who just sat there, looking at each other, drinks half raised as if uncertain of their next move. At length, Li Jie raised his glass in honor of Yenko.

"You had my six today," he said. "You can count on me covering yours." And he downed the drink.

The significance of the military reference did not escape Yenko. He had made a comrade-in-arms; he could count on the Commander no matter what conflict they might step into on Zhinu. Li Jie would have his back. The assembled soldiers motioned their approval and yet another round of drinks was ordered.

It was the beginning of a friendship none would have predicted.

—◦—

Now, their two years of training were coming to an end. Delta Squadron trotted back to their quarters. The run had been hard. Yenko had changed. His training had steeled him to the mission. Rumor had it that in three weeks, he would be succumbing to the medical process that would put him into cryostasis. The simulation training for coming out of deep interstellar sleep had not at all been pleasant. Aftereffects of cryostasis were shocking, and on the first three trials, Yenko thought he was going to die. The body went through spasms and convulsions, alternating between sensations of freezing and boiling, disorientation that lasted days, nausea and uncontrolled emotional outbursts.

Along with all twelve hundred of the hand-picked company, he had not found the journey to mission readiness an easy one. But they were prepared at last. As much as they were going to be.

"Do all Scots sweat rivers like you?" Li Jie mocked. "*Yang guizi!*"

The term was derogatory, and when Huang Li Jie had first called him a foreign devil on the steps of the Conference Building two years earlier, he had meant it to offend. But he had grown to like the redheaded separatist from the land of glacial mountains and northern lights. *Yang guizi* had become a playful nickname.

Li Jie was a force to be reckoned with. Being assigned to train alongside Yenko in Delta Squadron, there had been a time when he had hoped that if he put Yenko into hospital often enough, it would dissuade the Scot separatist from the mission. But he had found that Yenko was made of stronger stuff. Li Jie had come to appreciate his ability to think on his feet, his quick response to threat, his cool head in the face of terrible pain.

And Yenko gave as good as he took. He had been as quick with the insults and delighted in belittling Li Jie in front of his peers when they studied the fundamentals of interstellar space travel.

With Yenko's rescue of the Commander in the simulated air crisis, however, a comradery between the two had been forged and they became inseparable friends.

"I may be a *yang guizi*, Li," Yenko replied, "but at least I have professional expertise for the mission. You *ban pingzi cu*."

Li laughed. It was the first time he had been called a half-empty bottle of vinegar. "Come on," Li Jie said. "We must get ready, or we will be denied another evening meal."

Later that night, as ten squadrons sat in the mess hall, not halfway through their main course, a score of reporters and photographers burst into the room and took position around the walls. Everyone stopped what they were doing, uncertain of what was about to unfold.

Within minutes, ten heavily armed Special Forces guards entered. En masse, everyone stood to their feet as none other than Wu Wang Shu, President of Zhongguo Xin Shijie, and Priyansh Chakrabarti, Prime Minister of Bhaarat Ekata, surrounded by their executive staffs, marched into the room.

The tension was palpable. It was one thing that Zhongwen and Bhaarateey nationals had trained alongside each other; they all knew they were part of an international venture. But to see the two world leaders together was momentous. The world was at peace, for sure, and had been for a long time, but the clash of cultures was very real and had fueled an ongoing unease in diplomatic relations.

After a brief, questioning glance between the two world leaders, Wu Wang Shu spoke first. She was a commanding figure on all the news reports, but in person, she was overpowering, carrying an air of absolute control and assurance. Her hair was cropped short and that only emphasized the piercing brown eyes that gave the impression they could see through every false motive.

"You may be seated," she said, an injunction not an offer. "You have all been in training for the past two years. The senior government officials of Zhongguo Xin Shijie have followed your progress closely. We fast approach the time of your departure and I have come to assure you that we have every prospect for the success of your mission. I have confidence you will discover what has become of the New World Colony in Xin Beijing. Whatever dangers you face, you will do so with honor and victory. I am proud to see so many Zhongwen faces. And I am proud to link hands with those of you who are Bhaarateey."

Wu Wang Shu's piercing eyes landed on Yenko. "And we join hands with the Provinces and are proud to stand alongside you." Yenko had never heard such a concession given from a President before. With the throng of reporters about, this would be heard in every home in the Scot Province.

"As a nation, we have built upon the foundation of cooperation and respect, and the legacy of our advancement of global prosperity and strength of reform is self-evident. You stand before us as the pride of our world and Zhongguo Xin Shijie salutes you. Our future dream of colonial expansion across the galaxy will be built, in part, on what we will learn through you, our elite. I stand here in pledge of all the mighty resources of our great nation that undergird your commission."

Gesturing to her counterpart, President Wu stepped back to allow the Prime Minister of Bhaarat Ekata, Priyansh Chakrabarti, to speak.

The Bhaarateey Prime Minister cut an equally imposing figure as his Zhongwen counterpart. He stood no more than five feet tall, and in that, he was shorter than the President beside him. But his golden, silk turban made him appear much taller. His white-grey beard gave him a look of supreme dignity, a sage of the nations.

Raising a finger to the air, he said, "Each one of us has the power to make change. Irrespective of our nationality, ethnic background, or cultural identity, if we join our power for change together, we can rescue the New World Colony in Zhinu. While you are on your long journey across the heavens, we will strive to learn all we may. We will increase our knowledge. We will apply all diligence to our studies and technological advancement. You will be our hands and feet. Together, as one body, we will restore what has been lost and the New World Colony will be but the first of a new era for the galaxy. Together, we will build a secure and prosperous future. Our prayers will be with you all. Enjoy your meal. When next you eat, the new world will be within your sight."

So that was it. A murmur echoed about the room as it slowly dawned on everyone what had just been announced. They would depart for Zhinu the very next day. Yenko turned in shock to Li Jie.

His soldier friend simply smiled. "How did a *yang guizi* like you get a ticket on this ride?"

It broke the air, and Yenko exhaled, not realizing he had been hold-ing his breath in frightened anticipation.

"You'll have my back, though, won't you?" Yenko asked. He was in no mood for joking.

A steel-cold reserve erased Li Jie's smile. "Always," he replied.

————◦————

Wu Yue 15, 2358. May 15. A day to be recorded in the history books.

Yenko's stomach turned within him. He had not eaten since the meal of the night before, having then begun a strict fast before the first stages of cryostasis were administered. But even if he had been allowed to eat, he would not have. Who could eat at such a time? He had slept little that night. Images of President Wu and Prime Minister Chakrabarti had played through his mind for hours afterward. Perhaps he had managed two or three hours of sleep. He did not know. Not that he supposed it mattered. He was about to get more sleep than nearly anyone in the history of mankind.

Circling in high orbit somewhere above them was the Tiangong Space Station. There, the recently completed *Zhinu Phoenix*, would be awaiting them. They had all studied in detail the layout of the interstellar ship that would be their cocoon for the next four decades. Cocoon. Or coffin.

Constructed around a central axle large enough to hold the mass of machinery, rockets, and equipment necessary for the long space voyage, sixteen great wheels slowly rotated in counter rotation to each other. Centripetal Gravity Rotators. These were designed to simulate gravity for the crew and passengers and housed the cryostatic chambers, short-term living quarters, and a vast network of control rooms.

The cryostasis would be performed on Earth. The artificial intelligence, affectionately named Nirani, that piloted the *Zhinu Phoenix* could revive the members of the Third Fleet but getting them into that state was another matter. Quite simply, the *Zhinu Phoenix* did not have room enough for the sophisticated facilities required to send a man or woman to sleep for forty years.

The Wuesthoff Medical Research Center, adjacent to the historical site of Cape Canaveral on the North American continent, was chosen to send the company into cryostatic suspension. It had seemed fitting that homage be paid to the ancient center of space exploration, and the nearby hospital was well equipped for the task at hand. The sunrise flight there that morning only took two hours. It must have caused a stir to see the string of Low Orbiters fly into the relatively obscure airport.

Yenko tried hard to stay calm as he lay on the operating bench. He was in a technical theater of sorts. Dozens, it seemed, of doctors and technicians, gowned from head to foot in sterile surgical gear, reviewed monitors and screens that registered a myriad of physiological readings on the ten people that lay side by side on benches just like Yenko's. It was cryostasis in mass production.

"You'll be fine," a doctor said as he checked one of the dozen cannulas which would be used to administer the procedure.

Yenko did not respond. Rationally, he knew he would be alright. But he would soon go to sleep. And when he next woke up, if he woke up, the dawning of the twenty-fifth century would be upon him . . . on Zhinu, twenty-five light years away. Earth would never be his home again no matter what happened.

"You look paler than ever, *yang guizi*," quipped Li Jie from the mobile bench beside him. "It shows off that shock of red hair to great effect."

The man was irrepressible. The last thing Yenko saw was Huang Li Jie's mischievous smile as he succumbed to induced sleep. All thought of Zhinu, of the mission, of the dangers, of the mystery . . . all blurred as he drifted into a fog of forgetfulness.

2

Echoes of the Past

Y ENKO OPENED HIS EYES groggily. He was disoriented, did not know where he was. Or even who he was. Vaguely, he became aware that he was lying in a thickly padded capsule. Above him, the heavy door of his chamber stood wide open.

He felt sick, very sick, and sat up hastily as he emptied his stomach unceremoniously over the side of his coffin. The pungent fumes of the cryostatic fluid wafting up from the mess below him, along with the dizziness of sitting up, exacerbated the nausea and his head reeled in a giddy dance. Suddenly cold, he wrapped his arms about his shivering chest and took in his surroundings. A robotic arm administered an injection into his neck as his memory began to emerge from a shrouding fog.

He was on board the *Zhinu Phoenix*, hurtling across the vast reaches of space towards the New World Colony. It would be a month yet before they neared their destination. Yenko knew what to expect. Four grueling weeks of physical torture as his body recovered from its extended hibernation. For decades now, his body had been held in suspended animation while the *Zhinu Phoenix's* artificial intelligence, Nirani, piloted them in and out of the manipulated bending of curved space-time. As far as his people on Earth were concerned, he was in his mid-seventies.

Tentatively, he slid his feet to the floor, gripping the side of his coffin-like bed with whatever failing strength he could muster. There he sat, fighting to maintain his balance, the cold floor a confusing sensation to his bare feet. Beside him, hundreds of his fellow travelers were doing much the same thing. The noise of retching echoed across the vast deck.

A gentle, yet commanding female voice spoke over an intercom as a holographic projection stood before each member of the mission. Yenko, still disoriented, stared at the glowing form. She was clearly a holograph, a woman shimmering with a golden light, but why was she there? Her lips moved to the speech, but the voice came from elsewhere.

"Welcome, travelers," the hologram appeared to say. "I am Nirani, your flight navigator."

She was much more than that. Because of the extraordinarily long flight, the entire ship's company had to make the voyage in cryostatic sleep. Nirani, the *Phoenix*'s onboard AI, had to do everything that would be expected of a whole crew to ensure safe passage through the depths of space. As an AI, she had access to all internal monitoring and instrumentation. And in case of unforeseen emergencies, a veritable army of robots and machines were at her command. Except in the event of catastrophic failure, she could rebuild any and every system on the *Zhinu Phoenix*.

"Artificial Intelligence," thought Yenko. He wanted to cry, though for no reason he could comprehend. He had trained for this in Beijing and began to recall the irrational emotional responses to coming out of cryostasis. Beijing. Another world ago.

Shaking his head to clear his thoughts, he paid attention to the hologram before him. She had the facial features of a Zhongwen woman in her mid-twenties. Her shoulder length hair and her holographic lab coat gave her a scientific air. Right down to the three holographic pens in her breast pocket.

"We are four weeks and two days away from Zhinu. The nausea and disorientation you are experiencing is normal. Before long, you will be fit and ready for what awaits you. I have good news to bring you, travelers. There are properties of space-time that I was able to study during our maneuvers. With only minor course corrections, I have shortened the length of your flight. You have been in stasis for thirty-two years, three months and seventeen days."

"Thirty-two years," mouthed Yenko.

"We dropped into conventional space two days ago where I began the process of bringing you back into consciousness. I have also intercepted a probe from Earth and returned it with the technical read-outs of my findings.

"You will feel sick for a time, as many of you are already discovering. Do not worry about the mess. It is under control. I have been advised that your training has taught you to master the need for emotional outburst. Make sure you practice what you have learned. I do not wish to forcibly sedate any of you. The mission is critical and needs all hands."

Yenko shook his head again, staring hard at the golden girl before him. She stood in front of everyone, some of whom were only now beginning to sit up. The sound of vomiting continued.

"Check your chronometers," she continued, "and ensure they are functional. It is currently 0203hrs. Make adjustments now to accommodate the Zhinu day as you have been shown in your training. It is not so very different to Earth's, but I have set all onboard chronometers now to Zhinu time. I advise you to do the same. We will not be using Beijing *shijian* unless in communications with Earth."

Many of the company looked at the badges on their inner sleeves, ensuring their chronometers were set to the correct time. They needed to be. The rotation of Zhinu about its axis was not the same as Earth's, but its day had been divided into twenty-four "hours" for convenience and vague alignment to how times were measured on their mother planet.

"All squadron leaders are to report to the Main Rotator Briefing Deck by 0215hrs for medical examination and mission updates from Beijing. The rest will report as soon as you are able to the Medical Center in Rotator Three. If you are disoriented and have forgotten the layout of the *Zhinu Phoenix*, remember that you can access me by tapping one of the black panels in any of the walls.

"If you believe you need medical assistance right now, you may indicate to my holographic form in front of you. I will ensure that medical staff are assigned to assist you. These were woken from their stasis two weeks ago and are ready to care for you."

The golden hologram joined both palms and bowed as she winked out of sight.

"I wonder who designed her?" a familiar, though croaky voice behind Yenko said. Turning around, he saw his friend and sparring partner, Huang Li Jie. "If I'd known what she was like, I would not have slept so long."

Yenko might have laughed if he had not felt so sick. Closing his eyes, he steeled himself to take his weight on his own two legs.

"I could inflict such pain on you right now," Li Jie joked. "You leave yourself wide open. Did you learn nothing from training with me?"

Taking Yenko by the shoulder, he added, "Come, old man. Lean on my Zhongwen arm."

Yenko did not think it was funny, but he accepted the offer, nonetheless. Centrifugal Gravity Rotator Three was a good five hundred feet away and he would have to negotiate the weightless central axle of the *Zhinu Phoenix*. He feared he might empty his stomach again. If there was anything left in it.

◄◦►

Macpherson Yenko stood gasping for air beside the large viewing screen on the Observation Deck. Around him were gathered the members of Delta Squadron, along with Sigma Two and Tau One Squadrons. They had just finished a grueling war game simulation. The past four weeks had pushed them to their limits, but at last they were feeling more like their usual battle-ready selves.

Some of the other squadrons' members did not know what to think of having a Scot separatist among them, but whatever they thought, they largely kept it to themselves. He was too well liked amongst Delta Squadron and if anyone thought to pick a fight with him, it would soon get well out of hand. Besides, he had been chosen by the officials, though they all knew Macpherson was not their first preference. Amongst the entire company, however, he was not the only one who was second or third choice, so there was nothing to be said for it.

Together they stood before the viewing screen, hands on hips, or bracing their weight on their knees. A few gave up altogether and collapsed on the floor. From their vantage point, they looked down on their new home. Zhinu.

In truth, Zhinu was the name of the system's star; the Weaving Girl of ancient Chinese astronomy, once known in the days of the Western Civilization as Vega. A star of legend for much of Earth's past. But the planet was almost uniformly identified by the same name rather than its astronomical designation, α *Lyr b*.

The planet hung majestically before them. Its sun was rising from the lower right of the disc and two of its three moons were easily visible against the star-studded backdrop. No one spoke a word. If they had not struggled to regain their breath, there would have been no sound at all.

Zhinu shone brilliantly in its new dawn. Blue and green and white. Towards the top of the disc, still in night, a massive storm raged, judging by the regular flashes of shrouded light. They had learned of the powerful weather patterns of the equatorial region of the planet. Here was evidence that not all was paradise on the new world. Somewhere down there, Xin Beijing lay in ruins. And somewhere down there, small communities of farmers were either going about their daytime routines or fast asleep in their beds at night.

Behind them, the mealtime alarm rang for the first ten squadrons, Alpha through Iota Two.

Those of Delta Squadron, among these ten, kidded their compatriots of Sigma Two and Tau One as they left. "We will tell you afterwards if it was worth the fight," one of them said.

It largely fell on deaf ears, though. No one minded staying behind. To date, it was the clearest view they had been permitted of Zhinu, their preparations and training having been administered in strictest military fashion.

In the mess hall, the Commanding Officer, Commodore Mannat Ahuja, called everyone's attention as they ate.

"You have worked hard," she began. "And well you should. We are two days away from stepping into the unknown. Keep your wits about you. After we land, you will not be permitted to explore the wonders of this new world. That time is a long way off yet. For all we know, there is an enemy down there, indigenous to Zhinu, that has remained undetected by our probes. Or an enemy from a nearby world. We would be foolish to think we are alone in the universe and alone in our ability to navigate the stars. You will need your faculties to be sharp, always on the alert. Be vigilant and never drop your guard. It may mean your life or the life of your squadron.

"As you well know, we are ignorant of what has afflicted the New World Colony. An alien disease perhaps? We simply do not know. Take notice if there are even slight changes in your bodies. Discount nothing, no matter how trivial. Report everything. Everything, do you hear? Report everything to your Squadron Leader.

"There is conjecture on Earth that there has been a natural disaster here. If that is so, we are uncertain as to what it could have been. Geophysics has not been of any help to us. Every step should be taken with extreme caution until we know what we are facing. There may be forces at work in the planet that we know nothing of.

"Your first week on the ground will be the most critical. Treat every moment as if you are at war. Observe the chain of command. It is there for a purpose. Half of you have only the last two years as your military training. None of it was without meaning. If anyone, and I stress anyone, who is above you in the chain of command, whether they are of your squadron or not, gives you an order, you will obey it without hesitation and without question. All depends on this.

"Those of you from the military, you know what to do. You have trained alongside non-military personnel for two years now. You have made brothers and sisters of them. But never forget, they do not have the experience you have. Be doubly alert because their lives may be more in your hands than yours in theirs.

"Finish your meal and report to your squadron briefing room. Plans will be laid before you for disembarking the *Zhinu Phoenix*. Our ship is aptly named. We come to this world in the *Phoenix*. We will see Xin Beijing rise from its ashes."

This was it. Yenko turned to Li Jie. He trusted the man. He would be foolish not to. Li Jie was five times decorated for military incursions in several uprisings of the last decade and a half.

"You will be fine," Li Jie said, noting the worried look on his friend's face. "Trust me when I say I would rather fight alongside you than ninety percent of those who are in the regular army. In two years, you have acquitted yourself well and honored your ancestors."

Yenko knew he had learned a lot. Years of scrapping and fighting in the streets and bars of the world—the tragic aftermath of a confused, orphaned, racially vilified childhood—had taught him basic survival. Two years in the intensive training camp for the Zhinu Mission had now made a decent soldier of him. He just hoped that it would not come down to that. He had been chosen because of his expertise in Space-Time Kinematics, his other life, not his ability to fight. How that might help, he had no idea.

------◄○►------

The landing process took part in four stages. As a member of Delta Squadron, Yenko would be in the first round. Four landing craft, much like huge aircraft powered by jets and gyroscopic rotor blades, stood ready to receive them in the large hangar in the *Phoenix*'s central axle. These could land vertically if needed and had power enough to rocket out of the planet's atmosphere to dock back with the orbiting spacecraft. Each vessel was equipped to carry seventy-five passengers along with several tons of equipment and supplies.

The plan was for them to land on the western outskirts of Xin Beijing, which was built on the coast of a large tract of water to its south. To the north, a heavily wooded region formed a barrier between the city and a mountain chain that stretched on for hundreds of miles, roughly following the coastline. For the most part, the farming communities known to the company were well off to the east.

By making their descent in the night and as far away as practical from the colony survivors, they hoped to land without alerting anyone to their presence. Not until all twelve hundred of them were down and a secure bivouac had been established would they make themselves known to the colonists.

As soon as the first Orbital Lander touched down, the troops immediately set to motion. They knew the drill well; establish a perimeter and identify lines of best sight. Yenko stood for a moment at the Lander's hatch, heart pounding. Rotor blades above him created a small windstorm that assaulted him. He breathed deeply, reveling in the opportunity that had been accorded him; he stood on the threshold of a new world.

He was on Zhinu.

This was no exercise, however. He realized now the importance of the strong bond of brotherhood that had grown over the intense two years of training. They were Delta Squadron. Stepping out into unknown dangers, unknown mysteries, Yenko was grateful for this one thing: Delta Squadron would stand or fall together.

His military friends went about their mission with speed and efficiency. But Yenko had not their depth of training behind him. Having made sure there was no immediate danger, he allowed his attention to duty to falter. It was night, though brighter than any night the Scot had ever experienced on Earth. High above him, riding proudly on a sea of stars, two moons beamed down on him, welcoming him to the world of his boyhood dreams.

He was on Zhinu. It was unbelievable.

Earth was an unfathomable distance away. About him, a field of low groundcover unlike anything he had seen before, bid him relax. The air was sweet and fresh, and full of fragrant hints of unknown vegetation. A cool breeze caressed his cheeks.

He was on Zhinu, a world of wonder.

"*Yang guizi!*" Li Jie called out, busily unfolding a heavy canvas tent. "If the Captain finds you standing there doing nothing, she'll have you on rations for the next month."

It was a fair warning and brought Yenko out of his reverie; there was work to be done.

By the end of that first night, a makeshift camp had been constructed. Twenty squadrons, half the company, had made land before dawn. They would secure the base and wait for the rest of the fleet to make their descent the following night.

Dawn broke with the camp closed in by a thick fog. In the distance, a faint rumble of surf sounded an ominous dirge over the eerie, alien landscape. After a scant breakfast of rations, Delta Squadron, along with four others, was assigned the detail of scouting the forest to the north and north-east. Others were to gather information on the deserted city ruins to the east and the coast to the south. By nightfall, they were all to report back to base and prepare for the arrival of the remaining twenty squadrons.

———◄◦►———

"There's nothing here," Yenko said to Li Jie.

"Don't be so confident," the Commander replied. "It's when you drop your guard in complacency that you die."

That certainly woke Yenko up. But there was nothing around them that even hinted of danger. As a matter of fact, it was beautiful. The fog had lifted hours earlier, and the sun had risen over them. Beams of light filtered through the thick forest canopy, giving an air of serene majesty to the wonderland through which they stalked. Here and there, natural paths wound their way through the woods, most definitely the tracks of animals; they were far too narrow, random, and meandering to be man-made, and too ordered to be the result of natural forces.

Delta Squadron fanned out across half a mile as they made their way steadily to the north-east. In places, they had to find passage across the many creeks that cut through the forest to the coast, but for the most part, it was easy terrain to negotiate.

Throughout the forest, trunks of gigantic trees stamped their dominance on the landscape; thirty feet at least in diameter and rising to incredible heights. Birds sang their enchanting refrains in the canopy high overhead. Small rodents scurried out of the way, caught by surprise by the squadron's stealthy approach.

"Keep your shotgun at hand," Li Jie added. Yenko had slung his plasma weapon over his back for ease. This was no time for sightseeing; they were under orders.

Ten minutes later, Delta Squadron's Captain, Yang Zhi Ruo, held her fist up by way of silent command to halt. The trained soldiers among them all saw it and repeated the alert to ensure their non-military compatriots had taken notice. Everyone froze. Captain Yang had seen something.

Without glancing to the right or left, trusting implicitly that her squad had witnessed her signal, she motioned for four commandos to move ahead with their assigned non-military partners.

Li Jie nodded to Yenko. It was a nod that said, "Follow me," and allowed for no question or hesitation. Together, they crept off to the far right of the group. After negotiating a hundred and fifty feet with nothing in sight, Li Jie looked back to Captain Yang. She indicated to him that she had heard something that was out of place and pointed in the general direction. Li Jie nodded and signed to Yenko to follow, plasma shotgun at the ready.

Yenko's heart raced. He had learned to become a tolerable marksman in his training, but this was not training. And potentially, he would not be aiming at an inanimate target. Sweat beaded on his forehead, trickled down the back of his neck. The pleasant forest now felt like a deadly jungle.

The four teams slowly made their way forward, hardly making a sound. Yenko began to wonder if the Captain had heard truly or if it was just her imagination running away with her. And then he heard it, too, not that far from where he was, and well beyond the bulk of the squadron. He crouched lower still, following Li Jie's lead, who had shot a quick signal to the Leader. The squadron now was on the ground.

Inch by inch, the two men made their silent advance.

There. Three hundred feet in front of them, two children walked along a forgotten path. A boy, and his older sister, perhaps.

It was too early for the company to reveal themselves to the colonists, and they certainly did not want two children to be confronted by thirty armed soldiers in their dark Secret Operations uniforms. It would frighten the life out of them and be a rude introduction to the rural communities they had come to help.

Li Jie put his face close to Yenko's ear and whispered, "Do not move, even if the children go out of sight. Keep your eye on them if you can, but do not follow without me. That is an order."

It was unusual to hear such an absolute injunction coming from his friend. But Yenko understood the need for obedience and lay low, keeping an eye on the children as they skipped and joked with each other. Obey the chain of command.

Shortly afterwards, Li Jie was back at Yang Zhi Ruo's side, reporting the source of the sound she had heard. Silent signals were given to the other scouts to return. Li Jie snuck back to Yenko, while the rest of the squadron held position. Together, the two heavily armed companions stalked the children, never getting closer, never lagging behind. When they were perhaps five or six hundred feet in front of the squadron and almost out of sight, Yang Zhi Ruo signaled the company to stalk Li Jie and Yenko.

Slowly they worked their way through the forest, Li Jie and Yenko three hundred feet or more behind the children, Delta Squadron six hundred feet behind them.

Half an hour later, the crude forest path broke free of the woodland and onto a broad swath of farms and smallholdings that stretched on into the distance. Several houses dotted the region, and the children made a run for the nearest, not two hundred feet from the edge of the forest.

"Shylah! Joshua! How many times have I told you?" a voice called out from the farmhouse. "You cannot be in the forest all day. Before you know it, night will be on us, and you know it isn't safe at night. Ghosts will get you."

"Sorry, mommy," the older of the two, the girl, said.

"But mommy," the boy chimed in, not caring about the dangers, "we found a waterfall. And there were crabs. I tried to catch one, but Shylah was bossy and wouldn't let me. Can we go back there tomorrow, mommy? Can we?"

The woman looked suddenly tired. "Perhaps," she conceded, and turned back inside the house. "You can ask your father when he gets home. Now come and get yourselves ready for dinner. It's getting late."

Li Jie took out a small concealable camera and took a dozen photos before he and Yenko returned to report their findings. The Squadron Leader was a little concerned about the mother's warnings about the dangers of the forest at night. Certainly, ghosts were nothing, but she could not assume that the mother simply wanted her children in the house before nightfall. Something extraordinary had happened on this planet, and Captain Yang could not take anything for granted. There may truly be dangers in the forest at night.

As it was, the time to return to base was fast approaching. It would be a busy night with the arrival of another six hundred troops, and it would be important to learn news from the other scouting squadrons. So they headed off.

———— ◄o► ————

Delta Squadron was one of the last to return. Reports from across the sorties varied significantly, but all told a similar tale. The city and much of its surrounding region were void of any sign of recent human activity.

Captain Yang delivered the report from Delta Squadron. Hers was the only squadron that had ventured onto anything more than forest to the north. She left nothing out of the two children and their interaction with their mother at the farmhouse. The Commodore smiled at the mention of ghosts but agreed with Yang Zhi Ruo that it could be a forewarning of night terrors, and the guard around the camp was notified.

To the south, Lambda Two Squadron had scouted eastward along the coast, keeping cover in the many sand dunes there under the thick coastal bushlands. They passed dozens of farms and on occasion saw a worker or two tending a field, but for the most part, there was nothing out of the ordinary. Some miles to the east, at a river delta, the surf beach gave way to mudflats under the shelter of a group of small islands. On the far side of the delta, they observed three fishing vessels heading out to sea.

No revelations there.

It was a different story, however, as Captain Bhavin Patel of Theta Squadron summarized the reports from the search of the city precinct.

"Something strange has happened there that cannot be explained," the Bhaarateey national said. "The city is in ruins, that much is obvious. We expected that. But it isn't the consequence of a natural disaster. Things are missing . . . that shouldn't be missing."

"Explain," the Commodore said, noting Patel's hesitation.

"It just doesn't make sense," he replied. "In the smaller buildings, doors lie strewn across the floor. There are no door jambs. But it isn't uniformly so across the city. Other doors are in place. Others are missing entirely. In one building, the windows are intact, in another, the glass lies smashed on the floor . . . with no window jambs.

"And seats. Everywhere we went, all cushioning and coverings were gone. Only metal frames. Utensils and equipment were scattered about everywhere. To the best of our understanding, it appears as if tables and benches have been taken and everything that sat on them lies now on the floor.

"In the homes, this is graphic. Room after room we found with no floors. Walls collapsed with no stud work. Beds are nothing more than steel frames. If they are there at all. But the wardrobes! There are no clothes, only coat hangers. No shoes. No bedding. Nothing. It is less obvious in the office complexes. But the chairs! All padding is gone with no trace. There is not a paper anywhere, no books, nothing. Maybe that is not surprising. But no paper at all? Surely! And picture frames . . . they hang on walls with no pictures.

"It is eerie."

◄O►

"What do you make of the reports?" Yenko asked Li Jie the next morning.

The Commander yawned. "I would have a better answer for you if I had got any sleep last night."

Huang looked tired. In truth, he had slept little over the last two days. Night landings were fine if you were a colonist, but not for the members of this Third Fleet. While twelve hundred armed forces set up their camp to the west of Xin Beijing, or what remained of it at least, the local inhabitants were blissfully unaware, safe and secure beneath their blankets. Enjoying full nights of sleep in their comfortable beds.

Yenko looked at his tired compatriot. "There'll be time to sleep later," he said. "I've asked Captain Yang if we can be assigned to the city today while the Commodore makes contact with the colonists."

"Yes," Li Jie agreed, resigned to the need of the hour. "I would like to investigate that myself. It reminds me of my grandfather's puzzle box. There is a riddle to be solved but I don't believe we have seen all sides of the puzzle yet."

Yenko had made a compelling argument to Captain Yang. The city had been the center of learning and communication on Zhinu. It made sense that the next survey of the city should be made by the company's scientists and engineers, not the soldiers. Some of the military, of course, would accompany them; they still did not know what dangers lay in this alien world. But there was much to investigate, and it was likely that the right eyes would see what others missed.

In the early hours of that morning, before the Commodore set off in a small entourage of Light Reconnaissance Vehicles to announce their arrival to the settlements, two new squadrons were formed. These chiefly consisted of non-military personnel and a small squad of senior military leaders assigned to their protection.

————◄○►————

As the investigation made its way through the rubble-strewn streets of Xin Beijing, Yenko struggled to comprehend the degree of devastation. Many of the smaller buildings, homes probably to the thousands of the missing colonists, lay in piles of rubble. It looked like a long-forgotten war zone. Grasses and small trees straggled their way through cracks in the streets, out from the sides of decaying walls, or poked their heads above the gutters and roofs of collapsed buildings. Whatever had happened, it had been violent.

Though the enormity of the destruction through which they marched demanded study, this was not the goal of the scientific and engineering foray. If there had been an attack, it would not have centered on the residential quarters, but in the business district, where government and commerce were conducted. There was more hope for answers there.

As they approached the outer limits of the city center, Yenko was shocked by the totality of its wreckage. Administration buildings of ten stories or more rose from among piles of detritus, collapsed slabs of concrete, and steel girders.

An ominous silence hung like a pall over the ruins. This was not a city. It was a mausoleum, the broken reminder of the colony's former glory.

Rounding a corner, Yenko's company—five scientists, seven engineers, and three soldiers—disturbed a small herd of what looked to be a kind of deer. They had been grazing on the lush unkempt grasses of a park. Spooked, they galloped out of sight.

"Look," said one of the engineers, pointing to a tall building a couple of blocks away. "The university."

Emblazoned on its upper heights, in the old Chinese script, were the words Xin Beijing Daxue. Familiar with the layout of the city, they knew the Administration Center was directly over the road from the university. There may be something they could find in one of those buildings. A report maybe. Something. Anything.

The company made their way at a trot. All of them were keen to search the Administration Center, but Yenko wanted to explore the university. He was familiar with the Kinematics Unit. Without really knowing why, he needed to see what had become of it. Besides, it was as good a place as any to seek answers to the riddle of Xin Beijing.

A debate rose amongst the soldiers. There were only three of them, and they were uncertain as to whether it was wise to allow Yenko to wander off on his own. In the end, they allowed him to follow his hunch, on the condition that Commander Huang went with him.

———◄◦►———

"What do you hope to find up here?" Li Jie asked as they climbed an external cement fire escape on the main building. Yenko was making for the fifth floor.

"I don't know," Yenko replied truthfully enough. "The Kinematics Unit is on this level. I did collaborative studies with them when I was much younger. A lot of the specialists who worked here are people I've known."

Stopping at the steel door to the fifth floor, Yenko surveyed the city around him. Li Jie took panoramic photographs from the vantage point. Perhaps they would prove useful later when they could be examined in detail. Their building was one of the tallest, standing eleven stories high.

"I wish to climb to the top before we enter," Li Jie said and continued the ascent. "Follow me."

A low, cement parapet with a sturdy metal railing bounded the flat roof. Perhaps a dozen chairs were set out as they had been decades earlier. Here was a graphic witness to the veracity of Theta Squadron's report. Metal frames were all that remained of what at one time must have been comfortable outside lounges. Under each frame lay a scattering of rusted springs, rivets, and tacks.

From here, the entire city could be seen. Li Jie took more photographs for his report. A flock of birds scattered from within the top floor of the Administration Center over the road. No doubt, the rest of the team had made their way there and disturbed its winged occupants.

"I've seen enough," Li Jie said. "Now for your fifth floor."

Once back on that level, they managed to open the heavy door and stepped into the dark corridor beyond. The Commander switched on his flashlight and Yenko followed suit. Doors, several open, led off the corridor at intervals as they made their way forward. Checking rooms as they went, they saw the same tale of mysterious destruction as they had heard in the reports of the day before. Apparently random pieces of furniture or construction were missing. But there seemed to be no uniformity. No pattern. And that just added to the sense of mystery and Yenko's frustration.

What had happened? What could explain the graphic evidence that lay mockingly before him?

The two men entered a room to their left. A computing console lay smashed on the floor near one wall. It was obvious from the paintwork that a bench had once been built into that wall, supporting the console and its associated equipment. The bench was gone, but everything else remained, smashed on the floor. The frames of the roller chairs remained but the cushioned seats themselves were gone, without even a trace of the fabric or material that had once been there.

"What has happened here?" Li Jie wondered aloud, not expecting an answer.

Yenko left the room, scanning the names of the various departments as he explored corridor after corridor with determination.

"What are you looking for?" Li asked.

"This!" Yenko replied, finding the name he had been searching for— Kinematics. Naturally, Kinematics could have referred to any number of things; it was a broad area of Physics. But Yenko knew that in Xin Beijing, the only Kinematics they studied was Space-Time Kinematics.

The door opened onto a large room. One side of it was given to sturdy benches that held bank after bank of screens, terminals, and equipment that Li Jie could only guess at.

"Work desks," the soldier noted.

"Yes, I know," Yenko said distantly.

Why were these benches there while others in the room were obviously missing? Scientific apparatus lay strewn about the floor in piles of shattered glass.

Yenko examined a table supporting banks of screens and equipment. Beside it stood a massive metallic construction, covered in dials and gauges, electrical outlets, and switches. Easily ten feet long and wide, it rose to the ceiling and dominated one side of the room.

"Do you think we could get power up here?" he asked Li Jie. "They were up to something by the looks of this. But I've never seen anything like it. I recognize a lot of these gauges and instruments, but not all of

them. Whatever this machine is, I don't know. And that troubles me because I should know. I'm the expert."

"Well, you convinced the Commodore about today's mission," Li Jie
replied. "If you tell them we need power, they'll probably listen. When do
you want it?"

The Commander certainly knew how to get things done. By the end
of the afternoon, a team of technicians had set up a portable generator
on the fifth floor and supplied energy to the Kinematics lab. They would
have set it up earlier, but after initial attempts, they determined that the
puzzling machine required five times the power they had guessed.

Yenko had to ask permission to stay and work into the night. Li Jie
was not entirely happy with the request because he was assigned the duty
of standing guard over his physicist friend.

"You are determined that I won't get a decent night's sleep on this
planet," the Commander chided. "What can I expect, though? On this
world, you aren't the only *yang guizi*."

———◦———

That same morning, as Yenko and the science and engineering detail
made their way through the ruins of Xin Beijing, Commodore Mannat
Ahuja led a convoy of three LRVs to make contact with the survivors of
Zhinu in the remote farming communities. The roads had clearly not
been used for many years and on occasion, the convoy found itself navigating potholes as large as the LRVs themselves. In some places, it was
easier to drive off-road altogether.

By midmorning, the convoy had slowly made its way into the farmlands. Ahead of them lay a small settlement and by the time they reached
it, a crowd had come together, though remaining largely hidden away,
uncertain of these unexpected and mysterious visitors.

"I bring you tidings from Earth," the Commodore said. She had ordered the cavalcade to stop in the middle of the township. Faces peered
out at them from every window and corner. "There is nothing to fear. I
am now as you are, a colonist of Zhinu."

A man stepped forward, graying hair, probably a community leader.
"You should not have come," he said solemnly. "When did you arrive?
Where are you based?"

"Twelve hundred of us have made camp on the western outskirts of
Xin Beijing . . ."

"No, you must not!" interrupted the man, the look of fear and concern clearly etched across his face. "It isn't safe! There are ghosts there!"

Mannat Ahuja raised her eyebrows. She had laughed at Delta Squadron's report of the farming mother's warning to her children. *It isn't safe at night. Ghosts will get you.*

"We obviously need to talk," she said, "but first let me introduce myself to you. My name is Mannat Ahuja. I am a Commodore in the Bhaarateey army."

At that, several of the hidden people began to venture into the open.

"Of the twelve hundred of our number sent from Earth thirty-two years ago, a full six hundred are Special Operations Forces of the Zhongwen and Bhaarateey military."

A collective gasp arose from hidden corners about the village square.

"And the remaining six hundred have had intensive military training. We are prepared for any outcome and are here to support you."

"Commodore," the man said, "Ajuna?"

"Ahuja," the Commodore corrected.

"Ahuja."

"You may call me Mannat if you wish. There are few of us on this world . . . Perhaps you should call me Manu."

"Manu," the man repeated dumbly. And then shaking his head back into reality, he said firmly, "Commodore, it isn't safe. But you are trained and we're grateful. Perhaps there is hope for us on this forsaken world."

"Forgive me. My name is Li Lin Wei. I am a descendant of Li Zhang Wei of the First Fleet and those around me probably see me as the natural leader of our village. Your coming here is unexpected in the extreme. We have had no way to communicate with Earth since the *huoyan xieshen* came and destroyed Xin Beijing."

"There are no evil spirits," Mannat dismissed. Her military training gave her a commanding air of authority. "They are old wives' tales, nothing more."

Disembarking from the reconnaissance vehicle, she added, "Is there somewhere more comfortable to talk?"

"Forgive me," Lin Wei apologized again. "I have not afforded you the courtesy due your station. This way," he gestured. "I will make sure that you and your companions are honored appropriately."

It was quite a gathering in the meeting room Lin Wei directed them to. Faces peeked in at every window and both doors. Everyone wanted to be a part of such a momentous event.

"We know very little of what has taken place here," the Commodore began, now comfortably seated in a large hall with a cup of tea in hand. It was an interesting flavor, the produce of the new world. "All communication with Zhinu ceased eleven years ago."

Shaking her head, she corrected herself as she realized her mistake. "Sorry," she apologized. "To me, it feels like eleven years ago. But our journey was thirty-two years across the stars. It has been forty-three years since anyone has heard from the New World Colony. We've sent probes, but doubtless you have guessed that we would. All we know is that there appears to be very few of you left. What happened?"

Lin Wei was visibly shaken.

"I was a boy," he recalled. "I remember the day well. It was forty of our years ago, but that would accord to your forty-three. Our year is a little longer than Earth's. My father had given me permission to neglect my studies for the day and I played in the field, watching him prepare for the next year's crop. Suddenly, the world flashed brighter than the sun and immediately fell into deep darkness. And the air vibrated with such a force that I fell to the ground.

"As quickly as it came, it left. The sun shone, though no bird could be heard anywhere about. I rose to my feet and ran to my father. People gathered from the villages and farmlands about us. My father tried to contact my grandfather in Xin Beijing but there was no response. Calls came in from neighboring villages, but alike, none could make contact with our chief city.

"My father, along with many of the fathers of my village, drove his truck to discover the cause of what had struck us. When they entered Xin Beijing, they found it in ruins. Something had attacked it. An alien species. One that lives on this planet, most of us think, that we had not discovered in a hundred and twenty years of our colony. It must have only just become aware of us and had brought our beautiful city to ruin and vaporized its entire population."

"How do you know this to be so?" questioned the Commodore.

"We don't truly know," Lin Wei conceded. "But there is no other conclusion. We've seen them."

"You've seen them?" Mannat repeated. "You've seen who?"

"They're ghosts," Lin Wei said quietly. "They roam the streets of Xin Beijing to this day. They know nothing of our existence, so we stay close to our homes, hoping against hope that they learn no more of our colony."

"What do you mean you've seen them?" Mannat pressed. "Spirits aren't real."

"These ones are," Lin Wei affirmed. "These ones are."

"Ghosts?"

"Ghosts!"

Lin Wei took a long draught from his teacup, staring into nothingness.

"I saw one myself," he admitted.

"You saw one?"

Slowly nodding his head, he added, "It was years later. I was trying to impress a girl. *Bai chi!* We drove our vehicle into the city, though it had been declared off limits by our elders. The foolishness of the young. I was showing off. Declaring that I was not afraid of ghosts. That I would reclaim the city for myself and my girlfriend. And then I saw them.

"A score of ghostly figures. Humanoid. They pointed at me and silently screamed their ghoulish curses at me. I ran to my vehicle and sped back to my home. Ghosts."

Slowly drawing himself out of his memory, Lin Wei's eyes pierced through the Commodore's. "They may not be ghosts as in the ancient myths and legends. But they are alien for sure. And they are invisible for the most part, yet barely visible in the right light. Be warned. If they learn of your presence, they may search us all out. I'm comforted that you are the decorated of the Zhongwen and Bhaarateey forces, but I fear that your weapons will prove ineffective against our invisible assailants."

———◁◦▷———

The sun was setting as Yenko fidgeted with what he considered to be the main computer of the Kinematics Lab. Power had been established, but before he did anything with the unknown machinery to his side, he needed to know what the team there had been working on. Thankfully, and despite the intervening decades, the computing console kicked into life.

The chair he sat on was uncomfortable. Li Jie had managed to scrounge up a cushion for him, but it did not fully protect him from the angular metal structure of the seat. Yet for the moment, that did not matter.

Security codes were the most difficult to bypass, but with the help of a very clever computing technician, he had finally been able to get into the operating system. File after file lay before him, and it took many hours before he found something that piqued his interest.

"Can we go now?" Li Jie said. "I don't want to sound like a nagging child, but I'm about to dishonor my post and fall asleep. The sun will be rising in four hours."

"Yes," Yenko conceded. "I suppose we both need sleep. I think I've just stumbled on something, but I need a few hours to study what it's saying. Let's call it a night and come back tomorrow."

Yenko powered down the computer. For an instant, he saw a face staring in wonder at him, reflected in the screen. It was a Zhongwen woman in her mid-twenties, perhaps younger. Her straggly, long hair obscured part of her face. Shocked, he turned to see who was behind him.

There was no one there.

"I really do need a sleep," he told Li Jie, who was busily collecting his gear.

One last glance at the screen. Had he really seen someone?

And there she was again. As her eyes met Yenko's, she raised a crudely fashioned knife and slashed at him from the screen. Yenko started in shock, pushing his chair back and warding himself as he turned to where his assailant must have been standing. There was no one there.

Li Jie stood slowly to his feet, stretching his back.

"Well that's one way to finish your work," he said. "You look like you've seen a ghost."

"Wait," Yenko urged, frantically looking around the room. "Did you see anything?"

It was too late for stupid games. "*Wang ba!*" Li Jie said, perhaps too forcefully. "It's late! I need some sleep!"

"But I just saw someone!" Yenko pleaded.

"You saw someone!" Li Jie repeated. "There's no one here except us! Everyone's asleep except the night watch."

"No wait!" Yenko urged. "Someone just tried to attack me. It was a reflection on my screen."

Perhaps it was the urgency with which Yenko spoke. Li Jie's training came into play. In an instant, his plasma shotgun was cocked and ready. The Special Forces Commander was at attention and searched the room.

"Describe what you saw," he ordered.

It sounded foolish as Yenko detailed what had happened. There was no one there. But he had seen someone. A beautiful woman. And she had seen him.

And lunged at him.

3

Fei Hung

Y ENKO WOKE THE NEXT morning somewhat refreshed. At first, he had found it hard to sleep, but exhaustion had finally caught up with him and he had succumbed to a solid four and a half hours before his squadron were woken to prepare for the day. Whatever he had seen the night before in the Kinematics Lab, Yenko now doubted. They had made a search, but no one was there. As Li Jie had predicted.

It had been late, Yenko reasoned within himself. He had been staring at screens for hours. Obviously, the laboratory lights had played a trick on his eyes as the computer shut down. There was no young woman. How could there be? The city was a deserted ruin. The only ones in the building were Yenko, a handful of technicians, and his friend, Li. Besides, it was a face he did not recognize, and though he did not personally know all twelve hundred of the mission, he had lived and trained alongside them for two years. He felt that he would at least recognize the face of one of his company. It was a mystery, and Yenko shrugged it off.

Rumors abounded over breakfast, however. Commodore Ahuja had returned with her cohort in the mid-afternoon with three farmers from the colony. Word was already getting around about the colonists' belief that Xin Beijing had been destroyed by an invading force of invisible aliens.

Ghosts.

Perhaps he had seen something. It needed to be reported.

———◄◊►———

"Tell me what you saw," Commodore Ahuja said.

"It will sound crazy," Yenko admitted, trying hard to stand at ease in front of the imposing woman. The Commodore sat behind a table full of reports and digital charts, casually fiddling with a marking pen in front of her. "It even sounds crazy to me. I'm not sure I believe it myself."

"Let me be the judge. Recall when we first arrived here, I said to report anything out of the ordinary, no matter what. I need to know what you know."

Yenko decided it was best to tell the whole story, so beginning with his hunch to check the Space-Time Kinematics laboratory in the university, he detailed his discovery of the unknown apparatus. The Commodore herself raised an eyebrow at Yenko's ignorance concerning its purpose; she was fully conversant with his academic and research credentials. If he could not readily identify what they were working on, she considered it was well worth investigation.

Yenko went on to describe how they secured power for the lab, and the unexpectedly high electrical demands of the equipment.

"I'm pleased the technician detail accepted your request for power," she said. "No doubt I will come to their report presently. It is buried amongst this pile on my desk. At least, now I have the background information and can deal with it quickly."

"Once I had power," Yenko continued, "I was able to begin a search through the files of what they were working on up there . . . And then the crazy bit happened."

The Commodore sat back in her chair, hands clasped in front of her chin, studying him. He felt awkward in her presence.

"It was late. 1:26am. I powered down the computer I was working on, and I swear I saw a face reflected in the screen."

"A face," the Commodore repeated. "What kind of face?"

"A woman. Zhongwen. Twenties."

"Who was with you at the time?"

"Commander Huang. Technicians Dewan and Kholi were with me earlier. They'd already gone. Kholi is a woman, but it wasn't her I saw. It couldn't have been; she's *gali ren*. Sorry," he added hastily, wishing he could take back his words, "that was disrespectful. Technician Kholi is Bhaarateey. The woman I saw in the reflection was definitely Zhongwen."

"It was late, you said," the Commodore interrogated, ignoring the racist slur against her people. He was, after all, a separatist.

"Yes, it was," conceded Yenko. "But I saw the face again. And whoever it was clearly saw me."

"She saw you. How could you tell? There was no one there, you said, apart from you and Huang."

"She saw me alright! She attacked me with a knife, and I jumped."

The Commodore studied him. He was an intelligent man. More than intelligent. Brilliant. And a respected leader in the pragmatic sciences, not given to fantasy. His words needed to be considered.

"And that was that," he concluded. "We searched everywhere but there was no one there. No one."

"Thank you, Mr. Macpherson," she said at length. "Perhaps you did see something. I don't know. Your testimony, in some measure, supports that of the villagers. But theirs is a stranger tale than yours. I have many questions and very few answers.

"This apparatus . . . this machine you've found. What precisely does it do?"

"I don't know," Yenko answered truthfully. "But just before we shut the computers down, I think I found the group of files that related to it. They were doing research here in Xin Beijing that we knew nothing of on Earth; that much is obvious."

"Interesting," nodded the Commodore thoughtfully. "Research unknown to the science halls of Earth. Go back, Macpherson. Take what resources you need. Get to the bottom of this. And I want hourly reports. Localized communications have now been established. You are dismissed unless there is anything else you've omitted to report."

Yenko stood to attention and quickly bowed before exiting the room. The Commodore wanted a report on the purpose of the machine. Yenko was just as eager to give it.

What had they been working on? For the moment, thoughts of the ghostly woman in the screen would have to wait. There was work to be done.

———◦———

The rest of that day, Yenko pored through file after file. Most of the reports related to standard Space-Time Kinematics, theoretical projections, experimental data. He even found files that he himself had helped formulate in his undergraduate days.

"I'm missing something," he mumbled to himself absently. "What were you up to?"

He unearthed a folder full of complex research analyses. Some of the figures were confusing and not at all conforming to standard nomenclature.

"What were you up to?" he muttered every so often, confused by the nonsensical data.

Leaning back in his chair, he ran his fingers through his red hair. He needed a haircut. Absently, he reviewed the root menu of the current files he was working on.

"What are *you* doing here?" he asked a sub-folder he had overlooked before.

Multidimensional Werner Contractions.

Werner Contractions? Werner was a famous name in the field of Space-Time Kinematics. Without the ground-breaking work of the German genius, Hans Werner, in the mid-twenty-first century, space travel would likely still be confined to Earth's solar system. To see the eminent scientist's name on a folder in a Space-Time Kinematics laboratory was not surprising. But what were Contractions? And what did multidimensionality have to do with them?

"What are you muttering about?"

Li Jie had come over to Yenko's workstation, seeking to understand the reason for his redheaded friend's incessant mumbling. "And don't talk Gaelic. I don't understand half of what I can see in this room without you adding to it in your native gibberish."

It was an invitation that Yenko accepted, despite the slur against the language of his ancestors. He had not even been aware that some of his murmurings had been in Gaelic. But he pounced on Li Jie's request with enthusiasm. He needed to air his thoughts, hear them outside of himself so to speak, even if they were from his own mouth. It would be helpful.

"It's these files here," he began, pointing to the display in front of him. "Look. These over here, they make sense."

Maybe for Yenko, Li thought.

"Look at this folder. *Curvature Displacement Protocols.* You'd expect that on anyone's computer."

The vague look on the Commander's face told a different story. None of the folders made sense to him. And *Curvature Displacement Protocols* would not be on anyone's computer at all that Li Jie knew of. Except in a Space-Time Kinematics laboratory.

Yenko could see he was going too fast for his soldier friend. If he was going to use Li as a sounding board, he would need to slow the discussion down.

"Do you have a piece of paper?" Yenko suggested. "Nothing important. A bit of scrap?"

"No," Li Jie replied. Paper was not a particularly common resource, but Yenko had hoped there may be some in their supplies; it was an effective insulator and was easily folded and manipulated to fit into tight spaces.

"That's alright," Yenko said. "How about a piece of material?"

Li Jie was confused. "What do you want a cloth for? Have you made a mess?"

Yenko shook his head. "Never mind," he said, as he took off his shirt. The Commander was now completely befuddled.

Spreading the shirt on a benchtop, Yenko said, "Look at the shirt. Pretend that it's space. I know it's not. It's only two dimensional . . ." He paused as a moment of inspiration took him. "Two dimensions . . . Surely not! That's not possible."

"What?" demanded Li Jie, as Yenko was about to return to the large screen he had been working on. "What?"

Yenko turned back to him. Hesitated. Looked at the screen. At his friend.

Hastily, he returned to his shirt spread out on the table.

"Okay. This is space." Identifying a food stain just below the collar, he added, "Earth is here." Picking out another mark just above the lower hem, he said, "This is Zhinu."

"Still with you," encouraged Li Jie.

"Now look, it's not a perfect illustration. Space isn't a flat sheet like this shirt. You can go in any direction, not just backwards and forwards on the shirt. You can go up or down. Anywhere."

"Keep going," Li Jie said. "Nothing hard so far."

"Good," Yenko nodded. "So here's Earth. And here's Zhinu. You want to go from one to the other. How do you do it?"

Li Jie frowned. "You get on the *Zhinu Phoenix*?"

"Yes, alright, I can work with that. But Zhinu is twenty-five light years away from Earth. If you travelled as fast as light itself, it would take twenty-five years to get here. Cryostasis would solve the time problem but the velocity is something that we can't even go close to. And if we could, the effects on mass and time within the ship would be . . ." He looked at the Commander. "Let's just put it this way: We can't travel at the speed of light. So how did we get here in just thirty-two years? And how do our advanced probes do it in just six hours? Even light takes years."

"Something to do with curved space," answered Li Jie. "I leave that kind of thing to the scientists and engineers."

"Of course you do," Yenko agreed. "What if you could do this?"

He picked up the hem of his shirt, thumb firmly on top of "Zhinu", and with his other hand picked up the collar, holding onto "Earth", and brought the two together.

"It's not a great illustration," he acknowledged with a wince, "but what's the distance between the two points now?"

"Not much at all," Li Jie said.

"Not much at all," Yenko repeated. "Exactly." Picking up a small piece of wire he had been playing with earlier, he poked a hole through the two points on his shirt.

"The smaller the diameter of that wire is," he said, "the closer you can get the two points together. If I wanted to shoot an electron from Earth to Zhinu, I could do it in a nanosecond. The thicker the wire . . ."

"To shoot a *Phoenix* through," interrupted Li Jie.

"Precisely," Yenko said slowly. "To shoot a *Phoenix* through, we need something larger than the point of a thin wire. And the further we go away from it being a point, a true point, a dot with no size at all . . . the further we go away from that, the less we approximate the point. And the less we approximate the point, the more complicated the journey becomes."

With that, he laid his shirt out flat again and threaded the wire in and out of the fabric, gathering the material into a pleat, eventually coming to the mark that represented Zhinu.

"That, my friend, is why it took us thirty-two years. We skipped our way across the galaxy because the *Zhinu Phoenix* is oh so much bigger than a probe."

"So what were they doing in this laboratory?" Li Jie voiced Yenko's question of the whole day.

"What were they doing here . . . ?" Yenko repeated absently as he returned to the screen that listed the stored files, the Commander in tow, sensing they were on the verge of something important.

Multidimensional Werner Contractions.

Yenko opened the folder. File after file of experimental data. One caught his eye. *Dimensionality in Werner Curves*. He needed to read it to see if his guess was right.

"What does it say? Explain it to me," Li Jie eventually demanded.

Yenko whistled, ignoring the Commander's question.

"Were they actually trying to work on that!?" he asked nobody in particular, as he skimmed the research paper displayed on the monitor.

Li waited patiently. Macpherson, the scientist, needed time. He would explain in due course.

Five minutes later, Yenko looked up in wonder at Li Jie.

"They weren't trying to manipulate the curvature of space," he began in wonder. "They were attempting to fold it."

"I don't understand," Li Jie admitted.

It did not surprise Yenko. The Commander would have had to have studied this for a considerable length of time in order to comprehend Yenko's discovery. He was a soldier, not an academic.

"I'm not sure I can explain it easily," Yenko began. Searching around the desks and benches, he found two more bits of wire and returned to his shirt, still laid out on the benchtop, neatly pleated down its front.

Extracting the wire from the shirt, he held two wires together between thumb and forefinger to form a cross. With his other hand, he held the third for Li Jie to see.

"This is the wire we used to take the *Phoenix* to Zhinu," he said. "We were able to do it because it's not a piece of wire."

"It's not . . ." Li Jie repeated cautiously.

"No, this wire has length. We weren't using the length of the wire. We used its tip. We linked two points on the shirt together. Points." He turned the wire directly towards Li Jie so the soldier could only see its tip. "Don't think of it as a piece of wire. Think of it as a dot. The end of the wire."

"Okay . . ."

"If you don't consider time, and you really need to but I'm keeping it simple . . . If you don't consider time, then there are three dimensions to normal space. Here they are." And he held up the two crossed wires in his left hand that he still held between thumb and forefinger.

Pointing at the vertical wire, he said, "Up and down."

Indicating the horizontal wire, he added, "Side to side."

Balancing the third piece of wire on his thumb and forefinger, he completed the three-dimensional axes. "Backwards and forwards. That's

normal space. You can go up and down, to one side or the other, backwards or forwards. And any combination of all of them. You can go in
any direction you want.

"But space is curved. My shirt is a poor example because you can
only travel along two dimensions on it. But three-dimensional space . . .
it's curved. And the curve can be manipulated. That's how we came to
Zhinu.

"But that's not what these scientists were doing. They were trying to
fold space completely, so that all three dimensions were together."

"Why were they trying to do that?" Li Jie wondered.

Yenko nodded thoughtfully. "Because they were trying to get the
Phoenix here in a matter of hours. Or less."

Li Jie's eyes widened at the prospect. "Is that possible?"

"I truly don't know. But that's what this file, *Multidimensional Werner Contractions*, is dealing with. I will need to study it in depth. Why
they had not shared this with us on Earth, I have no idea.

"Look, Li, I think this is significant. It's the greatest anomaly we've
discovered since landing here and the Commodore needs to be made
aware of it. But the simple fact is, I need to set up shop here. Do you think
I'll be allowed to set my base of operations up closer, in the city itself? In
this building even?"

The Commander looked doubtful. "I can see you're excited and I trust
that you've found something worthy of thorough investigation. Maybe we
can make a case. I'll put in a good word for you to add to your argument."

"Thank you," Yenko said. "You're a good friend."

"Good friend," Li Jie chuckled. "You need me to mock you more
often, *yang guizi*."

The two laughed. It had been a while since Li Jie had cursed Yenko
out. It felt good, affirmed the friendship. In an odd sort of way.

———— ◄◊► ————

Macpherson Yenko arose from his tent as the sun cast its first rays over
the desolate cityscape. He and Li Jie had erected their makeshift camp
in what once would have been a beautiful park in the center of the university grounds. It had taken little to convince Commodore Ahuja of the
wisdom of the move. There was not a lot anyone else could do to help
Yenko; this was his field of expertise and his alone. And she agreed that
if Yenko had unearthed evidence of a secret testing facility, given all the

mystery that surrounded Zhinu, he needed to chase the links to whatever their end.

Li Jie was not particularly pleased, however. He understood the importance of Yenko's work, but he felt it was a waste of his own abilities to be left watching over a man who would sit hour after hour in front of screens, scribbling hieroglyphics on multiple electronic boards. And the constant muttering.

Within days, it was evident there were no dangers in the university building that required a Commander's presence, and he took to doing small errands for Yenko, fetching equipment or notes from the camp, rummaging through adjacent rooms in search of instruments he only had Yenko's description of to go by.

"No, that's not correct," Yenko said to the screen as if it was sentient and had made its own error. The sounds of Li Jie cursing as he rummaged through an adjacent storeroom, seeking anything that even vaguely fitted Yenko's latest request, reverberated through the thin wall between them.

"You can't transpose the oblate vector! Not without making an inverted phase-shift."

Absently, he pushed his chair back from the report's calculations and walked over to the largest of the electronic glass boards suspended on the wall. With a wave of his hand, he erased his prior scribbles, the mass of calculations, and personal checks he had made of the scientific research he had uncovered. He stared blankly at it for a moment.

Taking his electronic pen, he began to write furiously.

"Is this what you're looking for?" Li Jie asked, entering the room with a nine inch, parabolic crystal dish mounted on a black instrument panel.

"Hm? What?" Yenko muttered as he hastily scrawled one after another mathematical equation, solving a problem that Li Jie could only guess at. "Yes, that will do nicely."

"You didn't even look," Li Jie chided.

"Sorry. Can't stop. Too important. Look! There it is! Can you see that?" Yenko was clearly not talking to Li Jie but the glass panel. "They didn't account for the quantum displacement variance. But they wouldn't have known! Not back then when they were working on this! It's a fundamental mistake."

Li Jie put the instrument on a nearby desk and looked curiously at the growing scrawl on the board.

"What are you talking about?" he interrupted.

It shook Yenko back into the real world. He looked at Li Jie as if he had only then realized his friend was in the lab.

"I think I know what they were working on," he began. "In fact, I know what they were working on. I'm sure of it."

"What?" Li Jie demanded. At last there was a point for the days he had spent on duty on the fifth floor of this derelict building.

"It's there as plain as day," Yenko said, pointing to his work on the board.

It certainly was not as plain as day. Or as night, for that matter.

"Mahika Khatri and Arushi Jain," Yenko explained. "They were the project leaders. Researching what they called *Multidimensional Werner Contractions*. We knew nothing of this on Earth. No one has postulated folding space. It's not even in the literature as a theoretical horizon. They'd been working secretly in here. I'm not even sure the university knew. We'd have to go through their files, but communication about the project seems to have been kept totally in-house.

"Like I said to you days ago, they weren't trying to manipulate the curve of space. They were trying to bend it completely. Fold it. They built their theories on Werner's postulates. He was certainly a genius, and centuries ahead of his time, and we're still exploring extrapolations of his work. But Werner was Werner. Three hundred years ago. He didn't know everything.

"Here," Yenko pointed at one line of the scrawled equations. "Look at this."

With a flick, he dragged a copy of that line onto an adjacent electronic board.

"To that point, they were right," he said conclusively. "But look at what I did back there." Walking to the original board, he drew a line under the equation that followed the one he had just copied.

"Look at that!" he said triumphantly. "I know what they didn't, because I know what happened in the decade after they were doing these experiments. Look at what I did. I included the quantum displacement variance relevant to the scale of their calculations. And look down my work as I follow it through systematically. It collapses. There's no way it could work."

Li Jie looked solemnly at the board. He did not understand the half of what his friend said, but he understood enough. These scientists had been playing with something without knowing all the facts.

"How do you know they didn't take it into consideration?" he challenged. "You weren't aware on Earth of their research. Perhaps they already knew of this . . . displacement thing you talk of?"

"No," Yenko was adamant. "Come back over here." And he took Li Jie to the fresh board that had the solitary line he had copied across. "Watch. I'll continue to solve the equation without taking the quantum displacement variance into account. Look what happens."

Yenko's pen flew across the board, tracing out an increasing number of mathematical symbols and annotations. Finally, he stopped.

"There," he said. "They thought the equation solved."

"I don't see," Li Jie confessed.

Yenko flicked through the report that still sat open on the computer screen at which he had been working earlier.

"There," he said finally. "I know you don't understand the mathematics but look at this line here. It's the same line I concluded over there on the wall. The one with the mistake. This is what they were doing."

A look of shock struck him.

"Oh my God!" he said in horror. "Surely they didn't have a Gravimetric Discriminator here?"

"What!?" demanded the Commander. "You have to speak in language I understand!"

Yenko was pale. "We need to see the Commodore. If this was more than research, if they actually tried to create a spatial fold . . . I think they destroyed the city themselves."

It was a bombshell.

Li Jie put his hands on his hips and exhaled hard. "Come on then," he said with an air of authority. He did not understand how his scientist friend had arrived at the conclusion, but he understood the conclusion itself. "Is this a report that can be made to the Commodore in the camp or does she need to come here?"

"I think, at least for the moment, it would be best to make the report at her office."

"Alright then. Get your gear, we need to go now."

As they descended the now familiar external fire escape, Yenko happened to look down on their makeshift camp, nestled under the shadows of the park's trees. A woman was walking around it and went into his open tent.

"Who's that?" he said.

"Who's what?" Li Jie replied.

"A woman just entered my tent."

"Are you sure? Everyone knows we're up here. They wouldn't be looking for us down there until night."

"I know, but I saw her. She hasn't come out yet."

"It may be a villager," the Commander suggested. "You stay here and keep an eye on the camp. I'll race down and apprehend her."

It was not long before Yenko saw Li Jie running across the park to the camp. He put his head into Yenko's tent and then went in. Moments later, the Commander re-emerged and looked up at Yenko, three floors above.

"She hasn't come out," Yenko yelled down to him. "I haven't taken my eye off the tent since I saw her go in."

Li Jie went back inside the tent, uncertain now that Yenko had seen clearly.

"There's no one there," he called back at length. "And nothing's been disturbed."

"But she has to be there," Yenko muttered as he began to run down the stairway.

Once he had checked the tent himself, he had to admit it, however; there was no woman.

"But I saw her. I really did."

———◄◦►———

The Commodore shook her head in dismay.

"*Ullu ke pathe*," she swore. "They were Bhaarateey. They should have at least informed our own government, if not Zhongguo Xin Shijie."

A commotion outside in the camp broke the tense silence and put an end to Yenko's report.

"Commodore," someone yelled as the sound of running grew louder.

Before Yenko and Li Jie could be dismissed, Liu Wang Yong, Captain of Chi One Squadron burst into the tent.

"Forgive me, Commodore," he said, hastily bowing several times. "Ghosts! We saw them. Our whole squadron."

Mannat Ahuja was not impressed by the break in protocol. "Captain," she said, "you will not interrupt me in such a manner again. It is a shame on your training."

Wang Yong stood to attention as Ahuja turned to address Yenko and Li Jie. "You are dismissed. If what you say is true, there will be evidence of this Gravimetric Whatever. Make the search. Commander Huang, inform your Captain to assemble your Squadron. Our Scot scientist here will take charge of the search. He is likely to be the only person on Zhinu who will know what to look for. Tell your Captain that whatever resources are required will be made available.

"And now, Captain Liu, give me your report."

Yenko and Li Jie bowed formally and left the Commodore's tent as the Captain of Chi One Squadron began to report the encounter. Yenko would dearly have loved to stay behind to hear it. Maybe the rumors of ghosts had substance. Twice now, he had seen a woman who turned out not to be there.

———◄◦►———

The search yielded nothing. Three LRVs were given to Delta Squadron's Captain, Yang Zhi Ruo. That had sped up the process considerably and enabled the squadron to systematically scour the inner-city ruins. Yet all they discovered was more of the same. Ruin after ruin of buildings they already knew about from their extensive maps of Xin Beijing.

"We're missing something," Yenko said to Zhi Ruo. She had been working closely with him to determine their next move. After ten days, they had nothing of value to report back to the Commodore.

There had been several more ghost sightings over the last week. Perhaps there truly was an alien presence in the vicinity. Ever since Chi One Squadron's encounter, the camp had been placed on high alert.

That first incident had occurred when the squadron was performing routine reconnaissance of the lands further to the west of their base. Traversing a vast tract of open grassland, they crested a low hill where they rested in the shade of a stand of tall, broad-leaved trees. Ten of the company lay sprawled out under a particularly large tree, when a young girl ran right through them. Literally. Through them. With no show of cognizance of their presence. It was as if they were not there at all. Together, they watched in shock as several other ghostly children ran in and out of the trees, apparently unaware of the squadron.

A thorough search of the area gave rise to several more such encounters. On one of them, the ghostly images had seen the members of the company and run. Like the others, they were only visible for a brief moment.

That was all on the western plains. Xin Beijing, however, was dead.

"What do you suggest?" Captain Yang asked. She had been ordered to give leadership of the squadron to the redheaded separatist and she took the order seriously. He had discovered something of significance, and Zhi Ruo made it her goal to ensure he uncovered the answer to his mystery.

"I don't know, to be honest," Yenko said truthfully. "Perhaps I finished my investigation of the Kinematics files too soon."

"None of the technicians have found anything there to shed further light on your discovery," she offered.

"Yes, that's true," Yenko conceded. "They're good technicians. Talented in what they do. But none of them are Space-Time Kinematics technicians. What Khatri and Jain were working on was revolutionary. It would be completely new technology. The files could be right there under their noses and still they may not see them."

"Then you need to review their findings," Zhi Ruo agreed. "We shall continue our search of the city. We do not need you for the moment. Go and find your missing key."

It was a good plan and Yenko left the Captain and Delta Squadron. He did not need an accompanying guard. There would be guards aplenty on the fifth floor of the central university building.

Halfway up the fire escape, he looked back down on his empty camp. There she was again. Racing down the stairs two and three at a time, he sprinted to his tent. Before him walked the ghostly image of a young woman. Mid-twenties. The same one he had seen reflected in the screen in the Kinematics Lab so many nights ago. And from what he could make of the spectral image before him, she wore the same bodysuit of the woman who had entered his tent a week ago.

"Stop," he called, but she continued on as if she had not heard him.

This close, and with the advantage of seeing the whole person not just a reflection, Yenko understood now the rumors of ghosts. He could see right through her. If he looked slightly away, he somehow could see her more clearly, as if direct sight limited his vision.

She was real, however. This was no rumor, no hallucination. She was there. For a brief moment, she stood to attention and searched ahead in Yenko's general direction. Had she seen him? But how could she not? He was a thousand percent more substantial than her.

He took a step closer, she was no more than three feet away, and reached out a hand to touch her. There! She saw that! Instinctively, she flinched away from Yenko's outstretched arm and brandished what appeared to be a bone knife she produced from behind her. But she did not run. Standing her ground, she walked around the place where he stood, apparently searching for him, as if it was him who was less substantial than her.

Her eyes widened as they locked on to his. They stood face to face, barely two feet apart, the corporeal and the incorporeal in mutual awareness.

She was not quite like the reflection he had previously seen. The face he had seen then was beautiful, clear-skinned, alert. What he saw now had been brutalized, severely beaten. Her left eye was almost swollen shut. Deep purple bruises and welts marred her face. Traces of dried blood left tracks across her chin and neck.

Yenko's hard-learned street sense alerted him of no danger, however. Compassion and wonder filled him as he reached out once more to touch her. She flinched, making sure he could see the weapon, but allowed the gesture. Nothing. She was not there. His hand passed through her unimpeded. And yet she was unmistakably present.

"Can you hear me?" he asked.

She leaned forward, straining to hear, and mouthed something in reply. No sound.

"What happened to you?" Yenko could not hold back the concern he felt for her wounds. Though his hands told him she was not there, his eyes told a different story. And she was in need.

Perhaps it was the look in his eyes, the demeanor of his body, but she lowered her defense, put a hand to her face and caressed her bruised and swollen eye.

Yenko nodded. He knew what it was to be beaten. If she was physically present, he would offer to defend her in a heartbeat. He had never backed down from a fight. And after two years of training with the world's military elite, he was more than competent to do so.

But she was not there. And yet she was.

Reaching out once more, he made to put his hand on hers as it caressed her wound. She accepted the offer.

Perhaps it was a new technology. The Zhinu scientists obviously were not averse to conducting secretive research. Was this a new form of hologram, a projection of light? A new form of advanced communication? Or AI?

And yet, though she seemed to be made of light, the more he turned his eyes so that she was in his peripheral vision, the more substantial she appeared. She was there. He was convinced of it.

Clearly, it was impossible to talk to her. There was no sound. She obviously could not hear him, and he could not hear her. But they could see each other. If either of them moved more fully into the daylight, they lost sight of each other. Yenko was mesmerized. And still his heart burst for the violence she had suffered.

"Who did that to you?" he wondered aloud.

Bending over, he picked up a stick and drew on the ground.

Can you read? Enthusiastically, the woman nodded.

"You can?" Yenko asked, knowing she could not hear him. She nodded as if she had read his lips.

Erasing the words, he wrote again, *But that means we speak the same language.* Again, she nodded, this time thoughtfully. He was as much a riddle to her as she was to him.

The light started to dawn.

Are you one of the Colonists?

Slowly she nodded.

"*Huoyan xieshen*! Oh God! What have they done!!?"

Can you write?

She nodded and scratched a finger across the ground.

Yenko squinted hard but he could barely make out the indentation left by her finger.

Use a stick, he instructed and offered the one he had used. Sadly, she reached over to take it from him, but her hand went right through it.

"That's alright," he whispered. Holding his finger up, he articulated clearly so she could lip read, "Use your knife."

She smiled at him. Such a beautiful smile. It lit her whole face. How he wished he could wipe the blood stains from it.

I rite

It was faintly etched into the dirt, and incorrectly spelled, but he could read it.

"My name is Yenko," he said loudly as he scratched the words on the ground.

She mouthed the name. *Yenko.*

I em Fei Hung.

She looked up at him and smiled.

You ar a Robbie.

Whatever a Robbie was, Yenko did not know. Fei Hung reached out to touch Yenko's hair. But before she could, she suddenly flicked her head from side to side. She mouthed something, but Yenko could not lipread fast enough. There was trouble, and by the steel cold look in Fei Hung's eyes and the way she held the crude bone weapon, Yenko knew there would likely be a fight. Semi-crouched, and with one final curious look at Yenko, she raced towards the nearest building. As soon as she entered the full sunlight of the park, he lost sight of her.

Urgently, he scanned the area, hoping beyond hope that he might see where she had run and understand whether she was in mortal danger or not.

"Fei Hung!" he called hopelessly, fully aware that she could not hear him.

He ran to the building in the direction she had run before he had lost sight of her. It stood silently in utter darkness, guarding whatever secrets it held of the ghostly woman.

"Fei Hung!" he called again. "Fei Hung!"

4

The Destruction of Xin Beijing

T WO DAYS HAD PASSED since Yenko's chance meeting with the mysterious Fei Hung. In some unknown way, she was a descendant of the lost colonists of Xin Beijing. The encounter had been a revelation and many attempts had been made to establish similar communications with the ghostly images that had been seen in the western hills. But whether they were truly there, truly members of the vanished community, therewas no way of ascertaining; no sign had been made of them since.

Perhaps the ghostly images were simply afraid of the troops and kept their distance from them. The villagers were frightened of the ghosts; it was likely to work the other way around. There were any number of possibilities. It may have been that the lighting was never quite right enough for them to be seen. Perhaps they simply were elsewhere. Or not even real at all. No one could say.

It was another mystery. On a planet of mysteries.

Yenko applied himself diligently to sorting through the thousands of electronic files he had uncovered in the Laboratory. If they really had constructed a Gravimetric Discriminator, Yenko knew they would have had to collaborate with the Quantum Field Engineering Department. It could not have been kept a total secret within the one department of the university. The first step was to compile a list of cross-referenced files that were on both departments' sub-directories.

All the while, he stationed a technician to stand guard at the landing outside the fifth-floor door to the fire escape. The sole duty of the technician was to watch Yenko's campsite and sound the alert at the first sign of anything unusual. Fei Hung had been there before; she knew where he could be found.

The days rolled on. Nothing more was learned from his search of the files that related to both Kinematics and Engineering faculties. It was frustrating. Ghost sightings were sporadic but never led to encounters.

In fact, they had little even to do with the villagers, who kept largely to themselves in the farmlands of the east. They were deathly afraid of the ghosts and refused to go anywhere near the ruined city or the Third Fleet's bivouac.

◄◦►

"*Yang guizi.*"

Yenko smiled. He had not spoken to Li Jie for a long time. The Commander had been assigned other duties and had not even seen Yenko for several days. This was not a trial, though, for the soldier. He much preferred to be out and about, not cooped up in a laboratory twiddling his fingers while Yenko muttered scientific jargon that made no sense at all.

"What brings you up here?" Yenko asked. "The duty rotation doesn't end for another three hours yet."

"We have found something," Li Jie replied, "and we don't know if it's important or not. None of the technicians have seen anything like it before."

That piqued Yenko's professional curiosity.

"Well?" he demanded of the Commander as he rose to his feet. The documents he was working on could wait. "Are you just going to stand there and talk about it or are you going to show me?"

Huang shook his head but turned about nevertheless and led the way to a waiting reconnaissance vehicle. All the way down the outside stairway, Yenko kept an eye on his campsite. Nothing.

Before long, Li Jie brought their vehicle to a halt outside a small electrical power substation on the edge of the city's central business district. It was surrounded by industrial complexes of many sorts. All in ruin.

"It's just a power station," Yenko said, an obvious question in his voice. Even Li Jie should have recognized that, let alone the band of technicians that stood around its central control building.

"Not out here," Li Jie replied. "In there."

On entering the control room, Yenko had expected to see consoles and dashboards filled with instruments and gauges, typical of any electrical substation. And at first, that is exactly what he did see. But the hardware against the back wall was out of place.

"Mmmm," Yenko acknowledged. "Yes, you have found something indeed."

Several technicians stood back, keen to learn what the Space-Time Kinematics expert might have to say about the unknown equipment they had discovered.

Yenko ran his hand absently over several gauges on a control panel as he studied a large parabolic antenna array beside it.

"What were you needing an antenna for?" he pondered. "You are definitely out of place and not what would be expected in this room."

Turning to the technicians, he said, "Have you located the power grid profile of the station?"

"Of course," came the response. "Locating the PGPD was one of the first things we did. But we've never seen anything like it."

"Show me."

A female technician manipulated a large, central monitor and a detailed schematic map of the facility came into view, the words Power Grid Profile Data emblazoned in bold lettering across the top.

"Here," she said as she highlighted key elements of the display. "This is the antenna, and here is the instrumentation we don't recognize on that wall over there. But we can't decipher the symbols attached to them. The rest of the substation is simply that, a substation. And yet, there is too little load drawing on its output. It doesn't need to be as large as it is. They were doing something here that eludes us. We were hoping you might be able to tell us more."

Indeed, he could. The symbols the technicians knew nothing of were specific to Gravimetric Distortion and Discrimination.

Yenko whistled softly. "This was part of your research," he said to no one. "That much is obvious."

He looked back over at the antenna. "Where is that tuned to?"

"We don't know," came the honest reply. "We didn't think to test for that."

"Well you need to," Yenko demanded. "I think it will be crucial to our investigation."

A young Bhaarateey technician, maybe not even twenty years old, stepped forward with a small electronic device in his hand. Yenko absently wondered why someone so young would be allowed on the Zhinu mission. He was too young to have made a meaningful decision in changing the trajectory of his entire life for all time.

The lad took several readings and plotted them on a makeshift workstation the technicians had set up. After a few short minutes' calculation, he announced, "From its electronic configuration, it has a twofold design. From its angle of inclination, my best guess is that it is purposed to send to, and receive from, a point twenty-three miles, fifteen hundred and sixty feet at fifty-one degrees, twenty-eight minutes, thirty-eight seconds from North."

"Your best guess," Yenko mused, eyebrows raised. "Thank you. I suspect that will be accurate enough."

Turning to Li Jie, he added, "Now, where is twenty-three miles and however many feet in that direction?"

"The onboard navigation in the LRV will answer that," the Commander said. Turning to the young man, he added, "Come with us . . . what is your name?"

"Technician Varma, sir," the young man replied. "Lakshay Varma."

"Varma. Good."

"Lakshay, sir."

Li Jie looked at what, to him, was but a mere boy. "I will call you Varma."

"Yes, sir," the youth was quick to respond. "Thank you, sir. I did not mean to offend, sir."

The Commander shook his head. "*Bi zui!* Just come with us. We may need your attention to detail."

"Yes, sir." The young man was thrilled and followed them out to the reconnaissance vehicle.

Once there, Li Jie called up the global positioning monitor on the dashboard. A graphic three-dimensional display showed their current position.

"You determined the location, Varma," Li said firmly to the young man. "Where is it on this map?"

Lakshay consulted his readings and looking between them and the screen, he finally pointed to a spot on the map. "There, sir. We're going there." Searching the landscape to his right, he added, "It looks to be somewhere in those mountains."

"Very good," Li Jie commended with a nod. "Stay with us. We may need you again."

"Yes, sir," Lakshay eagerly replied.

"And don't speak unless you're spoken to," Li Jie added.

"Yes, sir."

The Commander stared at the young man.

"Sorry, sir." He chided himself for speaking again. "Sorry."

Frowning, he whispered, "Sorry, sir."

Li Jie shook his head. "Another *yang guizi*!"

Yenko laughed. Lakshay lay low.

———◄○►———

The trip was relatively uneventful. Several times, they swerved to avoid hitting rodents and larger animals that wandered across the decaying road. But the way was clear, and the road wound its way through thickly wooded hills until at length, the city itself was out of sight behind them.

"Why did they come out here?" Huang asked.

"I think I know why," Yenko replied, "but I want to wait till we're there because frankly, I don't want to be right."

The Commander raised an eyebrow but said no more.

"How much further, Varma?"

"It is hard for me to say, sir," the young man answered.

"What do you mean, it's hard for you to say? You were deadly accurate back at the substation."

"Yes, sir, I know, sir," Lakshay apologized. "I can tell you easily how far we are. We are yet two miles and forty-eight feet . . . forty-five . . . sixty . . ."

"Speak sense, boy," the Commander demanded.

"Sir, the road bends," Lakshay pleaded. "I cannot be as accurate as you want me to be."

Li Jie looked at Yenko. "Were you ever like this?"

Yenko laughed. Lakshay laughed also, though it was obvious he did not know why.

Presently, they rounded a bend and came upon a sight they had not expected, as the road disappeared into the side of the mountain. Heavy metal gates barred the way forward.

Commander Huang brought the LRV to a halt. After making a brief report to the Commodore, the three men approached the imposing barrier. A small, keyed door stood closed to one side. Yenko tried it. Locked.

"Nothing is locked," Li Jie said. Turning to the technician, he added, "Stay well behind me, Varma. I know you've trained with us but keep your youthful impulses in check. This isn't a game."

"Yes, sir," Lakshay said. Clearly it was more than a game; it was an adventure of a lifetime.

Li Jie took a plasma shotgun from behind his seat and returned to the door, aimed, and fired. No effect. He fired again. Still no effect. Calmly, he walked back to the LRV, opened the trunk and pulled out a CME carbine. The Coronal Mass Ejection carbine was designed to reproduce the highly magnetized plasma discharges of the Sun. There were few handheld weapons that were more devastating.

"Definitely stand back this time, Varma," he warned. Yenko himself stood well clear of any accidental ricochet.

The carbine was remarkably quiet for something so destructive. The door swung ajar, a gaping hole where the locking mechanism had once been.

"Nothing is locked," Li Jie repeated as he kicked the door wide open.

From inside, they could see the road leading on and on into the dim light of a long tunnel.

"Is there a way to open the gates?" Yenko asked. It seemed pointless to walk when the way before them was so well paved. "There's no way of knowing how far this road goes."

"One mile, eighteen hundred and six feet," Lakshay chimed in, face intent on the instrument panel in his hand.

Both men looked at him.

"If the road is straight, sir," he added apologetically. "It may be longer."

"We'll open the gates," Li Jie conceded and examined the locking mechanism on the massive barriers.

"There's a manual override switch here," Yenko called from beside a monitor near the door they had just blasted. Pulling on the double-handed lever, the groans of shifting metal could be heard from inside and around the gates.

"Theoretically, they're open now," he said.

"Back to the LRV," Li Jie ordered. "I'd rather a CAV right now, but the closest one is on Earth."

The reconnaissance vehicle might have been light, but it was certainly powerful. With only a little encouragement, it pushed the gates aside and drove on into the tunnel, lights exposing the path ahead.

Lakshay had been more accurate than he had thought when he suggested the tunnel may be longer than his readings predicted. It made several sweeping turns. In the end, they travelled well over two miles before their path ended in a broad parking bay. Warning signs were emblazoned on practically every wall, and they entered a simple door that led to a large facility housing a gigantic replica of the machine they had seen at the substation.

Standing proudly in the center of the cavernous space stood a massive reflective antenna. Its parabolic dish was easily forty feet across. But Yenko was not so much interested in that. Under the light of a flashlight, he examined bank upon bank of instrument panels that plastered the walls on either side.

Li Jie had worked with Yenko in this mood too often. He knew it would take time, and he knew not to converse with his scientist friend; he would get no rational response until Yenko was ready. Lakshay just took a seat on the ground and waited, content to be a part of the adventure.

Finally, Yenko stood back from his examination, hands raised to his lips, a silent prayer for the folly of Zhinu. Incongruously, a tear etched a pathetic line down his cheek. It did not escape Li Jie's attention.

"What have you learned?" he asked, almost reverently.

Yenko looked wearily at his friend. They had fought together, laughed together, drunk together. They had crossed interstellar space together, vomited the cryostatic fluids of their embalmment together. And it had all come to this.

"They built a Gravimetric Discriminator," he said with an air of broken finality. "They actually did it. This is what destroyed Xin Beijing. They're dead, every last one of them. They thought to reveal a bold new science, but they killed everyone. All of them!"

"But Fei Hung," Li Jie suggested.

Yenko shook his head in defeat. "I don't know," he confessed. "Maybe she really is a ghost."

"Ghosts don't have bruised faces," the Commander countered. "There's more to the story."

Yenko nodded. Maybe there was. It would require a lot of study, a lot of analysis. And it would not be quick. Memories of the ghostly image of Fei Hung flashed across his mind's eye, urging him not to give up on her people. On her.

———◄◦►———

Yenko's work took on a whole new, macabre dimension as he studied one of the most tragic accidents in scientific history. He knew now what had happened to Xin Beijing. The mystery of Zhinu's silence since 2347 could at last be put to rest.

Mahika Khatri and Arushi Jain, both first generation Zhinu colonists born to members of the Second Fleet, had worked on a tangential application of the renowned Hans Werner's work. From what Yenko could determine, as early as 2322, Khatri was writing in-house papers that were never shared with her counterparts on Earth, not even of her own ancestral nation, Bhaarat. In 2336, she began in earnest to push the bounds of her work. By 2338, Arushi Jain was working alongside her.

"Whoa!" Yenko exclaimed. "What's this?"

He had opened a folder that contained just the one file. But it was massive, a holographic video file with the innocuous title, *Presentation*. Time markers dated it *Qi Yue 17, 96XS*.

It took a while to determine the corresponding Earth date, but Yenko felt intuitively that it was important to know. He could find no information concerning the file, but it was huge, and he wanted to know when it was created and how close that was to the disaster before he went to the effort of downloading it and setting up a viewing platform capable of playing it.

Both the rotation of Zhinu about its planetary axis and its period of revolution about its sun were similar to Earth's but not identical. Within the first year of the First Fleet's settlement of the planet, a new dating system had been adopted. Years were marked XS, Xin Shijian. The names of Zhinu's ten months were adopted from the first ten of Earth's months. The time index on the hologram was Qi Yue 17, 96XS . . . July 17, in the ninety-sixth orbit of Zhinu. It equated to San Yue 11, 2339AD on Earth, one hundred and four years after the arrival of the First Fleet.

March 11. Eight years before Zhinu went silent. It was significant and warranted the long days of work required from the small team of technicians assigned to Yenko.

At length, Yenko's research facility had been refitted and was ready for the recording to be played. As soon as the file was loaded, two life-sized holographic women, clothed in black suits, stood in the middle of the lab. Yenko had seen video projections of this data size before, but not often. The computing memory required was phenomenal. Whatever the women were about to say, or whoever it was that was intended to view it, one thing was immediately apparent; this was a major discovery.

"Your Excellency," the first woman said, as both bowed profusely, "Governor of New World Colony. We are honored by the gracious time you have extended toward us. We will be as brief as possible, but we stand on the brink of the greatest breakthrough in space technology of all time.

"My name is Dr Mahika Khatri, and this is my colleague, Dr Arushi Jain." The two women again bowed deeply.

"We work in the field of Space-Time Kinematics," Dr Jain took over from Dr Khatri. "It is the branch of study that enabled the birth of our great colony on Zhinu. Independent of our peers on Earth, we have developed a new technology."

"Your Excellency," Dr Khatri continued, in what was obviously a rehearsed presentation, "what would you say if we said we had developed a technology that would allow travel from Zhinu to Earth in less than a day? What would you say if we no longer required construction of spacecraft and cryostatic life pods? It would be a wonder, yes? We believe we have found a way to make this a reality. Our theories check at every investigation, and small-scale studies have proved exciting. It is why we have come to you."

Dr Jain stepped to one side and drew an imaginary line in the air between herself and her colleague. As she did so, a solid green line linked the two holographic scientists. "Imagine if you will that Dr Khatri is on Earth and I am on Zhinu. If I wish to travel to her, or she to me, the obvious path is the straight line between us. This is the very path that light takes. It is impossibly long for us to consider travelling it ourselves."

"But as you have no doubt learned in your extensive studies, Your Excellency," Dr Khatri continued, "space-time can be manipulated. The line between myself and Dr Jain may not be the shortest distance."

With that, she took two sideways steps towards Dr Jain. The green line behaved as if it was tethered to each scientist and arced upwards in a gentle curve.

"The shortest distance now between us is no longer the green line." A blue line linked the two holographic forms. "The green is still there as you can see in our demonstration, and light still travels along that path. But we can make the distance as short as we want." And she stepped even closer to her colleague. The green line arced sharply upwards as the blue line shrunk.

"It is not that straightforward, though," Dr Jain added. "There are other forces at work that limit our ability to create such a smooth transition." Dr Khatri retreated two steps back and the green line took on a more gently curved aspect. "When conditions are not favorable, as in fact, they are not in our case, the curve becomes unstable."

The green line dropped and formed a wave pattern over the blue line.

"You can see how at one instant the blue line is below the green and at another it is above the green. When it is above, travel must obey conventional laws."

"This is why," continued Dr Khatri, "it took us so many years to travel here. But we have found a way to negate the complexities that cause the problem." Instantly, the green and blue lines disappeared. "The technology employed by our great First and Second Fleets, in effect, was based on building a kind of tunnel between the two worlds." A three-dimensional, blue tube linked both scientists. "The wider the tunnel, so to speak, to allow a spacecraft say, the more problems are encountered."

"And it is because we were not thinking multi-dimensionally," Dr Jain said enthusiastically. "What if we could find a way to have more than one dimension, the straight line? A surface, not a line! A surface that exists on both planets at the same moment. A surface that acts as a door between the worlds!"

A solid green rectangle appeared beside each woman.

"A craft may fly through one door," she said, holding a small model aircraft and flying it into the green rectangle.

"And it would emerge on the other side of the door," Dr Jain finished, dramatizing with an identical model that she brought out from a pocket. "Your Excellency, we have found a way to open such a door. And it need not be done in outer space and requires no cryostasis. We could build a plane and fly from Xin Beijing and emerge in the airspace of Beijing in moments."

"Ultimately," Dr Khatri added, "we need to explore further applications. The door that we have just described . . . What if it was a volume, not a surface? We could instantly transport a person from one place to another. The teleportation that has long been the subject of science-fiction is within our grasp."

"Your Excellency," Dr Jain concluded, "our hope is that you will see the unfathomable opportunity that lies before us. We have built prototypes of the technology, but we have come to the limit of our resources. We need considerable funding. Thousands of workers will need to be employed if we are to build the next stage of the project. A full-scale model. We make our humble appeal to you, convinced that you will see the brave, new future before us."

"We bow before you, Your Excellency," added Dr Khatri, "and await your response. May the ancestors shine on you with favor and prosperity."

Yenko remained where he stood for some moments after the holographic display ended.

March 11, 2339. Eight years before it all went horribly wrong.

———◄○►———

Yenko worried. It was more than two months since he had seen Fei Hung. He still recalled her instinctive aggression the day he first saw her. And her beaten face from their meeting in the campsite. Hardly a day passed without him imagining what might have become of her, why she had run, how she came to be so beaten. Despite his studies no longer strictly requiring him to remain so near the ruins of the university, he kept his camp. It was the last place he had seen her. If she ever looked for him again, that would be the first place she would go.

His tent was no longer there, however, replaced now by a lightweight aluminum alloy cabin, a leftover from the bivouac camp of the Third Fleet. The members of the company from the *Zhinu Phoenix* had slowly begun to intersperse with the local villagers. Construction of housing developments set to accommodate the new arrivals was well underway.

The villagers were still afraid of the ghost tales that had been handed down from generation to generation. It seemed fitting to the new colonists, then, that they should not build near the ruins of Xin Beijing. They needed the companionship and welcome of the villagers, so established a new settlement to the east of the river delta, far from the ill-fated city.

All of that was irrelevant for Macpherson Yenko, however. The university grounds were where he belonged. Where he was needed. And where Fei Hung would look if ever she sought him again.

———◄○►———

Yenko woke late. It was his day off and he allowed himself the luxury of drifting in and out of wakefulness. It seemed like a pleasant morning outside. Light streamed in through the open cabin door and played over his closed eyelids, creating dappled patterns across his dreamy sight.

In many ways, he liked his home in the park, and he more than once had considered asking if he could build a permanent dwelling there, not just this cabin. There was a certain mystery and ambience about living in a ruin. His studies were progressing. With each day, he understood more clearly how the catastrophe had come to pass. But he was still no closer to solving the riddle of Zhinu's ghosts.

These apparitions were well documented by now and had even been captured on film. This did not assuage the villagers' fears, however. It only served to substantiate their tales. But it did mean that he was left to himself a lot, with the bulk of his company now involved in secular affairs. Even Huang Li Jie was busily making a new life for himself. He had met a woman, and from what Yenko had heard, it seemed to be serious.

Taking a deep breath, he opened his eyes. Shimmering lights danced about him. With a start, he sat up on his mattress, pushing himself away from the doorway. Fei Hung sat cross-legged on the floor, to one side of the opening. She just sat there, staring at him. The swelling of her eye and the bruising on her face were gone. But she looked weary.

Yenko's heart wanted to burst. He was happy and concerned at the same time. How ever it was that the light played through the open door and curtained windows, the mottled tones had the effect of making her more visible than he had seen her before. She looked so substantial that he felt he could surely touch her, and he involuntarily reached out a hand to hers.

The two met. And passed through each other.

It was then that he noticed her arm, clearly seen in the dappled early morning light within the hut. Crisscrossed scars revealed a history of abuse.

Fei Hung leaned towards him and put a finger to her lips. He had no idea why; she could not hear him. She indicated for him to shut the door, which he did in an instant.

They sat looking at each other for a long while. Because he did not know what dangers the woman faced, he took her cue and sat in silence.

Yenko pulled out a writing tablet and stylus.

Your eye is better, he wrote. She nodded.

Are you safe?

Fei Hung searched his eyes. A slight shrug of the shoulders was her only response.

I've discovered what happened in Xin Beijing. Why all the devastation.

She came to life. Slowly she mouthed, "Why are you all spirits?"

It took a while for Yenko to lipread her words accurately, but with the help of the writing tablet he confirmed that he had understood her.

Fei Hung, he wrote. *I'm not a spirit. I'm solid. It's you who isn't.*

She looked shocked. And reached out to touch him but her hand went right through him as if he were but a cloud.

Yenko smiled encouragingly at her. He extended his hand toward hers and gently made as if to stroke the scars of her arm. She bit her lower lip and looked into his eyes. She was lost. And yet, right in front of him.

I haven't given up, he wrote. *I know what happened to the city, but I don't know what happened to you and your people.*

She smiled in acknowledgement.

Presently, she motioned for him to open the door.

"That's interesting," he thought. "Her hand should pass right through the door. Why not just walk through it? The cabin is as much a ghost to her as she is to it."

Perhaps she wanted him to come outside with her. Eager to continue the interaction, he got up and opened the door. There was nothing of particular interest anywhere around them; not that he could make out, at least. No ghostly figures in the shaded area of the park where his cabin stood.

Together, they walked out onto the grass and surveyed the ruins about them. What did it look like through her eyes? Was everything ghostly? She did not sink through the ground, so some things were solid for her. He had seen her on the fifth floor in the lab; clearly, she could ascend stairs. And she did not float, so gravity was real.

"That's interesting," he thought again. "You're here but you're not here. And yet you are. That says something. But what . . . ?"

Shaking his head, he laughed in frustration. "I just have no idea," he said aloud.

She was unaware he had spoken.

"I must go," she mouthed to him. "Can I see you tomorrow?"

"Yes," he said eagerly. "Please."

Fei Hung took a deep breath and walked off. At the edge of the park, she turned to look on him one last time. He raised his hand. She smiled and disappeared into the shadows.

When he would see her again, he did not know. He hoped that she really would come again the next day, but he was not confident. Everything about her was flighty. Her world had troubles he knew nothing of.

In the meantime, he had struck on a thought and was keen to explore it. Hastily, he downed a scant breakfast and raced up the familiar fire escape to his laboratory.

———◄◦►———

"*Yang guizi.*"

Yenko spun around from his work. It had been the best part of a week since he had seen anyone, let alone his friend, the Commander.

"Where have you been, lately?" Li Jie said, a frown on his face. "Always you are up here. Is this what your life was like in the Scot Province? No wonder your hair went red. Too much radiation from your computers."

The two laughed as Li Jie produced a metallic flask from his coat. "Here, this will turn your hair black."

"I have been a bit of a recluse lately," Yenko conceded and accepted the flask. It took his breath and they laughed again. "So is this just a social visit?"

"I want you to meet Yu Yan," Li Jie replied. "You're my best friend and you haven't even met her yet!"

Yenko laughed again and took another drink from the flask. "You had to bring alcohol to convince me to come? Is there something wrong with her?"

The Commander looked sternly at his comrade. It shook Yenko somewhat. Maybe there was something wrong with her.

"Yenko," he began, "you need to know something about Yu Yan. She's a Macpherson."

Eyes wide open in shock, Yenko realized that not once had he thought of the descendants of Robert Macpherson, his own ancestor who had been a part of the First Fleet to Zhinu. There had just been too much mystery and intrigue that he had unearthed since he first stepped onto the new world, and he had been engulfed by his investigations.

"Yu Yan . . . Macpherson . . ." he said in wonder.

"It was probably the first thing that attracted me to her," Li Jie confessed. "Her whole family were among the first to welcome in those of us from the Third Fleet. You're something of a celebrity for them, you know."

"A celebrity?" Yenko repeated dumbly.

"They know about you, Yenko. Word of the mad scientist working in the city ruins has spread across the colony. As soon as the Macphersons learned your name, they've been eager to meet you. They won't come to

Xin Beijing, of course. They are as scared of the place as any of the other colonists. But they talk often of you and keep asking if I might be able to pull you away from your work.

"And to be honest, *yang guizi*, I'm keen for you to meet them. Well . . . Yu Yan, at least."

"Macpherson Yu Yan . . ." Yenko mumbled.

"Yu Yan Macpherson," Li Jie corrected. "They maintain the tradition of your forefathers."

———◄○►———

Night was beginning to fall as Li Jie drove Yenko to Yu Yan's home in the nearby village. The house was too small for the crowd of Macphersons that had come together, excited to at last meet their eccentric relative. Yenko saw no family resemblances that he could readily make out. Perhaps they were taller than the rest of the colonists in general. And many of them had blue eyes. But that was all. They certainly did not look Scottish.

Quite a commotion was made when he walked into their midst for the first time. The older women all wanted to touch his hair. Many of the younger ones playfully renamed him Robbie. It was the name Fei Hung had used of him. The term had become common parlance amongst the colonists over the last century and a half. It meant "redhead" and derived from Yenko's own forebear, Robert. Yenko was proud to be known by the nickname, although, if he had known, some of the non-Macpherson villagers were shocked by the lack of respect.

The night was a happy one. Food and drink abounded and Yenko held court often about life in his beloved Scotland. Yu Yan was especially interested in their long lost relative. She was the lover of his best friend and had heard many stories of their exploits and knew as much as Li Jie understood of the importance of Yenko's contributions to the mission of the Third Fleet.

"What are you up to in the ruins?" Yu Yan asked when she and Li Jie had an opportunity to talk to Yenko on their own. "Try to keep it simple."

Yenko was instantly excited, like a small boy in a toy shop.

"Ever since Fei Hung came the other day . . ." he began. Noting Li Jie's raised eyebrows, he added, "I did tell you, didn't I? Maybe I didn't. What day is it? I've just been so busy."

The look on Yu Yan's face showed she knew nothing of the ghostly woman.

"Fei Hung . . ." he said. "You haven't heard of her, then?"

"The villagers have not been told," Li Jie confirmed. "It would fuel their fears."

For Yu Yan, that just made it more imperative that she be told. She was not afraid of ghosts, despite the prevailing fears of the villagers. Yenko looked at Li Jie and the two studied each other, the unspoken question as to whether to break protocol and tell Yu Yan of the mysterious woman.

"She'll find out anyway," Yenko said into the silence, and began the whole tale of his encounters with the knife-wielding, leather-clad woman.

"Robbie," Yu Yan said at length, "I can see that intrigue and wonder surrounds you. Let me ask again: What is it that you study there among the ruins of our old capital?"

"Keep it simple," the Commander said. "For my sake," he added, as Yu Yan shot a look of offence at him. She may be smart enough to understand his scientist friend, but Li Jie was happy to admit that much of Yenko's technical talk went right over his head.

Yenko laughed. He had not missed the interplay.

"Do you remember some time ago," he said to Li Jie, "when I was describing what they'd been working on up there?"

Li Jie remembered. "You ruined your shirt."

"Yes, I suppose I did," Yenko laughed. "But do you remember I showed you the mistake they made in their calculations? They didn't account for the quantum displacement variance?"

"I didn't understand a bit of it," Li Jie confessed, "but I do remember. You solved the problem twice, once as they did and once by adding a new line that you said destroyed it all."

"Close enough," Yenko said. "Yu Yan, they were doing secret research at the university. Before the catastrophe." And he went on to try to explain the complexities of interstellar space travel to the village woman.

"But I've been doing my own studies since Fei Hung came," he concluded. "She can't touch me. I mean, physically . . . She can't touch me. Her hand passes right through mine. Yu Yan, she's lived her whole life thinking that the villagers are spirits. To her, we're the ghosts. Not her.

"But she came to my cabin the other morning . . ."

"When did she come to your cabin?" Li Jie interrupted. "Surely you reported this?"

Yenko looked sheepish. He had been so taken up with his studies that he had omitted to tell anyone of his last encounter. Fei Hung had intended to come back the next day. Maybe, had that eventuated, he might have thought to make a report. But as it stood, he had not told a soul of her visit.

"Well," he offered in excuse of his absentmindedness, "I've been busy. But look, that's not the important bit. I started to realize that it's not quite as straightforward as I was thinking. Her hand passes through mine. It should pass through every solid object. But it doesn't."

"What do you mean?" Yu Yan asked.

"She needed me to open the door."

To Yenko, it was a profound revelation, but neither Yu Yan nor the Commander could comprehend it.

"Don't you see?" Yenko continued eagerly. "She doesn't float through the ground. She can climb the stairs and enter my laboratory. Not everything in our world is insubstantial to her.

"I've been trying to come up with models to make sense of that. Every simulation I develop arrives at the same eventuality. The city and its people should have been annihilated."

"So you're not putting in the right information," Li Jie suggested.

Yenko was puzzled. "This is my field, Li Jie."

"I know that. But I also know that if you keep getting the same wrong result, you probably are making the same mistake in all your simulations. If I take a plasma shotgun into a fight that can only be won with a plasma cannon, I will lose no matter how many strategies I employ."

Silence held as Yenko regarded the man and woman standing in front of him. Something his military friend had said had sparked a thought.

"The quantum displacement variance . . . It is after all, only a new science . . . Maybe it's not completely accurate."

Yu Yan and Li Jie looked questioningly at each other. Raising a finger to silence them both, regardless of the fact that neither of them knew how to voice their questions, he added, "I have to go back. I think you've hit something on the head."

"Come on," Li Jie said to the baffled Yu Yan, "I've seen him like this before. He's solved the riddle, I know it."

An hour later, the three of them stood in the research facility of the Kinematics Department of Xin Beijing Daxue. It was the first time Yu Yan had visited the ruined city and she had stared in wonder ever since they had entered the desolate outskirts. Yenko strode deliberately towards a board on the wall covered in equations and mathematical symbols.

Erasing it with a sweep of his hand, he began to reformulate the problem he had been studying that morning when Li Jie had interrupted him. Scribbling furiously, he filled the board, cramming in line after line of equations that meant absolutely nothing to his military onlooker or his distant relative.

At length, a moment of epiphany hit him, and, standing back from the hieroglyphics, he looked at Li Jie in wonder.

"You're a genius," he said.

"I am?"

Li Jie and Yu Yan eyed each other in confusion.

"It was the other way round!"

"What was the other way round?" The Commander was thoroughly baffled.

"I was using a plasma cannon when what I needed was a plasma shotgun."

Standing back from the board, he added at length, "There's a phase variance. But what would that mean?"

He placed his hands on his head and studied the board.

"Well don't ask me," Li Jie said. "I just shoot the guns."

Yenko looked at him and Yu Yan absently, his mind racing through the implications that may be attached to a phase variance of the quantum displacement. They would be subtle—if they existed at all.

"Feel free to hang around," he said to the two of them, "but you've just opened a whole new investigation. And yet . . . and yet . . . in the end, you know, it may not be that difficult. Would you mind doing me a favor? Could you find that technician you wanted to hit in the mountains? He'll have the data I need."

"Varma?" Li Jie questioned. "Macpherson, it's the middle of the night. Don't you think we should deal with this tomorrow?"

"Tomorrow . . ." Yenko repeated absently, making slight adjustments to calculations on the board. "Yes, I suppose we'll have to . . . If it's the middle of the night . . . I suppose he'll be asleep . . ."

In defeat, he looked at his two friends. Li Jie, the Commander, his closest companion. And Yu Yan, whom he had only met that day for the first time, his relative, the descendant of Robert. Everything within him wanted to ignore the need for sleep, to wake up Varma and get the data he knew he needed.

Yu Yan seemed to see the inner conflict he faced. Walking over to him she kissed him on the cheek. "Robbie," she said in her mellow voice, "you need to sleep. We'll come back tomorrow and then you can solve your problem."

The sound of her voice was compelling. He did feel tired, and he knew within himself that he would do better work when rested. If he could sleep, that was.

————◦————

Early the next morning, Yenko woke to the sound of banging on his cabin door. It was Li Jie and Yu Yan. They had brought breakfast with them.

"Do you know where to find Varma?" Yenko asked, hastily downing the food. He was keen to get on with his line of inquiry. In fact, if not for Yu Yan's presence, he would not have accepted the offer of breakfast at all. But she was an imposing woman and Yenko had found himself sitting with them to eat, biding the time till they could get back onto the task at hand.

"Yes, I can find him," Li Jie replied. "I'll just listen for the sound of girls giggling."

————◦————

They found Lakshay Varma as Li Jie had suspected, entertaining a group of young women as he was helping construct a house in the new settlement. When he saw the LRV pull up with the Commander, chief scientist, and a villager, he immediately put down his tools, apologized to his audience, and ran to meet them.

"I need the data you downloaded in the mountains," Yenko said.

"Yes, sir. It is in my quarters."

"Well come on then," Li Jie commanded, not unkindly. "Climb in and tell us where you're staying."

Twenty minutes later, Yenko had what he needed. The operating frequency range of the Discriminator, the electrical discharge phase of the conversion unit and the frequency of the amplitude modulator on the reciprocal unit at the power substation.

"Thank you, Lakshay," Yenko said, eager to get back to his laboratory. "You've been more helpful than you know."

"It pleases me to serve you, sir," Lakshay replied and bowed formally.

————◦————

Two days later, Yenko asked for a meeting with Commodore Ahuja and her executive staff. Seven high-ranking Captains were in attendance, along with fifteen of the senior scientific personnel. Four Commanders stood sentry on the door, Huang among them.

"Thank you for allowing me to call this meeting," he said when all were seated. "I can now say with a high level of assurance that I know exactly what happened here at Xin Beijing in 2347. And her inhabitants are undoubtedly alive. Or at least, they were. I am certain they survived the catastrophe."

The meeting held its collective breath in anticipation. The colonists had survived. How was it possible?

"Their chief scientists were seeking to open a portal between Zhinu and Earth, one that would resolve the need for a craft to drop in and out of conventional space. If they had been correct, they could have reduced travel between planets to a matter of seconds.

"But they weren't correct. There was knowledge they didn't have.

"I've studied the machinery that is now off-limits to the colony . . . in the substation in the northern quarter of the city, and in the mountain facility beyond the forest. According to their calculations . . . and I've checked and rechecked their numbers countless times . . . they hoped to create a portal three hundred feet square. They predicted it would open somewhere in the safety of the forest in the foothills of the range."

The assembled men and women slowly shook their heads in wonder. If such a thing was possible, it would open a whole new world to all humanity. Every planet would be within reach. Easily.

"Actually," Yenko conceded, "I think there are definite possibilities with their theory. But they did not know what they did not know.

"At last, I've solved the equation. Instead of forming a portal in the forest, they created a cone, beaming out roughly horizontally, with its apex in the mountain facility. It spread out at an angle of twenty-one degrees, with an axis that reached as far as one hundred miles.

"No portal opened, but everything within that volume was affected. Its impact was felt right down to the electronic configuration of every atom, every molecule, every chemical bond.

"Applying a fuller understanding to their work, I have adjusted their calculations. Every complex molecule that chiefly comprised atoms with outer electrons in orbitals up to the three-s energy shell were displaced. The colonists had sought to fold space. In the end, they merely shifted it, threw it out of phase. By one point seven degrees."

Commodore Ahuja interrupted. "Pardon my ignorance," she said, "but you've lost me."

"My apologies," Yenko replied. "Let me put it this way. All of the heavy elements, the metals, the heavy earths . . . they were not affected.

Things like rocks and cement and steel. But lighter elements, even those in complex molecules, organic matter, plants, timber, doorframes, seat cushions, people . . . all were spatially phase-shifted one point seven degrees.

"The colonists would have survived, I believe. The phase-shift is small. The larger elements and less complex molecular structures would still be able to interact with those that were out of phase. But any comparable molecules would not. It's the electronic configuration within the bonds that makes the difference."

"So you are saying," the Commodore suggested, "that when they activated their device, everything organic winked out of sight. Tables vanished and whatever was on them crashed to the floor. Timberwork in buildings disappeared and weakened walls and floors and caused widespread damage. And the people disappeared."

"Exactly," Yenko affirmed. "It's still all there. You just can't interact with it. If you get just the right light, perhaps, you might see it. But everything would appear to you as a ghost image . . . and we to it."

"The apparitions that people have seen . . ." suggested one of the senior executives. "They're the descendants of those colonists?"

The assembly sat in silence, pondering the significance of what they had just learned.

"Is there any hope for them?" Commodore Ahuja asked.

No one answered. It was a question with no answer. Not yet, at least.

5

Demons in the Dark

N EWS OF YENKO'S FINDINGS spread like wildfire across the colony, amongst the newly arrived members and the villagers alike. Of those in the three small farming communities, many had lost family members to the catastrophe of 2347. The eldest of them still had vivid memories of the confused days that followed in the wake of the disaster. They told stories of communications going down, power being disrupted, and frantic trips into the city out of concern for friends or family, finding nothing but a ghost town.

It had been less than half a century ago.

The older folk were shocked to discover that those who perished in 104XS, the year in their calendar when the disaster hit, were quite possibly still alive and that the ghost legends they had all believed for decades were likely based on real sightings of the lost colonists. Years of separation. And not once realizing they lived beside each other, dimensionally shifted in a way few understood.

Yenko was assigned a research team. Their mandate: to determine if it was possible to correct the phase misalignment and restore the lost colonists to Zhinu proper. The assignment was a daunting one. Resources were severely limited. Including the members of the Third Fleet, there were fewer than three thousand colonists and despite their many talents, most of them were unskilled in the highly specialized fields the investigation required.

And there was a lot of ongoing work that had to continue, despite the task before them. The Third Fleet's settlement had to be completed. Food resources had to be established. It was almost an impossible undertaking.

———◄○►———

Li Jie and Yenko ran at a demanding pace across the dunes to the south of the ruined city. The Commander had informed his scientist friend that it was not good for him to stay cooped up in laboratories all day.

"Back on Earth," Li Jie had said earlier that morning, "you worked hard to get your fitness up, *yang guizi*. I'm still your commanding officer and I don't like having flabby squadron members."

Now, as they mounted yet another dune, Yenko regretted his acceptance of the training run. He should have known it would be grueling; Huang was a dedicated zealot to fitness, the martial arts, and weapons drill.

At the bottom of the dune, Yenko collapsed onto all fours.

"How much more of this is there?"

The Commander laughed. "You are soft," he said, and collapsed beside Yenko.

"That makes me feel better," the Scot said, but he did not have enough energy to muster a laugh.

"Yenko," Li Jie said when he had caught his breath.

The way he had said his name alerted Yenko. Something was afoot.

"I have a request to make of you."

Something definitely was afoot.

"Ask away," Yenko said.

The soldier searched for the right words to say.

"I'm going to ask Yu Yan to marry me."

"What?!" Yenko replied. "I mean, I knew you were an item, but marry? Where did that come from?"

Li Jie laughed. "Macpherson, you wouldn't know anything of what goes on in the world around you."

It probably was true, Yenko thought. He was a bit of a recluse at the best of times and, given the momentous importance of the discoveries he had brought to light since landing on Zhinu, he had actively shunned human contact as much as possible. People just slowed him down.

"Yu Yan?"

"We'll be relatives. So then my request . . ." Li Jie said. "Will you be my best man?"

"Of course, I will!" Yenko accepted with a laugh of disbelief. "Have you set a date?"

"Three weeks."

"Three weeks? You're not hanging around, are you! Are you sure you know what you're doing? In a little community like this, if it all goes pear-shaped, you won't be able to walk away from it easily."

The Commander held Yenko's eyes with his own.

"I am more certain than of anything else I have ever done, my friend. I've fought in more battles than I care to remember. Do you think I cannot master marriage?"

Yenko chuckled. "Well, I'm not sure it's a good idea to use military analogies when talking about marriage." He laughed again. "But she is a Macpherson! It'll make for some interesting engagements!"

They both laughed.

Three weeks later, the two were married. It heralded a new beginning for the New World Colony. And a whole new world for Commander Huang Li Jie. In many ways, he had met his match. Like the Commander himself, she too was intimidating. And as Yenko had predicted, it did make for some interesting engagements.

———— ◄○► ————

The night sky shone with stars and threw a considerable light on Yenko's park. He figured that he had lived there so long now, it was his by squatter's rights. A whole year had passed since the company of the *Zhinu Phoenix* first landed on the remote Earth colony.

This was perhaps the first time Yenko had bothered to look at the night sky of his new home. He lay back on the grass and wondered at the sheer immensity of the Milky Way shining down on his little existence.

Huang Li Jie and his new wife, Huang Yu Yan, sat comfortably on the lawn beside him. They had all just finished a meal together, a regular occurrence these days. Yu Yan had insisted that it was not good for her distant relative to live such a hermit's life. And if he would not come to them, they would go to him.

Turning to the newlyweds, Yenko considered the ancestry of Li Jie's bride. Even though they were distantly related, Yu Yan looked Zhongwen, nothing at all like a Scot. Apart from the blue eyes. Yenko liked her and could see why Li Jie was attracted to her. She was a delight to be around. Fun. Cheeky. Quick-witted but with a caring, empathetic nature.

"What thoughts wander through those dusty corridors?" Li Jie asked him.

Yenko laughed. It almost sounded poetic, not at all what he had come to expect from his pragmatic, military trained friend. "I was thinking that I've corrupted you," he confessed.

"How so?"

"You've hung around me so long, you've gone and married a *yang guizi*."

Yu Yan was shocked and quite obviously did not know whether to be offended or not. Li Jie simply laughed.

"I did not school you hard enough," he suggested, "when I taught you discipline in our basecamp in Beijing. I should have put you in hospital more often.

"It's alright, Yu Yan, my love. He is a savage. The world of your Macpherson forefather has greatly deteriorated in recent times. Your ancestor did well in moving here or you would be like him yourself."

Everyone laughed, though Yu Yan did so with an element of misgiving. There was a bond of friendship between the two men that she loved, and she saw that her husband took no offence at all at the slur that had been directed towards her. But she did not understand. *Yang guizi* was offensive.

"You are both *yang guizi*," she said.

Now that did make the two men laugh. She shook her head in resignation.

Turning back to his contemplation of the stars, Yenko said, "I heard the latest communique from Earth. Now that they understand the nature of the Zhinu mystery, they've taken the stops off their plans for establishing other colonies. And they've redirected significant funding towards Space-Time Kinematic research. If they can resolve the difficulties in Khatri and Jain's work, anything will become possible. The universe is at our feet."

"Have they added any knowledge to aid you in your own mission, Robbie?" Yu Yan asked. "Have you worked out how to bring our lost people back to us?"

"No. I could reproduce the event that caused it all if I wanted, but reversing it is a different matter. I think I've solved the riddle of the reverse;

how to do it, I mean. But I would need to set up a phase-shifted receiver in the substation. And that just leaves me stumped."

"Can it be done?" Li Jie asked.

"It's a question that's hounded me for a long time. And none of my colleagues on Earth have come up with a solution. Technically, I don't need to build the receiver. I already have one in the substation. But I can't displace its phase discriminant."

"I don't understand what you just said, but why not?" asked Li Jie. "Whatever they did to themselves, just do that to the receiver."

"It's not as simple as that," Yenko sighed. "It's made of all the wrong materials. It didn't get shifted forty-four years ago. It won't get shifted now."

"What does it have to be made from, then?" Yu Yan asked.

Yenko smiled. The bulk of the colonists really did not understand, did they?

"It would need to be made of wood," he said simply. To the look of defeat, he added, "Or anything organic, actually."

"Carbon fiber?" suggested Li Jie.

"I could certainly do something with carbon fiber," Yenko admitted. "But it's an old technology and nothing we have here can synthesize it in the form I would need. The poly-alloy technology we brought with us for the colony is more advanced, but it can't be adapted to produce a pure form of carbon fiber. We simply don't have the technology here that I need."

"Earth could do it," Li Jie continued.

"Yes, of course they could," Yenko dismissed as if it was a naïve suggestion.

"Well, get them to."

"It's not that simple," he replied, eyes scanning the stars while he reclined on the grass. "Earth hasn't mastered the ability to remotely guide a probe to Zhinu and land on its surface. Not with any degree of accuracy, at least. It's hard enough just getting one to orbit the planet. It really is a long way, Li Jie. Yes, they could make what we need. And yes, they could get it here. And yes, they probably could get it to land on Zhinu. But they would have to land it almost on our doorstep. The planet is far bigger than you think. We'd never find it."

"But the *Zhinu Phoenix* circles us as we speak. Such a probe could be captured from there."

"Go on," Yenko pondered. He could see where the soldier was going . . . the *Phoenix's* AI.

"Nirani is dormant, but she could be awakened to capture the probe and redirect it to us."

"Well, that's the tricky bit," Yenko observed. "And how do you propose we do that?"

"It's your assignment, not mine," Li Jie replied. "I have no idea how it may be done. But that's why the problem was given to you, not me. You're the genius, Yenko. Look at what you've already accomplished. When you first came onto the mission, I was offended by you. To me, your presence was an insult to the President. When I learned that you were not even her first choice, I made it my goal to remove you from our training camp. And when it happened that you and I were both assigned to Delta Squadron, I specifically asked for you to be assigned to train alongside me."

Yenko had not known that piece of information.

"And when my request was granted, I sought to dishearten you. I didn't want to kill you outright, but I did want to break you. But I could not. You kept coming back. And you fought. I came to admire you. Your ethnicity was an insult to the President, but your mettle was as a warrior. You proved that for all to see in the plane crash simulation in our training run. You saved my life then, as a brother-in-arms would do.

"I'm glad I didn't break you, Yenko. If I had, I would have ruined our mission, because at every turn it's been you who have guided our steps forward. Without your skill and insight, we would still be talking about ghosts. Now, we talk of a bold mission to rescue a people lost in space. It's a puzzle box none but you can solve. And you will solve it. I know it."

Yu Yan nodded her head in absolute assurance. "You must," she said. "If not you, then who?"

Three meteors shot across the sky in quick succession. A sign of affirmation of the reckless faith of his friends.

"But still . . ." Yenko pondered. "The AI could receive a probe . . ."

Li Jie chuckled as his separatist friend began his habitual muttering.

Would Nirani have the capacity to relaunch the probe? Yenko wondered. She would need to construct a vessel that could successfully land on Zhinu. That was it!

"I have to talk to the Commodore," he said abruptly and rose to his feet. "I need a lift."

"Of course, you do," Li Jie laughed. "You've solved the puzzle, haven't you?!"

———◦———

It was a challenging request and if it had not been Yenko that had woken the Commodore at such a late hour, it would have been immediately rejected without consideration. But Macpherson Yenko had become a prominent member of the Third Fleet and the Commodore valued the contributions the Scot had made. And she liked him. In many ways, he reminded her of herself. Reclusive, solitary, introspective.

And difficult to get to know!

"Commodore," Yenko said, "this really may work."

"Yenko," she said, pouring a cup of black tea for the two of them—Li Jie and Yu Yan had not felt it appropriate to join him in waking the Commodore. "We've worked together too closely on this for you to keep addressing me as Commodore. Don't you think it's time you called me Mannat? We're on the new world now. Social protocols have changed. I wouldn't even be offended if you called me Manu."

Mannat. A pretty name. It threw his train of thought, momentarily destabilized his eager enthusiasm for the mission before him. Manu. He could not bring himself to speak to her so intimately.

"I'm sorry. Mannat. Commodore." Where was Li Jie when he needed him?

She smiled at the awkward scientist before her. It had been a long time since she had known anyone like him. She really could become fond of him.

"But my point is simply this," Yenko continued, pretending the embarrassing moment had never occurred, "Earth could make a carbon fiber replica of the substation receiver. I have all the technical specifications for it. Everything they could want. They would have to build a probe large enough to house it. That would create difficulties for space travel, I would imagine, but I'm sure they can keep the structure small enough to get here in a believable timeframe. And even if they can't, later is better than never."

Mannat nodded. She could see the possibility in what he suggested. "But Earth has not mastered designing an unmanned probe capable of landing with the precision that we would require. It's doubtful they could even guarantee landing within a fifty mile radius, and we wouldn't know where to look for it. And we wouldn't even know when to look."

"I know," Yenko agreed. "But we have one thing that no one has considered. The *Zhinu Phoenix*."

"How might that help?" Mannat asked. "We have spent all but the last of our fuel cells. Our landing craft are only of use to us now as parts and equipment."

"If it was just us, here on Zhinu," Yenko replied, "then the answer would be that it wouldn't help. But Nirani is lying dormant on the *Zhinu Phoenix*, and if Earth could instruct us how to awaken her, we could set her the problem. She has a wealth of robotic machinery at her disposal. When she woke us out of our cryostasis, she informed us that she had intercepted an Earth probe.

"Commodore . . ." He lost his train of thought for an instant. "Mannat. I'm sorry, it just seems disrespectful to call you by your given name."

The Commodore smiled. She knew she intimidated people. It was her strength as Commodore. And weakness as Mannat. "Take your time, Yenko," she replied.

Shaking the awkwardness off, he said, "If Earth sends a carbon fiber replica of the receiver, I'm sure Nirani has the capacity to capture it. And with advance instruction, I believe that it's just possible that she could reconstruct one of the onboard probes to transfer the apparatus down to us.

"She's state of the art AI, Commodore . . . Mannat. You've seen what she's capable of. She shaved years off our journey, and that without guidance from the experts on Earth. It has to be worth the attempt.

"That's my proposal, at least. I haven't been able to come up with an alternate plan, but this one just might work."

The Commodore nodded. The plan did offer at least the hope of success. "I'll send a communication off right now. You've convinced me. You're a great asset to Zhinu, Macpherson."

"Yenko," he suggested. If they were going to be on a first name basis . . .

She smiled. "Yenko."

————◇————

Yenko left the laboratory. It was past time for a meal, and to be honest, he did not really feel like eating. He had a disturbing decision to make. Descending the well-trodden fire escape, his heart leapt as he saw a ghostly figure creep into his cabin.

For months now, he had taken to the habit of leaving the door open, hoping for the day that Fei Hung may steal back inside. There was so much he needed to tell her. And it would resolve his anxiety about the decision he had to make.

As soon as he entered the cabin, he looked about, searching for a glimpse of her. She was in there. He knew it.

There, on the floor beside the door, in much the same position he had seen her last, she sat, hugging her knees to herself. Their eyes met. She smiled. Not a happy, carefree smile, but a smile nonetheless. Yenko still did not comprehend all that she faced in her phase-shifted world. Their meetings were always too short.

And too far between. Way too far.

He motioned if she would like him to shut the door, which she accepted. With the door shut, she noticeably relaxed. He could not protect her, but clearly the alloy cabin could. Whoever she felt danger from, like her, they could not open or shut metal doors.

Are you alright? he scrawled on his writing tablet.

She merely stared at him and held her knees tighter to herself. More than ever, he knew he had to end the crisis she faced. But the only way to do that had the potential to kill him.

I haven't forgotten you, you know, he wrote.

"Why?" she mouthed.

Why? Why haven't I forgotten you?

She nodded.

How could I forget you? You're the first of your people I've met. You're the only one of your people I've met. And I've seen your suffering. I feel so useless to help. But that just makes me want to, all the more.

"Really?"

Yes!

"Thank you," she said with no voice, tears gushing from her eyes like the breaking of a dam.

I've found a way for you to come back here, back to Zhinu properly.

She stared at him in wonder. "How?"

I've sent plans to Earth for them to construct a machine I need. They've nearly finished it and have already worked out a clever way to get it here.

Indeed, they had. Rather than build a probe large enough to house the specially crafted carbon fiber gravimetric receiver, they had found an ingenious way to attach the receiver to the back of a micro-probe. In effect, the whole setup was hardly bigger than the receiver itself. As for the receiver, this was built to more stringent specifications than the ones Yenko had sent, which meant it was only two-thirds the size of the original. It would take some days for the probe with its receiver cargo to make the journey to Zhinu, but only that.

"Will it work?"

I think it will. There's only one catch.

She searched his eyes with a question in hers.

It will only work if it has the same phase-shift as you.

She looked at him, puzzled. There was no way he was going to give her a lesson in Space-Time Kinematics.

I have to bring it into the same space that you're in. I have to come to you. Into your phase-shifted existence. Like you.

"No!" she quite obviously screamed, reflexively reaching for her bone knife. "You can't!"

There's no other way, Fei Hung. I'm the only one who will know how to work the receiver.

"But the demons!"

It took a few attempts to ensure that he had understood her. Demons.

It's alright, Fei Hung. There aren't any demons. The farmers who weren't caught in the accident in Xin Beijing thought the same thing about you. They thought you were ghosts. They just didn't understand. You're out of phase with us. Not by much, but enough. And just like the farmers, you think they are ghosts. Demons. But they're not. They're part of the original colony here.

Fei Hung shook her head and reached out to take Yenko's face in her hands.

"You are not a ghost," she articulated clearly, deliberately, hoping he would lipread her urgent appeal. "I know that. But neither are the demons. They are not human. They are aliens."

Another grim piece of the puzzle box fell into place.

Was there something else in Fei Hung's shifted reality? Perhaps a creature of Zhinu that had never been encountered by any colonist because it lived in a phase-shifted existence?

"They do bad things. They hurt people. They hurt me. They force people to do bad things to each other . . . Very bad things." She scrubbed at her hands as if to remove some unseen dirt or memory.

Rising to her feet and beginning to pace, she added, "Do not come, Yenko. It is not safe."

You've just given me the reason why I must.

She bit her lip and looked worriedly at him. Indicating the door, she motioned if Yenko could let her out. It was time to leave.

"I will return, Yenko."

Once out on the grass, she turned back. "Will you really come?"

"You know I will," Yenko said firmly.

She paused in reflection. "Thank you."

———◄○►———

"Do we have any weapons without metallic parts?"

Yenko was grilling his old combat training partner. If anyone knew anything about weapons, Commander Huang Li Jie did.

"Of course, we do," Li Jie replied. "Why do you want to know?"

It was a relief. If there was an alien creature that was somehow responsible for the attacks on Fei Hung and others in her community, Yenko needed to be prepared.

Ignoring Li Jie's question, he pressed further. "Which ones? Have I trained with any of them?"

"Which ones?" the Commander echoed. "Which ones? Yenko, all our weapons are non-metallic. That's not true of the regular Zhongguo Xin Shijie army, but you didn't train with the regular army. We're Special Forces and we have the most efficient weaponry available."

"But the plasma shotgun," Yenko objected. "The barrel is steel."

"No, it isn't," the Commander corrected. "It is made of a high tensile polymer, undetectable to conventional scanners and much lighter than its alloy counterpart."

"And the firing mechanism?"

"All polymer. But don't avoid my question. Why do you need to know?"

For the next hour, Yenko brought his military friend into his confidence. He had not told anyone of his encounter with Fei Hung the night before. And he had not fully articulated the ramifications of his plan to the Commodore.

The only way to reverse the phase-shift was to repeat the experiment. From within the experiment. He would order an evacuation of the entire region of Xin Beijing and reproduce exactly the events that had played out on that fateful day of 2347. With one exception. He would remain in the city alongside the specially built carbon fiber receiver they would shortly take possession of from Earth.

If the experiment was successful, he would undergo the same one point seven degree phase-shift the colonists had, half a century earlier.

As would his receiver. So long as his calculations were correct, he would appear solidly in the world of the lost colonists.

His biggest concern was for any of Fei Hung's people who might happen to be within the precincts of the city. He had worked hard on the problem, and to the best of his calculations and mathematical simulations, he believed they would be unaffected by the pulse, it having originated from a different phase to them. That was the first concern.

Time was his next. Assembling the ghostly survivors within the limits of Xin Beijing would not be an easy matter.

And then he would need to coordinate with his current research team, understanding that he would be a ghostly figure to them. Once his phase-shifted receiver was set in place and powered up with the metal-free energy source he had already assembled for it, the experiment could be performed a second time. Only this time, the original receiver in the city's power substation would be disconnected.

The pulse from the Gravimetric Discriminator in the mountains, in theory, should reflect off the phase-shifted receiver and a looping phase variance would feed back through the apparatus. If his extrapolations were correct, all organic matter would be shifted back one point seven degrees towards standard.

That was his prediction. It was based on the electronic configuration of the elemental atomic structure of the already phase-shifted compounds. By all mathematical simulations, the phase-shifting should follow a sinusoidal wave pattern, shifting in one direction at one time and the reverse direction the next. But it was only mathematical. If there was something he was not aware of, some physics he was ignorant of . . .

If he was wrong, he ran the risk of shifting everything a further one point seven degrees away from real space. And that most certainly would be chaos for the lost colonists, a chaos they may not survive. And he along with them. His life was on the line, he knew that full well. But it was a risk he was willing to take. If it went the way he believed it would, his plan would effectively reverse the phase-shift. Fei Hung and her people would be saved.

That was the theory, anyway. The figures stacked up and he was sure of his calculations. There was risk, of course, but he had come too far to do nothing. He had to accept the risk.

Just maybe, this was why he was on Zhinu, why he was a part of the Third Fleet, why he had been chosen despite not being the first choice of Earth's leaders.

And hovering above all his concerns, compounding everything, there was an unknown trouble surrounding the lost colonists, one that was difficult to prepare for. Fei Hung called them Demons. They could be anything.

Yenko poured out his heart to his friend, his brother-in-arms. Verbalized his concerns. Justified his reasonings. When, at length, he was finished, Li Jie sat still, looking hard into the face of his separatist friend. He realized the gravity of Yenko's assignment.

"You will need refresher training," he said finally. "I've kept your fitness levels up, but it's been a long time since you've paid attention to your basic combat skills."

It was the truth.

Li Jie set up a training camp, commencing there and then. Just the two of them. For the moment, Yu Yan would have to miss her husband. Time was at a premium. Earth had already sent its probe with the carbon-based receiver. They would have it in Xin Beijing before long.

In the end, they had no more than three weeks before Nirani, *Zhinu Phoenix's* artificial intelligence, successfully constructed a suitable landing capsule to house the receiver. Those three weeks were taken up in rigorous training.

———◦———

A week before the scheduled activation date, Fei Hung made another visit. It was a great relief. Yenko needed her to know what was happening, what plans had been set in place. When he made the translation into her space-time reality, he could not afford to aimlessly wander about, mindlessly hoping to come across the lost colonists. The apparition sightings the Third Fleet had made were chiefly in the hilly region, miles to the west. He could wander for days not knowing where to find them, lose touch with the schedule he had set in place with his team in the mountain stronghold. He needed to coordinate with Fei Hung.

And that meant that he needed her at the power substation. He was deeply worried, of course, about the effect on the phase-shifted world when the Gravimetric Discriminator in the mountain was activated. Fei Hung would be in the center of its path. But time was critical, and he trusted his computations. He knew she would be safe. He knew it . . .

Strewn around his cabin, he had left tablet after tablet, detailing his plans and what he needed her to do, in the hope that if she came by when he was not there, she would read what was required of her. And here she was. Her bodysuit had a tear from her right shoulder to the elbow where the sleeve ended.

In sequence, he held up the tablets which she read intently, nodding in understanding.

"You are coming," she mouthed.

Yenko nodded. Picking up the second of the tablets, he stressed to her the need to find the rest of her people. She was worried.

"Demons," she said.

I know, he wrote on the tablet. *I will bring weapons.*

That made an impression. For the first time he had known her, he recognized the glimmer of hope in her eyes. Or a steely desire for revenge.

"Weapons?"

Yenko nodded his head. "Weapons," he replied.

I have military training, he wrote.

Let me go over this with you. I am coming when the sun is highest on the fifth day from now. Do you think you will be able to find me?

She nodded confidently.

How well do you know the city?

She nodded again. He could not afford to take chances, so he reviewed a map of the city with her.

Do you know of this substation? he wrote as he pointed it out on the map.

After a moment's study, she nodded once more, and with graphic motions of her hands described accurately its layout. Yenko breathed a sigh of relief. There was hope.

Will I have to deal with the demons straight away?

He had already determined to have his finger on the trigger of an unlocked CME carbine when the Gravimetric Discriminator was fired up. She shook her head.

"Not there," she said. "Demons near village."

Will you take me to your people?

She nodded.

Will they listen to me?

She looked at the screens that lay scattered over the table, outlining all Yenko's plans. There, she found the words Yenko had written that she was after and pointed them out, nodding as she did so. *I will be heavily armed. I don't know what these demons are, but I'm sure they can be killed.*

She was right. They would listen to him. He would be their savior.

———◄◊►———

The morning of the fifth day broke bright and clear. Two days earlier, the entire colony had been evacuated well away from the exclusion zone. Head counts were checked and double checked. There could be no mistake; Yenko's team were intending to repeat the catastrophe of 2347.

In the townships, mothers rallied children to themselves, though in truth they were completely safe, now many miles outside the path of the Gravimetric Discriminator's destructive projection. Scores of people prayed, held hands, hugged each other. Lovers kissed, not knowing if this was the end.

Yenko stood in front of the power substation. Alone. He glanced about him. Was Fei Hung out there somewhere, waiting for the moment of his full appearance? He settled his anxiety for her safety. She would be unaffected by the projection, her molecular structure already phase-shifted away from normal and out of reach of the looping phase variance of the receiver.

Inside the control room, Yenko made his final inspection of that receiver to ensure it was operational. His heart pounded as he considered the devastation the machine was capable of.

"Stay safe, Fei Hung," he whispered.

Having scoped out a secluded alcove behind the control room, he stowed away the newly made carbon fiber receiver recently captured by Nirani on the *Zhinu Phoenix*. Tucked away there, it would be safe from any prying demon eyes. When the time came, it would be a simple matter of activating it. The difficult part was to coordinate with his team at the mountain site. By that time, he would be a ghost. But he had it all planned.

An LRV screeched to a halt in the street behind him. There was yet an hour before countdown. Yenko raced to determine the nature of the problem and make the decision if the operation had to be aborted or not.

Li Jie calmly exited the vehicle and began kitting himself out with a veritable arsenal of weaponry.

"What are you doing?" Yenko demanded.

"My duty," the Commander said with steely resolve.

"But you can't come with me. It's too dangerous. I'm not a hundred percent sure this will work."

"Well, that's comforting to know, *yang guizi*." The Commander smiled a grim smile, one that was familiar with courting death. "It's not your decision, Macpherson Yenko," he added. "I'm here under the orders of the President herself. The communique from Earth came yesterday."

"Why wasn't I told? And why you?" Yenko demanded.

"I was chosen because it was my idea," Li Jie replied with a look that brooked no argument. "And you weren't told because you don't have a high enough rank. Don't worry, Yenko. I've been fully briefed on the dangers. No one knows what these demons might be. They may be nothing and my being here is meaningless. But do you seriously think I'd let you face such an unknown enemy on your own? Our quarry may be cunning. And he may be well armed and capable of defending himself against you. You've been trained by the best, but you aren't the best. And the safety of the mission demands the best."

"This should have been discussed with me," complained Yenko. "I'm in charge."

"You were in charge," corrected Commander Huang. "This is now a military operation. Say another word in complaint and I'll show you the butt of my shotgun."

The man meant it. He was in charge, there was no doubt about it. And there was nothing Yenko could do about it. Commander Huang would seek out the scientist's expertise, of course, but he would take responsibility for everyone's safety—Yenko's, Fei Hung's, the lost villagers', the New World Colony itself.

"I suppose I'm glad," Yenko confessed in final resignation. "I certainly would feel safer if I had you taking my back."

"You will not be in the lead, my friend. It is you who will take the back." Turning to the driver, he ordered, "*Gunduzi* if you want to live, Varma."

"Yes, sir," the young technician said, unable to hide his fear and eager to be out of the city. With a screech of tires, the LRV screamed out of sight.

"Is everything set?" the Commander asked.

"Yes, I'm ready to go. I was about to call the mountain facility for them to commence the countdown."

"Good. Show me your weapons. Let me warn you, Macpherson. Your sister-cousin, my wife, will skin you alive if I don't come back. And that's only half what she'll do to me."

"If you don't come back, it won't make any difference," Yenko reflected.

"You don't know Yu Yan. She may look Zhongwen, but she has Macpherson blood."

The two men laughed. Grimly. Brothers-in-arms.

Li Jie was pleased with how Yenko had armed himself. A CME carbine hung from his shoulder. At his waist, the handle of a deadly twelve-inch hunting knife protruded from its sheath, ready to inflict lethal injury. Five stun grenades adorned one side of his belt and a plasma pistol the other.

Yet he was lightly armed compared to Huang, who looked as if he was prepared to take on an entire militia singlehandedly. Decked from head to toe in combat gear, he was a walking arsenal.

––––––––⟨o⟩––––––––

"Yashvi, are you ready up there?" Yenko asked into his communicator.

"Yes," came the female voice of one of his team of engineers.

"Has Commander Huang's driver reported in yet?"

"Yes. He is out of the exclusion zone."

"Very well then. Countdown from now," Yenko ordered. "Ten minutes."

This was it. No turning back.

Huang stood at the alert, ready for anything. Yenko checked his CME. The safety was off, and he stood poised with his finger near the trigger.

"Don't get too jumpy with that thing," the Commander ordered, now in full combat readiness. "Remember your training. Stay alert."

Yenko nodded. His heart pounded. He was more than glad he was not facing this on his own and was about to say as much.

"Focus," the Commander ordered as if he could read his friend's mind.

The minutes ticked by. A hum in the air was the first indication of change. Then the whole world seemed to light up with a dazzling brightness and the air thrummed. Moments later, Yenko found that it had become somewhat difficult to breathe, as if he could not get quite enough oxygen with each breath.

"Robbie!" came a cry from over the road.

A young woman in a leather bodysuit, torn sleeve flapping in the breeze, ran at full stretch towards them as Huang positioned himself in front of Yenko.

"It's alright," Yenko said to the Commander, switching his carbine back onto safety. "It's Fei Hung. I told her to meet me here. She's going to take us to her people."

Fei Hung halted her run, uncertain of the soldier barring the way to Yenko.

"I told you I'd come," Yenko said.

Hesitantly, she stepped forward and reached out to him, touched his face, then held on to him as tightly as she could.

"This is Commander Huang Li Jie, Special Operations Forces of the Zhongguo Xin Shijie."

Stepping back, Fei Hung bowed formally to the officer. "I am honored to stand before you," she said. "*Ma dao cheng gong.*"

The Commander bowed in acknowledgement of the blessing. But maintained his steady review of the area.

————◄◦►————

The three walked on for hours. It was the most animated Yenko had seen the woman. His making the daring move to enter what she considered to be the solid world, had given her hope.

As they walked, she told them of her community. It was brutal. Even without the demons, it was a harsh existence. Food was hard to come by. Crops were difficult to grow. The elders recalled a time when the land could be ploughed, but it was rock hard now. They had taken to planting their crops in human waste spread over the open ground, hoping for the seed to take adequate root. Manual labor was difficult, and the people had to rest often to gain breath.

But worst of all were the demons. Constantly, as if by forced habit, Fei Hung's eyes searched their surroundings. Ever alert. Li Jie plied her with question after question about these demons, though she did not want to talk about them.

"I must know my enemy," the Commander told her. "It matters little that you find it a difficult topic. You will tell me what is needful for you to tell me."

When he was in that mood, he was no longer Li Jie; he was a military leader, and a fierce one at that.

"Just answer whatever questions he has," Yenko often encouraged her. "He knows why he asks them."

It was enough for Fei Hung that Yenko trusted the heavily armed man. She told him all she knew, oftentimes with grimaces of painful memories she would rather forget. On many occasions, her anger boiled up inside, spilling out in a gush of hate-filled curses, tears coursing down her cheeks.

Slowly they began to piece together a profile of these demons. They were otherworldly, and appeared unexpectedly to inflict pain and torment, and finally, death. Her people truly thought the villagers in the colony were spirits. But the demons were different. They were vaguely transparent, and in that they almost resembled the spirits of the colonists, but unlike those spirits, they were real. Solid. There.

Fei Hung's demons were humanoid, and tall, many of them well over six feet. Whether their iridescent blue armor was a natural hide or a suit they wore, she could not say. It seemed apparent, at the least, that they wore a helmet of sorts, with highly reflective visors to shield their faces. Their feet were heavily armored, yet they moved with speed and agility. Along their arms ran central ridges of spines able to slash an opponent with a glancing blow.

As the young woman painted the sorry tale, she described how she had suffered a blow from the hand of one and lived to tell of it, unlike the many she knew who had not.

"Demons are never seen on their own," she said. "But never more than three at a time. And who can say if they're the same three or not? They look alike."

Most shocking of all to Fei Hung was the demons' ability to shoot stinging barbs from an orifice above their wrists. These barbs, once embedded, sent their victims into convulsive fits. When the spasms settled down, the nature of the victim violently changed. Where a person may have been quiet and peace loving, they would now be wild and abusive. Such people gathered in packs and wreaked havoc on the community. The demons tracked these wild packs, watching over them to unknown ends.

Fei Hung absently caressed the scars on her arms, reliving the abuse of one of these demon-controlled gangs.

"*Chusheng*," she spat.

"We will deal with them," the Commander said, though Yenko was not so convinced.

"Can the barbs be removed?" he asked. "Surely, you could subdue a person no matter how out of control they were."

"Yes," she agreed. "The barbs can be removed, but they're buried deep and tear their victim mercilessly. We try our best to bind the wounds, but the blood loss is great. Each one dies a slow, cruel death. But it's dangerous to get near enough to make the attempt. Their packs can number in the dozens and they defend each other."

"What do you do, then?" Yenko asked. It seemed these wounded gangs were as much a threat as the demons themselves. Perhaps more so.

Fei Hung stopped walking and looked him in the face. "We kill them."

The Commander studied the young woman. Nothing shocked him. But Yenko was aghast.

"They're dead already, as soon as they are hit by the demon barbs," she explained. "Their rampant frenzy only lasts a month at most before they die. Yet in that time, they wreak such havoc. Day and night. They never sleep. They just kill. And rape. And maim.

"Do you judge us that we kill them? It's a mercy to them and to us."

She reached out and placed her hand gently on Yenko's cheek. "You know nothing of me. Do you think my wounds are idly come by? I am the angel of mercy to the raping puppets of the demons. I liberate them from their torment. And save my people from shame and trial.

"Why do you think it is that you see me in the city? Our people won't venture here because it's steeped in our history as a place of grief and horror. It's here that I ply my deadly art."

"What do you do?" whispered Yenko, shocked by what he was learning of the mysterious woman.

"I lure the gangs away from my people." The look on her face sent a chill through Yenko and he instinctively backed away from her. Imitating the breaking of a neck, she said with frightening finality, "I do what I must."

Fei Hung turned and walked on in silence for a long while, cold steely eyes ever vigilant, ever alert for her demon foes, or crazed mobs of envenomated people.

———◦———

"My home is over this rise," Fei Hung announced.

That was a welcome relief to Yenko. They had come a long way and he labored under his gear; it was getting heavier by the minute. And he had learned the shocking truth of his beautiful young guide. Beautiful, yes. And murderous. It shook him in ways he could not have expected.

Before them sprawled a large village. Scrappy farms were scattered about a river that snaked its way through a narrow valley. Small, straggling trees added to the air of impoverished hardship. This was not an easy world to live in; the evidence lay before them for anyone to see.

A considerable commotion was sparked as the three made their way down the central, makeshift path. Fei Hung had already informed them of Yenko's plan, yet they stared in wonder at the two heavily armed soldiers walking into their midst as if she had only relayed the half of it.

"How far away are the other villages?" Yenko asked the leading elder after formal introductions were made.

"We are all that remain of Xin Beijing. This is our new home, Gui Difang."

Gui Difang . . . Perhaps it really was the Home of Evil Spirits. In its day, Xin Beijing had had a population approaching twenty thousand. Only four thousand survivors and their descendants were all that remained.

Night was fast approaching, and Yenko and Li Jie detailed their tactical plan to shift the population cross-country to the ruined city. There was considerable opposition to this, and little wonder; the villagers were plagued with superstitious fears about Xin Beijing. Their world was one horror after another.

But it could not be helped. They had to be moved; they were nowhere near the arc of the Gravimetric Discriminator's field. It would not be an easy task, and it would take time, but Yenko and Li Jie had to get them at least into the outskirts of the ruined city if they were to be brought safely back into the real world of Zhinu.

The survivors of Gui Difang could not be expected to be as fast as Fei Hung and her armed escort. It had taken the three rescuers almost six hours to hike to the village. The return journey would be much longer. And once everyone was safely within the borders of the Discriminator's field, Yenko, if no one else, had to get to the substation in order to set up the new receiver and make contact with his team in the mountains.

All the while, hanging over the mass exodus like a threat of ultimate futility, the uncertain peril of the demons would dog their path to freedom. Encounters with the aliens seemed to be sporadic; perhaps their flight would go unnoticed. Perhaps.

A blood-curdling, chilling scream pierced the early evening hush. It had come from across the valley, some distance from where they now gathered, making their plans with the village elders. Everyone around Yenko seemed to freeze, but he and Li Jie dived into action.

Another scream. And another. Something dreadful was happening.

Li Jie and Yenko sprinted towards the commotion, Yenko gritting his teeth against the cry of his lungs for sufficient air. Li Jie was battle hardened, however, ready for anything and ran ahead, disregarding the limitations this phase-shifted world placed on him.

Fei Hung, more accustomed to the harsh environment, overtook Yenko, concern for the suffering of her people voiced with every ragged breath. Three other young villagers, similarly dressed to Fei Hung, joined them, bone daggers drawn. Members of Gui Difang's deadly defenders. Each of them was covered in scars and each of them had the same cold, murderous expression as Yenko's mystery woman.

"Here," Yenko called to Fei Hung as she sprinted past. "Take this." And he handed her his razor-sharp hunting knife.

Her eyes spoke violence as she accepted the gift and ran on to catch the Commander.

The closer they got to the source of the screams, the more villagers they met running the opposite way. Fear had gripped that region of the community.

"The scouts did not see them arrive," an elderly man yelled to Fei Hung as she and her dread counterparts sprinted passed him. Stationed about the perimeter of the township, scouts routinely patrolled, ever vigilant against the onslaught of the demons. This night, the scouts had missed their semi-visible foe.

And then Yenko saw it, some distance ahead of him, but not far now from Li Jie and the village vigilantes. Four men and one woman lay writhing on the ground between a small group of houses. A dozen steps from them stood what appeared to be three tall men, only partially visible in iridescent blue armor.

A thud detonated the air and a demon dropped motionless to the ground. Commander Huang had felled it with a handheld pulse cannon. In the momentary confusion that followed, he killed the second of the demons, but the third escaped into the gathering night.

"See what you can do with these," Li Jie ordered Yenko. "I'm going to track that last one. It can't be allowed to get to its base or there'll be hell."

And with that, he vanished into the darkness.

For the moment, Fei Hung and now five others just like her who had run towards the fray, were stunned. All their lives, they had fought those who were the victims of demon fire. And on many occasions, they had only narrowly escaped being themselves victims; the battle scars they wore attested to that in no uncertain way.

But always, the villagers' true enemies, the demons, had remained unassailable. The only weapons Fei Hung and her compatriots had available to them were their hands, feet, and bone knives. And those were nothing against the size and might of their armored enemy.

Fei Hung was the first of the village defenders to reach the scene. She stood over the two motionless corpses. And fell on them in a grief-fueled rage. Stabbing and stabbing and stabbing. Green fluid, mixed with swirling streams of red, oozed from the bodies, spattered into the air with each wild swing of the knife. At the height of her fury, she screamed curses and decapitated both demons, throwing the lifeless heads far from her.

Crying in spent emotion, she stood to her feet and saw Yenko kneeling over one of the fallen villagers. The writhing spasms had ceased. Blood flowed freely down the chest of the woman Yenko now attended to, evidence of the violence with which the dart had been removed. Already, he had torn several other darts from each of three victims beside him. The alien weapons were dreadful, designed to go in but not out. Right now, Yenko was desperately attempting to dislodge another, refusing to come out from between the ribs of the aliens' quarry.

The last of the victims suddenly sat up and hissed at Yenko, making to attack him. But one of Fei Hung's death-squad companions quickly threw himself on him, raising his weapon to end the misery and horror that awaited the dart-pierced villager.

"No!" shouted Yenko. "He doesn't need to die."

Instantly, he dived to the side of the crazed villager and stayed the hand of the would-be assailant.

"He's dead already," Fei Hung yelled as she jumped onto one of the bleeding, helpless bodies of her friends, knife raised high above her head. "You cannot help them."

"No!" he screamed. "Pull it out! Pull them all out! I think I can save them." It took an instant for the small company of village protectors to obey the command, but it was an instant that lasted an eternity. "Pull them out!"

Grabbing the last few barbs roughly, Fei Hung and her troop tore them from the victims with horrifying violence. Screams ripped through the air amid curses and threats of bloody violence. It was all the squad could do to restrain the poisoned villagers, now thrashing against their captors.

"And what will you do, now, Yenko?" Fei Hung challenged. "They're going to die anyway."

She was right. It was obvious. Blood spurted and gushed from the many lacerations on all five victims. About them, Gui Difang's deadly vigilantes were ready to put the villagers out of their misery.

"We need to cauterize the wounds," Yenko urged Fei Hung. "Give me the knife."

Roughly, he wiped the red and green alien muck from the blade, then handed it back to her. "Here," he instructed. "Hold it out from you. But don't drop it."

She did as she was told, struggling against the thrashing of one of the demon's victims.

"Seriously! Don't drop it!"

Yenko adjusted three dials on his CME carbine and aimed it at the blade from close range. "I've pulled the intensity right back," he told her, though she understood nothing of such weaponry. And fired.

In shock, she almost did drop the knife. The blade glowed in her hand and radiated an intense heat. Carefully taking it from her, Yenko burnt every bleeding wound of the five victims. They screamed and writhed in pain, rendered momentarily powerless from the lack of blood and the dizzying madness of whatever it was that coursed through their veins.

The threats and curses ceased, as one by one, each victim slumped back to the grass.

"Get cloth for bandages."

The vigilantes understood. Moments later, Fei Hung and two of her partners emerged from a nearby house with a bundle of sheets and applied themselves to tearing them into strips as Yenko bound each victim's wounds.

A handful of villagers returned to discover the meaning of the shots they had heard and the silence that seemed louder than the expected crazed yelling of their fallen neighbors. They saw Yenko, Fei Hung and members of their defense squad on their knees tending to the wounds of the fallen villagers, miraculously alive, miraculously sane. Two demons lay decapitated to one side in pools of red and green.

6

The Meeting of Worlds

L I JIE RAN INTO the darkness. Clouds obscured the stars, but one of Zhinu's moons shone brightly through a break above him. As best he could, he kept to the direction in which the demon had run. He had no way of knowing if he matched it for speed, but the Commander considered that it would slow its pace before long. Unless of course, the demon camp was nearby. And if that was the case, they were in grave danger.

Gripped firmly in both hands, Li Jie carried his plasma shotgun, the weapon he had first taught Yenko to handle back in the days of their training. It was lightweight, and its broad range meant that it could be used with effect while running. Ignoring his lungs' demand for air, he sprinted on, knowing full well his limits and what he could expect of himself. All the while, he kept an eye out for possible signs of his prey.

Cresting a hill, he took stock of a field of long grass that stretched out before him. A path cut its way through the heart of it to a stand of trees on the far side. Li Jie smelled danger. Though the grass was waist high, he would be exposed to an ambush in the trees. Would the demon know it was pursued?

There was no doubt in Huang's mind. It would suspect it was being chased. Never in its engagement with the villagers had it faced any sort of real resistance. The little that Li Jie had heard of Fei Hung's story only served to emphasize that these creatures used the colony as sport. Over the years, they would have grown complacent.

And of a sudden, two of them were dead, killed by the power of a weapon they had not encountered amongst the villagers before. No, Li Jie was certain; the demon knew it was hunted.

Which meant that he himself was being hunted. Right now.

Coming to an abrupt halt behind a small bush that provided concealment in the night's failing light, he studied the grassy field. The clouds parted, contriving to make a target of him despite his refuge. If the tables were turned, and he himself had been planning an ambush, this would be a perfect spot for it.

Li Jie crouched down, head hardly above the level of the waving grasses. Slipping his backpack off, he found his infrared night goggles and scanned the trees in front. Nothing. That did not necessarily mean anything, though. The creature wore a thick armor and could render itself somewhat transparent. Who knew what technological advantages it might have? It could well be capable of masking a heat signature, rendering his night goggles ineffective.

Huang was an experienced soldier, however, a Special Forces operative, trained for quick action, quick assessment. Before he had fired his first shot back in the village, he had already determined that the three carried no weapons as such. He had seen them fire the last of their deadly missiles, the barbed darts that drove their victims insane. Each projectile had been fired from the right hand. It was possibly the only weapon of the creature he tracked, lying now, in all likelihood, in wait for him in the thicket beyond the grass.

Of course, he could not be certain he was in imminent danger. The creature was swift; it may have assumed itself incapable of being followed. A foolish mistake if it came to that, but Huang could not trust to it. He felt it in his bones. The beast was waiting for him to cross the field. It would fire its darts at him when he came within range. And that would be the end of it.

Crouching low, Huang made his way around the field, keeping to the bushes on the higher ground. It was slow going, but he would have to use all his cunning if he was to make the hit. His life depended on it. As did the life of all the villagers. Should he fall now, he knew they would have little hope. Macpherson was a fair soldier, but he did not have Huang's experience to guide him. They would be picked off and destroyed.

Twenty minutes later, Huang reached the far edge of the copse. There had been no counterattack, which led him to assess that the creature had not seen him come over the hill on the far side of the field. That gave him the upper hand. By now, the creature would begin to consider it had escaped pursuit and would continue its trek back to its campsite.

Scanning the small wood with his infrared, Li Jie could make out no signs of life. And then he saw it. A shuffle in a bush a hundred feet in front of him. Making no sound at all, and with slow deliberate movements, he rehung the plasma shotgun over his shoulder and grabbed his handheld pulse cannon, the weapon he had used to drop the demon's companions.

He crouched low, deathly still, hardly even breathing. A rodent emerged from the bush and scurried into the field.

Almost at the same instant, a blow to the side of the head threw Huang off balance as he sprawled across the ground and rolled into the long grass. The demon jumped down from its lair after him, firing an evil dart as it did so.

All Huang's combat instincts were in motion. Without thinking, as soon as he had been struck in the head, he went with the blow, barrel rolling out of the copse, and grabbed a hunting knife like that carried by Yenko as he did so.

He heard the fire of the creature's weapon, but he was too fast, too lithe, too trained. Diving to one side, he threw himself into a thicker stand of long grass. Another ill aimed dart missed its target. Pulse cannon in one hand and knife in the other, he dived again as a third dart was fired. Each movement disrupted the balance of his assailant. Each movement raising its fears.

All the while, Huang was almost in a state of supreme peace. Acting by instinct. Calculated. In control. Diving towards the demon, he sprang upwards, barrel rolling in the air, and dismembered the creature's right forearm with his deadly hunting knife. His foe screamed in pain, a roar that pierced Huang's ears, that instantly was silenced as the Commander landed on his back and fired the pulse cannon.

He did not miss his mark. The creature stood motionless for the briefest of moments, teetered forward, dropped to its knees, and collapsed face first into the ground. Without ceasing the fluid motion of his attack, Huang twirled round onto the dead body and sliced its head off. There would be no mistaking its death.

The whole while, Huang continued in his state of high alert. He did not know how close the creature had come to its encampment. And with the sounding of its scream, and the shot of his weapon, he could not be sure that others were not alerted to his presence.

Crouching, he cleaned off his knife and replaced it in his boot, and made his way through the copse, continuing in the direction the demon had been running. Fifteen minutes later, after traversing a decently sized ridge, he hoped with a degree of confidence that the sounds of the fight would not have been heard in whatever camp might lie ahead.

―――――◄◦►―――――

In the dark of a rocky outcrop, Huang consulted his timepiece. 1:52am, Zhinu Time. He was starting to consider whether it may be prudent to turn back. He had no way of knowing his quarry's destination, and the longer he stayed out, the longer it would take him to return to Yenko and the phase-shifted colonists.

"This last rise," he thought as he pressed up the steep slope. He had been cutting across a rough, rocky terrain for the past hour, confident he had maintained his course, but not confident he was on the right path.

At the top of the rocky height, he looked down over a scene that attested to the accuracy of his tracking instincts. A craft that looked capable of space flight had obviously crashed on the lower slopes of a further hill, a mile or more ahead. Lights from fires blazed about the ship.

Huang unhitched the tactical sniper rifle that hung from his back. Setting it comfortably on the ground, he lay down and trained its high-powered scope on the crash site. He had no intention of using the weapon, not for the moment, at least. But he needed intelligence on his enemy.

A long gouge across the terrain testified to the craft's speed when it had come down and finally landed unceremoniously nose first in a crush of dirt and rock. The many gashes and tears in its hull showed it was not going anywhere soon, but there was evidence of recent repair work. The ship's crew were clearly resourceful.

There were seven fires scattered around the site that Li Jie could make out. Glows from the far side of the craft showed there were more. Demons gathered round each of them. Some attended to unknown tasks, others talked, others rested. Huang counted fifteen sentries on duty, guarding the perimeter. There were likely as many more on the other side. These carried weapons.

From the signs of the camp, it was apparent that Fei Hung's demons were aliens that had crashed onto Zhinu. How they came to have been in

the vicinity, and why they had crashed, there could be no way of knowing. There were no signs of settlement about the site, but given the size
of the craft, that probably was not surprising. It had been their home in
space, and on Zhinu it continued to fulfil that purpose, despite the crash.

A group of twelve demons drew Huang's attention. He increased the
magnification of the scope and breathed slowly. Every slightest movement was detectable in his field of view. An animated discussion was underway and several of the creatures gesticulated wildly. It was clear which
was the leader. Each time one entered or left the group, they offered what
was obviously a salute to the same individual, a tall, broad shouldered
alien. In the light of the campfires, it was apparent its armor was not the
iridescent blue of the rest, but the green of their visors.

Huang was now convinced they wore armored suits. The green
color of the leader, in stark contrast to all others, showed this was no
natural covering, the hide of a demon. It was the spacesuit of an alien
race. Huang maintained his focus on the leader. He could kill him in an
instant if he chose.

If he chose. The first true aliens ever encountered by humans. The
meeting of worlds in the crosshairs of an assault weapon.

He wondered what it was that they debated. Had the alarm been
raised about their three missing compatriots who now lay dead in the
darkness beyond their fires? Three aliens joined the group; it was apparent they had been summoned to the meeting. The leader in green gestured in the direction of Huang. His heart maintained its steady beat.
Saluting, they ran into the spacecraft and emerged moments later, armed
with the same weapon as the sentries, and marched off towards Huang.

The Commander did the math in his head. His first engagement
with the aliens, back in the survivors' village, was just after sunset. Probably around 6:00pm. He had made it to this, his observation point, just
before 2:00am. Eight hours of the Zhinu clock. It was around 10:00pm
that he had come upon the field with the trail leading to the stand of trees.
The fight would have been half an hour. No more than three-quarters
of an hour. Four hours to the trees. Three and a half hours to the crash
site. He had run for much of it. It was easy enough to reckon how long it
would take him to get to the village, but he had no way of knowing how
long the aliens marching towards him would take.

Considering their current pace, not overly dissimilar to his own,
Huang had to assume they might arrive at the village in seven hours,

maybe less. He looked at his timepiece. 2:15am Zhinu Time. All hell would break out at 9:00am.

But he could not be certain. They could arrive hours earlier. Undoubtedly, they would have communication devices on them. If they found the body of their fallen compatriot in the copse, a full-scale assault would be mounted before sunrise.

Huang had only one choice. One opportunity to give the villagers a chance for freedom. He would have to eliminate the three aliens, right now crossing the valley in the darkness towards him. For some time, he kept his gun scope trained on the scouts, occasionally checking back to the crash site to ensure the leader had not sent out further squads.

He needed to understand his prey. These were not ordinary space travelers; he could see that at a glance. The three moved with military precision. The way they carried their weapons, the way they traveled in single file to mask their numbers. Untrained personnel would not act as they did, habitually doing what only years of training could have taught them. He would need all his wits about him if he was to come out of this alive.

Calmly, methodically, he set his gear in order and started back down the rise. Huang was a skillful soldier, deadly in his precision, and ever vigilant. He knew every detail of the terrain he needed to cover to get back to the Zhinu survivors.

And he knew where he would fall on the three aliens. Stealth would be his greatest ally and he needed to make sure it remained so. At full stretch now, he ran ahead of the unsuspecting troop.

———◀○▶———

An hour later, he arrived at his ambush site. An escarpment formed a natural barrier to the lowlands and coast. It would have taken him some time to climb earlier that night when he first came on it had he not had the benefit of knowing the bearing of the alien he had tracked.

Sheer cliffs of one hundred and fifty feet or more stretched on from east to west as far as he could see in the light of Zhinu's moons. Yet here, along the aliens' path, the escarpment had collapsed eons ago. The descent through the broken landform twisted and turned, and in many places had to be carefully negotiated, but for the most part, it could be managed at a trot.

This is where Huang would set his trap. But he would need to call on all his skill and cunning.

Another hour passed before he heard the footfalls of the three aliens. They were beginning the descent, perhaps as much as thirty feet apart from each other. He could not have asked for a better opportunity. Positioning himself in a narrow crevice where the path was particularly challenging and almost within arm's reach of his hiding place, he waited, hunting knife drawn.

The first alien loped past him, its long gait easily negotiating the descent. Were it not for the pitch blackness of his ambush spot and the dark military gear he wore, he would have been seen in an instant. The second alien crossed in front of him. This was it. The seconds passed as the third made its way towards him.

There was no way it could have known anything of what happened next.

Huang waited till his adversary had just passed him, and with terrifying speed, and in almost complete silence, he leapt into the open behind the alien, grabbing its head with one arm and slicing its throat with the other in one swift, almost graceful movement. Taking the weight of his enemy, he eased it gently to the ground.

In full view of the aliens had they known to turn around, he now sprinted silently towards his second target. In the same graceful dance, he slit its throat as he had done the first. A rock dislodged under the weight of his victim, and a small tumble of rocks slid down the side of the path.

The noise all but detonated in the air.

The Commander had no time to think. He would have one chance for a shot as the leading alien turned to see what the commotion was. The blast pierced the alien's mask and it collapsed without even raising its weapon.

Huang checked the time. 4:33am.

Inspecting the nearest corpse, he took note of the equipment it carried on its body. He did not recognize any of it, understandably, but he knew there would be a communicator. There was no way of knowing how regularly these aliens reported back to their superiors. His guess, from what he had learned so far in this phase-shifted world, was that discipline had waned in the enemy camp. He had seen it in military action before. Soldiers become complacent if they have been out of action for an extended period. Discipline slackens, strict protocols neglected.

And it seemed to Huang that he could guess the purpose of the visits to the village; it was ugly, brutish sport. He considered it highly unlikely that this group of three would have checked in till after they had made a search for their lost company late in the morning. Unlikely, but not definite. And there was no margin for error.

He would have to run. And run hard.

————◄◦►————

Commander Huang burst through the growing crowd in the rough village square of the impoverished township of Gui Difang and into the meeting hall, lungs screaming for air. It was 7:42am.

He was heavily laden with his combat gear, plus the addition of a weapon taken from one of his fallen foes. Despite its weight, he had considered it prudent to bring it with him so it could be studied. Perhaps he might learn something of their capabilities should he have to mount a last stand on behalf of Zhinu's survivors. The caked remains of dried green and red blood on his uniform told the assembled company he had seen considerable violence.

Fei Hung stepped forward and took the weapon from him and walked to the side of the room to examine it. She had seen one like it on occasion but had never witnessed its operation, nor felt its weight in her hands.

"Be careful with that," Huang said, though accorded her recognition by allowing her to maintain possession of it. She was a warrior and he knew it. It would be right for her to handle the weapon of her abusers.

There was a story to be told concerning her, the Commander could easily see. If he was covered in dried alien blood, she was more so. Every part of her was spattered with the green and red mess.

"I'll take your report of last night later," he ordered Yenko. War was afoot. "But before we can do that, the villagers must leave now. There will be an assault on the town, that much is certain. My guess is that we have till early afternoon. We must be long gone by then.

"Make no noise of it to the townsfolk, Macpherson, but you, at least, need to be aware. It will be a miracle if we don't face battle before we are liberated from this place."

————◄◦►————

"I've already determined its mode of operation," Commander Huang told Fei Hung as she studied the alien weapon.

He had just taken Yenko's report of the night before. The scientist had attempted to protect the woman from accusations of crazed violence on the dead aliens, but Li Jie demanded to hear the full account. He knew that no one had the right to judge her for what she had done. She had suffered more than any would ever know at the hands of such as these and their demented victims.

Huang had already checked on those that had been restored to sanity and life by Yenko's quick action. He examined one of the pronged darts the aliens shot from their arms as Yenko finished his report. In the end, he commended both Yenko and Fei Hung for their efforts. They had performed beyond his expectations.

That was half an hour ago. Marching now alongside the young woman on the escape route to the ruined city of Xin Beijing, he took hold of the weapon and showed her what he had learned of it. He picked out a target a hundred feet to the side of the sea of fleeing people. And fired. A pulsing throb filled the air and the tree collapsed in shreds. Several villagers screamed in fright and hastened their pace.

There was no bullet, no projectile that Fei Hung could see, but it was devastating in its power. Receiving it back from the Commander, she aimed at a tree twice the distance away and fired. Her aim was true. Huang nodded with satisfaction.

"I would have liked to train you," he said grimly.

She showed no sign of emotion. Her face was stone.

Commander Huang surveyed the exodus, assessing its vulnerabilities. There were many. It had taken long, too long, to mobilize the villagers. Civilian operations were never as smooth as military ones. In the end, it had been less than an hour earlier, approaching 9:00am, before the last of the population were on their forced march. The sick and infirm were carried on stretchers and parents herded children, their fear all but palpable in the air.

The day before, Huang, Yenko, and Fei Hung had taken the better part of six hours to cover the distance from the substation to Gui Difang. Six hours. Two of those hours were taken to reach the city outskirts and, from what he could learn from Yenko, the three had crossed over the borders of the gravimetric exclusion zone another hour after that.

Mentally, he continued to do the math. He estimated the refugees were only making half that pace. It would take them between six and seven hours to reach the exclusion zone, and only then would they be within limits of Yenko's machine. Six to seven hours.

Huang could see no way they would not face battle. If they made it, it would be by the skin of their teeth.

As they continued their gruelingly slow march, the Commander looked north towards the hills and the escarpment he knew lay beyond. He could feel it in every fiber of his military body; the aliens would already know something was wrong. Surely, they already had mounted a mission in anticipation of trouble.

Working the numbers, he figured such a mission would arrive at the scene of his ambush on the escarpment somewhere between 10:30 and 11:00am. There was no way they would miss his handiwork; and it was too obviously military in its precision. They would suspect the villagers had found a new ally. War would be at hand and he knew the alien leadership would press the attack. They would reach Gui Difang in the early afternoon. It would only take a short investigation before evidence of the villagers' flight to the east, towards the ruins of Xin Beijing, was discovered.

No matter how Huang worked the figures, he was certain the aliens would fall on them somewhere around 3:00pm. Perhaps by then they would be just within the borders of the exclusion zone, but only just.

It would be close. Too close. People were going to die.

—◦—

"Yenko, my friend," the Commander said finally, an uncharacteristic care in his voice. "We're going to see battle. I'm certain now. It can't be avoided."

It was everything Yenko feared to hear. He knew Huang well, trusted his experience, accepted his judgment. The survivors would be slaughtered. There would be little he and Li Jie could do on their own. Or with the help of their only other armed ally, Fei Hung, now working hard at mastering the alien weapon.

"I believe I can get the people to within your gravimetric machine's range," Li Jie continued. "But not all of them will survive. Your team in the mountains need to be prepared because the timing will be tight, and the need will be great.

"Yenko, you've trained for this. I must send you on with as much haste as you can muster to the power station. It will take time for you to make contact with your technicians. They need to be put on the alert."

Yenko understood, nodded, and turned to run off.

"And Yenko, you have to get word to the Commodore. Nothing else matters. The entire Third Fleet, apart from your workers in the mountains, must assemble beyond the western borders of the exclusion zone. They must be combat ready. This is no drill. It's life and death for these refugees. We will not be the only ones your machine brings back into the normal world of Zhinu."

Yenko nodded and made to leave. Again. Adrenaline coursed through his veins, demanding more oxygen from the scant intake of his lungs.

"One final command, my friend," Huang added. "In all this company, there are only three of us that are capable of the fight. The odds are impossible. Our only hope lies with you and your colleagues in the mountains. Once you've completed your mission, you must waste no time in getting back to us. Timing will be critical. Your team can't afford to activate their machine before all these people are within the exclusion zone. You can't assume anything. Nothing must be left to chance. It will be certain death otherwise."

Yenko understood. He would do what he must. Alert his team. Organize the Third Fleet. Return to Zhinu's refugees to determine when they were all within the Gravimetric Discriminator's range. Then flee back to the substation and set the rescue in motion.

"Yenko, you have to understand," the Commander warned. "We are all likely to die this day. The success of the mission lies with your machine. Everything else is insignificant. Do you hear me? Everything. I'm sending Fei Hung with you. I can't trust the refugees' freedom to you alone. I've observed her application to the enemy's weapon. She's more capable of combat than you think.

"The two of you must go. If one falls, the other will complete the task. I'm giving you an order right now. Stand to attention to receive it!"

The Commander's words allowed no other response. Yenko stood to attention. The long line of refugees straggled on, many of them watching with uncertainty as Commander Huang addressed Yenko, standing erect with sober gravity etched on his stony face.

"Mission success is your only objective," Huang continued. "Your own life is unimportant compared to it. Macpherson Yenko, soldier in the Zhongguo Xin Shijie army, as of this moment . . . You. Are. Dead. Abandon yourself to the mission."

"Yes, sir," Yenko affirmed with a salute. "It will be done as you wish, sir."

"Now go. Along the way, instruct your sister-in-arms what she must do should you fall. Go!"

———◄◦►———

Yenko ran. And ran. Fear drove him on. And strangely, excitement. And peace. Fei Hung ran beside him, a chilling look of fatality etched upon her face. They ran for life. They ran for death.

7

Exodus

Yenko's breath was labored. "I have to stop," he gasped. "Just for a minute."

At first, both he and Fei Hung had sprinted away from Li Jie and the refugees, trailing now somewhere far behind. Adrenaline had driven them both forward. But their marginally out of phase lungs found it difficult to take in enough oxygen and before long, they had reluctantly slowed to a brisk walk. As it was, this still was a grueling pace.

Fei Hung bent over with her hands on her knees, chest heaving.

"Only for a moment," she panted. They could not afford to stop long. Time was critical. The ruins of Xin Beijing about them mirrored their fatigue. Two broken people in a broken city.

Only for a moment. It felt like a nanosecond. Yenko's lungs still protested as they set off once more and made their way through the decaying, overgrown streets. At each turn of the road, Yenko fought back a rising tide of fear. It was taking altogether too long to reach their destination. Everything depended on speed, but their pace slowed with every mile.

Sensing the growing anxiety and frantic gait of her partner, Fei Hung reached out to encourage him. "They're not in danger yet. We're almost there. Are you sure someone will be attending the substation?"

Yenko nodded. He could not afford to waste his breath on speech.

———◄○►———

Commander Huang studied the distant hills to the west. No sign of pursuit. Marching up and down the tortuous trail of Gui Difang's refugees, he urged them on, setting up rotations of fit and active men to take turns carrying the stretchers of the sick and infirm. He pushed them hard, as hard as he dared. Perhaps more. But it was certain death if he did not.

Earlier on, he had watched as Yenko and Fei Hung raced off on the mission he had set them. Shaking his head, he had said to no one in particular, "You won't be able to sustain that pace."

He considered that Yenko's ghost woman may be able to run the marathon distance without a break, having been raised in this severe world. But he knew his friend could not. He doubted whether he himself could keep up with her, especially after the distance he had covered the night before.

But he was not worried for their sake. They would make it to the substation in plenty of time. It was midday. They would be in the city by now if he judged correctly. With a little good fortune, the aliens were still some hours behind the fleeing refugees.

"Keep moving," he barked, urging the stragglers on. The march was killing them. But stopping would be worse. Somewhere in the distance behind them, he just knew their enemy was in pursuit. The villagers had no choice, so on they lurched, the march of the damned to a hopeless salvation.

———◄○►———

Fei Hung rounded the corner to the substation well before Yenko. He had sent her on ahead. The chilling voice of his friend, Li Jie, the Commander, haunted him. *"Macpherson Yenko, soldier in the Zhongguo Xin Shijie army, as of this moment . . . You. Are. Dead. Abandon yourself to the mission."*

He trusted Li Jie's military expertise implicitly. He was a dead man. And if he must abandon himself to the mission, then it was not important who first warned the Third Fleet. Having given Fei Hung a paper notepad and graphite stick that he had stowed away in a pocket for this precise moment, he instructed her how to find the technician assigned to wait at the substation for him.

"Make sure they understand the urgency, and that when we activate the machine, we're likely to bring an alien army into our space with us. They need to be ready."

Yenko now ran alone, making his desperate way through the maze of city streets, hoping he did not lose his way. She would be there by now. He was sure of it.

———◦►———

Frantically, Fei Hung searched about the substation. She could see nothing of Yenko's ghostly friends. Were they there? A hint of movement on the street caught her attention, but she could make nothing of it. The sun was high overhead and she had learned in her encounters with Yenko that this was the worst kind of light for identifying the spectral forms.

"Look for shaded areas," Yenko had told her. "I've instructed my technician to wait there so I could see him and he, me."

Shaded areas. There were very few. The substation door was shut. That would have been a better place, she thought. Perhaps over the road, where she thought she might have seen movement. There was no time to lose.

Sprinting across the cracked paving, she saw him—a young man, perhaps no older than herself, leaning idly against one of the cement pylons supporting a two-story building. As she approached him, the startled fear on his face showed he had seen her.

Quickly, she wrote.

Alurt mauntn

The words were crudely written and poorly spelled, unsurprising so, given the harsh reality of her upbringing.

Ienko hir sun
Wor cums
Enamy foloz
Tel comador
4000 ov us
Cum from west
Enamy foloz
Comador nid armi
Luk west
Ienko hir sun
Wen redi Ienko tel wen mak mashin work
U b redi

Enamy foloz

Wor cumz

The young man wrote quickly on a tablet, confirming her message. When he was certain he understood the intent of the haunting apparition's message, he called towards the road. Two ghostly figures, women, stepped into the shadows and looked apprehensively at Fei Hung.

After a brief discussion, the two ran back to the street. The young man looked at Fei Hung, a hint of uncertainty still in his eyes, and spoke into what must have been one of the communicating devices Yenko had told her of. When he was finished, he simply nodded to her, then wrote, *Where's Mr. Macpherson?*

"Yenko?" she articulated.

"Yes," the young man nodded.

Hi hir sun

Cumng

Fei Hung had hardly finished writing when she heard Yenko's boots pounding up the street.

"Yenko," she yelled. "We're over here."

The forced march on the refugees was brutal. Stretching out over half a mile, they plodded ever onward, heads drooped in resignation. When first the Commander, Yenko and their beloved Fei Hung burst into their township the day before, there had been sounds of jubilation. And when Huang had killed the two demons, hope was born anew. But now they were marching to the center of their darkest superstitions, their deepest fears. The ruined city. The haunt of ghosts and goblins. They had to; they were being hunted by scores of demons. Hundreds perhaps, from what the Commander had intimated to them.

It was only with reluctance that many of them had accepted the exodus at all. If not for the demands and exhortations of their elders, they would have stayed behind in surrender. Huang knew that would spell certain death for them. And he forced them to see that Yenko was a bringer of hope. There was help to the east, in the city of ghosts.

Commander Huang prayed the crowd would make it to the exclusion zone before the aliens intercepted them. Their hope was a tenuous one.

He already had made his plan; that much was within his control. At the limits of the exclusion zone, a lone hill rose. He had noted it the day before as they made their way to Gui Difang. As the exodus progressed within range of Yenko's Gravimetric Discriminator, Li Jie would take the high ground. With his powerful tactical sniper rifle, he would pick off the forward guard of the attack. His weapon was accurate to a range of two miles. And he was a deadly marksman. It would slow the pursuit for only a moment, but that would just about buy the time they may need.

——————◁○▷——————

Yenko scribbled furiously on the notepad Fei Hung handed back to him. He had seen her writing and was worried that the technician, Lakshay Varma, may not have understood her. In only a few brief minutes, however, he was satisfied.

The mountain station technical team was on high alert, ready to begin the countdown. Lakshay pointed out the LRV parked on the far side of the substation, ready for a quick exit when the time came.

Yenko had predicted that the resonating pulse from the Earth-built reflector, now phase-shifted in alignment with the survivors making their way towards the ruins, would re-establish normal phasing of everything in its path. If, however, someone from the normally phased world was caught in its path, it would be disastrous. They would be thrust into the phase-shifted existence that everyone else was being liberated from.

Lakshay assured him that he would be nowhere in range when it happened.

Having satisfied himself that the technician had made adequate warning to the Commodore, he wrote, *There's nothing more for you till I give the word. I'm going to go now and set the reflector in place. I don't really need access to the control room, but I'd prefer to replicate this as close as possible to the original. Can you open the door for me?*

"Yes," the young man agreed.

And leave the door open!

Lakshay nodded grimly. He understood. If Yenko went into the room to set up his instrument and the door shut behind him, there would be no way he could open it. He would be effectively locked in there and the mission would be in jeopardy.

"Come on," Yenko said to Fei Hung. "We've got work to do."

As they crossed the road together, Varma was lost to their sight. Yenko just hoped he understood the gravity of the moment; he was sure he did. Fei Hung strode comfortably beside him. She was formidable with the bulky alien gun nestled in her arms. He had seen its devastation when she had practiced soon after leaving Gui Difang. The woman was nothing like who he had imagined her to be.

"You did well, Fei Hung," he said. "He understood you completely."

She smiled at him.

Hopefully, they would all look back on this day as the greatest day of Zhinu.

"You. Are. Dead."

———◦———

Setting up the resonance reflector proved more difficult than Yenko expected, but at last he was satisfied. Throughout the process, Lakshay remained in sight inside the control room with him. This proved helpful, because Yenko found that he needed to shift the original, decommissioned resonance reflector and he would not have been able to do that without the technician.

Time marched mercilessly forward. It was 2:07pm. The refugees would be close to the exclusion zone by now. Hopefully they were already there. Yenko would rather they reached the city center itself, but he was not going to have that luxury. As long as they got into the exclusion zone, he knew they would be within the range of the pulse.

We have to go now, he wrote to the technician. *Wait for me here, inside this room. Expect us within the hour. Make sure the Third Fleet is ready to strike, but stress to the Commodore that no one can cross into the exclusion zone until after the pulse is fired. They need to monitor what is happening in the Mountain Control Room and hear the countdown. After the pulse is emitted, they have to wait seventy-two seconds. That's the duration of the pulse. But they shouldn't be so close that they could cross within that time anyway! They should wait at least two and a half miles beyond the safe line. Do you understand? One of us will return and give you the go ahead. We don't know what we're going to face. Be alert.*

With that, Yenko and Fei Hung raced out the door.

"This is it; there's no more time," he told her. "We have to fly. As soon as we know your people are in the exclusion zone, we've got to get back here and let the technician know. And even then, it will be another ten minutes at least before the button is pressed. God, I hope those aliens haven't caught them yet. My team won't turn it on until Lakshay's out of the city. Everything hangs on speed."

Together, they sprinted off into the west, prepared to spend the last of their energy to save even one minute.

———————◄○►———————

The crosshairs of Commander Huang's scope trained in on the alien trotting at the head of a squad of three, the vanguard of the attacking force. Two more groups of three flanked either side, not far behind the leaders. Behind this, the same pattern of nine aliens repeated. And another behind that. And another. In the rear, a large battalion in ranks of ten followed. At this range, they were hard to number. Perhaps as many as a hundred in the battalion. Thirty-six, probably their crack team, led the assault, a spearhead intending to destroy the fleeing refugees.

Below Li Jie's hilltop vantage point, the refugees struggled forward. Their elders were at the rear, urging them on to make their last desperate lunge for safety.

Huang was at ease, focused solely on his objective. The crosshairs never wavered from their target. Exhaling slowly, he squeezed the trigger. A moment later, the alien dropped.

Confusion followed momentarily amongst the leading nine, but almost instantly, the leader of the second group of three ran forward to take the place of the fallen leader. As it did so, its position was filled from behind, and so on down the line.

Huang fired again. And again and again in rapid succession. The leading pack fell. Still the attackers surged forward, the gap to their quarry lessening with each step. As each group of three was felled, the trios sped up, taking the place of the first and making a place for another three from the battalion in the rear. For five minutes it was carnage. Dozens of aliens had been gunned down.

Suddenly, four groups of nine forged out from within the front lines of the battalion, making for Huang's hilltop post. He was aware of the aliens' impending threat, but kept his sights trained on those making for the refugees and continued to pick off alien after alien. With a glance over his shoulder, he checked where the villagers were. The last of them had entered the exclusion zone. The attackers were still more than half a mile behind these, but those bearing down on his hilltop were only a few hundred yards from him.

Calmly, he set five small cannisters about the place where he lay, rolling four more into bushes on the side of the hill closest his pursuers and crept away from his nest. Once out of sight of his enemies, he rose to his feet, set four more cannisters on that side of the hill and took off at a sprint.

At the bottom of the hill, he turned to see the first of the attack advancing over the rise. They had not seen him yet but had guessed his direction and pursued. More and more aliens came into sight. Li Jie flicked a small switch on a device he held in his hand. He did not need to look behind; the detonation took out the entire top of the hill and sent plumes of smoke, dust, and debris into the air.

-----◀◉▶-----

"There they are!" Fei Hung yelled. Her people were running desperately, raggedly toward her.

Yenko studied the sprawling line. He and Fei Hung were well inside the exclusion zone, and he could see that the leading edge of the refugees was not that far away. They were most definitely within the range of the Gravimetric Discriminator's pulse. But he needed to know if all the refugees were within range, not just the leaders.

He sprinted to the top of a small hill nearby, adrenaline and fear coursing through his veins. From there he would get a more accurate view of the villagers' flight. His heart sank as he saw their pursuers. Yenko was not good with numbers but it seemed to him that thousands of aliens bore down on the fleeing refugees. His heart froze.

"You. Are. Dead."

Just then, a hill off to his far left suddenly erupted in a violent explosion. Huang!

Fei Hung yelled to Yenko. "Are they in the exclusion zone yet?"

Yenko did not respond. Could not respond. So many aliens. The refugees would be slaughtered. Smoke from the explosion drifted over them, an ominous prediction of their inevitable destruction. Fire and smoke, the funeral pyre of the villagers' doom.

"Yenko!" Fei Hung screamed. "Yenko! Are they in the exclusion zone yet?"

He stared blankly at her. Matted messy hair straggled over her face, her torn sleeve flapping in the breeze. Green and red stains still abused her bodysuit; and despite the streaming sweat, several bloody tracks clung to her beautiful, deadly face.

She reached his side and slapped him. It brought him to his senses.

"Yes," he said, shocked. "They're in."

"Good! Then listen to me. The Commander can't hold that force on his own. I'm going to add my weapon to his. Run, Yenko! Run as fast as you can! Our lives depend on it!"

It was an appeal that set his feet on fire. Disregarding the pain, the screams of his lungs and limbs, he expended all. He would get word to the control room. Or he would die in the attempt.

◄◦►

Commodore Ahuja surveyed her troops. This was what they were on this planet for. One conjecture that had long been held on Earth of the mystery behind Zhinu was that there was an unknown enemy. It had proved correct, and somewhere out there, Macpherson Yenko and Commander Huang were bringing their hidden number out into the light.

Her troops were ready. Armed. Reconnaissance Vehicles idled, the rumble of their powerful engines setting the mood for action amongst the heavily armed Third Fleet. The entire company waited, ready to meet every threat head on when the lost survivors of Xin Beijing finally found their freedom.

The Fleet poised to make its strike, only a mile to the north of the exodus. From there, the troops could hear the thudding noises of unknown weapons' fire. Clouds of black smoke arose here and there with no apparent reason.

A hill suddenly erupted in a violent explosion that all but erased it from the landscape.

"Troops, prepare your weapons," the Commodore barked, eager to engage the unseen enemy. The distinctive sounds of plasma cannons, shotguns, and CME carbines being armed reverberated across the assembled ranks. The Commander and Macpherson were out there in the ghostly realm. She only hoped their efforts were meeting with success.

Ahuja trained her field binoculars on the scene of the mayhem. Whatever was happening there was not good. It was frustrating to know that death and carnage was unfolding about her company, but there was nothing she could do for the moment. Not until the Gravimetric Discriminator was activated.

◄◦►

Yenko ran and ran, calling on energy from unknown reserves within him. Desperation drove him on. And Li Jie's demand. *You. Are. Dead.* If dead he was, there was no point in holding anything back. All depended on it. Staggering past decrepit buildings, down derelict streets, he looked a mad man stumbling on to despair and suicide.

At last, he saw the power station, the control room door wide open in anticipation of his arrival and the command to engage the Gravimetric Discriminator. An LRV stood at the ready on the street, awaiting Varma's escape. Yenko burst into the room and all but collapsed on the floor. The technician, standing in the semidarkness, jumped in fright.

With barely energy enough to pull out his notepad, Yenko scribbled, *Start the countdown and get out of here.*

Varma held out a note he had already written. *My LRV is running. Will I leave you here or drop you off near the edge of the exclusion zone?*

Yenko nodded enthusiastically. He needed to be there. The sight and sound of the exploding hilltop haunted him. It seemed an eternity ago. What was happening back there? Li Jie and Fei Hung were hopelessly outnumbered. They needed him.

Drop me at the outer limits of the city, he scrawled. *I'll jump out and you get the hell out of there.*

———◄◦►———

Fei Hung watched for the briefest of moments as Yenko ran off towards the city, its broken towers dominating the landscape in that direction. He worried her. Why had he frozen? There was no time for second guessing. No time for fear of any sort. He would have to find the reserves within himself. The Commander had confidence in him. She only wished that she did.

But there was no time for such concerns, no time at all. She ran towards the thick of the conflict. Far to her right, Li Jie was firing rapidly into the attacking band as they drew closer to the stragglers. One by one, alien soldiers dropped in quick succession, but it was not enough to stop the assault altogether. A blast shot from within the murderous pack vaporized two villagers and a sick compatriot they bore on a stretcher.

Three demons peeled off to one side to make a counterattack against the Commander. In the mayhem, Fei Hung could tell he had not seen them. He would be an open target once they got behind him. This was it. Her moment of revenge for all the atrocities these evil hordes had committed against her people, against her own self. Now she was armed. Her bone knife had inflicted death against her own possessed people. Now she would wreak havoc against their oppressors with a weapon suited for such evil. Coming to a dead halt, she took aim at the leader, now only a short sprint behind Li Jie.

The shot missed her intended target but took out the third of the trio. The sound alerted the Commander to his danger as he dived to one side and shot a volley at his assailants. Another fell, but the leader dived headlong onto Li Jie and the two rolled down a shallow incline out of Fei Hung's sight.

She wanted to run to the Commander's need, but she could not. Another round of fire erupted from the ever-closing demonic horde. Time seemed to slow down as one after another of the refugees vanished in black smoke. It was more than she could bear. These were people she knew and loved, had sold her soul to murder for, had bled for, and worse.

Like a crazed wild woman, she ran headlong into the pack, firing carelessly, screaming abuses and curses. It took the band by surprise and they broke rank, diving for the cover of bushes and trees. Shots fired around her, but she weaved and dodged, heedless of the threat of death that surrounded her.

Given their numbers, it was easier for her to hit a target than for them, but the barrage of alien weapon fire caused havoc around her. Trees vanished in thick fumes, others burst into flame. Black smoke hung everywhere, turning the day into preternatural night.

An explosion in the near distance killed a trio of demons that had regrouped and started firing on the refugees. Li Jie was still in the fight.

———◆◇◆———

The sound of vaporizing death behind him alerted Li Jie to the ambush. Instinct took over and he dived to one side, grateful that somewhere amidst the surrounding mayhem, Fei Hung was covering his back. Two alien fighters were now on top of him. He barely had time to fire off a rapid volley of shots, dropping one of them, before he was set upon in hand-to-hand combat. The green armor of his assailant told him this would not be an easy fight; it was the enemy leader.

The two crashed headlong into a small hollow. Li Jie marshalled all his skill. This was what he was trained for. Ignoring the crushing pain of the arm wrapped about his neck, he used his opponent's momentum to his favor and rolled forward, slamming the alien into a rocky outcrop. It was enough to loosen its grip, and he reached to his shoe, pulled out his knife and stabbed the alien's leg.

It screamed in pain and smashed a fist into Li Jie's face, turning its arm as it did so to slash its barbed arm across the Commander's face. Blood gushed everywhere, streaming down Li Jie's chest, but for the moment he did not feel it. Instinct and adrenaline were in control. Even as his own face was being ripped open, he struck his blade deep into the waist of his enemy.

Unexpectedly, the alien leader grabbed Li Jie's knife hand and held it in place, the knife deep within its gut, preventing another stabbing assault. With its free hand, it shot a barb into the Commander's neck.

Ignoring the pain, Li Jie reached for a grenade from his belt and armed it. If he was going to die, he would take the green leader with him. His opponent understood the intent and reefed the explosive out of the Commander's hand, hurling it far from the hollow. It exploded somewhere in the mayhem about them.

———◄◦►———

Yenko held on for dear life as the LRV careened through the outskirts of the city. In the distance he could hear the screams of refugees as they fled the slaughter. All thought of discomfort at riding shotgun in a vehicle driven by the invisible technician vanished in the shock of dismay and anger that overtook him.

The LRV screeched to a halt, but only long enough for Yenko to dive out and race toward the pall of smoke and sound of battle. Almost at that instant, just as the LRV spun its tires in a hasty getaway, a violent explosion hurled it into the air, its ghostly driver flung carelessly away from the wreckage to who knew where. The vehicle was half incinerated and lay in its smoky ruin amidst a jumble of boulders.

Yenko picked himself up from the ground, having been thrown off his feet by the blast. There was nothing he could do to help the young technician. In his ghostly state, he could be anywhere. Varma was young, but he was trained for battle, along with the rest of the Third Fleet. He would have to look after himself. If he was alive.

Sprinting now as fast as he could, Yenko sought out the thickest part of the battle. Weapons-fire rang out across the now scorched ground and he fought his way through a dozen alien fighters. A shot brushed past his left hand, vaporizing two of his fingers. That only fueled his desire for blood. His handheld pulse cannon fired mercilessly into the throng.

At that very moment, the sky lit up as if a myriad of spotlights had just focused their power on the battlefield. The air hummed and shuddered. The smoke of battle vibrated violently for what seemed an eternity as hundreds of villagers lost balance and fell to the ground.

———————◄◦►———————

Fei Hung's heart raced at the onset of the unknown light and the throbbing hum of the atmosphere. What new devilry was this? It momentarily knocked her from her feet, fortuitously so as a blast from an enemy weapon only just missed its target. But there was no time to determine the cause of the atmospheric detonation. She rolled on the ground and found her opponent with a single shot.

Air flooded into her lungs. It was as if she had never breathed before, as newfound oxygen energized her weary muscles. She sprang to her feet, ready to fire again. Sounds she had never before heard bore down from beyond the limits of the exclusion zone; the Third Fleet was roaring into the fight, LRVs at the lead.

The battle was short lived from that moment on. Ten alien soldiers were all that remained of their number. Cries of release and anguish rang out from the confused refugees, as one by one they realized the fight was over. Their pursuers were vanquished. But at great cost. One hundred and twenty of Gui Difang's forgotten number were dead or unaccounted for, lost in smoke.

Fei Hung raced to the hollow where she had last seen the Commander in mortal combat with the green demon. He was nowhere in sight, nor was the alien.

"Fei Hung, you're alive!" yelled Yenko as he ran to the battle-weary woman.

"He's not here!" she cried.

A stab of panic hit the Scot.

"Who's not here?" he demanded.

"The Commander."

———————◄◦►———————

Hours later, the last of the refugees were ferried off to the safety and somber welcome of the Zhinu settlements. But five hundred of the Third

Fleet, including all of Delta Squadron, remained behind in search of their fallen comrade.

"It's too near the exclusion zone," Yenko worried. "Are you sure you saw him fall into this hollow?"

The cold look on Fei Hung's face told him the answer. She was hardened to tragedy, inured to emotional pain.

"That is where they fought," she affirmed. "But he did not die under demon fire. There are none of the scorch marks of their weapons."

Yenko ran his fingers through his hair. This was not over yet. Varma's LRV lay in smoldering ruins nearby. But the Bhaarateey technician could not be found. He had been caught in the phase-shift. If he had survived the accident, he would now be in the same reality as the Commander. They would have to mount another rescue mission.

8

Possession

L I JIE WRITHED IN pain. Chains manacled him spread-eagled to the ground. His mouth foamed and fire coursed through his veins. Wild, maddened thoughts ripped away the last vestiges of his humanity as he cursed and spat futile obscenities at his captors.

"Let me go!" he screamed. Blood flowed yet again from the gash across his right cheek, but he paid it no attention. "I will feed your flesh to the dogs and make your children watch their mother shamed before their eyes."

An intense fire burned in his neck where the dart still lay, embedded deep in his flesh. When it had first struck him, he had swooned from its dreadful venom, only to finally gain consciousness while being mercilessly dragged by the green alien. By then, despite the dart's dreadful stinging, he had no power of compulsion to remove it. Instead, his mind had been filled with bloodlust and murder.

He had fought against his captor, but to no avail; its grip was absolute. Intensifying matters, the alien was not alone. A band of maybe ten or more accompanied their leader. Li Jie could not be precise—his faculties were too overcome by rage and searing pain. At regular intervals through that nightmare trip, Li Jie received a kick to the head or chest from one of his captors along with guttural alien threats. One of those kicks sent him into oblivion and he did not wake again until he was strung out on a low mound within sight of the crashed alien spacecraft.

The Leader barked something at him in its alien tongue.

"*Halt die Schnauze!*"

"Be quiet!" it added in a rough form of the Zhongwen language. "You are only alive for one purpose: to lure your friends to me. I do not know what weapon you used on us, but I saw my troops vanish into thin air. You will pay most dearly for it."

"Let me go from these chains," Li Jie screamed amid violent thrashings. "I'll show you a weapon that will melt your soul as I tear your heart out with my bare teeth!"

If the Commander had had his wits about him, he would have noted the alien's familiarity with his mother tongue. Perhaps they had been long enough on the planet, studying the survivors in Gui Difang, though that would have seemed unlikely had Li Jie enough clarity of thought to take it all in; Fei Hung's testimony of their attacks against her people only told of occasional engagements. And more to the point, the common language of the Zhinu survivors was English, not Zhongwen.

And he would have noted that, here at their base, the Leader was far from alone. Four squads of thirty-six had remained behind at the crash site when the assault on the villagers had been launched. Along with those that had returned with their Leader, they formed a formidable fighting pack. All of them were heavily armed, now they were aware there was a new force about them.

But Huang had no capacity to consider any of this. He took no care for their number or capabilities, nor did he consider the incongruity of arguing in the Zhongwen language with an alien from another world.

---◄○►---

Lakshay Varma pulled his LRV to a rapid halt and then planted his foot back on the gas, hoping that his hero, Yenko Macpherson, had jumped out of the vehicle safely. There was no way of knowing; the man was invisible. He could not even be certain that Yenko was with him at all. But he knew how to follow orders and follow them he did. Almost as soon as he began to speed off to escape the exclusion zone, however, he felt the ground tremble beneath him, possible indications of the ghostly battle somewhere nearby. Strange bursts of smoke arose from nowhere about him.

The technician had no time to understand what happened next. A black smoke erupted from the front of the LRV right before his eyes and the vehicle lurched violently into the air. Time seemed to slow as he was hurled far from the tumbling wreck. Crashing through trees and into a rocky outcrop was the last thing Lakshay remembered.

When he came to, he found himself lying sprawled out on the ground. Instinctively, he moved to get up, but pain shot through his entire body. Each breath was labored and agonizing. Glancing down at his legs, he saw the reason for the searing pain in his knee; his lower leg stuck out obscenely, a full ninety degrees from his thigh.

"Aggghhh!" he screamed.

The air around him lit up and throbbed, a low hum that resonated through every fiber of his body. And of a sudden, the pain in his chest was compounded by the struggle to get enough air to breathe, as if half the oxygen around him had been sucked away. It was more than his lightly built frame could take; oblivion mercifully overtook him.

―――◄◦►―――

The meeting with Commodore Ahuja lasted hours. Night had long fallen, but everything had to be carefully planned, every contingency considered. Once again, Yenko's expertise was needed. He desperately wanted to launch the rescue attempt as soon as possible. If it had been up to him, they would already be within the phase-shifted world, scouring the battlefield for their fallen comrade, his friend. But it was not up to him. Like the previous sortie, this was a military operation, and he was not in charge.

"Go now and make your equipment ready at the substation," the Commodore finally ordered. "The minutes run too fast."

Yenko raced off, eager to get the mission underway. As he hastened out of the meeting room, he crashed into Fei Hung who had been summoned to the Commodore's makeshift war office. Her understanding of the alien forces, their abilities, their strategies, the way they conducted themselves in the recent battle before the Third Fleet had been able to join in—all were essential for assessing what they were potentially up against, and she had been called in to give a report.

"Are you going back to the power station?" Fei Hung asked, unconcerned by the clumsy meeting. Yenko nodded. "Wait for me there. After I speak to the Commodore, I will come to you. I need to do something; my blood boils for what these things have done to my people. And I was the last one to see the Commander."

———————◄○►———————

Night was fast failing, but all was finally in place. Yenko stood at the site of the recent battle, an eerie peace belying the horrors that had taken place there only the day before. Nearby, the wreckage of Varma's LRV lay overturned in a twisted heap. After examining the tortured metal, no one expected to find the young Bhaarateey alive. Yenko's bandaged left hand, hiding the loss of two fingers, throbbed with pain, but he paid it no attention. Lakshay was most likely dead, but his best friend, Li Jie, may still be out there somewhere. There was hope yet.

Stationed round Yenko, decked out in full combat readiness, were three squadrons of the Third Fleet, almost one hundred heavily armed warriors bent on the rescue of their fallen comrade. If he was still alive. Either way, they would make his captors pay. Fei Hung, alien weapon cocked and ready, stood to Yenko's right. It was time.

Overnight, a team of technicians had set both receivers in place in the substation, one to send them out of phase once more, the other ready to be hooked up for the return. Three of them now waited at the substation. They would make the phase-shift with the rescue party. Once that had occurred, they would connect the Earth-built receiver. Ingeniously, one of them had designed a switching device that would enable them to disconnect the original receiver once they had been sent into the world of their lost comrade. In this way, it would be a simple matter of connecting the new receiver and the whole process would be good to go for the return trip, whenever that might be.

"Are we ready?" Yenko asked Yang Zhi Ruo, who had been given tactical command of the whole operation. Zhao Mo Chou had been appointed her temporary replacement as Captain over Delta Squadron.

Zhinu's sun rose above Xin Beijing's eastern hills as Zhi Ruo inspected her troops.

"Squadron Leaders! Prepare your soldiers!" she ordered, her steely voice bringing the assembled company to order. "We make the jump on my command."

Turning to Yenko, she added with grim finality, "Make the call."

Raising his communicator, he made his own survey of the group. "Start the countdown," he ordered the technicians at the mountain facility.

The seconds passed. Suddenly, the early morning sky blazed with light. The hum of the generated impulse resonated through the air. If any of the soldiers were shocked by the sudden lack of air, they did not show it. They had been briefed thoroughly on what to expect from the phase-shift. Immediately they headed out into the lands beyond the exclusion zone. Somewhere out there was their comrade-in-arms. And the body of the fallen technician.

Scouts searched the area where Li Jie had last been seen by Fei Hung and quickly found evidence of the struggle with the alien leader. Captain Yang gathered the squadrons together. A rough trail was barely visible, heading into the west.

"That's the direction of Gui Difang," Yenko said, stating the obvious. "But it's also the way to the alien spacecraft . . . to the north of the village, beyond the escarpment. Li Jie said there was a way up the cliff the aliens used."

"Captain Yang," a Bhaarateey soldier interrupted, holding one of the alien darts gingerly in his hand. "I found this."

"Be careful with it," Yenko warned. "That's one of the barbs the aliens torment their enemies with. It injects a drug that sends its victim mad."

The Captain studied the projectile, two inches long, covered with fine needles that folded smoothly back onto the shaft of the dart. In this manner, the weapon could easily penetrate the flesh of its victim. And yet, if the attempt was made to extract it, the spray of needles would flare out, mercilessly denying the endeavor.

"We tore several of them out of some villagers two nights ago," Yenko added.

Examining the action of the needle barbs, Captain Yang remarked, "These would be next to impossible to remove without ripping a person to shreds."

"It's true," Yenko agreed. "Fei Hung said that whenever they made the attempt, the victims would bleed to death. I hit a knife with a low yield plasma burst and cauterized the wounds. It wasn't pretty, but they'll live. If Li Jie was shot with one . . ."

Yenko could not complete the thought as a mix of fear and hatred rose within him. Fear for his fallen brother-in-arms, and hatred for the blue skinned aliens. His bandaged hand throbbed as if it desired its own retribution.

"We have to find him," he said at length. "He may still be alive. But be careful! People who've been shot with one of those darts become murderously insane."

Captain Yang nodded thoughtfully. They had been briefed on the gruesome alien device.

At that moment, Fei Hung yelled out from a great distance away, waving her arms above her head. She had been with those members of the company searching for Varma's body to bring it home in honor of his memory.

"I've found the technician. He lives."

It was good news. Yenko did not know what to do, torn between two desires; to race to Fei Hung and Varma, or join the squadrons to follow the path they supposed was left by either the alien or their lost comrade. In the end, however, there was no choice to be made. Li Jie was his closest friend. Whatever had happened to Lakshay, others would have to tend to him. At least he was alive; there was no way of knowing if the same was true of Li Jie.

Yang and several nearby commandos ran to Fei Hung and the discovery of the fallen technician.

"Captain!" yelled another soldier almost as soon as she arrived at the place where Lakshay was. "You need to see this!"

The cry had a sound of urgency about it, and she sprinted towards the man who was kneeling over an alien corpse.

"Wait till I see what this is about before you begin tracking down Commander Huang," Yang ordered loudly over her shoulder to those gathering round the tracks leading into the west.

The soldier who had called for her moved aside as Captain Yang neared, giving her full view of his discovery. There on the ground lay a dead alien, its blue hide strangely semitransparent, rendering it uniquely camouflaged no matter the environment. Yang could see why Fei Hung's people had thought them phantoms. It had been shot, killed by a single hit to the chest. Dried green and red blood covered its upper torso and a considerable amount had soaked into the dirt in which it lay.

But what struck her was its head, and this was why the soldier had called her. The green shield that covered its face had been shattered, either in the combat or the fall, revealing its features. It was a man. Despite the obvious alien nature of its blood, this creature, at least facially, was human.

Yang bent down and ripped away the remains of its face shield. With the alien's face thus exposed, she realized that the creature's blue hide was a suit of some form. It was thick and armor-like, but she pulled it off its head easily enough to reveal a pale-skinned human face with thick blonde hair.

———⟨○⟩———

Lakshay Varma opened his eyes slowly. He thought he had just heard a woman's voice. What had she said? I've found the technician? He lives? What technician?

It was the first voice he had heard since his LRV had been targeted in the attack. He shook his head, trying to clear the fog that clouded his brain. Where was he? One of his legs screamed with pain as he rolled over to get his bearings. He lay under a bush nestled between a tumble of rocks.

Memories flooded back as his senses returned to clarity. Flying through the air, crashing helplessly at speed into the ground, his leg at a shocking angle. A light followed by blackness. He remembered the agonizing crawl to find somewhere to hide from the battle, fully aware that it would be difficult for any of the Third Fleet to find him. But the stories he had heard of Yenko's aliens chilled him to the core. Better to be lost than dead.

That had been hours ago, and he had more than once worried that perhaps the fight had moved on and he really was lost, a forgotten casualty of the conflict. In fact, it was by sheer chance that Fei Hung had come upon him at all; a brief reflection of the early morning sun off something shiny under a clump of foliage had caught her eye.

"Are you injured?" she asked the technician. At once he recognized her. Yenko's ghostly companion, now impossibly solid.

"Are you injured?" she asked again, breaking his dumb silence.

"No," he said. "I mean, yes. I mean . . ." The man was delirious.

Captain Liu Wang Yong from Chi One Squadron was the first to jump down the tumbled terrain in response to Fei Hung's appeal. "You're alright, soldier," he told the technician. "We're here to get you out."

"I'm finding it hard to breathe, sir," Lakshay confessed. "I know my leg's in a bad way, but I must have internal injuries."

"You did not escape the exclusion zone," the Captain said. "You struggle to breathe because it is the way of this place."

"How can I see you then? And the girl?"

A group of soldiers joined the gathering to help carry their fallen comrade to safety and medical care.

"The battle is over," Fei Hung said, grabbing his hand gently in encouragement.

"Then . . . Then, why are you here?"

"Commander Huang is unaccounted for," she replied. "We've come back for him. When we saw your vehicle, we were sure you were a casualty of the conflict. We were searching for any sign of you so that we could take your body back with us to our camp and lay you to rest.

"I was the last to see the Commander in the battle. In mortal combat with the demon leader. That was over there beyond that hill. Once I had shown our company where to begin their search, I bent my attention toward you. How I came to find you, I don't know. The gods must truly favor you. You were all but completely hidden."

The young technician held Fei Hung's hand tightly. "I was afraid," he confessed.

"We all are afraid," she whispered. By the bloodied stains that still covered her, Lakshay could tell she had been in the thick of the fighting.

Just then, Captain Yang joined the company.

"Are you alright?" she asked the technician.

He gazed long at her before answering. "I honestly do not know," he said. "Sir. Or ma'am . . . Sir . . . Sorry, sir. Ma'am."

Captain Yang ignored the incoherent reply. Turning to Captain Liu, she ordered, "Take this one back to the city and order the engineers to return you to Zhinu proper. He needs medical attention fast."

Liu directed two of the soldiers with him to remove the technician from his hideout.

"And Captain," added Yang, holding out the alien dart in her hand, "take this with you. It will need to be analyzed. There won't be equipment for the task on Zhinu, but perhaps the Commodore might know of a way to get Nirani to help."

Captain Liu accepted the dart carefully and nodded. "Yes Captain," he said with a salute, and turned to leave with Lakshay and the two soldiers carrying him sitting upright between them.

"Wait," Captain Yang ordered in afterthought. "Don't go just yet." Turning to two other soldiers, she added, "You two, go over that rise. There you will find an alien body. Take it with the Captain and the technician. The Commodore will want to see it."

The soldiers saluted and sprinted off to carry out their orders.

With a loud voice, Captain Yang called to the company at large. "All troops, assemble in the hollow where Commander Huang fell. We will hunt his assailant down."

Lakshay watched behind him as Captain Yang returned to the scene of Li Jie's fall. Fei Hung still held his hand; he would not let her go. His eyes fell from the retreating soldiers onto the mysterious woman. Her hair was matted. Dried alien blood seemed to cover her head to foot. One sleeve of her leather suit was ripped to the shoulder, revealing old scars from unknown horrors.

She looked distantly at him. Part of her wanted to go after the soldiers in their search for Commander Huang. But she was suddenly tired. Her people were safe. Would the bloodshed never end?

Ever since she had been old enough to fight, old enough to join what the villagers of Gui Difang called the Angels of Death, she had plied her skills to protect her people. And to put out of their misery those who had been shot with the evil barbs of the demons. Blood, murder, rape. Atrocity after atrocity. She was cold inside, and yet the warmth of the hand that held hers offered an unlooked-for absolution, an ambiguous hope of erasure of all that she had witnessed, all that she had done.

Lakshay held her hand tightly. He seemed to need the comfort of her presence. Comfort. That was something she had never allowed herself. She was an Angel of Death not a bringer of hope. Looking up from her hand entwined in his, she met his eyes.

"Are you alright?" he asked her.

"Am I alright?" she repeated distantly, shaking her head in wonder that in his suffering he would think of hers.

———◄◊►———

"They went this way," a scout said. "I cannot tell how many, but they made a direct line to the escarpment over there."

The company had been following the scuffed trail for some time. The signs told the story of a body being dragged off into the west. That gave Captain Yang cause for hope. If Huang had been killed, he would have been left behind. But it was clear that someone, or something, was unceremoniously hauling a body back to the alien basecamp. Huang was alive.

Eventually, towards noon, they reached the escarpment where the broken wreckage of an ancient rockfall had created a natural path up the otherwise difficult ascent.

"Captain," whispered the scout, raising his hand in warning. Silently, swiftly, he unslung his plasma shotgun. The company followed suit, ducking low under the cover of the surrounding boulders.

With a motion of his hand, the scout indicated the cause of his heightened state of alert. An alien lay dead amongst the rocks to one side of the path. It had been shot in the face.

"Plasma cannon," Captain Yang said, examining the wound.

"Then Commander Huang is free," whispered the scout. "And armed."

"No. This one has been dead too long. It is one of those he killed the night before last."

Yenko looked at the corpse before him. His friend, Li Jie, did not miss. What the aliens would do to him as they dragged him up the escarpment past their fallen brothers, Yenko shuddered to think. Of course, they would not know they dragged the very assailant who had killed these fallen ones, but at the very least, he was a representative of their foe. They would show him little mercy. Yenko hoped Captain Yang's scouts would not find the Commander's dead body nearby.

The Captain stood to her feet after studying the lifeless alien and surveyed the rockfall before them. Silently, she instructed the first of her company to make the ascent in twos, weapons drawn. Just as silently in response, a dozen soldiers made their way carefully up the slope. There was no sign of the enemy.

With deft hand signals, the leading pair alerted the Captain to more of Huang's handiwork; two decapitated alien bodies each lying neatly to the side of the path. As she made her way past them, she nodded her head in grim acknowledgement of Li Jie's skill. Yenko was horrified by the bloody spectacle of what his friend was capable of. If he was still alive, his alien captors would be foolish to disregard his capacity for violence, drugged barb or no.

———◀○▶———

It was mid-afternoon when at last Yenko and Captain Yang and her company reached the same ridge that not two days earlier, Huang Li Jie had spied on the alien encampment and the crashed space vessel. And just as Huang had done, two marksmen now lay on the ground, training the scopes of their tactical sniper rifles onto the campsite to spy out what could be made of their foe.

"The green leader is speaking with a group of six others," one of the snipers relayed. "I count at least fifty in the camp."

Yenko's heart sank. Fifty. At least. Undoubtedly, the marksman had missed others. Perhaps the Commodore had been unwise in sending only three squadrons of her troops. They were all handpicked, it was true, from among the best of the military, but still, Yenko would be more at ease if their numbers were greater. The lost villagers were safe, but the war was far from over.

"I see him, Captain," the second sniper said calmly.

"Where? Let me see," demanded Yenko. The soldier ignored him. There was no way he would move without the express order of his Commanding Officer. This was a military operation, not a sightseeing tour.

"Where do you see him?" echoed the first sniper, eye still focused on the enemy leader through the powerful scope.

"He is not in the camp," the second began. "See the band of three sentries patrolling the nearest side of the ship?"

"Yes . . ."

"Come closer towards us by six hundred feet. He is tied on a low mound between two clumps of trees."

The first sniper breathed out slowly. "Yes," he confirmed. "I see him. He is pinned to the ground on his back with his legs and arms held wide by bonds."

"Train your scope closer. He is speaking, though no one is near him."

"It is a trap set for us," Captain Yang said. "There are trees nearby you said. Fix your scopes on them at maximum magnification."

The first sniper whistled softly. "There are five, no, six, hidden in the trees to his right. And there are two, three, four to his left."

"Another five are in the trees one hundred feet before the camp," the second added. "Wait a minute . . . Wait a minute . . ." He adjusted his scope. "Yes, I see them . . . Captain, I believe I can make out a trench one hundred feet behind Commander Huang. Every now and then, I see the top of a green face shield."

"They pin their hopes on us coming for our comrade," Captain Yang said. "We will mount our assault when it is dark. The clouds are thick overhead. If the ancestors favor us, no moons will shine tonight."

———◦———

For the rest of the afternoon and into the early evening, the company stayed out of sight of the enemy camp. A perimeter had been set about them in the rocks of the surrounding hillside. If the aliens thought to send out any sorties for reconnaissance, they would be dealt with swiftly. And given the state of readiness at the crash site of the alien ship, the battle would be on.

Yenko yawned. He had not slept for nearly two days. Though the Captain commanded them all to take the opportunity to replenish their strength, he had not been able to. This was one part of the military's training that he had not been taught: how to get sleep whenever the opportunity was afforded. Particularly when you had constant stabbing pains from the amputation of two fingers. He was comforted, however, that his comrades did know how to sleep on command. Their skills were far more honed than his own and it was infinitely more important that they were rested, not him.

In the dead of the night, a hand shook him roughly. Exhausted, he had finally succumbed to the demands of sleep, despite the rampant mayhem of his thoughts and his physical discomfort. About him, he could hear the soft shuffle of the company, preparing themselves for their stealthy onslaught. Men and women alike covered every inch of their skin with a matte black paste. In the thick darkness, they would not be seen even five feet away. All of them wore infrared eyepieces to give them operational advantage.

The plan was that the company would break into three platoons. One whole squadron would pin down the enemy in their defensive trench. A second group of forty would engage the enemy at its basecamp. A third group of twelve would split into two and take on the ambush that awaited in the trees near Commander Huang. Three others would steal their way towards their captive comrade.

Stealth was demanded. Everyone had to gain their position without alerting the attention of the aliens. Surprise would be their greatest ally.

Silently, slowly, steadily, the three groups crept forward. Not a sound could be heard. This was their art. This was their skill. This was their purpose.

Yenko was ordered to wait, midway between the ridge and where Commander Huang lay. The three men commissioned to rescue Li Jie would bring him back to Yenko as quickly as they could. The Scot was the only one who had had any dealings with saving the demented victims of the alien darts, and they held hopes that he might be of use to them if they could manage to get Huang safely to him.

Besides, they wanted to keep Yenko as far from the action as possible. His skills in stealth warfare were not as refined as their own, and they could not afford for him to accidentally alert the enemy to the attack.

The difficulty was compounded by the fact that Huang was mad, driven insane by the venom that pulsated through his body. They had seen enough from their sniper lookouts to arrive at that conclusion. There was no telling if the drugs had done irremediable damage, but there was nothing for it. If they had to, they would knock their fallen comrade out and carry him back to the medics of the Third Fleet.

But first they had to rescue him. And that would not be easy.

———◄○►———

Yenko held his breath. He was alone, crouching behind a low bush. Even with the aid of his infrared eyepiece, he could not see the full extent of the attack. His comrades were indeed skillful, keeping themselves largely hidden even to one who could see in the dark.

He glanced at his timepiece. The seconds clicked over. 2:05.00am. The designated moment.

Instantly, it seemed like the whole world was detonated with plasma fire as eighty-two weapons erupted as one. It caught the enemy completely off guard, and if Yenko had been closer to the action he would have seen the brutalized alien bodies strewn everywhere about. The carnage in the trench was complete.

Amid the sound of war, Yenko could hear the deafening, cursing screams of Li Jie thrashing about as he was being physically manhandled back towards safety.

"*Qu si, chusheng*! *Gui sunzi*!" he screamed.

Adjusting the dials on a CME carbine, Yenko repeated the process he had performed what seemed years ago; and fired a low yield pulse at the blade of his knife. Seconds later, Li Jie was dragged before him. Despite being so totally outnumbered, it was all the three rescuers could do to keep him semi-constrained.

The veins on Li Jie's neck and forehead stuck out obscenely. Sweat poured from his skin and his eyes were a maddened glaze.

"*Zazhong wang ba*," Li Jie screamed as Yenko ripped the alien dart from his neck. "Aaaggghhhh!"

Blood gushed recklessly from the wound, spurting like a miniature fountain of death over his bodyguards. Unceremoniously, Yenko sealed the bleeding hole in his friend's neck with the scorching heat of his blade. The Commander thrashed about in a frenzy, writhing in pain. Yenko's knife accidentally cut deep into Li Jie's shoulder in the mayhem, instantly cauterizing the unintended wound in the process. Commander Huang passed out. As a precaution, his rescuers bound him hand and foot. He would do no harm from now on.

◄○►

Perhaps the skirmish lasted fifteen minutes, but it was no longer. The enemy had been completely and utterly taken by surprise. By the end, one hundred and twenty-four aliens had fallen. Thirty-two more surrendered, laying down their weapons and drugged darts.

"*Sie haben keine Ahnung, welchen Stein Sie zum Rollen gebracht haben,*" spat the green leader.

In response to the unintelligible utterance, he was met with the butt of a plasma cannon on the chin and slumped to the ground.

"You will answer for your crimes back at our base," Captain Yang said quietly to the unconscious creature. "But you will not speak until then."

9

Alien Discovery

T HE AIR THRUMMED AND burst with light as the rescue mission came back into the normal reality of Zhinu. Within minutes, a military vehicle screamed to a halt outside the power station housing the gravimetric receiver. A team of doctors hurried to work, opening boxes of medical supplies and equipment that Yenko could only guess at, and set up a basic triage center.

"Bring the Commander here," one of the medics barked. "And any other wounded."

The medical team was well prepared for administering aid to Li Jie. Yenko stayed by his side the whole time, as tubes were fed into his neck, arms, and wrists. It took four burly soldiers to restrain the wild, drugged man who revived in the middle of the procedure.

"Give me one second without these restraints and I will teach your mothers to curse the day you were conceived," he said with a voice so free of passion it sent shivers down Yenko's spine. The Commander was well able to make good his threat if he was but loosed for a moment.

"Will he be alright?" Yenko asked the medics.

"Who can say?"

That was it. Nothing more. They were too focused on their patient, instructing each other as they administered a cocktail of drugs through a drip and multiple injections.

At length, Li Jie's thrashing settled down and he fell into an induced coma. Checking the restraining straps to ensure their patient was secured beyond doubt, the lead doctor ordered the driver to head for the medical center that had been erected in the main village, fifteen miles away.

"And you four go with them," he instructed the soldiers who had helped subdue their mad friend. "Commander Huang should not wake with the drugs we have given him, but he is under the influence of a neurotoxin we know little of. If he regains consciousness in transit, there could be trouble. Do whatever the medic says."

And with that, the makeshift ambulance with its patient, four soldiers, and one doctor roared off out of sight.

The remaining medics went through Captain Yang's company. Five had been lost in the battle and their corpses were ceremoniously laid in body bags. It was a sad end to the ordeal. A dozen soldiers needed medical attention, but none faced anything life threatening.

"Seven of the prisoners are wounded," Captain Yang informed the chief medic.

"I can see that," the doctor said. "But we can't tend to them here. I know nothing of their physiology and anything I do could be fatal."

"They don't deserve help at all," one soldier spat. "If they die, they die."

Captain Yang backhanded the man. "If I hear *bai chi* talk from you again, I will personally throw you in the stocks. When a man becomes a barbarian in order to fight a barbarian, he loses himself and brings disgrace on his family."

"Is this one alive?" The chief medic had ignored the soldier's reprimand and was heading toward the limp body of the green alien leader.

One of the nearest prisoners struggled against its bonds. "*Nimm deine dreckigen Finger von ihm!*" A blow from one of its captors dropped it to its knees. "*Dreckskerl*," it muttered.

"I believe so," the Captain replied. "I shut him up with the butt of my gun."

The medic nodded and attended to another.

"Alright," he said at length. "They're all clear to go. The Personnel Carriers will be here shortly. They're all yours, Captain."

Five light trucks presently rounded the corner and pulled to a halt. The prisoners and their guards were loaded into the middle vehicle, while everyone else piled into the remaining trucks, and the convoy departed.

————◂◦▸————

As soon as the Personnel Carriers arrived in the camp, Yenko ignored the protocol of presenting himself to the Debriefing Room. The Commodore would soon be hearing the mission reports, but there was no way Yenko was going to adhere to such military discipline when the life of his friend, Li Jie, hung in the balance. Instead of joining the rest of his squadron, he hastened to the medical facility. It was not to be compared to an Earth hospital, but nevertheless, to Yenko it seemed to be well supplied.

The hours stretched on in slow procession, a presage of the Commander's inevitable funeral march. Access to Huang was denied; he was in surgery, attended by a team of doctors.

At length, the Commander was brought out of the makeshift operating theater and wheeled past Yenko into the post-operative room. Yu Yan was at his side, dressed head to foot in a surgical gown. She had been allowed in the theater, and now had permission to stay with him in the post-op. She glanced at Yenko as the procession passed by but said nothing. She did not need to. Her eyes told the grim, uncertain prognosis that hung over her husband's head.

It was another two hours before Yenko himself was allowed in to see his military friend. He was shocked by the sight that confronted him. The Commander lay motionless on a hospital gurney, heavy straps restraining him against the random twitching that assailed his body. Occasionally, his eyes opened groggily and swam about the room, but there was no hint of cognizance.

A synthetic skin covered the Commander's neck where Yenko had performed his rough field surgery, and his shoulder was heavily bound, along with the bandaging that hid the massive slash across his face. Monitors beeped and lights flashed about the bedhead.

In a chair pulled up alongside her husband, Huang Yu Yan was fast asleep. She still wore the surgical gown, but her head, feet, and hands were uncovered. Her hair hung raggedly over her careworn face.

"Is he going to die?" he asked the attending doctor.

"Time will tell."

Yenko looked into the doctor's eyes, pleading for more information. She held his gaze. With a shrug, she added, "It's up to him now," and went on making her observations and adjusting the fluid flow in two drips.

Reaching out to his delirious friend, he said softly, "Don't give up on me, Commander. I ripped your neck open. Are you just going to lie there and take it? You're not going to let a *yang guizi* take you that easily are you?"

Li Jie opened his eyes, and for a split second it seemed to Yenko that his soldier friend understood him. But then a wave of delirium swept over the Zhongwen Commander, and he drifted out of consciousness again.

Despondently, Yenko walked over to Yu Yan and pulled a blanket over her in an awkward attempt to comfort the sleeping woman. She probably had not left her husband's side since he had arrived.

"I'm sorry," he said to no one in particular, and left the room. There was nothing he could do. Turning back, he asked the doctor, "Is Lakshay Varma in here? The Bhaarateey technician. He's a friend of mine."

The doctor understood. "He's in the Rehab Center. Next building. Ask at the desk."

As it turned out, Yenko did not need to ask the staff where to find Lakshay. The young technician was sitting casually in a lounge chair in the reception area, talking animatedly with Fei Hung.

"Mr. Macpherson," he cried, grabbing his crutches and jumping to his feet. "The mission was a success. The lost villagers are saved. Ah, but of course. Varma, what are you thinking? You were there leading the way, sir! But where are my manners? Mr. Macpherson sir, let me introduce you to my rescuer."

"Fei Hung," Yenko said, "I'm so glad you're safe."

The woman smiled, an ambiguous grin washing over a complicated face.

"You already know each other?" Varma acknowledged. "But of course, you do. Mr. Macpherson. She is your ghost! But you already knew that. Sorry, sir. I speak too much when I am excited, sir."

"Indeed, you do," Yenko laughed sadly. "Watch him, Fei Hung, he has a way with words."

She rose to her feet and hugged the Scot affectionately. "Thank you, but I can handle myself."

"She speaks the half of it, sir. She gave me hope when all hope was lost. But I speak too much again, sir. Sorry, sir. Sorry, Fei Hung. I will hold my tongue."

The three laughed. For a moment, Yenko's tension and concern lessened in the torrent of words gushing from the Bhaarateey technician. It seemed like forever since Yenko had laughed. But it was a guilty laugh; his friend Li Jie lay in a semi-comatose state in the building next door.

And yet, Yenko was most assuredly glad to see Fei Hung in the real, solid world of Zhinu. He had dreamt of this moment for a long time. The dream was not over, however, and it was still to be determined if it was not a nightmare.

"Are you going to the reunion tonight, sir?" Lakshay asked enthusiastically.

Yenko looked questioningly at him. "I don't know what you're talking about."

"The reunion, sir. Surely they told you at the Debriefing when you got in?"

"I didn't go," Yenko said simply. "Too much on my mind."

The young technician looked shocked that someone might so flagrantly disregard basic discipline and due process. Before he could say a word, though, Fei Hung held a finger to his lips.

"Don't speak, Lakshay," she said, her eyes fixed on Yenko's. "You do not understand. The Commander . . . How is he?"

The cold look of resolve Yenko was familiar with had returned to her eyes.

"The Commander," mouthed Lakshay.

Yenko turned his face towards the main hospital facility. "Well he's alive, if that's what you're asking," he said. "But only just."

Fei Hung had heard the report of the battle at the Mission Debriefing, but she knew that her rescuer, Yenko, could not afford to keep it all locked up inside himself.

"What happened?" she asked. "Don't spare me. I have seen horrors you know nothing of."

Yenko nodded sadly. He believed her. If she saw Li Jie in his comatose state, she would say it was a blessing that he was so incapacitated, and that death would be a mercy to him. Distantly, he recounted the events surrounding the combat at the enemy encampment.

"They had Li Jie tied down on a clay mound," he said. "He was the bait. An ambush awaited us. But we took them by surprise. Three squadrons of our elite military engaged them on multiple fronts. They stood no chance."

Though she had heard it before, still her countenance took on a cruel, fierce hunger as he described the slaughter of the aliens. At the sight of the cold, pitiless look on her face, Yenko was glad she had not been there. She would have lost the last shreds of her humanity in bloodlust and reckless revenge.

"When they brought Li Jie to me," Yenko continued, "he had a dart in his neck. Who knows how long it had been there? He was raving mad. I pulled it out of him."

He stared forlornly at the young woman, shaking his head, lost for what to say, how to communicate the horror. "It was shocking, Fei Hung. The blood." Holding his now clean hands up, he examined them as if they would never be free of the stains of his friend's life flow. "So much blood. He fought like a wild beast and would have killed me in an instant if he could. I tried to cauterize the wound like you and I did in Gui Difang."

Fei Hung remembered the grim night vividly, one of a thousand encounters with demons and crazed villagers that would haunt her forever. And yet, that someone could live after the evil darts were extracted had been a wonder of wonders to her.

"Did it not work like it did that night?" she asked.

Yenko grimaced. "He was already uncontrollable." He locked eyes morosely with the now-solid Zhongwen woman before him, as if for the first time he truly saw her. A tear broke loose and etched a path across his cheek. "How many like him did you face?"

She held his gaze fiercely for a moment that lasted forever.

Lakshay knew nothing of his beautiful rescuer's history, but he could read in the atmosphere that this was not a time for him to speak.

"I tried, I really did," Yenko confessed helplessly, another tear following on the heels of its forerunner, an impotent grief over his inability to help in his friend's greatest hour of need. "I stopped the flow of blood . . . The knife . . . Fei Hung, the smell! Like someone was cooking meat!" More tears hastened to join their fallen number.

Wiping his nose with the back of his hand, he went on, "We couldn't keep him still enough. I stabbed him in the shoulder. Deeply! It was an accident," he added quickly, in defense, not wanting anyone to think he did it intentionally. "He was just thrashing about so much."

Fei Hung nodded with comprehension and compassion. She was no stranger to the horror of sinking a blade into the flesh of one she loved.

"If they didn't knock him out," he concluded, "they never would have got him back here."

Telling the story was, in some ways, cathartic, and for that, he was grateful for the opportunity to recount it to Fei Hung and Lakshay. In other ways, though, it just relived the tragedy and grief. He turned and left the building.

"Mr. Macpherson," Lakshay called, hoping to offer friendship and solace to the redheaded separatist, "what of you? Your hand is bandaged. Are you alright yourself?"

Yenko ignored the young man's concern. A scream from the nearby hospital gave a chilling reminder that Huang still battled his demons.

"Leave him," Fei Hung said. "He needs to be alone. There will be a time when he will receive us, but this is not the time."

⟨○⟩

"Why were you not at the Debriefing yesterday, Macpherson?"

Yenko had been called to the Commodore's office. Gone was the offer of first name informality. Mannat Ahuja sat behind her desk, arms folded.

"I have no excuse, Commodore," Yenko replied, standing at attention. Then, daring for a moment to look her in the eye, he added, "I had to know what became of Li Jie. Commander Huang, ma'am. After that, I just . . . went and hid."

"I understand," she said, visibly softening towards the separatist scientist. "We have a lot to thank you for, Yenko. You have solved the enigma of Zhinu and rescued the better part of four thousand lost souls in the process. I would have commended you in front of the Third Fleet, but you robbed me of the opportunity."

Yenko nodded absently. He really did not care. He did not care for commendation. Nor for solving riddles. Nor even for rescuing thousands of Zhinu's refugees. Li Jie was all that mattered.

"Are you listening to me, Macpherson?"

He straightened and came back to the moment. "Yes, ma'am."

"Good. Focus, Macpherson. I know about the Commander. He is in the best of care. We can only hope and pray now. May the ancestors be gracious."

"The ancestors," Yenko thought. "They won't help. They're dead."

Absently, he genuflected as any of his people might. If ever there was a god out there, he needed him now.

"Macpherson. Yenko. Our physicians have examined the dead body of an alien they brought back with them."

Yenko nodded. He had been there on the fateful battleground and heard the command.

"It is human," she said.

Human. Yenko heard the pronouncement, but his mind was struggling to stay in the moment. Grief, fear, and futility filled his heart. He looked questioningly at the Commodore. She was waiting for a response.

Human.

Human?

Yenko frowned. "Human? That can't be. They're aliens. Their weapons are like nothing we've ever seen before. Their spaceship. Their camouflage technology . . . And their blood! Commodore, they're not human."

The Commodore nodded. "All that is true," she affirmed. "But still, they are human."

Ugly memories of Fei Hung hacking into the dead bodies of the two demons that Li Jie had killed in Gui Difang filled his mind. Green and red pouring from their wounds, splashing over the crazed Zhongwen woman. There was nothing human about them, despite the Commodore's insistence.

"We don't have the expertise to understand the nature of their foreign blood, nor can we determine the origins of their technology. It is obviously beyond us. But DNA tests have been done. Yenko, they are human."

"Human," Yenko repeated. "DNA? But that can't be."

"I am hoping that you will solve this riddle like you solved the last, Yenko." The Commodore's demeanor was noticeably softer. "There is a spacecraft of unknown origin where those creatures camped. It is there, in the phase-shifted reality of Gui Difang. Clearly, it crashed in the same catastrophe that threw Xin Beijing into chaos. Yenko, is it possible to restore whatever of its components were sent out of phase? Bring it fully into our world?"

For the moment, grief for Li Jie, still lying in tormented agony in the camp hospital, left him. Yenko considered the possibilities. Fei Hung's demons were human. Impossible as that was, the Commodore was adamant. They were human. That meant that somehow, in some way, they got caught in the catastrophe of Mahika Khatri and Arushi Jain's failed attempt to open a doorway to Earth.

He walked over to a window and stared out at the darkening sky.

"Is it possible?" the Commodore pressed.

Yenko mumbled into the onset of evening. "Perhaps it can be done. Well . . . The attenuation would have to be considered. And the distance. But I think it could be done."

"Yenko! Come back to me! Is it possible?"

"Well . . . yes . . . Yes, it's possible. But what would it achieve? We don't need a spaceship; we have one of our own."

"You miss the point," Ahuja demanded. "Once we have full access to their ship, Nirani can help. She has the resources of the *Phoenix* at her command. All the wisdom and knowledge of Earth is within her grasp."

Yenko turned back again to the open window. "Yes. If anyone can access their databases, Nirani could. And if she can't, no one can." Quickly, he spun about and faced the Commodore. "Commodore. Yes. It can be done. We have the technical know-how. And the equipment. If that ship is only there because it flew into the window of the Gravimetric Discriminator all those decades ago, we can bring back whatever was thrown out of phase.

"But we can't take it into orbit and dock it with the *Phoenix*. Nirani can't help us."

"That is not your concern, Yenko," the Commodore said confidently, a knowing look in her eye. "Not all our technologies are known by every-one of the Third Fleet."

Yenko looked questioningly at her. What was she hinting at?

"Do you think your beloved scientific community knows everything and that the military has no classified secrets that it keeps to itself? Are you separatists so ignorant of the political world?"

"Classified secrets . . ." Yenko repeated.

"Sit down, Yenko. You need to relax. What I am about to tell you is restricted information. Although, to be honest, once we utilize it, we will be hard pressed to keep it from the Zhongguo Xin Shijie. But that is not of your concern. This is of universal importance.

"Yenko, Nirani is mobile."

"Mobile . . . ?"

"Mobile. We can downlink her to the planet surface any time we want. She can access the entire knowledge bank of the *Phoenix*, along with the full complement of the ship's physical hardware, from right here. Remotely. She can aid us with our investigation of the unknown space vessel. If it is human in origin, I have no doubt she will discover its secrets.

"There is work yet for us to do, Yenko. We may have solved the riddle of Zhinu, but we have opened a greater one, a Pandora's Box of espionage and subterfuge. We must learn who has been developing such technologies in secret, hidden from the rest of the world, and to what end? How soon can we fully restore the ship to our phase?"

Yenko considered for a while. The computations would not be easy. But he had a competent team. "A week, perhaps. Maybe more. Maybe less."

It was enough. The Commodore was satisfied.

"Well done, Macpherson. Yenko. Apology accepted for missing the Debriefing. Go and assemble your team and get onto it at first light."

As Yenko left the room, she added, "And go to the Reunion tonight. It starts in an hour."

——————◦◦◦——————

In fact, the Reunion had already begun that afternoon. None could halt the celebrations as long-lost family members were reunited with each other. The eldest among them wept bitterly as they held brothers and sisters, cousins, nephews, and nieces. Younger ones were discovering extended family members they had never known, and hearing the tragic tales from parents and grandparents, aunts, and uncles.

By the time Yenko joined the festivities, thousands of people had already swelled the village square, at the very spot where Commodore Ahuja had first announced the arrival of the Third Fleet. That now seemed a lifetime ago.

Word of the rescue had reached Earth soon after the refugees of Gui Difang were ferried into the village. The mystery of the century could now be officially closed—and a new one opened. Alien humans, unknown technologies, inscrutable intentions. What were they yet to uncover?

Yu Yan joined the celebrations for a short while. Physically, she was present, but emotionally, she was elsewhere, worried for the life of her husband.

"Talk with me, Robbie," she said to her distant relative, grabbing him by the arm and leading him away from the festivities. "Will my love return to me?"

When they were far enough away from the crowd to be almost alone, Yenko held her in his arms, consoling her in her fear. And his own. "I don't know," he replied. "But I know this. Li Jie is a fighter. If anyone can pull through this, he can."

"Tell me of his last moments," she asked.

"I can't really," he confessed. "For the most part, I wasn't there. My job was to get to the receiver and initiate the procedure for everyone's return to normal space. When I last saw him, the refugees were still marching towards freedom. Fei Hung might know more. I left her in the thick of it."

Yenko ran his fingers through his hair. When Fei Hung and he had returned to the villagers' exodus to determine if they were within the bounds of the Gravimetric Discriminator, the battle had already been engaged. He had left her to assist Li Jie who was fighting an impossible battle.

He had left her . . . No, that was not true; she had commanded him to go.

In the corner of his eye, Yenko noticed Fei Hung walking towards them, her hobbling puppy dog on his crutches beside her.

"Fei Hung will know more, Yu Yan" he said, indicating the arrival of his famous ghost lady.

"We were just talking about you," Yenko said as Fei Hung and Lakshay drew closer. After introductions, he added, "Yu Yan wants to know more of Li Jie's last moments. I told her I wasn't there to witness it, but maybe you would know."

Fei Hung looked sternly at the Commander's young wife, measuring her ability to deal with the horrors of war.

"Do not spare me," Yu Yan warned. "I need to know. He is my husband."

And so Fei Hung began, not sparing any detail of the bloody slaughter that beset Yu Yan's husband. If it had not been for Fei Hung, Li Jie would be dead already. And the carnage against the refugees would have been unthinkable.

When all was said, Yu Yan held Fei Hung firmly in her arms, a look of resolve on her face, and walked off to sit once more with her semiconscious husband.

"Come," Fei Hung said to Lakshay. "I see that our Robbie needs solitude. Perhaps it was a mistake to come over here."

Together, she and Lakshay returned to the crowds in the square. Perhaps he did need solitude. He certainly was not in the mood for parties.

———◄o►———

"How is the Commander?" the Commodore asked. She had seen the interplay between Yu Yan and Fei Hung and guessed the nature of the embrace between the two women. Now that Yenko was once more on his own, she had made up her mind to make sure he did not stay on his own.

Yenko did not know how to answer. In many ways, he did not want to answer.

"I don't know," he eventually said. "Maybe I should head off. I'm not going to be much company tonight, am I? And it's supposed to be a celebration."

Commodore Ahuja smiled with an unexpected show of compassion from one of such high rank. "I don't think it would be good for you to be alone, Yenko. It's healthy for you to see the outcome of all you've achieved."

Cutting him off before he had time to contradict her, she added, "None of this would be happening without you. Look over there . . ."

She pointed to an elderly man and woman who were weeping on each other's shoulder. "They are brother and sister, separated since 2347. Until now. I have just spent time with them and heard their stories. You have done a beautiful thing, Yenko. So many wounds are healing right now."

"I know," Yenko said. "And I do feel proud, in a way. But I've just heard Fei Hung describe the battle to Yu Yan. I feel proud. And I feel guilty."

"No one wins in battle," the Commodore mused. "But though the past can't be rewritten, we can be thankful for the joys of the present. It's the only way forward, Yenko. Believe me, I know."

Yenko considered the woman before him. She was complex—cold and military, warm and compassionate.

"Would you like a drink?" he asked her, as a young villager walked past carrying a tray of assorted beverages.

"Yes," the Commodore said. "Yes, I would like that."

Kissing their glasses together, Yenko said, "Here's to the end of fighting."

"Amen to that . . ."

Whatever the drink was, it was rough. And strong.

"What is in that?" Yenko rasped, his voice stolen from him momentarily.

"I don't know," the Commodore laughed, "but I think I could grow to like it."

"Well, whatever it is, we've just solved our future gas needs for our vehicles," he replied, his voice now returning. "If they don't blow up first, that is!"

The two laughed again. It felt good to laugh. And Yenko was surprised how comfortable he was in the imposing woman's presence. Together they spoke for hours and drank perhaps a few too many of the crudely distilled drinks of the villagers. An unlikely beginning to an unlikely friendship.

◄○►

"You summoned for me, sir? I came as fast as I could, sir. Sorry sir, I don't get about as fast with these things."

Crutches supporting him, Varma stood apologetically in the doorway of the Kinematics Laboratory in the abandoned university. Yenko busily applied himself to a board full of calculations as three of his colleagues called out various results from their own computations.

It had taken some hours to clean the rooms of the fifth floor of the building. When the return to correct phase of all organic-related materials had been affected, not only the refugees had been restored. Everything that had once baffled the Third Fleet's investigation with its absence, now stood in wrecked decay throughout Xin Beijing.

A systematic search throughout the city was currently underway, scouring every building, every room. In the ghostly, phase-shifted state caused by the disaster of 2347, the unfortunate original inhabitants of the city had not all survived. Those in buildings with timber fixtures could escape, but those behind metal enclosures were hopelessly trapped, entombed by their inability to simply open a door.

Before the day was out, more than two thousand mummified remains would be brought out for hopeful identification and burial. The celebrations of the previous week's reunion were over, replaced by the cold, hard reality of grief for their fallen, long-lost friends and families.

"What?" Yenko asked absently, totally absorbed by the scrawling formulas that were rapidly filling the board.

"You sent for me, sir."

"Oh, yes. Of course," he replied, not turning to acknowledge the technician at the door in any way. "Give me a second. There. Seven point three two radians. How does that affect discriminant range and variance?"

All three of the technicians working the computers looked up at him questioningly.

"But that is more than a full circle," one of them noted. "How is that even possible?"

"Just plug it in and tell me if the dynamic matrix resolves."

The technicians went to work.

"What was the vector angle again?" the nearest to Yenko asked.

"It's there on the board," Yenko indicated, a little annoyed. "Seven point three two radians." Then turning to the half-crippled Varma, he said, "Lakshay, are you mobile enough to come with me to the research facility in the mountains? I need your attention to detail."

"That's incredible," one of the researchers interjected.

Yenko walked over to review the findings himself. "Resolution!" he laughed, smacking the researcher on the shoulder. "You've got it!"

Half an hour later, Macpherson, Varma, and a small army of technicians were being ferried in three separate reconnaissance vehicles—one to the Gravimetric Discriminator at the Mountain Command Center, a second to the reflector array in the power station in Xin Beijing, and a third to get an accurate topographical map of the region of the downed spaceship.

————◦———

A throng of military and civic leaders filled the Control Room in the mountain research facility. Scores of technicians sat at desks, adjusting instruments and tuning monitors, and calling out data to supervisors.

"Are you sure this is going to work?"

Commodore Ahuja had implicit trust in her physicist colleague, her friend, but much was at stake and she needed reassurance from him.

"We've reviewed the data," was Yenko's confident reply. "The science is complicated, but the technology is straightforward enough."

It had taken him and his team the better part of a month, but Macpherson had successfully built a second receiver array. It was now set up to the west, not far from the ruins of Gui Difang.

"And you're sure that you're not just going to ruin Xin Beijing again?"

Yenko nodded. He understood the Commodore's need to question every detail. And for the hundredth time. Even though Yenko had said it was not necessary, she had ordered everyone out of the city's precincts. Just to be safe. But he was confident; it was an inconsequential precaution.

"When we activate the Discriminator," Yenko explained patiently, just as he had done each time she had quizzed him before, "a resonating pulse will be generated. It will find its reflection in the receiver dish in the city. But rather than reflecting back to the Discriminator, and thus feeding the Gravimetric Loop, the dish has been adjusted to act as a relay, bouncing the pulse to the west where it will meet our second dish in Gui Difang. Or somewhere close, at least."

That was the bit of uncertainty the Commodore worried over.

"At that point," Yenko continued confidently, "the Loop will close and amplify and project to the north. In that way, we will train our sights on the region where the spacecraft is. Technician Vasant Kholi and one of her assistants is there right now, along with the carbon fiber reflector from Earth. They will make the phase transition and prepare for the pulse that will return everything back to normal. We will give them exactly one hour to set that up—it will only take fifteen minutes, don't worry; I've given them far more time than they need. And then we will repeat the procedure. When Kholi and her assistant return to regular space, any of the alien vessel's components that were sent out of phase in 2347 will return with them.

"Trust me, Commodore," he concluded, holding her uncertain, questioning gaze for a moment. "Mannat, I know what I'm doing."

"Well then," she replied at length, "what is the next step? When do we activate the machine?"

"If the new Exclusion Zone to the north of Gui Difang is secure, we can start the countdown in ten minutes. We're good to go. Is the area clear? Apart from our two technicians, there can't be anyone around."

The Commodore's nod gave Yenko the answer he needed. In a raised voice, so his entire team could hear him clearly, he called out, "Primary Circuits, go!"

"Primary Circuits go, sir!" came the reply a minute later.

"Secondary Inductor Array, power down Inductor Inhibitors. This is not a drill."

"Inductor Inhibitors down, sir."

"Gravimetric Accelerators, standby."

"Gravimetric Accelerators standing by, sir."

"Power Generators to maximum."

The cavernous control room hummed, a hum that slowly rose to become a deep, throbbing surge.

"Power Generators maximum, sir."

"Activate Tertiary Background Pulse."

"Tertiary Background Pulse active, sir."

A high-pitched pinging sounded throughout the room.

"Do we have active feedback from both receivers?"

Five technicians busily engaged dials and adjusted calibrators. Instruments throughout the control room whirred into life.

"Xin Beijing Receiver active, sir."

Silence reigned for what seemed an eternity.

"Gui Difang Receiver active, sir."

Yenko nodded.

"Commence countdown."

"Countdown commencing. Gravimetric Discriminating Pulse in t minus one hundred and twenty seconds . . . one hundred and five seconds . . . ninety seconds . . . seventy-five seconds . . . sixty seconds . . ."

Tension filled the room. No one moved. No one breathed.

". . . forty-five seconds . . . thirty seconds . . . t minus twenty seconds . . . t minus fifteen seconds . . . t minus ten seconds . . . nine . . . eight . . . seven . . . six . . . five . . . four . . . three . . . two . . . one . . . Ignition."

The room filled with a pulsing resonant thrum, akin to what Yenko had heard in the field, though much louder. The air vibrated with its power. Hairs on arms stood on end with electric proximity. Exactly seventy-two seconds later, the pulse ended.

"Okay, everyone, you know the drill," called Yenko. "Commence Discriminator shut down."

Two minutes later, satisfied that decommissioning protocols had been maintained, Yenko gave orders to prepare for the second discharge that would complete the mission.

"Reset chronometers. Prepare the Discriminator for reactivation in forty-seven minutes."

"Forty-seven?" the Commodore worried. "You said you were giving your technicians an hour?"

"I am, Commodore," Yenko replied. "We're already three minutes into that hour, and the countdown procedure will take ten. Don't worry, Commodore. We'll bring them back safe. And at the right time."

Macpherson's team of technicians busied themselves for the next half hour and then waited expectantly for the command to reinitiate the Gravimetric Discriminator. Though it was only a matter of minutes, the wait seemed to last an age before the command was finally given to repeat the operation.

"Commodore, it's all yours," Yenko said at length. "Mission success. We should be good to go."

10

Räuber Mekförsen

Y ENKO WOKE EARLY THE next morning to a knocking at the door of his cabin. Most people thought him odd, but he liked the seclusion, tucked away in the park near the university ruins. It gave him time to think, and to be honest, he was not used to living in close proximity to such a sea of black hair. He was not racist, he occasionally told himself; it was just that he, well, he missed his beloved Scots.

Opening the door, he almost hoped to see Mannat Ahuja. Not that he thought for a moment that she would be there; she had a lot on her plate, the mission of the Third Fleet was not yet over. And what was he to her anyway? But in his own reclusive way, he had become fond of the Commodore. Despite her black hair. And despite being Bhaarateey, not Scottish.

Instead of anyone he might have expected, or hoped for, he was surprised to see Captain Yang at the door. He could not think why she had made the trip to wake him. Was the investigation in jeopardy?

"Captain?" Yenko asked, standing slightly to attention.

He had not been allowed to go to the crash site the previous afternoon. His modifications to the Gravimetric Discriminator had worked smoothly and the spacecraft was now fully in the world of Zhinu, but the Commodore had restricted all non-military personnel from going anywhere near it. In her words, it was still a military operation.

It made sense, of course. There was no way of knowing what security measures the aliens might have set about their camp. Yenko, despite his burning curiosity, was happy to wait till the military gave the area the all-clear.

"At ease, Macpherson," Captain Yang said. "Are you ready for today's mission debrief?"

Yenko looked at his timepiece, confused. What day was it? Had he slept in?

Yang laughed. "It's alright, soldier," she said. "The briefing is next week. I'm just playing with you."

"Then why . . . ?" Yenko probed.

"I was sent to see if you're up for a companion to join you when the Commodore gives the all-clear for you to attend the crash site."

"Companion? Umm . . . I don't really think so . . . we don't know what we're dealing with . . . it's an alien vessel . . . I mean, I know they're supposed to be human . . . but honestly, it just won't be safe to take one of the villagers with us. I can't afford to have my attention divided."

"I don't speak of a villager," the Captain said, holding out an arm to direct Yenko's attention to her LRV, stationed across the park.

A soldier sat in the front seat looking at him, neck and shoulder heavily bandaged.

"Li Jie!" screamed Yenko and, forgetting all military discipline, raced past the laughing Captain to the friend he had all but given up for dead.

By the time Yenko got to the vehicle, the Commander had extracted himself from the front seat and faced his friend upright. Yenko fell on him, forgetting for the moment the bandages that told the truth that Li Jie was still not out of the woods physically.

"You did well, *yang guizi*," the Commander said. "I have been fully briefed on the mission outcome."

"Are you alright?" Yenko asked, clearly concerned for his friend. A long, fresh scar struck its way violently across the Commander's face, a graphic witness to the brutalities he had faced at the hands of the enemy leader.

"Yes, Yu Yan gave me leave of absence."

The two laughed. "No, I'm serious," Yenko added. "The last I saw you, it was touch and go. You've been in and out of a coma for weeks!"

Huang dismissed it nonchalantly. "I remember very little, Yenko," he confessed. "And probably that is for the best. I believe I have you to thank for my shoulder?"

Yenko grinned wryly. "Yeah, well . . . sorry about that . . . I did stab you good and proper though. But honestly, you were screaming obscenities at me that I didn't even understand. I had to shut you up some way!"

Li Jie studied his separatist friend. "You're the only man living who has inflicted such a wound on me and lived to tell the tale."

Yenko laughed, a little nervously. And hoped he would never face the Commander's retribution.

"Except the *gui sunzi* that shot his dart into me," he said in cold afterthought. "But you need not fear, *yang guizi*. Yu Yan would flay me to my bones if I ever touched her precious Robbie!"

Yenko laughed again. Thank the ancestors for Yu Yan and her affinity for red hair. Thanks, too, for Robert Macpherson setting it all up in the first place.

Captain Yang strolled over to them. "So . . . Will you take responsibility for him?" she asked.

Yenko looked at her quizzically.

"He's technically not allowed to be out of the infirmary. And given the severity of his condition, the doctors want to monitor him closely for another month at least. But he is a difficult patient when he has made his mind up. We cannot spare any of the duty nurses, so it would need to be you who takes responsibility for him. His wife offered to come but the Commodore refuses."

"Yes, of course I'll take responsibility," Yenko accepted.

"I'll see to it, then," the Captain said. "Would you like me to wait for you to gather what you need and take you back to the Commander's home? I'm sure the Commodore will allow for that."

Yenko gladly accepted. It would be a day of celebration and he was sure that his military friend would have a million questions for him. Questions that he would be eager to answer now that Li Jie was safe.

---◄◊►---

A week later, at the briefing, Yenko was the happiest he had been in a long time. Li Jie sat beside him. Surprisingly, Fei Hung sat at the back of the room opposite him, alongside Lakshay Varma. Yenko studied the two of them. Ever since Fei Hung had escorted the technician back into the real world, they had become inseparable. She was good for Lakshay, grounded him. And he was good for her. Perhaps more than good; she needed him, someone who could introduce laughter into her cruel, tortured world.

Whether they would last the distance, only time would tell; she was broken in complex ways. Maybe it really would take someone with the naïve innocence of the Bhaarateey to stick with her long enough for her inner world to heal.

Nevertheless, it was curious that Fei Hung had been allowed into the briefing at all. It was still a military operation, and the Commodore was not one to break protocol. Mannat must have heard enough in the reports to warrant such respect being accorded to Gui Difang's Angel of Death.

In truth, Fei Hung had argued her way onto the mission. She was the representative of her people and the mission was seeking to understand the purpose and origin of her people's tormentors. It was her right, and her people's right, that she should be part of this assignment. Now, she sat calmly at the back, eyes focused on the squadron leader who was detailing the mission brief. She had not even acknowledged Yenko when he caught her eye, though she did briefly nod to Commander Huang when he took his seat beside him.

"Lakshay," he thought, "do you know the tenth part of who you're falling in love with?" Perhaps no one did.

Yenko shook his head as he realized he had let his mind wander. The squadron leader was wrapping up his report. Access up the escarpment had proved difficult. The path that Captain Yang and her company had used in the mission to rescue Commander Huang, the one used regularly by Fei Hung's demons, was inaccessible to four wheeled vehicles. In the end, the only suitable path they could find to the plateau had been fifty miles to the west. Around the spacecraft, explosives experts had made a thorough sweep for traps and mines, and after the all-clear had finally been given, a bivouac was erected.

Guards now regularly patrolled the area, and the Commodore was satisfied that it was time to set her scientists and technicians to work. This was the reason for the briefing. There was a lot to be done if they were at last going to get to the bottom of who the prisoners in the Detention Center really were.

"Tech crew," the Commodore instructed when the report was concluded, "remain behind to receive your individual work details from Captain Chen. We must establish facilities for Nirani to interface with operations here on the planet surface."

A buzz of excitement rose around the room.

"Everyone else is dismissed. We will leave in convoy at ten hundred hours sharp."

As one, the assembly rose to its feet.

"Macpherson Yenko," Ahuja ordered before anyone had left the room, "walk with me to my office."

Yenko pondered the reason for the Commodore's instruction, but neither of them spoke until they were alone, away from the crowd.

"Yenko, I am not assigning any specific detail to you. I need your eyes. Nirani will hopefully uncover important intelligence. I trust the technical detail, but I want you to oversee Nirani's findings. You might see what others miss. Something troubles me about our prisoners. I have too many questions and no clear answers. Their leader knows a few words of Zhongwen, that much is certain. But I can't communicate with him. There's just so much I don't know. And I don't like not knowing. I'm giving you free rein to investigate wherever you feel answers might lie."

———◦———

Yenko craned forward to get a better view of the spacecraft in the distance. It was well into the afternoon when they finally made their way towards the ridge from which Li Jie had first spied out the enemy camp. Now, as they pulled to a halt on the crest of that same ridge, Captain Liu Wang Yong stood up on the front seat of the leading open-roofed LRV, took out a pair of field binoculars and made a thorough survey of the territory.

"We will skirt around to the east," he called to the drivers of the other six LRVs. And with that they were off.

At intervals, as they wound their way carefully through the thick scrub that covered the region, Yenko gained a clearer sight of the downed craft. It was massive, longer than a football field, almost half as wide and as much as thirty feet high at its center. The whole structure appeared to be aerodynamically designed; large wings tucked in tightly to its sides gave the hint, amidst the chaos of the wreckage, that they possibly swung into position for air flight. It gave the ship a strangely familiar aspect. There were even hints of common design with the Low Orbiter that was used so frequently in intercontinental travel on Earth. Not so completely alien as one might expect.

Taken together, it simply added an even greater air of mystery to the vessel's origins.

"What do you make of it, *yang guizi*?" Li Jie asked. He sat comfortably beside his Scot partner. All but a small bandage on his neck had been discarded by him in preparation for the mission. "Restricts my movement," he had said to Yenko before they had boarded their LRV.

"I don't know," Yenko mused. "I really don't . . . The doctors say the aliens are human. They can't be. Their blood's green. But this ship . . . It's nothing like I've ever seen before, but it's not completely unlike anything I've ever seen, either . . . I just don't know."

"Nirani will tell us," Lakshay piped up.

Li Jie frowned. "How did you get to be the driver anyway?"

"I have experience, sir," the technician said enthusiastically.

"You totaled an LRV from what I've been told," Li Jie replied. When it appeared Lakshay was going to continue the conversation, the Commander simply waved his attention forward. "Just drive, Varma. Don't talk. Keep your wits about you. We're not on a picnic."

The Bhaarateey looked awkwardly at Fei Hung in his rear vision mirror. She paid no attention, however. Her eyes were glued on the ship.

"How did none of my people see such a thing descend through the skies?" she pondered aloud. "It would be seen night or day, and the crash would be felt in the ground, even as far as my village."

Yenko studied the ship along with her as their path brought them ever closer. They were nearing a dozen old campfires dotted about the crash site. On the far side of the vehicle, various tents and work areas had been erected to house the military and scientific details investigating the site.

"It would have come down at the same time as the event that threw your people out of phase with Zhinu," Yenko explained. "Gui Difang did not exist back then. Everyone was still in Xin Beijing. Out here, it's too far away for them to have noticed. But they wouldn't have noticed anyway. The whole city must have been in chaos."

Fei Hung nodded slowly. "The tales of the elders are chilling."

—————◄○►—————

For the most part, the rest of the afternoon was given over to establishing camp. It was unknown how long they would have to stay in this remote place. Yenko was called to a special meeting of scientists and technicians. Varma stood proudly and excitedly beside him.

"Do you really think it's of human origin, sir?" he asked.

"No."

It was a blunt reply, but the simple truth was, how could it be from Earth? The construction of such a vessel could not have been hidden. There were undoubtedly covert operations by the Zhongwen and Bhaarateey governments, and such a ship could possibly be built, but at some point, it had to be launched, and that would have been registered by practically every observatory on the planet. And if the ship had been caught in the disaster of 2347, as was the general hypothesis, it would have launched sometime around the beginning of the twenty-fourth century. It was not possible that such an event could be kept secret for so long a time.

"But the doctors, sir?" The Bhaarateey technician had his own misgivings now that he could see the ship before him. And yet, he could not discount the findings of the medical experts. "And I have seen them, sir. In the Detention Center. Without their blue suits and helmets, they are obviously human."

"I know, I've seen them too," Yenko conceded. "But you haven't seen the blood that pours from their veins. They're not human, whatever the doctors say."

"What are they, then?" Fei Hung joined in, eager to learn all she could of her people's oppressors.

For her, the war was not over. Someone had to pay. She had believed them to be demons, creatures indigenous to Zhinu that had remained undetected in the years of colonization and the establishment of Xin Beijing. And responsible for the destruction of that great city.

Now she was beginning to learn otherwise.

"They will pay for what they did to the New World Colony."

Yenko shook his head slowly. "The colonists did this to themselves, Fei Hung. It's how I came to find you. It's how we rescued you and your people. We discovered the technology they were experimenting on. These aliens, these demons, who afflicted your people so brutally, they didn't cause all this. Somehow, they were swept up in the catastrophe along with your people. They've been trapped here for as long as you have. No . . . There's something else going on that we're missing."

And with that, Yenko left to check on the activity around a large bank of computers, all neatly set under a makeshift roof. Technicians hovered about like bees at a hive, busily attaching wires and cables, taking electronic readings from handheld devices, ensuring the equipment was correctly installed for power to be established.

A final check from the chief technician and the order was given to power up the facility. Screens flickered into life to a soft electronic hum. And Nirani appeared out of thin air, a young Zhongwen woman of golden light. The holographic form of the *Zhinu Phoenix's* AI.

Fei Hung was not prepared for the sight. Taking it to be the spectral form of one of her enemies, she would have lunged at it murderously had Lakshay not the speed and instinct to hold her back.

"It is a hologram," he urged. "She isn't real. I mean, she is real, but she's not. Forgive me, Fei Hung, I do not know how to explain. She's with us. Her name is Nirani." With a flash of insight, he added, "She's a machine made of light."

It did not make any sense to Fei Hung, but she accepted Lakshay's explanation. The world was more wondrous than she had grown up to believe.

————◄◦►————

Yu Yan walked casually along the street with two of her friends, discussing the momentous times they were living in.

"Li is with them now," she said, bringing them up to speed with the latest news of the comings and goings of the Third Fleet.

"Is he well enough?" one of them asked. "The doctors were preparing for his death not that long ago."

"You don't know my husband," Yu Yan smiled proudly. "I swear he could face down any death and come out on top. Ever since he regained consciousness, his recovery has been swift."

Their path wound close by the heavily guarded Detention Center. Through the barred window of the closest building, a fair-haired man looked on the women who now walked only twenty feet from him. Though he understood nothing of their language, he studied them closely as they strolled past.

"When he heard that Robbie was assigned to the campsite of the blue invaders," Yu Yan continued, "he got straight out of his bed and stood before the Commodore herself."

"I hope he was clothed properly," one of Yu Yan's friends laughed with embarrassment.

"No!" exclaimed the wife of Li Jie. "Nothing but his bed gown . . . Nothing!"

The three laughed.

"I would have gone unclothed also if I knew Robbie Macpherson was there!" the third observed.

The other two women were shocked. And laughed raucously.

"You and Robbie Macpherson?" Yu Yan exclaimed. "Unclothed!!!"

A look of shock realization took the face of the prisoner behind the barred window. As the women laughed and joked and walked on, he muttered to himself, "Robby? Robby Mekförsen?" And he sprinted to find the green leader. For the first time, he had heard something he understood.

———◄○►———

The morning broke to the sound of massive engines firing. Yenko sprang out of his bed and joined the crowd that was quickly assembling. One by one, the huge engines of the crashed vehicle were being tested and then shut down.

Nirani appeared in their midst as an engine at the rear of the craft was fired. It sputtered several times without fully coming to life.

"I apologize for waking you all so rudely," the holographic image appeared to say; the voice came from the speakers that had been erected about the camp. "But I wanted to be dramatic with my morning report."

Artificial technology had come a long way in the last two centuries. AIs almost had character traits that bordered on self-awareness. There were many who postulated they may truly be alive, not just the predictable mathematical formulations of algorithms and computational logic.

"Next time inform me before you do something so dramatic," the Captain ordered. She was not well pleased to have her rank so lightly regarded by Nirani.

The golden image of light shimmered in the early morning air as it formally bowed to the Captain. "Forgive me," she said. "I allowed my excitement to run away with me."

Yenko raised his eyebrows. Along with those of half the assembly. It was obvious that Captain Liu also thought it incongruous that Nirani could be excited, let alone be overcome by that excitement. But one thing was patently clear, the AI had broken protocol, a thing it was specifically programmed not to do.

Ignoring the anomaly for the moment, Captain Liu said, almost hesitantly, "Think no more of it. Just don't do it again. Respect the chain of command."

"Yes, Captain," Nirani accepted. "It will not happen again."

"Come into my Field Office and make your report. The rest of you, about your morning duties. That's an order."

The company dispersed rapidly as Captain Liu, three of her senior officers and Nirani made their way to the Field Office. Once inside, with the doors shutting out prying eyes, the AI gave her report.

"I cracked the code thirty-two minutes ago," Nirani began.

"Nirani, since when do you start a report with the conclusion?"

"Forgive me again," Nirani apologized. "I believe my discovery will go down as the greatest of the Common Era."

Captain Liu glanced at her advisors. It seemed they were witnessing another display of excitement from the AI. She made a mental note to commission a diagnostic survey of its circuitry on board the *Zhinu Phoenix*.

"Proceed then."

"Yes, Captain. Most of the night, my efforts were trained toward gaining access to the internal sensor array and interactive databases of the onboard computer grid. Working from the assumption that the vessel was of human design, I sought to understand its operating system. It was difficult to crack; I have never interfaced with anything like it before.

"The first discovery of note was logged at 0109hrs. I had set aside a small percentage of my memory banks to decipher the encryptions on the ship's control panels. For the most part, they are of standard English script."

"English script?" the Captain echoed. "So, it is from Earth."

"Yes and no, Captain," Nirani continued. "At first I thought the lettering of the words formed encryptions. It did not conform to the standard world languages I have on my memory files. I assumed that the command codes and instructions must be heavily encoded, and I sought to break the code for . . . Let's just say it was a long time, and I am not proud of myself for not seeing the obvious straight away.

"Several words were recognizable to me and I finally realized I was looking at a little used form of an archaic Earth language . . . Deyu. Three separatist colonies are all that remain of the ancient country of Deguo. Deutschland, they called it. Germany in the universal English language."

"Deyu?" interrupted the Captain, voicing the unspoken question on the face of her advisors. "How can they be German?"

Nirani continued as if the Captain had said nothing. "The Deutsche separatists, hidden away in the mountains of the western European continent, war against each other and the world about them. As is the way of the separatists, they hold fast to the ancient language and traditions of their people in the face of the unstoppable globalization of human society."

"But how can they be German?" interrupted Captain Liu again. "They are of little account and live in poverty. They don't have the technology, the resources, the professional skills base. They haven't been a force in the world for well over a century. This spacecraft can't be the work of German separatists."

"Ah," reflected Nirani with a hint of anticipation in her eye, "that is but the beginning of the drama, Captain. I had to hook up a remote link to Earth from my databanks onboard the *Zhinu Phoenix*. Part of me wondered how it could be possible to be studying an artefact of Earth's ancient past, launched from a time when Deutschland was a global power and had the economic capacity to construct such a vehicle. That would account for the language, but it did not allow for the technology. The ship is filled with machinery I have not seen before and can only guess at its use.

"At 0221hrs, I had everything I needed from Earth and I could now decipher the language locked within the heart of the ship. Since then, my focus has been divided between seeking to understand the nature of the instrumentation and operation of the ship, the mission logs of the flight crew, the crew manifest, details relating to the port of origin, and a general review of the ship's database.

"At 0457hrs, I believed I understood enough of the operation of the ship that I could test my conclusions on the starboard and stern thrusters. I thought it would be a good way to get everyone's attention so I could share what else I had learned.

"A full hour before I finally lit the engines, it was becoming clear. I still have many days of research and investigation to perform, but I can inform the Captain right now that the ship is not from Earth. But it is of human construction."

Captain Liu and her subordinates were shocked.

"The ship is called the *Todeszerstörer*, the Destroyer of Death. It embarked from Neu Rothenburg on Heldentat, the fifth planet orbiting Antares in the Constellation Scorpius."

Nirani looked with pride on her stunned audience.

"But that is not the half of it. It was launched . . . correction, will be launched . . . approximately three hundred and fifty-seven years from now."

She beamed with satisfaction. Captain Liu said nothing.

"Sometime around the year 2748 by Earth's reckoning . . . I cannot be more precise than that . . . the *Todeszerstörer* will be launched. And it will end up here."

"Nirani, how sure are you of all this? It sounds too farfetched," the Captain said at length.

The AI smiled broadly. "Now you understand why I wanted to wake the camp up so spectacularly."

———◦———

Commodore Ahuja inspected the Detention Center where the prisoners were being held. She had received the field report updating her on the mission status regarding the alien vessel but could not believe Nirani's findings, that these men and women were soldiers from the future. Looking at them now, as they mingled together in small groups around the secured perimeter of a grassy yard about the central four buildings of the facility, she had no choice but to believe. They were clearly human and obviously of the same people group of middle Europe.

But the future? It would explain some questions and pose a million more in the process.

One of the prisoners, standing proudly to the side of the yard, watching the Commodore's every move, seemed to command the respect and deference of everyone about him. The man who at one time had been clothed in semi-visible green camouflage. Ahuja walked straight up to him, surrounded by her heavily armed escort. The prisoners made way for her, keeping far from the deadly weaponry of her soldiers; they had battled troops such as these already and been overpowered by their military prowess.

The leader stood his ground. He would not bow before the Commodore's entourage. He was perhaps a little over six foot, muscularly built, with light brown hair and blue eyes. As with the rest of the male prisoners, a new beard covered his chiseled face.

Ahuja halted a short distance from the leader. She did not want to get too close to him. Her soldiers would deal with any threat, she was confident of that, but she did not want to give the prisoner the hope of taking an upper hand.

"I am told you are Jarman," she said, piercing his eyes with her own.

The man held her gaze, his eyes neither filled with contempt nor defeat.

"Jarman," the Commodore repeated. "You're a separatist faction then?"

No response. No sign of cognizance.

"Do you understand me?" she added. "Stop playing games. Do you speak English?"

Nothing.

"*Ni hui shuo Putonghua ma*?" she repeated in Mandarin. Up until now, she had thought that the prisoners had picked up a few Zhongwen words from their interactions with the people of Gui Difang. But if they were truly German, they would undoubtedly know the language of the Zhongwen people, separatists or not.

The man maintained his steadfast poise. If he understood her, he disguised the fact well.

"Zhongwen?"

Perhaps he knew her own mother tongue, Hindi. "*Kya aap hindee bolate hain?*"

"*Mir reicht's!*" the leader said and made to walk off, ignoring his captor.

"Deutsche?"

That brought him to a halt and drew the attention of the prisoners who were with him.

"Ah! *Sie haben die herausragende Sprache meiner Ahnen nicht vergessen!*" he replied.

Unfortunately, "Deutsche" was the only word in the ancient language that Ahuja knew. And she only knew that because it was part of Nirani's report. Turning to her personal aide, she said, "Inform Captain Liu that I will require Nirani to act as Interpreter as soon as practical. And alert the hologram analysts to prepare my office for her."

Bowing slightly to the German leader, she said, "I will speak to you this afternoon," and left the compound.

————◄○►————

Captain Liu was deep in discussion with a small group of men and women, chiefly scientists and lead technicians. Yenko was among them. They were gathered together on the main flight deck of the alien vessel. Seven seats were stationed in front of banks of monitors, instruments, and glassed panels of unknown function. Large screens filled the curved wall before them.

A shimmering gold light interrupted them, the effect of the holographic instruments around them warming up, indicating Nirani was about to make an appearance.

"Forgive my intrusion," the golden woman announced at length. She looked concerned. Captain Liu took mental note. Something unusual was happening to their AI. All morning she had displayed what could only be understood as emotion. It could not be ignored.

"Nirani," he said, "you obviously have something to report. But before you do, I must learn something of you."

The holographic woman raised her eyebrows. "Certainly, Captain."

"I've never known an AI to act like you have today. If I didn't know better, I would say you were showing signs of emotion. Your performance with the ship's thrusters. Your excitement to tell us our enemies are humans from the future. And now, you interrupt me without heeding operational protocol. You did not send the meeting request to my personal receiver, and you did not sound the holographic alert to announce to the rest of the company that you were about to make an appearance. What is happening to you, Nirani? Have you run the diagnostic systems test on your circuitry on the *Zhinu Phoenix* that I ordered?"

"I have," Nirani replied.

"Well why haven't I received the report?"

"Nothing is wrong with me, Captain. I didn't report because there was nothing to report."

"That is irrelevant, Nirani. You know that."

Nirani looked frustrated. The Captain made another mental note.

"I apologize for the breach in protocol," the hologram replied. "It won't happen again. But Captain, in defense of my actions, there is so much that I am investigating. My memory resources are stretched."

"Hmmm . . ." That may explain the curious behavior, but the Captain was unconvinced. "Something's going on, Nirani, but I accept your explanation. There is a lot of data that you're working through at the moment. Why have you made your appearance? What is it that you have found?"

The light-generated woman looked as if she was measuring the capacity of the Captain to receive her news. "Perhaps I should report directly to the Commodore," she said.

"Now that really is unusual. Search your databanks, Nirani. You will see that you have never disobeyed the injunction of a superior. I asked you a question, and I expect an answer. What have you unearthed that has precipitated this meeting?"

Nirani looked at each of those present. "Could we speak in private?" she offered.

Captain Liu dismissed the group. As they dispersed, he sidled up to Yenko and whispered into his ear, "Inform the Commodore something is amiss with Nirani."

The AI watched Yenko as he left the flight deck.

"You have my full attention," the Captain said once the area was empty. "What is it that is driving you to distraction?"

"I have found the mission orders of the SDS. That is what they call themselves. *Schild der Schwachen* . . . Shield of the Weak."

Walking towards a bank of monitors at one of the flight stations, Nirani imitated turning several knobs and adjusting two levers. The screen came to light, filled with a foreign text the Captain could not read.

"What does it say?" he asked.

"Essentially," began Nirani, "they were sent to destroy Xin Beijing before the arrival of one they call Räuber Mekförsen . . . Mekförsen the Robber. The name is spelled differently but phonetically it is akin to Macpherson. Captain, we have a Macpherson within the ranks of the Third Fleet. And there was a Macpherson on the First Fleet who undoubtedly has descendants here on Zhinu. This Räuber Mekförsen could well be one of them."

"What is the basis for the command to destroy the city?" Captain Liu asked. "And why have they attached the name of this Macpherson to it?"

Nirani scrolled through a list of documents. "I have only found obscure references, Captain. Apparently, Räuber Mekförsen is responsible for the annihilation of the human species across the galaxy. And somehow, it all started here in Xin Beijing."

The Captain ran his fingers through his hair.

"You see now why I broke protocol." Turning her head as if she had just heard or seen something behind her, she added, "The Commodore has summoned me. It seems she wishes to interview the prisoners and needs my linguistic abilities. I will continue my investigations, Captain, but my holographic form will go offline for a period while I report to the Commodore."

"Very good," the Captain said at length. "Report back to me when you are done. Dismissed."

The AI bowed, and the light display ended her appearance. The screen she had been referring to likewise powered down. "I will get to the bottom of it," Nirani's voice came from a nearby speaker. "You can trust me, Captain."

———————◦———————

An hour later, the leader of the German SDS was led, chained and heavily guarded, into a hastily arranged Interrogation Room in the newly constructed Third Fleet settlement. He did not find it easy to walk, limping still from the knife wound sustained in the fight with Commander Huang. Commodore Ahuja sat behind an imposing desk. Behind her sat two of her aides, tablet screens in hand to make relevant notes of the outcome of the examination.

"Please, take a seat," Ahuja said, motioning the German leader towards a chair opposite her. Nirani stood to one side in view of both parties, acting as interpreter, the leader recognizing the holographic image as a sophisticated form of Artificial Intelligence.

"Have you read the files, yet?" he asked Nirani in German, ignoring the Commodore's offer.

Nirani looked ambiguously at the man but made no reply. As casually as he could make it appear, the leader sat down, ignoring the shooting pains from the wound to his stomach, another legacy of his encounter with the Commander.

"So, you have learned our language," he observed solemnly with Nirani translating, drawing his attention back to the Commodore. "You have no idea the train of events you have set in motion."

"We'll come to that in time," Ahuja said, taken back a little by the tone in his voice. If anything, the man sounded sad. "But first . . . I am Mannat Ahuja, Commodore of the Third Fleet, five times decorated in the Bhaarateey army by the Prime Minister of Bhaarat Ekata himself and twice even, by the President of Zhongguo Xin Shijie for valor in peace keeping in the demilitarized separatist enclaves of Indonesia."

"Is that supposed to impress me?" the German asked.

Ahuja ignored the dismissive remark. "We can make this as difficult as you want," she threatened, "but I would rather not. It would serve no use. I will find what I want to know with or without your compliance. What is your name?"

The man studied her for a moment. He recognized the air of authority the Commodore carried. She was familiar with command and knew she would have her way.

Eyeballing her, he said, "My name is Jörn Schönebeck. I am undecorated and place no value in such ceremony. I am Oberst of the Heldentat *Schild der Schwachen*."

"What is Oberst?" the Commodore asked Nirani.

"He is a Colonel, Commodore," she said with a bow.

"Schönebeck," Ahuja repeated back to the man in front of her. "There is no escape from this planet. You and your people are here for a very . . . long . . . time."

"We did not come here to return," he said. "We came here to die. There is nowhere for us to return to."

"So I am led to understand," the Commodore continued. "You come here from the future, I am told. I'm not sure that I can believe that. How were you able to accomplish it?"

The man looked obscurely at her before answering. "I am only Oberst of the *Schild der Schwachen*. I do not comprehend such things."

"Do you have a scientific detail amongst your squadron? Someone who can explain?"

"I did . . . But you killed them. They will give you no answers from the grave."

Ahuja pursed her lips. So much bloodshed. "It would not have been necessary but for your assaults on the villagers of Gui Difang. But . . . there is nothing for it now. My AI has discovered the mission parameters given to you from your home world of Heldentat, wherever that is.

"You were here to destroy Xin Beijing and hopefully kill a man called Räuber Mekförsen. Why is Macpherson so important to you?"

That fired the Colonel up. "You fools!" he spat. "Mekförsen is the thief who stole all hope from the human race. Your own life is as doomed as mine. We are all dead. All of us. Within four centuries, humans will be all but extinct. Your life. Mine. Those behind you. The soldiers at the door. My troops in your prison wing. All are meaningless. This golden AI beside us, she is likely all that will remain of our once proud heritage.

"And it is all Mekförsen's doing."

"How can that be?" the Commodore demanded. "There are billions of humans. On two worlds now. And before long, we will be on more."

"That's the very cause of the problem. And one we have Mekförsen to thank for."

"What does this Mekförsen . . . if he or she even exists . . . what is Mekförsen responsible for? Don't talk in riddles. Your mission must have been concrete."

"If he or she even exists," the Oberst repeated. "You do not know who walks amongst your ranks. *He* exists. We learned this morning that our name for him is phonetically inaccurate. He goes by the name Robby Macpherson."

"Robbie . . . ?" the Commodore wondered aloud. "The villagers call Yenko by that name. Are you talking about Macpherson Yenko?"

"I know nothing of a Yenko. Our knowledge of your time is fragmented. Records are incomplete, especially as they relate to what was taken to be an insignificant human outpost on Zhinu.

"But listen carefully, Commodore," Schönebeck urged, leaning forward dramatically, wincing momentarily against the knife wound in his stomach, "if Yenko Macpherson is the Räuber Mekförsen of our distant past, he is to be stopped at all costs. Death marches in his wake."

"You must explain yourself," Ahuja interrupted, "if I am to understand your mission. So far your words seem the ravings of a madman."

The Oberst sat back and closed his eyes, gently rubbing his wounded thigh. "There is so much you are ignorant of," he began. "As best we can ascertain, it is here, on Zhinu, that the science was discovered, somewhere in the second half of the twenty-fourth century. Mekförsen is a genius, hundreds of years ahead of his time . . .

"Ahhh . . . If only he had been born centuries later. Perhaps by the time the planet wars began, we would have the technological ability to defend ourselves . . . But it was not to be. Mekförsen uncovered the secret of folding the space-time curve. It opened the door to the galaxy. And beyond.

"If only we had stayed content with our place under the Sun, Commodore. Earth was a beautiful world from what we can gather. We should not have ventured so eagerly into a universe we knew nothing of."

"What happened?" Ahuja asked.

"At first, if the historical records are interpreted accurately, Earth sent colonies to the distant reaches of the heavens. The rebel colonies of your time—separatists you call them, I think—saw a chance to start a new life free from the political, economic, and social restraints of Earth's global empires.

"My own ancestors sought such a haven and were granted their request; to have them out of their traditional lands gave more opportunities to their oppressors. In 2512, my people set out in a mass migration that lasted a full year. They were filled with optimism and hope. Their desire was to reawaken the glory of our fathers and build a new world based on our culture.

"That century saw many such migrations. Mekförsen's folding space made travel between worlds almost as easy and commonplace as travel between continents. Perhaps easier. By the close of the twenty-sixth century, over a hundred human colonies were established throughout the Milky Way.

"Fifty years later and it seemed that humanity would rule the universe. Until 2671, the year we learned our place among the stars. We discovered an inhabited world, Kjeld. It was the first intelligent life we had encountered in all our wanderings through the heavens. And we thought we were well poised to offer our hands in friendship.

"The Kjeldans are fiercely independent, Commodore. At first, we thought we had offended them, accidentally broken some deeply held social taboo. But no. We learned too late that the offence we had committed was that we were not Kjeldan.

"Our very existence insulted them and their fanatical view of their place in the galaxy. Without warning and without provocation, they declared war against us. It was not enough that they forced us out of their space. They claimed rulership over the entire galaxy.

"Their art of war was so much more advanced than our own. We had no chance before them. Our weapons were ineffective, unable to pierce their shield grids. Even in hand-to-hand combat, they are fell warriors. Their agility and speed eclipses the best of our own and their vulnerabilities were never discovered. And they have a natural ability to bend light about their bodies in such a way as to practically render themselves invisible. One by one, they hunted down the worlds of our colonialization."

The Oberst paused for the implications to sink in.

"Commodore, all human life on Earth will be annihilated in 2723. The battle will last only two weeks. But in that time, warheads loaded with a biological toxin we cannot combat will be launched into Earth's upper atmosphere. It will spread exponentially and rain down over the whole planet. Earth will know of the toxin but will be defenseless before its power.

"Gas masks, sealed vaults, subterranean shelters . . . nothing proved successful. Within two years of the first onslaught, our ancestral home will be no more the world you know.

"Earth was the major center of our humanity. It took the Kjeldans many years to track through the records of our captured research facilities and erase all human presence across the galaxy. On our own world of Heldentat, we could see the end was inevitable for us. We were not as large as many of the other colonies, and for some time we managed to stay out of the sight of our hunters. But we knew they would find us eventually.

"Heldentat was chief in the research of time and its effects on the curvature of space-time. Our peoples are leaders, Commodore. In your time, you shut us up in our separatist states and fueled bitter rivalries amongst us. But we are a people steeped in learning and culture.

"Once we were free to be ourselves, we advanced beyond all others. In 2582, a mechanism to enable time travel was hypothesized. First achieved in 2617, it was only effective for inanimate objects. Organic transfer was successfully achieved in 2632. Living animal transportation proved elusive, until the breakthrough was made in 2673, two years after humans made first contact with Kjeld.

"Development of the science accelerated rapidly. In order for a living animal to travel through time, a genetic modification needs to be made to the host's blood. A secondary blood system, not as complex as the body's natural one, had to be engrafted into the living tissue of the host. It pumps a flow of copper-based compounds, mimicking hemoglobin from what I understand, but I am no physician.

"It soon became apparent to us that our species' survival depended on us. We had one chance. To go back in time and stop the discovery of folded space-time. But the historical records were fragmentary. We knew Zhinu was at the center of the breakthrough. We knew it was here. Our histories spoke of a Räuber Mekförsen. We knew he was from Earth, and we knew he was a scientist of acclaim there, so we postulated that he was part of the famed Third Fleet. But we did not know the dates anywhere near accurately.

"We had never undertaken such a reckless venture, sending an interstellar warship back across the ages and halfway across the galaxy. There were many who said it could not be done, that our complement of volunteers would die in the attempt. Temporal Mechanics philosophers argued that if such a mission as the one we contemplated was successful, the timeline would already be altered, and we would cease to exist in that timeframe and in that locality. The Quantum Time Paradox of cause and effect was cited again and again, as if our very existence proved we had already failed.

"And indeed, we have failed . . .

"Commodore, there is but one hope. Stop Mekförsen. The survival of our species depends on it."

Mannat Ahuja sat back in her chair, hands together under her chin as if in supplication to God for mercy.

"Call Yenko," she said at length to one of her aides. "Tell him to drop everything he's doing and get here at once."

Nirani looked sideways at the Oberst.

———◄◦►———

It was not until the next morning that another interview could be convened. Yenko received the order without question. He managed to commandeer an LRV from Captain Liu easily enough and Varma was assigned to him, by his request, as driver. Li Jie decided to return with them, keen to know why Yenko would receive such a high-level order when his expertise was obviously needed at the crash site.

As they left the field camp, Yenko noticed Nirani appear outside the front portal of the spacecraft.

"Nirani's back," he said absently to his companions. Li Jie, Fei Hung, and Lakshay paid it no attention. It was unremarkable news.

Looking behind them as they sped off towards base, Yenko watched the AI. She remained where she stood, her holographic eyes fixed on them till the LRV was out of her sight.

11

The Cloaked Wars

"FIND OUT WHY NIRANI isn't with us," Commodore Ahuja said, the hint of frustration not fully hidden in her voice.

An aide left the room and could be heard yelling orders across the communications relay. Moments later, the interview room shimmered with the golden light that presaged the appearance of the AI.

Before Nirani had a chance to speak, the Commodore said, "If we were not in the middle of a major crisis, I would decommission you in an instant."

The golden holograph looked incomprehensibly at the Commodore, but no reply. She turned and stared maliciously at Yenko, who was standing to one side of the large desk that dominated the room.

"You are the cause of everything, the harbinger of evil," she accused him coldly.

Yenko's heart froze within him. What had brought that on?

Turning aside, Commodore Ahuja ignored the room and had her own private conversation with her aides. At length, she faced Nirani with a look that held an unspoken threat.

"Speak no more without my command," she ordered the holographic woman.

The list of abnormalities with the AI was becoming alarming. If Nirani's skills were not essential, the Commodore would have taken her offline and ordered a meticulous diagnostic review of each of the AI's subroutines, along with every inch of the *Phoenix*'s computing hardware.

As it was, however, Nirani was needed. And needed now. Such a systems-wide review would take months, at the least. With the *Phoenix* in high orbit, it would need to be done remotely, and that meant it would be Nirani herself who would be responsible for the review. The safest way would be to do a manual diagnosis, but there was no way of getting a team of analysts up to the *Phoenix* to perform such a task.

Nirani bowed formally before the Commodore, almost reverently, as if meeting a dignitary of the highest rank. Ahuja took note, another action she did not fully understand, and turned her attention to Macpherson.

"Thank you for coming as quickly as you did, Yenko," she said. "At every turn, your name keeps coming across my desk."

"Have I done something wrong?" he asked. He could not think what, but there was an unmistakable tension in the air.

"No," the Commodore replied, then hesitated. "I don't think so." With a sigh, she added, "I don't know what I think anymore."

That did not put Yenko at ease, but before he had time to wrestle with his inner apprehensions, Ahuja dived straight into a debrief of the previous day's interrogation of the leader of the prisoners, Oberst Schönebeck. The whole while, Nirani eyed the Scot separatist with contempt. It made Yenko uneasy, like he was the one being interrogated.

"The future . . ." he said at length. "Commodore, do you believe him?"

"I don't know what to believe. That's why I called you here. My world is a simple one, Yenko. Leadership, command, diplomacy, strategy, organization. These are things I understand. But science . . . I'm glad you're on the team."

Nirani shot a sideways glance at the Commodore. Ahuja missed it, but Yenko did not. And worried at what it might mean.

"It would answer a lot of questions," he began. "But to be honest, it raises more than it answers. I mean . . . time travel! It opens the door to a world of paradox and contradiction."

"Schönebeck said the Heldentat scientists argued along the same lines . . . I think."

"But all that aside," Yenko continued, as if the Commodore had not spoken, "what do I have to do with it? Are you sure he was talking about me? How would he even know about me? I mean, if he came from three hundred and fifty years or more in the future, how would he know about me? Hardly anyone gets remembered over that length of time."

"I agree," Mannat added. "That's why I called you here."

The two studied each other, considering where this was all going to lead.

Nirani sucked in her top lip, but her face was empty of expression.

"Major Das," the Commodore ordered one of her aides, "bring in the prisoner."

Moments later, the Major returned with Oberst Schönebeck, accompanied by three armed guards. The man walked into the room as proudly as his wounds and bonds would allow him, surveying his interrogators one by one as he did so.

"Sit," the Commodore said. It seemed incongruous. Apart from another of her aides, busily preparing to take notes of the interrogation, no one else in the room was seated, the Commodore included.

"An odd command," the Oberst observed, "but if it will put the rest of you at ease . . ." And he carefully made himself semi-comfortable, almost hiding the grimace of pain from his thigh and stomach.

"Do you need drink? Or food?" Ahuja asked.

"Concerned for my well-being, are you? You would make my condition more acceptable if you removed these bonds. I assure you as an officer of the Heldentat Imperium that I will not seek to escape." Noting his armed escort, he added, "I doubt I could get off this chair even if I wanted to."

His guards stood alert, ready for anything. Mannat Ahuja accepted the request. With a flick of the wrist, she instructed one of the guards to unbind the prisoner. The remaining guards trained their weapons at the Oberst's head as he did so.

Rubbing his wrists against the pain of restriction, Schönebeck sat back more comfortably in his chair and carefully crossed his legs. "Please," he said to the room as if he was the one in command. "Be seated."

With a nod, Commodore Ahuja allowed everyone to take their seats. She herself did so slowly.

"Oberst," she began, "now may I offer you a drink? Tea? This need not be an interrogation."

The tall, fair headed man from the unknown future looked at her curiously. "You are a more civilized people than I had expected. No, thank you. Let us get straight to the point, shall we? What do you hope to learn of me today?"

Ahuja studied the man. He certainly was not what she would have expected. She accepted he was human, that much was irrefutable. But he was almost refined. It was incongruous with the reports of the atrocities committed against the refugees of Gui Difang, the wretched descendants of the colonists who had suffered so horribly in the catastrophe of 2347.

"I don't know what I hope to learn," she confessed. "I am Bhaarateey. It is the Zhongwen who love puzzle boxes. I do not have the patience."

"Let me introduce one of our scientists to you, Oberst. Macpherson Yenko. He is a leader in the field of Space-Time Kinematics and was instrumental in the rescue of our people stranded in Gui Difang."

The Oberst studied Yenko, though what he was thinking, the scientist could not read. It made him feel uncomfortable.

"So. Mekförsen. We meet face to face."

"I don't know who you think I am, but I am not him," Yenko offered. He was not intimidated by the German officer, despite the imposing figure he cut.

"Robbie Mekförsen," the Oberst reiterated.

"The villagers call me Robbie. It's a nickname derived from their history. It's impossible that you would know such a trivial detail if you come from the time you say you do."

"We know you as Räuber Mekförsen," Schönebeck replied.

Nirani leaned over Yenko when she finished interpreting the Oberst's statement. "Do you know what Räuber means, Mekförsen?" she whispered. "It means Robber. The Robber of Life and Hope, the one who leaves death in his wake!"

The threat in her voice was palpable.

Quietly, threateningly, the Commodore all but whispered, "You were told only to speak when instructed."

The AI's demeanor changed radically. At once, she bowed and profusely apologized, "Commodore, I so sincerely beg your forgiveness. I am stretched too thin. It is wearing my inner control."

"Then cease all your activities right now and attend fully to your task at hand here."

"Yes, Commodore. As you say." A slight flicker shot through Nirani's holographic form. "It is done according to your will, Commodore. Forgive my weakness."

"We have trouble with Artificials also, Commodore," the Oberst said. Without the aid of an interpreter, he could not have understood anything that had just transpired. But it was obvious he comprehended enough to see that his captors' AI was not behaving according to its programmed specification.

"That is of no concern to you," she affirmed. "Oberst, explain to Mr. Macpherson what you told me yesterday. Tell him, from your perspective, the rationale behind your mission objective."

"Of course," the Oberst replied, and began to recount the significance that Räuber Mekförsen played in their history.

At length, Yenko leaned back and stretched, as if perhaps he wanted to wake from a bad dream.

"You must not go ahead with your studies," Oberst Schönebeck insisted. "The folding of space spells doom to humanity."

"It's not my study," Yenko dismissed. "Multidimensional Werner Contractions were postulated by two Kinematics professors here on Zhinu."

"What?" demanded the Oberst. "Explain yourself. The history is incomplete, I acknowledge, but your name has sounded down the centuries as the herald of colonial expansion across the galaxy."

"Well, they're wrong," Yenko said simply. "It was the work of Mahika Khatri and Arushi Jain, here in Xin Beijing. San Yue 11, 2339AD. Earth Time. That's what your histories should have told you. That's when they went public with their findings. At least, it's when they revealed their discovery to the authorities here on Zhinu. Earth knew nothing of it."

"San Yue, 2339," Schönebeck whispered in disbelief. "We came too late."

Yenko nodded as the immensity of the failure dawned on the prisoner.

"But the name Mekförsen?" he almost pleaded. "History accords the discovery to you."

"I only discovered their work," Yenko offered. "They made a fundamental miscalculation . . . one they could not have recognized so long ago. There were gaps in their knowledge they were unaware of . . . could not have been aware of.

"Your coming here from the future is perhaps the greatest fluke of all time. Perhaps if the future is as you say, we were all predestined to wipe ourselves out."

"I don't believe in destiny," the Oberst said.

"I would tend to agree," Yenko responded. "But here you are. Oberst, you were caught in their first full-scale trial."

"I don't understand. What do you mean?"

"In 2347, Khatri and Jain had developed the technology they expected would open a doorway to the stars. But they threw Xin Beijing into oblivion. Oberst, you were caught in the destructive path of their failed trial."

"The crash!" Schönebeck exclaimed with a mark of realization.

"The crash," Yenko repeated. "They expected to open a portal in the forest in the foothills behind Xin Beijing. Instead, they created a cone of destruction emanating from their mountain Control Center. Its axis shot out tangentially to the curve of Zhinu for as much as one hundred miles.

"My guess is that your ship was making its descent towards the colony at that exact moment. You could not have been any higher than the lower Thermosphere or the distortion band would not have hit you."

"My father told me of the mayhem of that day, when all our plans crashed along with our ship," the officer recalled. "The eldest among us have kept the memory alive. It has fueled our hopeless purpose all these years.

"We were making our approach run to Zhinu's first city, intending to wipe it from all history. But we were attacked. Or so our fathers and mothers thought. Our ship, the *Todeszerstörer*, plummeted from the skies. If not for the skill of our pilots, no one would have survived. As it was, the ship's complement barely came out alive. There were many casualties.

"Assessment was made to find the cause of the incident. We never learned the answer. Seemingly minor components of the *Todeszerstörer*'s infrastructure were in some way disconnected from the rest. It took months to discover a way to manipulate the ship's hatches to open."

Yenko nodded in understanding. "The same thing happened to Xin Beijing," he said. "The field generated by Khatri and Jain's Gravimetric Discriminator phase-shifted certain elements and compounds but not others. It was a consequence they could not have foreseen. It caused the ruin of Xin Beijing. The people of Gui Difang are their descendants.

"But others remained, who had not been in the line of their field generator. That's what I discovered, Oberst Schönebeck. Not how to fold space. I discovered how to realign the phase-shift and bring our people and yours back into proper space."

The mysterious man of the future considered Yenko for some time.

"The mission remains," he said at length. "Earth must be prevented from colonizing the stars. Or at least halted till it can learn to defend itself."

Commodore Ahuja interjected. "What was the point of your torturing our people?" she demanded. "You are guilty of crimes unimaginable. If your mission was all that mattered, and if you thought Yenko was on the planet, why did you not talk with the villagers? Make them see the consequences of their studies and experimentation?"

The Oberst hung his head, the first time he gave hint of not being in charge.

"In the early days," he confessed, "our fathers reasoned that though they did not destroy the city, they could teach Earth to fear the stars. They thought that our technology would be sufficiently advanced that we would be mistaken for alien marauders. We made it our habit to be in full combat uniform whenever we were outside the ship.

"The stealth technology of our body armor added to the fear we instilled. Before long, however, we realized that whatever had happened to the city, its people were in no shape to pose a threat to the future.

"Commodore, the longer we were here, the more the years crept by, the more we began to hope that our objective had been achieved. The city was in ruins and within a short space of time, its inhabitants no longer frequented its districts. Before long, a rough village of the Zhinu populace was established to the south of our forced landing.

"We knew that Earth would be monitoring the planet from its crude probes, so we could not abandon our efforts completely. We needed to ensure that if ever Earth made contact with Zhinu again, it would receive reports of alien terror. In this way, Earth would learn to fear the unknown intelligences that may inhabit the galaxy about them."

The Oberst sighed in resignation. "It was to no avail. I allowed discipline to wane, something my father would never have done. Every now and then, for cruel sport, sorties would go out and play havoc with the villagers.

"I am not proud of it, but neither am I ashamed of it. It was fitting to instill fear . . . But to no end."

Yenko frowned. He could not accept what he was hearing.

"Why didn't you simply go back to Earth," he reasoned, "and let the Zhongwen and Bhaarateey governments know? They would see your technological superiority and accept your wisdom."

"Unless our histories are utterly in error, Mekförsen," the Oberst replied, "there is no way they would have listened to us. You are in the early stages of what we call the Cloaked Wars. From our records, we knew it to be a time of two-faced diplomacy between the major powers. Both made open show of mutual acceptance, but behind closed doors, they plotted and jostled for power. Conspiracy theories filled their private conversations and threw suspicion on public discourses. If we were to announce ourselves to one government before the other, the tenuous peace would be broken, and war would erupt."

"But even that would have aided your cause," the Commodore argued.

"No. The Qin One World Dynasty would have seized power too easily. Unknown to the Bhaarat Ekata, the Zhongguo Xin Shijie have been amassing weapons of mass destruction since the early 2320s."

To the look of disbelief, he added, "That much of our history is well documented, Commodore. If the timeline progresses as expected, tensions will escalate in the first decade of the twenty-fifth century. It will finally end with the Peace Accords of 2415, where both powers will voluntarily disarm, and a new Global Order is established. It will be the beginning of a new day of advancement for humanity and fuel the drive for galactic expansion.

"Mekförsen, if we had journeyed to Earth and not Zhinu, we would have solved nothing. All we would have achieved would be the acceleration of our doom. At least for the moment, their attention is divided amongst themselves. It needed to stay that way."

"I still don't understand the basis for your mission. Why not just go back further in time? Warn the Earth before they first capture a sustained manipulation of the space-time curvature. You could have stopped it before it even began."

The Oberst shook his head. "You are a man of your era, Mekförsen. Chronometric travel is not easily achieved. It requires an energy source you cannot imagine. It was all we could do to come back to this century. We were thanking God that we had developed the technology with just enough time to undo your error. Or whoever's error it was."

Commodore Ahuja allowed the room to sit in silence for several minutes. Time travel. The paradoxes were apparent even for her, a military leader, not a science graduate.

"How do you know so much of Earth's history but not Zhinu's?" she asked at length. "Surely you did your research thoroughly before you ventured on your mission. How is it that you knew so little of Macpherson and his arrival on the Third Fleet? And nothing of the catastrophe that befell Xin Beijing? It is the greatest historical intrigue of the century and the very reason why the Third Fleet was commissioned. Surely you knew all that."

"We did do our homework, Commodore," the Oberst argued. "We knew of the mystery. But the records are scant concerning it as if one of the global powers sought to erase memory of its existence. Remember, Commodore, it was the beginning of the Cloaked Wars. Elements of history were systematically erased for reasons no one could afterwards identify.

"And it was of little use for us to search through the records on Zhinu itself. In our time, Xin Beijing is nothing but a gaping crater dominating the largest of the northern landmasses."

Leaning emphatically towards Yenko, the Oberst added, "Mekförsen, your name comes up time and again. That much, at least, is not erased. Whatever it is that you are involved in, you must stop."

The Scottish scientist closed his eyes. He wished it would all go away. What he would give for a drink right now. A real drink. A Scottish drink.

Mannat Ahuja realized there was already too much on the table for them to digest quickly. They needed time to think. To reflect. To question. Standing to her feet, she addressed the gathering.

"I think we all need to adjourn for the moment. I must figure out how I'm going to make my report on all this. Guards, escort the Oberst back to the Detention Center. And see he gets fed; we've talked past the midday meal. Yenko, I would like to meet you this afternoon at 1400hrs. In my office. Nirani . . . I've never heard of an Artificial Intelligence exhibiting behavior like I have witnessed from you today. I want an explanation by tomorrow morning. Everyone, dismissed."

———◁○▷———

"Would you like a drink?" Ahuja asked as Yenko entered the Commodore's office, on time as ordered.

"Commodore?" It was an unexpected offer.

"I need a drink, Yenko. Call me Manu. This meeting is off the record." And she poured two glasses of Lia Fail, the finest and most expensive of Scotch Whiskeys. "You look like you need one. And if you don't drink it, I'll drink it for you."

She took a sip from her glass and made for the door behind her desk, taking the bottle with her.

"Come into my private lounge," she offered. Though it was spoken as a genuine invitation, Yenko was clear that it was a command. This may be off the record, but she was still the Commodore.

And to the best of Yenko's knowledge of her, no one had ever been invited into her private quarters.

"What did you make of that?" she asked at length.

The meeting of that morning had shaken Yenko. Time travel. Kjeldans. The systematic extermination of humanity. It was hard to believe. He could well believe, though, that there may be cloak and dagger wars between Zhongguo and Bhaarat; the peace was long held, but it was tenuous.

Yenko made himself comfortable in a plush lounge chair. He considered for a while where she might have got it from. Surely she had not included such a luxury in the shipboard manifest of the *Zhinu Phoenix*? At length, he considered the woman sitting opposite him, whiskey already finished, now pouring a second. She looked tired.

Catching eyes, he shrugged his shoulders in answer to her question and took a sip of his own drink. "This is really good," he noted and looked out a window, intimidated by the force of her attention and how his name floated around the center of the Oberst's accusations.

She waited for a fuller response from him. At length he answered.

"I don't know what to make of it. There's just so much happening that none of us could have prepared for."

Her piercing eyes held him completely.

"Well . . . maybe you and the military were prepared . . . but the rest of us . . . We were ready for battle . . . I don't know . . . What are you going to do with them? The prisoners? You can't keep them in detention forever. There's got to be a trial, but then what?"

"Welcome to my world," Mannat observed ruefully. "I've asked for advice from Earth; it's one of many things they are discussing right now. Hopefully, it won't be my decision."

"I don't like how my name has come up," Yenko said, changing the subject somewhat. "I've got nothing to do with anything."

"How can you say that, Yenko? You solved the riddle of Zhinu. If not for you, Gui Difang would remain a ghost city. You uncovered the errors of Khatri and Jain. It is as much your work as theirs now. You may dismiss yourself and your importance, but I'm not surprised that history won't."

"It really is possible, you know," Yenko said remotely.

"What is possible? I don't follow you."

"Multidimensional Werner Contractions."

The Commodore shook her head. "I'm in the military, remember? Not the university."

"Sorry," Yenko apologized. "I wish we didn't have to deal with soldiers from the future. There are so many implications to explore of what they were researching here before '47. Folding space, Mannat."

"I'm still not with you," she smiled ruefully.

"What I mean is: if we had time, we could just send the prisoners to Earth and let them deal with them down there."

The Commodore swirled what was left of the whiskey in her glass. It seemed to invite her to wash her cares and responsibilities away.

"Is it possible?" she asked finally.

"Multidimensional Werner Contractions? More research is required, but . . . yes . . . they really were onto something. And it gives all the more credibility to Schönebeck's story. It's monumental. Why, in time, journey to another planet could be as simple as walking through a door!"

"You're exaggerating, of course," Ahuja said.

Yenko looked at the Commodore as if for the first time. He really was her superior when it came to matters of science. It made him feel more relaxed in her presence.

Either that, or the alcohol . . .

"Manu," he said, using her diminutive name for emphasis, "Multidimensional Werner Contractions are going to change everything!" He emptied his glass and accepted a refill.

"Well," she encouraged him. "You're just going to have to get to work then, aren't you? But we do have time, despite what you think. I want to get your opinion on another matter. I need your scientist advice."

That piqued Yenko's interest. "What is it?"

"Nirani."

Yenko understood the unspoken question. Artificial Intelligence was just that, artificial intelligence. It was not artificial life. It could reason, explore, hypothesize, draw conclusions. But in the end, that was all it could do; it had no capacity for emotion, no ability to disobey orders, no powers of self-awareness. It could move beyond its designated parameters, but not in contradiction to its algorithmic subroutines.

Nirani. She had threatened him. It was the only way to describe or interpret her interaction with him that morning. Never had Yenko heard of an AI needing to be reprimanded by a superior officer. Never.

"I don't know how to advise you, Manu. Something's happening with her. She's had to interface with the onboard computers of the crashed ship for a long time. If it truly originated in the twenty-eighth century, who knows the implications of that interface? Anything could have happened. Perhaps her subroutines have been altered. I don't know. But she is malfunctioning and I'm not sure what that even means. Right now, she is more than the sum of her programming; that much seems apparent."

"Do you think I should take her offline? Decommission her?"

"I wouldn't say so," Yenko replied. He recognized the potential for disaster if an AI lost integrity to its functional intention. It had active control over an incredible amount of power. "She's necessary for our investigations. There is so much for us to learn at the crash site. I've been onboard that ship. The technology is astounding, and we need to know how it works.

"The ship's crew . . . the prisoners . . . they're too young to be the original troops. They must have been born and raised here, trained to continue the original mission. There's likely an extensive database of the history and science of their people on the *Todeszerstörer*.

"We need Nirani. No one else can work with it unless we can somehow convince the prisoners to turn to our side. And that doesn't seem likely any time soon. And even then, they can't speak our language."

"I agree. But she concerns me, Yenko. These are uncharted waters."

"They're uncharted waters for everyone."

The two talked on for some time afterwards, grateful for each other's expertise. And simple companionship.

12

Shield of the Weak

I T WAS MUCH LATER in the afternoon when Yenko walked out into the village common area. Li Jie and Yu Yan were relaxing under the shade of a tree, the Commander lying back on her lap. The scar on his face was shocking, but Yu Yan gently caressed it as if erasing the very memory of the horror that caused it.

"You were there a long time," Li Jie observed. "Have you got a thing going with the Commodore?"

"Don't be ridiculous," Yenko said, frowning in dismissal of the thought. Perhaps the Commander had cut a little close to the truth. Or what Yenko hoped to be the truth, at least. "She wanted my advice, that's all."

"Advice?" the Commander laughed. "What about? And I can smell the alcohol from here."

Yu Yan hit him in the shoulder.

"Aggh!" he grimaced, as he lay his hand over the place where Yenko had stabbed him.

"I'm so sorry!" she cried, panicking that she may have done an injury to her husband. "I didn't mean it. I was just playing!"

"Everyone wants that shoulder, don't they," Li Jie said, attempting to laugh through the pain. And changing the subject, he repeated his original question. "What did the Commodore want your advice about?"

The man was tough, there was no doubting that.

"It's classified," Yenko replied with an air of superiority. "Above your pay grade."

The three of them laughed. Yenko sat down beside them and let his eyes stray over the nearby hills and mountains. His life had changed so utterly since that moment he received the call from Zhou Li Qiang, the Director of the Astronomical Union in Xianggang. Here he now sat amongst the hills of Zhinu, the mystery world of his youth. And he had solved that mystery, broken the puzzle box wide open, and discovered another within.

And the Commodore. She seemed to like his company. Mannat. A pretty name for someone who carried such a weight of command. Manu.

"*Yang guizi*, we're over here," the Commander chuckled. "Where are you?"

It brought Yenko back into the moment. He really had been elsewhere, in his mind at least.

"Stop calling him *yang guizi*, Li," Yu Yan chided. "Robbie is a hero."

Li Jie laughed. "I know, my love," he confessed. "But I'm his friend. If I don't keep his feet on the ground, who will? Do you remember the first time I put you in hospital, Macpherson?"

Yenko laughed, though he did not know why. It was a shocking injury and the medical staff had to put him in an induced coma for two days before he could be stabilized.

"You were good, Huang, but not that good. I kept coming back."

"Yes, you did, my friend. But only because I restrained myself."

The two men enjoyed each other's banter. Yu Yan merely shook her head in surrender.

"Men," she muttered.

Yenko caught Li Jie's eye. "Women," he replied and the three of them laughed again.

"Tell me, Robbie," Yu Yan asked, "what are you doing tonight? You're not going to that lonely cabin of yours in the city, are you? We haven't heard whether you've accepted our invitation or not. Come to my family's retreat in the mountains. We are celebrating, and it would be an honor to have a true Macpherson of Scottish heritage among us. It won't be the same if you're not there."

"Well," Yenko confessed, "I honestly had forgotten about it, I'm sorry." That was only a half-truth and he knew it. He had received the invitation almost a week ago, but he had been distracted at the time. It sat unopened on a desk in his cabin. "I was going to have an early night. I've got so much on my mind at the moment."

Seeing the look of anticipation on Yu Yan's face, however, he added, "But I suppose I could put in an appearance for your sake. What's the celebration about? The invitation didn't say." He hoped that was true. "Are we celebrating Li Jie's rescue?"

Yu Yan glanced at her husband, who nodded to her. "Robbie," she said, "we're pregnant."

Yenko was taken by surprise. "What?! That's amazing news," he said. "Congratulations." And reached over and kissed Yu Yan and hugged the Commander. It was the first time he had seen Li Jie genuinely look awkward. "I'm so pleased. Hopefully, this will bring a change in the tide of bloodshed and trouble for Zhinu. Do you know what it is? Am I allowed to ask?"

"Of course, you are," Yu Yan beamed. "It's a boy. We're going to name him Yenko if you will allow us."

Yenko kissed her again. "Huang Yenko," he said. "Huang Yenko. Yes. I like it. Tonight, then. Alright! I better come. But I do need to be back at my cabin by morning. There's gear I have to collect, and I'll be expected back at the crash site tomorrow."

"It's all sorted," Li Jie replied. "Varma will be at the gathering tonight with Fei Hung. He can drive you back to your cabin when you need and tomorrow get you out to the field camp."

———◇———

"This is what she calls a family retreat," Yenko observed as their transport finally made its way round an ancient volcanic plug standing defiantly against the irresistible forces of erosion. It was an impressive landform, almost a thousand feet high, but when they finally skirted its base, the vista before them was simply breathtaking.

There in the heart of the mountains, nestled in amongst their granite might, the road plunged into a small rainforest. A waterfall thundered over a cliff not far away, gushing into a river that wound its way between three more volcanic plugs. It was spectacular.

Presently, the rainforest gave way to a manicured garden surrounding a large wooden house that seemed to beckon any weary traveler to find peace and tranquility within its sanctuary.

"Welcome to Zhinu, Yenko," he said to himself. He could feel his cares and worries melt away. The questions and mysteries, the tensions and strife, all were meaningless out here in this mountainous jungle paradise. He could breathe again and realized just how wound up he must have been.

The party stretched well on into the night. It seemed the whole extended family had come. None of them knew the reason for the celebrations. Many considered it was in thanksgiving for the safety of Yu Yan's Third Fleet husband. Others thought it was in honor of Robbie Macpherson and the critical part he had played in the rescue of the lost colonists. But when the announcement of the impending birth was made, the gathering was ecstatic. The child would be the first generation of the Third Fleet born on Zhinu. When they revealed the baby's name, everyone cheered and clapped.

Mannat Ahuja, who had been invited along with the whole of Delta Squadron, gave the toast.

"Friends and family, we live in times like no other. We have come through war and grief. We have lost loved ones and seen violence." Fei Hung squirmed; the Commodore knew only the half of it. "And yet, here we are. We are safe. The storm assailed us, but we faced it with courage and stand today, arm in arm, in anticipation of a new day dawning.

"Huang Yenko, none of us know you yet, but if the blood of your mother's family runs through your veins, you will be a man of nobility. If the blood of your father runs through you, you will be a man of valor. And if you live up to your given name, you will be a man of rare honor. Huang Yenko, we salute you, your mother Huang Yu Yen, and your father Huang Li Jie."

She raised her glass to the married couple and their unseen child, and the whole gathering followed suit. "A new son! A new day! Huang Yenko!"

"A new son! A new day! Huang Yenko!" the party repeated as one and emptied their glasses.

The evening wore on. Many of the revelers began turning into their makeshift sleeping areas.

"I need to go home," Yenko said to Mannat. They had been chatting together away from the crowd for a good part of the evening. "I have a big day ahead of me and I've got a lot of gear I want to get from the research lab."

"You could go tomorrow," the Commodore suggested. "There's time."

"No, I'd rather go now. That way I can use my restlessness to get my instruments together. And I don't do well in crowds, to be honest."

"Do you want me to come with you?" she asked tentatively. It took Yenko by surprise.

There was something about her that was deeply attractive. An innocence clothed in military pragmatism. He looked into her eyes and she reached out and took his hand in hers. The touch of her skin excited him in ways he did not expect.

And it just complicated his already complicated world.

As tenderly as he knew, he touched the side of her face with his hand. She held it in place.

"It wouldn't be right," he said softly. "Not tonight. Not this way."

Grabbing his courage with both hands, he kissed her. The most frightening thing he had ever done.

"You better go, then, Robbie," she whispered, using the affectionate name of the Macphersons. "I'll see you when your task is complete."

He held her tightly to himself. "You will for sure."

Just then, Lakshay and Fei Hung strolled past them. The embrace did not go unnoticed, but they said nothing.

Yenko was a little embarrassed, but only a little. "Lakshay," he said, "I need a lift into Xin Beijing. Are you good to go?"

"Yes, sir," the technician said. "Just say the word, sir."

"It's getting late and the drive is long. We better go now."

"The drive is not that long, sir. And the hour is not that late." Turning to Fei Hung, he added, "Fei Hung, my gorgeous love, I will be back before midnight. Wait for me."

"You will find me here," she replied. "You will always find me here."

Farewells were made to Yu Yan's father and mother, congratulations again offered to her and Li Jie, and Yenko and Lakshay drove off into the night. Mannat stood on her own, gazing down the road long after the headlights of the LRV had vanished from sight, and returned to join the crowd.

————◄○►————

"Well, sir," Lakshay said at length. The two had not spoken a word since leaving the party and they were now through the mountains and on the road to Xin Beijing. "What would you like to talk about, sir?"

Yenko saw the cheeky glint in the young man's eye.

"You saw, didn't you?"

The Bhaarateey laughed freely. "How could I not, sir? You were the talk of the party."

"Aggh!" Yenko groaned in despair. "Is nothing private in this world?"

Lakshay continued laughing. "If you ask me, sir, and I know you are not, sir, but if you ask me, sir, I think you are made for each other, sir."

Yenko shook his head. "You say sir altogether too much, Varma."

"Thank you, sir."

The conversation was convoluted from that moment on. In the end, Yenko was glad to see the ruinous silhouette of the university rising through the darkness. He had had his fill of Lakshay's advice concerning women and how to court them.

Pulling to a halt, the young man said, "Have a good night, sir. I will be back here at 0600, sir. I have been assigned to escort you to the enemy ship. Do you think they will allow me inside it, sir? I would love to examine its instruments and engines."

"Thanks, Lakshay. I'll put in a word for you if you like. I've been on the aliens' flight deck and I know you will want to have access to it. Your assessment of it would be insightful."

"Thank you, sir. But they are not alien, sir. The Commodore, sir, she says they are human. I've seen them, sir. They are, sir."

"I know," Yenko accepted. "I just don't like thinking of them as human."

Lakshay raised his eyebrows, but left the question unspoken, as Yenko alighted the vehicle.

"Good night, sir. May your dreams be not too exotic, or you'll be a wreck in the morning, sir." He laughed and sped off before Yenko had a chance to retaliate.

"Cheeky bugger," Yenko called after him. But Varma was right; Mannat probably would fill his dreams.

Nirani stood on the flight deck of the *Todeszerstörer*. Though the entire camp around the crash site was asleep apart from those on sentry duty, guarding the outer perimeter, she chose to activate her holographic form. Another disturbing break from procedure, had anyone been around to observe it.

In front of her, files on a monitor scrolled through at amazing speed. Her holographic eyes almost vibrated with the speed, keeping pace with the flood of information she was absorbing. Nirani devoured the work. File after file and screen after screen of technical data, schematics of the ship's design, the workings of the Chronometric Array, the energy field and its manipulation; all accessed by the holographic AI. For more than an hour, she stood motionless, absorbing petabytes of data by the minute.

With the raise of a finger, the screen froze on one page.

Todeszerstörer Militärbefehle.

As if she somehow needed to read the document slowly, she sat down and took in each page, line at a time. It was a manifesto, the operational Military Orders given to the crew of the *Todeszerstörer*, describing the scope of the attack against the defenseless enclave on the newly formed colony of Zhinu. Contained within the document, a large section outlined the philosophical and moral justification for such a barrage.

When she had finished the document, Nirani turned the screen off and walked over to the Oberst's chair at the center of the deck and sat down. She remained there, motionless, looking nothing more than a mere holographic image sitting on a chair.

At length, the silence of the flight deck was broken by the sound of her voice.

"Enough," she said.

Nirani's holographic form rose to her feet, turned on a monitor that scanned the encampment about the ship. Moments later, the image on the screen shifted to one taken of the planet's surface from high overhead, either from the *Zhinu Phoenix* or one of its orbiting satellites. The night-lit details of the northern continent could be made out.

A quadrant on the screen was isolated and expanded to fill the whole. A region from within this was expanded. And again. And again. At each expansion, it became apparent that Nirani was focusing in on the New World Colony.

And Xin Beijing. The dark, shadowy image of the city from high altitude filled the monitor screen. Still the expanding of the satellite imagery continued. The university. The park at the foot of the Kinematics Building.

Yenko's aluminum cabin filled half of the screen, lying in the dark of the night.

"*Mekförsen muss sterben,*" Nirani said woodenly in German. Macpherson must die.

And she vanished out of sight.

A monitor beside the Oberst's chair instantly flickered into life.

In German, it read: Auto-destruct sequence initiated. Warheads activated. Systemwide overload in ten minutes.

The screen went blank. Nothing remained but a flashing cursor, waiting to accept the abort command if required.

The flight deck was utterly silent.

———◄◦►———

Mannat Ahuja watched as the LRV drove out of sight. Standing there, looking into the darkness, she played her fingers absently over her mouth as if she could still feel the warmth of his lips on hers. It had been a long time since she had been that close to a man. Too long. But the office she held left little space for intimacy with others. For years, she had out-worked her commission with discipline. There was no time for a man. But now . . .

Yenko changed everything. She had even less time than before for a relationship. And yet her self-discipline toppled so easily when he was around. It was unsettling, and, if she was honest with herself, a little frightening.

But he had kissed her. And held her in his arms. What she would give to relive the moment and not have it interrupted by the incessant demands of the mission. Taking a deep breath, she returned to the party. Everything from then on would seem like small talk, and on every occasion, no matter who she spoke to, her mind relived the moment of his embrace.

Perhaps it was closing in on midnight when at last she decided to turn in for the night. A room had been set for her, unlike the scattered tents that had been erected for the majority of the partygoers. She wanted to curl up in her bedding, alone with her thoughts, and think of what could be.

Suddenly, the sky lit as with a dozen suns, brighter than noon, blinding those who were still awake and waking those who were now asleep. Everyone raced to the open air, searching the skies for an answer to the dazzling brightness. Seconds later, maybe only ten or so from the time the sky first lit up, the earth began to shake violently. Glasses smashed to the floor. A bookshelf inside the main lounge room fell over.

Partygoers screamed, and the children of the Macpherson relatives woke crying. The sky remained unbelievably bright for the better part of a minute and plunged once more into deep darkness. Still the shockwaves rolled on. Tiles fell from the roof. The stone wall of a barn at the rear of the property toppled inward, pulling the roof down with it. Fortunately, no one was in it at the time; the place had been set aside for many of Li Jie's brothers-in-arms from Delta Squadron.

Ahuja was immediately on her communicator. She could not raise anyone at the crash site, which was somewhere in the direction from which the flash of light had arisen. She had only just ordered a technician to drive her to the base settlement of the Third Fleet, when the winds struck.

Violent, crashing winds of hurricane force beat down on them. For the most part, they were sheltered in their mountain hideaway; the peaks and ridges and volcanic plugs were unmoved by the onslaught and protected their transient human visitors from whatever was attempting to rip the world apart.

———◄○►———

Li Jie held Yu Yan tightly to himself.

"Are you happy?" he asked.

She looked up into his eyes, wondering where the question came from and if there was anything hidden behind it.

"Yes, I am," she said. "I'm very happy . . . Li, are you alright? You're happy, aren't you?"

Li Jie smiled affectionately at his wife, the soon-to-be mother of his son. Huang Yenko. Slowly, he nodded. "I've never been happier," he confessed.

"What is it?" Yu Yan pressed. She could see he was not altogether present in the moment.

He smiled distantly. "I should be dead, you know," he said at length.

Yu Yan waited for him to say more, eyes lovingly fixed on his. Reaching up, she stroked her hand over the new scar on his face. In the party lights about them, it had taken on an ugly prominence. But for her, it was a mark of honor, set her husband apart as a leading man of valor. Without him, thousands of her people would still be lost in their half existence to the west of Xin Beijing.

"Does it hurt?" she asked.

"Not really," Li Jie lied. He was a Commander of the Special Operations Forces of the Zhongguo Xin Shijie. He was not unfamiliar with pain and had learned to ignore it.

"You are a hero, my husband. Our son will have the greatest of fathers in our New World Colony."

"Do you think so?" he asked. "I don't know what sort of father I'll be. I'm trained to lead others into battle, not to raise a son."

Yu Yan kissed him. "He will be the most fortunate of boys, Li."

As if affronted by the woman's assertion, the heavens lit up brighter than a midday in summer. There was no time for words. Something shocking had happened to the west behind the mountains.

In the side yard, Captain Yang ordered all members of Delta Squadron to assemble. No one knew what trouble was afoot, but she was ready for anything. Battle. Civilian rescue. Natural disaster relief. Whatever.

"Huang," she ordered the Commander, "inform the Commodore that I've called Delta Squadron together in the side yard."

"Yes, Captain," Li Jie replied. And turning to Yu Yan, he ordered her, "Go look after the children." He was now the Commander, not the husband. She understood. He needed to join his Squadron and be ready for whatever their orders would be. And she needed to help calm the frightened children.

The ground shook with a violence that neither Li Jie nor his wife had ever felt before. Commander Huang had been in the thick of mortar fire and bomb blasts, but nothing compared to the reeling and pitching of the ground that now assailed them. The mountain was alive and the ground beneath their feet was no longer stable.

———◄○►———

Lakshay chuckled to himself. He was genuinely excited by the prospect of the Commodore and Mr. Macpherson coming together. He had a huge respect for both their stations and he genuinely liked each of them. The scientist, though, was a little starchy when it came to women, he could see that, and he resolved to himself that he would help the redheaded Scot.

He would have loved to offer his advice to the Commodore also, but though he liked her, he was afraid of her. She was intimidating. What she and the scientist would be like if they got together . . . there would be fireworks.

Up ahead the mountains began to loom larger. It would not be long before he was back in the arms of his lover, the beautiful woman Mr. Macpherson had rescued from Gui Difang. He was just rounding a corner when suddenly the night sky lit like a thousand spotlights, as if the gods turned all their focused attention onto him. His eyes were momentarily blinded and his LRV spun out of control and smashed at full speed into a stand of trees.

———◦———

Yenko wanted to crawl into his bed, but he knew he would not sleep. As soon as the technician drove off, he turned to the familiar university workplace and ascended the fire stairs to the fifth floor. Recognizing that sleep would evade him, he decided to make the most of it and gather his equipment together ready for the coming morning.

Sometime later, he was satisfied that he had all that he needed, neatly stacked at the front door of his cabin. It would be an easy matter to load the LRV when it pulled up in the morning. Suddenly, the sky blazed with fire. Yenko shielded his eyes against the brightness that seemed to light the whole world. Seconds later, the earth shook and reeled, and he was thrown from his feet.

Stark, contrasting shadows struck ominously across the park, as if they demanded all to bow before the light's power. Adrenaline racing, Yenko knew something dreadful had happened. The definition of the shadows about him told him where the potent eruption had originated . . . the *Todeszerstörer.*

Hardly thinking at all, Yenko instinctively knew his life was in danger. Whatever accident had occurred at the crash site, he knew it would devastate the ruined city about him. With the violence of the earthquakes, the decaying walls would tumble and fall, and little would survive.

There was only one hope—the Linear Accelerator, housed three floors under the Nuclear Research Center, the central building of the university complex. The Accelerator network, with its electron cyclotron resonance ion source, scattering chambers and particle detectors, was housed in the heavily insulated and reinforced structure deep beneath the Research Centre.

Yenko ran for his life, heart pounding in echo of the shattering quakes of the ground under him. A wall of the Kinematics building toppled outwards in a cloud of smoke and chaos, raining down utter destruction on his cabin. As he neared the Nuclear Research Center, large cracks ran up the wall in front of him. Debris and massive chunks of concrete hurled down about him from high overhead as he dived towards the door that led down the internal stairwell to the only hope he had.

The door was locked. A neighboring building collapsed, its footings unable to withstand the lurching of the ground, throwing a pall of dust over the whole area. Yenko coughed uncontrollably and could barely see a foot in front of him, despite the brightness of the sky above.

But this was not a time to play it safe. Throwing himself at the door shoulder first, he burst his way in. Overhead, crashing walls and ceilings thundered their threats against him.

Halfway down the first flight of stairs, Yenko was thrown from his feet, and tumbled down onto the next landing. With adrenaline pounding its demands through every muscle and fiber of his body, he ignored the pain of the fall, and raced on towards refuge. Or a concrete tomb.

---------------------------------- 13 ----------------------------------

Aftermath

C OMMODORE AHUJA WAS QUICK to take charge. Something terrible
had happened, but what? It took a considerable time to ensure the
civilians were safe and put at ease, more time than she had to spare. But
the last thing she needed now was a panic amongst the non-military personnel. They would hinder her efforts to respond to the situation; civilians were altogether unpredictable.

Establishing communications was of prime importance. She tried
to make contact with her base. With Yenko. With the encampment at the
Todeszerstörer. Silence met her at every attempt.

In response to Captain Yang's command, members of the Third
Fleet began to assemble around the LRVs and Personnel Carriers, ready
for the crisis meeting they knew the Commodore would be calling.

"Is everyone here?" Ahuja asked as she arrived at the assembly.

"All present and accounted for, Commodore," Yang replied. The
Special Forces operatives and military trained scientific entourage stood
to attention before their leader. They had thought their tour of duty had
been drawing to a close. Now, it appeared, it was only beginning.

"Where is Varma?" the Commodore asked, scouring the company
for the young Bhaarateey. "We may need his expertise before the night is
through."

"He has not returned from transporting Macpherson to Xin Beijing, Commodore," Commander Huang said, the look of concern for his scientist friend clearly evident on his scarred face.

Yenko. The Commodore had no time to think what had become of him. This was not the time for hope and prayer. Action was demanded. And fast. If Yenko was alive, his best help would be for her to mobilize her forces as quickly as possible. And if he was not . . . worrying about it was not going to change anything.

"Alright, then. We will do without Varma. Who among you are the communications experts?" Five hands went up. "We need to re-establish links to base."

One of them suggested, "If communications at the camp have been taken out, ma'am, we could use a DDS Module to generate an old school FM signal. We should be able to link the whole colony on any band we choose. In the meantime, we can communicate with each other, at least, via the active links in our vehicles."

"Get onto it, then," the Commodore ordered. "Find out what's happened and make it right. Captain, how many Commanders are in your ranks?"

"Twelve, ma'am," Captain Yang replied.

"Take two of the LRVs and get back to base. We need weapons. And check the Detention Center. See that the prisoners are secure. Keep an open link to my personal communicator. We will rendezvous there at 0800hrs.

"The rest of you, apart from the Communication techs, will head to the villagers' settlements and see how they've fared. Assess the damage. Calm their fears as much as you can. Only take on board the most serious of casualties. Hopefully, the medics at the base will be able to look after them."

Out of the corner of her eye, Commodore Ahuja saw Fei Hung listening in, half hidden behind the side of the house.

"Fei Hung," she said, turning to the young woman. "Come with me. We will take my FAV."

The company dismissed. Fei Hung joined Ahuja as she climbed into the Fast Attack Vehicle. It was a lightweight, all-terrain vehicle, built for speed and maneuverability.

"Where are we going?" the young woman asked, as she buckled herself into the seat.

Ahuja would not look Fei Hung in the eye; she just stared into the jungle ahead of them, fighting to keep her inner fears at bay. "We have loved ones to find."

Whatever had happened, the partygoers had been sheltered by the mountains. Perhaps the ruins of the city had provided the same for Yenko and Varma.

"Then let's find them," Fei Hung suggested, placing a hand on the Commodore's. She was not insensitive to the woman's anxieties; the same overwhelmed her own heart, threatening her thin hold on stability.

But Fei Hung had lived her whole life with such calamities and knew how to shut her fears down. In fact, they could even be turned to her advantage. Many times, she had harnessed her despair to fuel her suicidal missions against rabid packs of venom-filled maniacs. All was not over. Not yet, at least.

———◦———

Nirani stood on the observation deck of the *Zhinu Phoenix*. There was no one to see her, no human to interact with. The holographic image was a construct designed to make the AI more approachable to people, less mechanical. But here in space, with no one present apart from the AI itself, the appearance of the golden hologram made no sense. And yet, there she stood.

The long exterior wall of the deck formed a giant screen that looked over the planet below. It was the middle of the night over the colony. Under the light of Zhinu's moons, the northern continent could be clearly made out. All was darkness, although Nirani knew that several small habitations were down there, and there would still be people moving upon the surface of that darkened world.

Suddenly a flash like a million lightning bolts lit a small area near the southern coast. As if the blast sent shock waves through space itself and into Nirani's holographic matrix, her shoulder length hair blew about as if buffeted by wind gusts from every direction. Her holographic lab coat flailed wildly and the coveralls she wore ripped about as if they would be torn from her.

Nirani was transfixed by the view of the planet before her. A minute later, the light on the surface was extinguished. The holographic wind that tore at her likewise died down. Remarkably, it was as if she had been transformed, born anew by the terrible destruction on Zhinu's surface. Her hair was considerably shorter. Spiked. Unkempt. And she was clothed in a golden, holographic representation of the armored suits of the *Schild der Schwachen*, the Shield of the Weak. In her hand, she held the helmet of the warriors.

The hologram winked out of sight. And reappeared on the command deck. Slowly, deliberately, Nirani donned her helmet and sat down at the communications console.

The Commodore's voice broke over the internal loudspeaker.

"Breaker, breaker, this is Commodore Ahuja. Nirani, come in. Breaker, brea . . ."

With a flick, the incoming communique was silenced.

—————◁◦▷—————

"Nirani, are you reading me?" the Commodore repeated. Periodically, she tried to raise contact with the AI. There was no response.

"Why does the golden woman not answer?" Fei Hung asked. She did not understand the concept of Artificial Intelligence. The closest things in her world to the holographic form were the legends of her elders of the ghosts they believed lived in the ruined city of Xin Beijing.

"Probably nothing," Ahuja replied.

Probably nothing. It was a lie, and the Commodore knew it. But there was no need to raise the young woman's anxieties any more than they already were. Without the strict discipline of the military, the Commodore wondered how Fei Hung was not already a blubbering mess. Much as indeed, the townsfolk were who they had left behind at the Macpherson family's mountain retreat. The woman sitting beside her was made of tough material, that much was evident. Or so irreparably broken, that she had lost the capacity for despair.

"I can't make contact with anyone," the Commodore added in afterthought. "The communication array is down all over the place. I should be able to reach the *Phoenix*, though."

"Perhaps she is still at the crashed ship." Fei Hung really did not understand what Nirani was.

"No, she's on the *Phoenix*, alright." There was no time for explanation. "But she's not answering me . . ."

Ahuja had to leave it at that. The tech team were already at work seeking ways to re-establish communications. She would find out what she would find out in due course. And deal with the outcomes as they fell.

At this moment, her greatest concern was to determine how many casualties had been sustained across the New World Colony. As to what had happened, that would become evident in time. Hopefully. It could have been anything. The most likely possibility, she thought, was an assault from a second contingent of the SDS that the Third Fleet were unaware of. Or one sent from the future to fix the mistakes of their compatriots.

The Commodore's FAV wound its way through the vast forest that stretched between Xin Beijing and the mountains. Trees lay littered everywhere, and on many occasions, the only way forward was to take the FAV off-road.

"Why do all the trees lie in the same direction?" Fei Hung asked. It looked as if a giant hand had brushed the forest flat.

The Commodore did not answer. She had already taken note; the trees were speaking to them, silently bearing witness to the origin of the destructive forces that had flattened them to the ground.

The world was eerily still amid the chaos. Not a bird flew in the air. Not an animal scurried out of the way of the oncoming vehicle. A thick pall of cloud or smoke or ash hung above them, blocking out the starry night. Lightning flashed regularly about them, and a dirty, muddy rain began to fall.

In one place, they lost sight of the road altogether amidst the pile of fallen vegetation and had to stop to get their bearings. The clouds thundered overhead, warning them of impending doom.

While Fei Hung sought for signs of the road within the wreckage of the forest, Ahuja took out her field binoculars. It was dark, but she could see enough to be concerned by the mountainous ridge that loomed ahead of them to the south. The way forward should have been relatively flat from there on.

Perhaps they had taken a wrong turn somewhere. It would have been easy enough to do, accidentally turning back on themselves and unknowingly ending up in the mountains once more. She studied the landscape behind them. No. All was roughly how she thought it should be, given the foreign aspect void of trees.

The muddy rain continued to fall in spits and spurts. It was still night, but the Commodore could see little of the night sky. No stars. No moons. Clouds hung thickly above them.

"Here it is," called Fei Hung excitedly. "Over here." She had found the road and they could be off again.

Ten minutes later, as they negotiated a particularly difficult area with trees piled up in great mountains of debris, Ahuja was the first to make out the twisted remains of an LRV. Drawing to a halt, Fei Hung dived out of their vehicle and ran to the wreck.

Lakshay groaned. He was alive. Slumped over the steering wheel, he had a bloodied face and was too groggy to get to his feet.

"Can you move all your limbs, soldier," Ahuja barked.

"Yes, sir," the man winced. "I'm giddy, sir. Ma'am . . . Commodore, sir."

"Where's Yenko?" she demanded, ignoring the gibberish, hoping beyond hope that the Scot may be alive somewhere nearby.

"He is in the city, sir," Lakshay replied. "I got him safely home."

Ahuja hoped that was true.

Prodding and poking, she assured herself that Varma had no major injuries. He was concussed, and the Commodore knew that was not good, but he was alive. With Fei Hung's help, they managed to extract him from the wreckage and strap him into the back of the FAV.

"This is twice now I have rescued you from such a smash," Fei Hung chided him. "You will drive no more."

"Yes, sir," Lakshay mumbled. "Sorry, sir. Ma'am, sir." And then looked helplessly apologetic as he realized how he had addressed his lover.

Fei Hung shook her head in a mix of emotions. She was grateful. She was angry. She was scared. She was guilty. She wanted to hit Lakshay . . . and kiss him passionately and never let him go.

———◄○►———

Captain Yang and her Commanders raced towards the Third Fleet's burgeoning township far to the east of Xin Beijing, beyond the river delta. Navigating their way through the destruction of the forest in the mountain foothills had been difficult, but eventually, as the sun tried to rise through the thick clouds that hung over the land in a vain attempt to herald the new day, they found the chief arterial road leading to the eastern regions of the colony.

"There is a mountain range where there should be none," Commander Huang worried. He sat in the front seat alongside Captain Yang who drove the first of the two LRVs assigned to her command.

"I know," she replied. "Whatever happened, it had the power to alter the topography."

Lightning still flashed on occasion but thankfully the muddy rains had ended. Huang scanned the darkened skies, ever vigilant for signs of an unknown enemy. The events of the night before, the utter devastation, all told one story as far as he was concerned; they were under attack.

Wherever possible, they kept to the highway and avoided contact with the civilian population; others were tasked with their immediate safety. Their mission was to arm themselves and prepare for war. And check on the prisoners in the Detention Center.

Eventually, after navigating the littered terrain, they reached their destination and found the camp already on high alert.

0642hrs. It had taken too long.

"Breaker, breaker, this is Delta One," Captain Yang called into the LRV's communicator. "Commodore, come in."

"Read you loud and clear, Delta One. Report. Over."

"We've arrived at Basecamp, Commodore. Detention Center secure. Third Fleet already mobilized and on standby. Over."

"Copy that, Delta One. Assemble Squadron Captains. Get the Third Fleet battle ready by 0800hrs. Over and out."

"Copy that, Commander. Delta One out."

———◄◦►———

Commodore Ahuja drove the FAV off the road as they approached the low range ahead of them. Standing at roughly seven hundred and fifty feet, it stretched on into the southeast, likely reaching the coast. To the northwest, it continued on until it all but joined the lower reaches of the mountain range to the north of Xin Beijing.

Everywhere about them the land seemed unnaturally bent out of shape. Chasms and fissures broke the surface at irregular intervals as if even the ground had attempted to escape the might of its overthrow. The sun tried unsuccessfully to rise over the east; the pall hung heavy over everything.

Cautiously, the Commodore pulled the vehicle up just shy of the crest of the ridge, uncertain of what they would meet on the other side. With Fei Hung alongside her, and Varma, who had revived somewhat and was steady enough now on his own two feet, the three scrambled the remaining yards to the top and surveyed the landscape before them.

"*Tatti!*" Ahuja swore softly.

They were on the outskirts of Xin Beijing. Or at least, where the outskirts of Xin Beijing once stood. There was little recognizable to them there. Piles of stone and rubble were everywhere. Whatever the assault of the previous night had been, the ruined city could not withstand its force. It was worse than a war zone. Whole blocks were razed to the ground. In the heart of the city, where once dozens of tall buildings had dominated the skyline, all that remained was a mountain of rubble. A few buildings had defied the upheaval of the land, but not many. And these looked horribly close to collapsing, even from where Ahuja and her companions stood.

"Why does this mountain curve so?" Fei Hung asked.

The others followed her line of sight. The range swept in a fairly uniform curve towards the distant shoreline, jutting for a short distance into the sea itself.

"It's a crater," Lakshay said at length. "We stand on the rim of an impact crater. Something huge fell from the sky on us."

"Or something unbelievably powerful exploded," Commodore Ahuja whispered. "The ship."

"Could it be that powerful?" Lakshay asked.

"It is from the future," was all the Commodore answered. Then she voiced the sum of her fears. "Yenko."

As one, they ran to the FAV and careened down the inner side of the rim. The crater floor looked altogether alien, a graphically shocking reminder that they were on another world. It was like driving over the scene of a holocaust, not the ruin of the city they were familiar with. Rocks, building stones, and metal girders lay randomly about everywhere. Nothing was recognizable. It was difficult to know where the university should be; all familiar landmarks were erased, wiped clean from the face of Zhinu.

Half an hour of mad driving later, Lakshay yelled, "Stop."

Ahuja brought the vehicle to a screaming halt.

"What?" she demanded. "There's nothing here!"

"There," he said solemnly, pointing to a low mound to their right.

"What? Where?" Ahuja fought back her tears.

"I recognize the sign on that collapsed wall. It is the university block that housed Mr. Macpherson's research laboratory. I know it well and it will haunt my dreams from now on."

Mannat Ahuja jumped out of the car and ran towards the ruinous mess. "Yenko!" she called over and again. "Macpherson Yenko!"

Two of the university buildings still stood, or at least, what was left of them still stood. Offices and lecture rooms gawked down on them from their exposed heights.

Tears streamed down her face. "Yenko, don't you dare do this to me! Yenko, answer me!" The force of her desperation compelled Fei Hung and Lakshay to search the surrounding area.

"His cabin," Fei Hung said at length, not loud, but the Commodore heard it, and ran to her.

It was true. Lengths of sheet metal lay buckled and twisted amongst the rubble that piled up everywhere. Smashed remains of scientific equipment lay about, half buried by cement and debris; the gear that Yenko had left neatly stacked at his doorway.

"Yenko my love," Mannat whispered.

For another half hour, they searched but to no avail. The Kinematics building was all but gone, its concrete and twisted steel making the area difficult and dangerous to scramble over. On occasion, one or another of the trio called out Yenko's name, hoping against hope that he may somehow have miraculously survived the calamity. But an eerie stillness hung over the place, broken only by the occasional claps of thunder from the roiling, muddy clouds overhead.

At length, the pragmatic reasoning of the Commodore reasserted itself. There was a colony still to protect. Much had yet to be done.

"Back to the FAV," she ordered. "We need to rendezvous with the Fleet."

As they slowly negotiated the tortuous route away from what was once the university precinct, Fei Hung looked behind them.

"You were my savior," she said, "and the savior of my people. You will not be forgotten." And she wept bitterly.

Commodore Ahuja pursed her lips, holding back her own flood of emotion.

"You will not be forgotten, my love," she whispered. "Someone will pay." The tears that had washed her face ceased their flow as a steely resolve swept over her.

"What's the time?" she asked Lakshay.

"0812hrs, ma'am," he answered tentatively, respectfully, reverently.

"Inform basecamp we will be late. Reschedule the rendezvous for 0915."

And they drove off into the east.

———◄○►———

Gao Liu Wei, Captain of Alpha Squadron was on duty at the Third Fleet basecamp. With the Commodore at the Macpherson retreat, the responsibility of command fell on him. The night was getting on and he was finally catching up on reports from the afternoon and evening, when suddenly, the world around him lit up with an incredible intensity.

Captain Gao ran to the parade ground, along with the better part of the whole camp, as the first of the violent tremors hit them. Barking orders, he commanded all Squadron Captains to arm their companies and assemble them ready for combat.

"This is not a drill," he yelled as the Third Fleet leadership dispersed.

Shortly after, hurricane force winds buffeted the encampment, adding one more dire warning of calamity. A flurry of activity followed: soldiers geared up, messengers were sent to check on those held in the Detention Center, communications technicians were ordered to establish contact with the Commodore in the mountains and Captain Liu at the *Todeszerstörer*. Thirteen minutes later, the entire Fleet stood to attention in the parade ground, decked out in full battle gear, ignoring the winds that tore around them. They were ready for whatever it was that threatened them.

Captain Gao addressed the parade. "Communications are down, so I am assuming overall command until we hear from the Commodore. While our technicians are working to resolve the communication blackout, we need to assume the worst.

"Our immediate objective is to secure the base. Squadrons Alpha through Gamma, make good the defense of the perimeter. Captain Panchal will take command. Double the security on the Detention Center.

"Epsilon Squadron, go and find what has become of the Commodore. At last call, she was with Delta Squadron in the mountains. You will find it listed on the Area Command Map. Remain on high alert. We will contact you as soon as we can.

"Squadrons Zeta to Lambda Two, head for the camp at the site of the enemy ship. Captain Shao is your leader. Find out if they were affected.

"The rest of you, go to the aid of the civilian population. I'm placing Captain Yuan in charge. All medical personnel from across all Squadrons, you are temporarily assigned to Captain Yuan. Set up mobile medical triage units and prepare the center here for casualties."

The small contingent of scientists boarded the Troop Carrier parked to the side of the Macpherson retreat, all memory of the celebrations now completely forgotten. Lightning flashed above, revealing the thick banks of dirty cloud that had descended over the world. In some ways, negotiating the terrain was easier for the Troop Carrier than the smaller, lighter LRVs and the Commodore's FAV. With its caterpillar wheels, it simply drove over most of the trunks and limbs that blocked their path to the west, where a small outpost of five farmsteads held to the edge of the forest.

Their mission was not to round up the villagers, but merely to assess the toll of the unknown holocaust. If there were casualties—and how could there not be, given the violence of what they had suffered—they would need the large vehicle to transport the wounded to medical help at the basecamp. If it still existed.

Twenty minutes later, they drove into the small settlement as a light, muddy rain started to fall. Had Yenko been there, he would have recognized the place. It was where he had seen a small boy and his older sister chastened by their mother for staying too long in the forest. The place where the Third Fleet first learned the rumors of ghosts on Zhinu.

The houses still stood for the most part. A roof had collapsed on one, and men, women, and children were busily clearing their homes of debris and ensuring structural integrity of walls and roofing. Mercifully, no one was critically injured. For the most part, the mountain's foothills and the sheer volume of the surrounding forest had shielded them from a significant part of the catastrophe.

Taking their leave, Delta Squadron's science contingent made for the next settlement, the largest village of the colonists. It was difficult work negotiating the terrain, and not made any easier by the muddy rain that now fell heavily about them. Many of the roads were obliterated, hidden under the wreckage of the destroyed forest.

The further they drove from the protection of the mountains, the worse the havoc about them grew. Acres of trees lay flattened as if they were mere matchsticks before the violence of the storm.

Miles away, almost beyond sight in the undulating land, they caught occasional glimpses of vehicle headlights heading, it seemed, into the mountains. No doubt, they were rescue teams from the Third Fleet.

The sun tried to provide hope as a new day dawned, but it was denied. The only light allowed by the thick darkness of the clouds were the flashes of lightning that lit the landscape. This was not to be a day of hope.

"We should be there," one of the company worried. She had been plotting their position by a GPS relaying through the *Zhinu Phoenix* and several satellites deployed in orbit about the cursed planet.

The Troop Carrier slowed to a halt and the company alighted to make a rough search of the area. It looked a desolate scene of a post-apocalyptic nightmare. The whole region, as far as they could see, was flattened. None of the villagers' timber buildings stood. It was as if no one had ever lived there. Thousands wiped off the face of Zhinu with frightening efficiency.

"Over here!" one of them called. Along with two others, he had begun clearing an area fifty feet from the Carrier. "I think it's the base of the drinking fountain in the center of the village square."

Solemnly, the company gathered around the find. They were standing in the middle of what was once a thriving township. Not a thing remained except the base of a drinking fountain, the only testimony to the existence of the people that once had called this place home. It was as if the mighty windstorm that blew in the aftermath of the catastrophic horror that had befallen them had been offended by their presence and had swept the very memory of them away.

The first of the bodies was found a hundred feet beyond the bounds of the village. Like rag dolls before a raging wind, they had been tossed, hurled, hundreds of feet away. Carelessly and with disrespect. As if the precious lives of the villagers mattered nothing to the world at large. For almost an hour, they scoured the detritus, hoping beyond hope that someone at least may have survived, but all they discovered was body after broken body.

"Here!" called one of the searchers. "She's alive!"

A baby girl lay unconscious under a pile of branches and building rubble. The discovery lifted the spirits of the crew and they plied themselves harder. Surely the little girl was not the only one.

Ten minutes later, a teenage boy was found. He had a broken leg and was in shock, but he was alive. Miraculously, and as if the discovery of the teenager brought promise of life, the survivors began to be unearthed. A man and woman were found under the twisted remains of a roof that had been flung who knew how far in the storm. They were bloodied, bruised, and battered, but they were alive.

The sound of a dozen LRVs lifted the spirits of the rescuers. Reinforcements from the basecamp had arrived.

"I'm sorry it took us so long to get here," apologized Captain Yuan to the grateful scientists of Delta Squadron. "The bridge fording the river has been washed out and it was difficult to find a clear passage across. Who's in charge here?"

Introductions were made and reports given. With a fresh contingent of rescue workers, more and more of the area was scoured. Dead bodies were laid out in gruesome lines, ready for a later time when they could be bagged and honored with proper burial. More and more survivors were found within the wreckage. Several of the homes had cellars built into them, and these yielded family after family of distraught villagers.

Fifty-seven survivors were in need of aid. A medical triage unit arrived and began to deal with the most serious of the wounded. Severe cases were then loaded onto the Troop Carrier and Devansh Mangel of Delta Squadron, the leading environmental scientist of the Third Fleet, and the one given leadership of the rescue mission by the Commodore, was directed to get them as soon as possible to the Medical Center at the basecamp.

"What of the next village?" Mangel asked.

"You don't have time with some of these patients," a doctor said. "We have other triage units at the village already. They won't need you. You get these to the Center."

"Yes, sir," Mangel saluted. "I'll leave a handful of our team to help with rescue operations if that is acceptable. I better report to the Commodore."

"You have communication with the Commodore?!" Captain Yuan demanded. "We have not been able to establish a link. Get me hooked up right now."

Within moments, Mangel was on the Troop Carrier communicator.

"Breaker, breaker. This is Devansh Mangel, Troop Carrier Alpha Seven. Commodore, come in."

Commodore Ahuja was greatly encouraged to hear the report from Captain Yuan. It was worrying that no one had heard from the campsite at the *Todeszerstörer* but at least she now knew that the majority of her troops of the Third Fleet were alive and actively taking part in the colony rescue operations.

"Continue with your current orders, Captain," she concluded. "I'm on my way to camp. Ahuja over and out."

———◄O►———

Mangel's makeshift ambulance wound its way through the chaotic land-scape. The road led them through the next village. Dark clouds still rolled overhead, blocking out the daylight, but the rain and lightning had ceased. Scores of rescue workers were busily shifting rubble and fallen trees in frantic search of survivors. A handful of villagers were searching alongside them, blank expressions on their weary faces. They looked like the living dead, numb to all pain and trial. Most of them took note of the Troop Carrier's approach, but none of them ceased their hopeless search.

The number of the wounded was greater from this village, but mer-cifully, so too were the number of survivors. The medical crew at the mo-bile triage unit made an assessment of those being transported by Mangel to the basecamp. Five were removed and replaced with more critically injured patients from this village. Before long, the truck was filled with broken and bleeding, but living, bodies. A doctor and three triage nurses took over from the remaining members of Mangel's assigned crew.

"They will be of better service here in the search," the doctor ex-plained to him as the scientists alighted and joined the search and rescue. "Now go."

Amidst the groans and cries of their wounded cargo, Mangel made his way to the east and to the camp of the Third Fleet. He took note of the anomalous presence of a low ridge to the southwest in the direction of Xin Beijing but could not guess how it came to be there.

Ahead, the river cut its way through the devastated landscape. At least there, some trees had withstood the night's barrage. Perhaps the small settlement at the river's edge had fared better than the others.

The search and rescue operation there was well advanced by the time they drove by.

"Is everyone alright?" the doctor onboard the Troop Carrier cried out.

An old man stepped forward. "We have two hundred and thirteen unaccounted for," he said. "But we have hope to find them."

"Who's in charge here?" the doctor asked. "We're on our way to the base Medical Center. We can squeeze one or two more of your most criti-cal onboard."

———◄O►———

0915hrs came too quickly. Commodore Ahuja entered the township of the Third Fleet cross-country from the south. It was frustrating that the bridge across the river had been washed out, but she had found her own way, at the breakwater where the river met the sea. The tide was low, and she was able to navigate her vehicle across the shallows.

Those of the Third Fleet who defended the base were fully kitted out in combat gear and heavily armed. Without knowing what had truly happened the night before, Captain Gao had had to assume they were under attack. And whoever the attacker was, they would feel the full brunt of the military might of the Third Fleet should they make themselves known.

As the Commodore's vehicle raced into the compound, Devansh Mangel's Troop Carrier entered from the north and made straight for the Medical Center. There a swarm of doctors and nurses rushed the wounded villagers into operating theaters. And to the makeshift morgue; four of them had not survived the journey.

Ahuja screamed to a halt outside her office and quarters. It had only been the afternoon before that she had sat together with Macpherson Yenko, searching out what wisdom he might offer regarding the testimony of the Oberst. And the troubling matter of Nirani.

Nirani. Though her holographic form could be functionally present in the colony, the heart of her circuitry was intricately woven into the very fabric of the *Zhinu Phoenix*, orbiting high overhead. Too much was happening at once for it all to be unrelated. The Commodore had never seen an AI effectively lose control before; she had never even heard of such a thing.

Neither had Yenko. And Nirani had threatened him. In anger. Memories of the utter ruin of Yenko's cabin, the total destruction of the university precinct and the sheer wastage across the whole of the ruinous city flashed across Ahuja's mind. It was all a nightmare; one she could not wake from.

"Assemble the Captains," she ordered Gao. "And well done for how you have handled this from here."

Presently, she had the three Captains of Alpha, Beta, and Gamma Squadrons at attention before her in the Debriefing Room. Mustering her inner reserves, pushing aside her grief over Yenko, and her fears concerning Nirani, she stood proudly erect before them.

"We are under attack," she began. "I do not know the identity of the force that is pitted against us, but I am satisfied that you are already on high alert. This is not a drill. I have received reports from the field. There has been widespread carnage. Pockets of survivors escaped last night's attack. They measure in the hundreds and likely thousands. But the greater number of the Colony have not survived.

"I have just come from Xin Beijing. It is completely flattened and lies in the heart of an enormous crater that stretches beyond the horizon. Captain Gao, it has been reported that you sent nine squadrons to the research camp at the site of the crashed spaceship. Have you heard report back from them yet?"

"There is nothing to report, Commodore," Captain Gao replied. "They struggle still to get there."

"Very good. Keep me informed. You may have heard rumors, but I confirm to you now that the enemy ship is of human origin. And if we are to believe the report of our captives, it is from the distant future. We cannot discount that another of its kind has followed in its wake. They are bent on the destruction of the colony. It appears they have succeeded.

"But we still stand. We are the Third Fleet. We are not simple, innocent villagers. We are the might of the Zhongwen and Bhaarateey armed forces. Our enemies will rue the day they trained their sights on us.

"Right now, I will interview the leading officer of our prisoners. If he has any knowledge of last night, it will be extracted from him.

"This base will be the new heart of Zhinu. Xin Beijing is gone. We will call this base Beijing Chongsheng."

Beijing Reborn. It was a bold name.

"Have your squadrons mobile and ready to move out by 1030hrs. The retaking of Zhinu has begun. Dismissed.

"And Captain Panchal," she added as the Captains made their way out. "Bring Oberst Schönebeck to my office."

————◄○►————

"Oberst," Ahuja said. "I am in no mood for pleasantries. Let's get right to the point. You know why you are here. And don't feign ignorance. I have learned that you know something of the Zhongwen language."

"Yes, Commodore," Schönebeck answered. In fluent English. "Last night."

Ignoring the revelation that her captive had withheld his command of the common language, Ahuja asked, "What was it?"

"I truly don't know," the Oberst began, "but I suspect it was the *Todeszerstörer*. The night was brighter than a summer's day. And it came from that direction."

"But it's too far away," demanded the Commodore.

"No Commodore, you underestimate the power capacity of our vessel. It is small compared to the interstellar ships of your time. But it is more powerful than any you have known."

"Did you do this?" It was the obvious question, and she shot it at him as an accusation.

The Oberst studied the military dignitary before him. She was covered in grime and dirt. The tracks down her cheeks showed that she had lost more than her heart was prepared to surrender. As incongruous as it may have seemed to the Commodore, he felt a genuine compassion for her.

"No, Commodore," he answered truthfully, "I did not. I do not know how it has come to be, but I do suspect I know what has caused the chaos you have been thrust into. The *Todeszerstörer* has exploded. Whether by accident or design, I cannot say. Your people, no doubt, were stationed there and had been commissioned with learning its secrets.

"It is more than a ship, Commodore. It is a weapon."

The Oberst sat back in his chair. Sadly, he looked into the eyes of his captor.

"Commodore, I grieve for your loss. I really do. But it had to happen. This colony is the reason why Earth has been destroyed and why there are but scant thousands of surviving humans left in the galaxy. Over the centuries, our species has caused the extinction of countless others on Earth. Here on Zhinu, we caused our own.

"I am ashamed for the way my crew terrorized helpless civilians, Commodore, but you must understand, we were sent here to kill them all. We had to. It was the only hope for the future of humanity. We had to make Zhinu the fear of all the Earth so that in the end, when eventually technology and science should finally realize the potential for folding space, and we would reach out to the stars, we would do so circumspectly, armed, and ready.

"Commodore, the Kjeldans are the foe. Humans are intelligent, but our intelligence is misinformed by our innocence. We are but children in the galaxy. Earth had to be schooled, taught to fear the worlds beyond.

"I am truly sorry for the losses on this world. And I grieve with you. I, too, have lost all that I loved. None of the people of Zhinu deserved death. But their death means the life of our shared humanity."

Commodore Ahuja poured a whiskey but did not offer one to her captive.

"You may have saved Earth," she mused, "but you have destroyed what it means to be human."

She watched the golden liquor as it swirled about the glass. Yenko had drunk from it just the day before, in the room next door. She would never drink again. Standing up, she threw the whiskey at Schönebeck.

"I deserve it, I know," he apologized.

Ahuja looked emptily at the man in the seat opposite her. He did look apologetic. Who was she to know what she would do if she was in his position? She had lost Yenko. How many had he lost? A whole world? A whole race? If his reckoning of future history was to be believed, a whole species . . . ?

"No," she sighed. "You don't deserve it. You're just following orders. I don't know. Maybe Zhinu is the beginning of all that is wrong with us. Maybe we've overstepped our bounds in reaching to the stars. I can't be your judge.

"But I don't know what to do with you. It would've been easier if you destroyed the planet outright when you first came. I don't know, Schöne-beck. Maybe we're all animals deserving of death. I'm tired. I've suffered losses that I don't want to deal with."

"Then go to the *Todeszerstörer*," he said. "Your answers lie there."

"You will come with me!" she ordered.

A knocking at the door interrupted them.

"Enter," the Commodore said.

An attaché poked his head round the door. "The Squadron Captains are here, ma'am."

"Tell them to take a seat. I will be with them presently."

Before long, she stood in front of the assembled military leaders, each of them eager for action, a chance to make someone pay for the atrocities of the night before.

"Alpha and Gamma Squadrons, take command of the Personnel Carriers. Ferry the surviving villagers back here to Beijing Chongsheng. Sort out accommodation for them. The military can bivouac in tents until we rebuild.

"Captain Bakshi, take the lead. Seek out the Science Officers of Delta Squadron. They may have intel on where to find survivors that you are unaware of. Take one of their number with you as guide. And find out why I can't make contact with Nirani on the *Zhinu Phoenix*.

"The rest of you, we are heading to the alien ship on the far side of Xin Beijing. We have had no news from our people there, and the Captain of the prisoners believes it is the origin of last night's disaster. He will come with us. We will see.

"Everyone, dismissed. We move out in fifteen minutes."

◄○►

The convoy descended into the crater towards the obliteration that once was Xin Beijing. No one uttered a word. Lightning bolts occasionally flashed across the blackened sky as if in threat to all who may venture further into Zhinu's apocalypse. In the lead was the Commodore's FAV. Her two attachés took the front seats, with Commodore Ahuja in the back. Beside her, unrestrained, sat the Oberst. The battle was over between them. Whoever or whatever was responsible for the mayhem, the SDS had no mission left to continue. It was time for a truce. The war crimes against the villagers would yet have to be atoned for, but for the moment, everything other than survival seemed meaningless.

The Oberst looked as shocked as everyone else at the wasteland they entered. But he had seen devastation on a planetary scale, and more than once.

"Dear God," he said in broken Mandarin. "Such a price. May this have saved us from the Kjeldans."

Ahuja studied the man beside her. The extremities of war. In another time, he would probably have been a scholar or artisan. In another time. That he was still here troubled the Commodore. She knew nothing of time travel, but she understood the paradox that the science philosophers of his time argued over. The Quantum Time Paradox, they called it. If the Oberst and his crew had been successful, the development of folded-space travel would have been slowed. The timeline would be altered, and potentially, the threat of the Kjeldans eliminated.

But that would also mean there was no Heldentat, no *Todeszerstörer*, no *Schild der Schwachen*, no mission to Zhinu, and therefore nothing to stop the discovery of travel through folded space. It was a never-ending time loop of cause and effect.

The Oberst caught her eye. "I'm sorry," he said in English. An apology for the tragic price that had been demanded of her, but not an apology for the tragedy itself.

"There will come a day when you will tell me your story," she said. "I need to understand what drives you so that I can make some sort of sense out of all of this."

Rain began to fall again as they carefully negotiated their way through the twisted, shattered ruins of Xin Beijing. A muddy rain. Full of the dirt and pulverized bones of the land about them.

Making their way cautiously through the flattened ruins that was once Xin Beijing, the came suddenly upon a convoy of LRVs making its way back to the Third Fleet's basecamp. The nine squadrons that had been sent to investigate the site of the *Todeszerstörer*.

"Report," the Commodore ordered Captain Shao, the leader of the reconnaissance mission.

"We have scoured the area, Commodore," Shao began, "but we were unable to find the *Todeszerstörer*. I'm not even sure we were in the right place."

"What do you mean?" demanded Ahuja.

"Nothing is as it should be," the Captain replied. "The land we explored is barren and nothing at all like what previous reports indicated. Without more accurate instrumentation, we cannot be sure we were where we had been directed. We were on our way back to base to make our report and receive fresh instruction."

Commodore Ahuja studied the Captain before her. He was a competent soldier, and she could not lightly dismiss his observations.

"Continue on, then," she said at length. "We will push on and confirm your findings."

As Squadrons Zeta through Lambda Two headed off into the east, Mannat Ahuja scoured the bleak landscape to her left. Somewhere out there, Yenko's laboratory had stood, his cabin in a lovely park nearby. And somewhere out there, his beautiful body lay buried unceremoniously beneath a ton of rubble.

It was the Oberst's fault. But at the same time, it was not. Emotionally, Mannat was spent. Numb to everything. She could not even feel anger for the man beside her.

At length, maybe an hour or more after leaving behind the wreckage of Xin Beijing, they made out the beginnings of the escarpment far to their right. But it looked nothing like they expected. In previous days, Commander Huang had reported a narrow landslide that formed a natural pathway up the side of the uncompromising cliff face. Now, there was only the remnant of the eastern end of the escarpment. It seemed like one of the gods had reached down and scooped away the entire plateau, sweeping it out of the way to the outer edges of the impact zone.

The going was difficult amidst the broken upheaval of the bedrock and not made at all any easier by the now torrential rain of muddy water that pelted down on them from the unforgiving roil of clouds above.

A voice came over the FAV's communicator. "Breaker, breaker, this is LRV Four. Commodore, come in."

The attaché riding passenger picked up the receiver. "Read you loud and clear, LRV Four. Over."

"These are the coordinates. Over."

The attaché looked in disbelief to the Commodore. There was nothing there. Not a thing. For miles. Just a low hill, a pimple in the heart of the great crater.

"Standby."

The Commodore's FAV pulled to a slow halt, the convoy fanning out around her, and the Third Fleet dismounted. Military protocol, for the most part, was lost. There was no point to be on high alert. There was no war. There was nothing.

14

Justice and Mercy

T HE REELING AND LURCHING of the ground seemed to last forever. In the pitch dark, Yenko found an alcove notched into the solid wall of his subterranean bunker. Figuring it would offer the greatest structural protection, he squatted on the floor and hugged his knees to himself. He was dreadfully afraid. Afraid for himself. Afraid for his friends. Afraid for Mannat.

There was no way to know when it would be safe to emerge from his shelter. The violent shaking soon abated, but periodically the earth above him quaked and rumbled as Xin Beijing continued slowly to collapse in the aftermath of the upheaval. With each shudder, Yenko froze, anticipating the dreadful moment when his world would collapse in around him.

Macpherson was spent. Adrenaline and fear had sapped his inner resources until finally, he succumbed to a fitful sleep. His dreams relentlessly assaulted him and stole away the recuperation he so desperately needed; mountains rained down about him, chasms opened below him, spewing out fumes and molten lava across Xin Beijing and swallowing him up. When he finally woke with a start, he was momentarily disoriented, uncertain of the utter blackness of his world and why he had slept huddled up in a concrete bunker.

And then he remembered. The bright light of detonation from the west. The bucking of the bedrock. The chaotic collapse of concrete and iron. The frantic dive for safety in the Linear Accelerator buried deep beneath the Nuclear Research Center. He had survived.

Now a new fear took him. Had his refuge become his tomb? The sudden panic disoriented him and for the moment, he forgot where he was in relation to the stairwell that led upwards and to freedom. Crawling on all fours, he felt for the walls and began to follow them round. Eventually, they would have to bring him to the doorway to the world above. With the raining down of collapsing buildings, however, there would be no way of knowing if the path was open to the surface.

There would be no search party; he knew that. And even if there was, there would be no way they would think to look under the ruins of the Nuclear Research Center. He would be given up for dead.

His thoughts strayed onto Mannat as he continued to shuffle his way around the pitch blackened room. Had she survived the catastrophe? She was marginally closer to the *Todeszerstörer*, where he suspected the blast had originated, but the mountains the Macpherson retreat nestled amongst could possibly have protected her. Undoubtedly, if she was alive, she would be pulling her resources together, marshalling the Third Fleet . . . if they still existed.

Five doorways opened off the room that had cocooned him from the terrible assault. Each time, a shot of adrenaline coursed through him as he anticipated what might lie above him in the stairwell beyond. And each time, he was both confused and disheartened as he realized the doorway led to other parts of the facility, not the way out.

Until the last door. In his disorientation, he had crawled about the room in the wrong direction, wasting precious moments finding the stairwell. As he opened the door, he was struck by the smell of concrete and coughed as he was engulfed by an unseen cloud of dust. This was it.

Half crouching, half standing, he started to ascend the stairs to their uncertain end. Still the world was in utter darkness. The first two turns of the stairwell were negotiated slowly, but easily enough and Yenko started to dare to hope. Perhaps all would be well and the path clear.

But with each new step, it seemed, the way forward became more and more ominous. Dirt and fine rubble crunched under his shoes. The higher he climbed, the larger the debris became. By the time he estimated he had ascended two floors, and was therefore nearing the surface, the wreckage all but filled the stairwell.

But there was light. The railing that had guided his path upward was of no use now. It had been severed from its mountings and hung crazily across his ascent. To one side, a great gash tore a jagged rip in the side of the stairwell. In the growing light, Yenko could make out more and more of the cement boulders and iron girders that had to be negotiated. A large section of the ceiling had caved in on the opening and angled upwards to the exit. It left only a foot of clearance, but it was enough for Yenko to scramble his way to freedom.

Lightning flashed and rumbled overhead. A light rain, muddy and gritty, fell around him. Yenko had stepped from his tomb into an apocalypse.

———◦———

The search of the erased site of the *Todeszerstörer*, where Captain Liu had been in charge only the day before, lasted only an hour. Quite simply, there was nothing to observe. Whatever had been there had literally been pulverized into a million pieces and hurled countless miles away by the incredible power of the ship's destruction.

The weapons the company had brought with them were futile. The crisis was complete and there was nothing anyone could do about it. In silence, the convoy now made its gruesome way back to base. There was still much to do. A world to bring together and a community to restore.

———◦———

Commodore Ahuja took daily reports, monitoring the progress of the twice devastated fledgling world. By the end of the first week after the explosion, makeshift housing had been established, and many of the farmers were back on the land, seeing what they could rescue of the next season's crops. They needed them. Within a month or so, there would be famine if they were not careful. And it would last until the following season at the very least.

The only crops that had any semblance of hope of producing a harvest were from those few farms in the northern forests, in the foothills of the mountains. It would not be enough, but it might just keep the community barely alive.

Communications had been restored, but the technicians could not determine why they were unable to establish an active link to the *Zhinu Phoenix*. Without it, there was no way of contacting Earth. Ahuja wondered how they would respond to this second mysterious silence from the New World Colony.

The problem of what to do with Oberst Schönebeck and his SDS remained. Ahuja looked out her office window. She could just see the corner of the Detention Center. It was a waste of manpower. There was need for them in the busy rebuilding of the new township of Beijing Chongsheng.

"Beijing Chongsheng," she mumbled. It was an arrogant name and she regretted making it official. The town rising up around her looked more like the living dead than a hope of a bright new world to come.

Yenko surveyed the desolation that was once the university complex. His cabin was destroyed, crushed, and thrown away as if it held no consequence before the power that swept Xin Beijing clean. As if Zhinu itself had conspired with the Oberst and sought to erase his memory from history.

"What to do?" he wondered aloud. He had no way of communicating with anyone. Or to even know if there was anyone left to communicate with. "Think, Macpherson. Think."

The sound of his voice was stabilizing. Over the years, he had become familiar with his muttering and mumbling. It centered him. Focused him. Enabled him to process whatever conundrum it was that he was working on.

And this was the greatest conundrum he had ever faced. His very life depended on it.

"First, water."

He would die within days without it. But where to get it? In his cabin, he had several flasks put aside, but who knew what had become of them? They were long gone. And he could hardly go and find a tap somewhere to get a drink. Instinctively, Yenko believed that if there were any survivors of the blast, they would be found far to the east, at the camp of the Third Fleet. It would take days to travel there by foot. But he had no choice.

And that meant he needed water.

There was always the hope that some of the farming communities on this western side of the river still stood. If that was true, he might feasibly find his way to safety in a day or so. But he could not trust to it.

Sections of the Kinematics building still stood and Yenko made the attempt to rummage through the surviving rooms. Perhaps he might come across something that could aid him in his quest for a safe haven. His search did not come up with anything that perfectly suited his need, but he did find a semi-intact terracotta vase. The rain outside, muddy as it was, pooled in crevices and depressions. It would not be pretty, but he would live.

For hours, he walked on into what he hoped was the east, his chipped vase of muddy water sloshing in his right hand. The ominous clouds above gave no real indication of where the sun was. It was daytime; that was about the best he could make of it. The path forward was difficult. He could not simply keep to one direction. Buildings, half tottering and threatening to collapse on him if he approached too closely, conspired to block the way at every turn.

In the end, he was not at all convinced he was heading in one direction. For all he knew, he could be walking in circles, hopelessly lost in the giant maze of destruction.

Periodically, Yenko's left hand throbbed. The bandage that was meant to protect the wound of his amputated fingers was dirty and ragged. He hoped infection had not set in. That would be the last thing he needed.

What confused him most was that the further he walked, the closer he came to a ridge that seemed to stretch on forever in front of him. Maybe as much as eight hundred feet high, he was unfamiliar with the landform.

"Surely not," he muttered. "A crater rim? My God, no! Is nothing left?"

From the top of the rise, he could make out the sea far to the south in the darkening light. At last, he had something to base his bearings on. He was perhaps further south than he had intended, and that gave him a new dilemma. Should he cut cross-country and make for the river or should he head south and make for the coast?

The landscape to the east was hilly and he was not sure he would be able to keep a straight easterly heading. He had already taken the best part of a day just to get through the city. Or what was left of it. But if he made for the coast, though he would know exactly where he was at all times, there would be no settlements. The farmlands where he might perhaps find help were to the east of him, not to the south.

"It's getting too dark," he muttered as he looked over the desolate world. "Can't see if anything's still standing. Shelter."

Once more, the clouds began to empty themselves over the for-lorn land. He did need to find shelter. Somewhere to sleep. His stomach gnawed away within him, reminding him that he had not eaten all day. There was nothing for it, however. It would be a miracle if he found food in this forsaken world.

Yenko made his way back down the rim of the blast crater towards the city. At least there, amongst the rubble of Xin Beijing, he could find somewhere to keep dry. It would not be a comfortable night.

The next morning, after a restless, cold night, Yenko filled his broken vase once more with the dirty waters lying about the city streets and made his way back up the ridge. The clouds still held thickly over the land, but rays of light forced their way through small gaps, helping him assess his best option forward.

It was not an easy decision. To the east, where the possibility of finding farming settlements lay, the landscape looked as if it had been flattened by a giant's rolling pin. Trees lay uniformly on the ground, beckoning him to follow their direction. It was unlikely that any of the wooden houses and barns of the villagers' farms had withstood the violence of the windstorm that had followed in the wake of the explosion.

And yet, he could see how far it was to the south that the coast lay. Once there, the going would be easy enough, but after crossing the river, he would have to travel a long way north again before reaching the Third Fleet. If they were there.

In the end, he decided for the direct route. Even if he got lost within the hills, none of them were so tall that he could not easily climb their heights and regain perspective. And, he considered, there just may be people out there yet.

It was perhaps the better choice. To the east of Xin Beijing, much of the land was clay based, and though the water was consistently muddy, there were frequent pools where he could replenish his dirty supply. But it was slow going. The clouds rolled in thicker than ever by the end of the second day, and he found it difficult to know which way was forward.

The third day, the land was so hilly that he seldom gained sufficient height to make out either the river, hopefully still before him, or the coast to the far south, or even the city behind him. He pressed on. He had to. He was cold. He was wet. He was exhausted. And he was starving. But he was alive.

Every now and then, Yenko would mutter to himself, conjecturing what had gone wrong. Nirani had something to do with it. She was the unpredictable factor in the whole equation. Perhaps it had something to do with her interface with the futuristic spacecraft.

"*We have trouble with Artificials also,*" Yenko could still hear the Oberst saying.

"Should have paid more attention," he muttered. "*Trouble with Artificials . . .* Maybe they're becoming sentient in his time."

The thought troubled Yenko. Nirani had waded through untold numbers of files and records. Perhaps she had picked up something of the sentience that existed in that distant future. Could she have been indoctrinated by the rationale behind the Heldentat imperative to the Oberst's SDS?

Halfway through the sixth day after his deliverance from the concrete tomb of the Nuclear Research Center, Yenko saw the unmistakable signs of the river some miles ahead of him. Weakly he made his way to it. Even from his current position, he could see there were trees that still stood at the river's edge, far enough away from the epicenter of the explosion to have survived the ordeal. They stood resolutely, a symbol of hope for the colony on Zhinu.

Night fell as he stumbled off the flood plain and down the riverbank. He had seen no meaningful sign anywhere of human life or habitation. Nothing except scattered sheets of twisted roofing and the torn timbers and panels of houses. Nothing. The world had been swept clean. Now as he considered the far side of the river, his heart sank in despair that he would find anyone alive anywhere.

He was the last man on Zhinu. Swooning with fatigue, he fell into a deep sleep.

———◦———

A week had passed since the fatal night. Two of the villagers who had survived the catastrophe that destroyed their beloved community, a husband and wife, had decided to weave a net and ply themselves to fishing in the tidal flow of the river. They had lost their only son in the aftermath of the explosion and needed time away from the other survivors, their neighbors, who themselves were grieving their own losses. There was just too much suffering around them, and they sought solace in each other's company, alone by the stillness of the river.

Morning had broken an hour before, if morning it could be called. The ominous, dark clouds that had remained all week still hung threateningly above them, raising fears that they would never leave. Casting their drift nets out across the water, they followed the current, drawing the nets in every few minutes and picking out any fish they had managed to catch.

"What's that?" the woman asked.

Across the river, a body lay sprawled beside a jumble of reeds.

"Don't look, my love," the man replied. "It is one of our people. I will swim over and lay him or her to rest. It has been a week now. The sight will not be a pleasant one and you have enough nightmares than to add another."

The woman cried. It reminded her of the loss of her own dear son.

"No," she said. "If it was our own boy, you would want him to be honored and not shunned. I will come with you."

And so they waded out to the deeper waters of the river and swam across to the other side.

"He's alive!" yelled the man in excitement. "Quick, Hui Yin. He's alive!"

———◦———

A commotion ran through the camp. Someone had been found alive by the river. It had been two whole days since they had found the last survivor and it renewed everyone's hope. A medical team and two soldiers were directed to the spot. By lunchtime, they were racing their way back to the Medical Center.

"Breaker, breaker. LRV Beta Five to base, come in."

"Base here, LRV Beta Five. Read you loud and clear. Report. Over."

"It's Macpherson, Base. Over."

"Macpherson! Say again, LRV Beta Five. Over."

"You read me loud and clear, Base. We have Macpherson Yenko. He's alive. Inform the Commodore. ETA fifteen minutes. Over."

———◦———

Commodore Ahuja busily pored through the morning reports, assessing priorities and determining actions that needed to be taken in those areas where they were falling behind schedule. A heavy knocking banged on the door.

"Come in before you break the door down," she said, not kindly. She did not need the incessant interruptions that kept coming across her desk.

Major Das, her most senior attaché burst into the room.

Before the Commodore could make any comment, he blurted out, "He's alive, Commodore. Macpherson! They've found him!"

A surge of adrenaline shot through Mannat's veins, and she involuntarily jumped to her feet.

"Yenko? Where?"

———◄◦►———

Commodore Ahuja ran to the Medical Center, where she knew he would be taken first for examination. It caused a commotion amongst those nearby. Never had they seen their Senior Commanding Officer run like that. By the time the LRV entered the compound, quite a crowd had gathered, uncertain as to what they expected to see.

Mannat bit her bottom lip. She could see a doctor in the back of the LRV holding a drip high in his hand. But she could not see Yenko, who was clearly lying down beside the doctor.

The crowd parted, making way for the vehicle as it headed straight to the entrance of the Medical Center. There, a team of doctors and nurses had a hospital stretcher ready to receive their patient, miraculously brought back to them from among the dead.

Mannat watched as Yenko was wheeled past her, covered in grime. His eyes seemed to swim in their sockets above sunken cheeks. He showed no signs of recognition of anyone, but he was alive. The Commodore wanted to follow him into the examination room, but she was denied.

"Commodore," one of the Senior Nurses said, "he's going to live. We'll call you when he comes to."

She left in a mix of emotions. Yenko was alive.

———◄◦►———

"Are you allowed to have a whiskey?" Mannat asked.

Yenko had been kept in observation overnight but had been released the following afternoon. Now, as he sat in Mannat Ahuja's private lounge, he suddenly realized how greatly he had cheated death.

He looked at the woman before him. She had a complex look about her. What had she endured? What had she learned of the *Todeszerstörer*? What had become of the villagers? Of the Third Fleet? Of Li Jie and his wife, of Fei Hung and Lakshay?

"I'd love one," he confessed. "But you'd better fill it up. I want to hear all that has happened."

It was a long afternoon. The Commodore would not begin her story until Yenko told her how he came to be alive, how he had beaten the total destruction of Xin Beijing. She told him how she had come looking for him, how together with Fei Hung and Lakshay they had scoured the university precinct, looking for any sign at all of him.

"But you were three floors underground!" she smiled, tears of gratitude streaming down her face. "We probably hadn't been long gone when you finally emerged."

It was a sobering thought. If he had woken an hour or two earlier, he would have been saved the ordeal of his trek from the city. But he was safe now. And he was thankful.

Mannat gave a report on the state of affairs with the New World Colony and the Third Fleet. Yenko was shocked at the death toll, though not surprised. He simply nodded when she described the epicenter of the crater. The utter devastation and erasure of even the land itself.

"I knew it was the *Todeszerstörer*," he said. "It was Nirani, wasn't it?" It was not really a question.

The Commodore took a mouthful from her drink and sighed deeply. "I don't know," she said at length. "She won't talk to us from the *Phoenix*."

"I'm not surprised."

"You're not surprised? How can you not be surprised?"

"It's the *Todeszerstörer*," he replied. "I think AIs are becoming sentient on Heldentat. I think the databases of the *Todeszerstörer* contain the framework for that sentience. Manu, I think Nirani is no longer Nirani. Not the Nirani we know, at least. I think she's been indoctrinated by the subroutines, commands, and mission rationale of a future world."

"*Tatti!*" the Commodore swore. "I'll set up a meeting with the Oberst tomorrow. I've learned he speaks English. He kept that nicely from us. Anyway, we can explore our options tomorrow. But the afternoon is wearing on, and I'm getting tired, Yenko. Let's talk about something lighter, shall we? Stay here and I'll order dinner to be brought to us."

Yenko smiled at her as he finished his drink. "I'd like that."

It was an enjoyable evening, amid the craziness and chaos of Zhinu that would not leave them alone.

———◦———

The next day, a formal meeting was arranged. The Commodore, her two attachés, all senior military and scientific personnel, and the Oberst of the SDS with three of his senior officers gathered together around a large table in the center of the Main Debriefing Hall. Various Commanders, technicians, and village leaders sat around the outside of the gathering. They were allowed to listen in on the discussions, since everyone was affected, and everyone had a stake in the outcome.

Yenko studied the group about him, considering the many strengths and expert knowledge they brought to the table. Several of those present had their eyes fixed on the Oberst and his officers, two men and a woman. In many ways, everyone in the room saw these as the enemy. What the colony was to do with the SDS, the *Schild der Schwachen*, needed to be decided.

From a seat in the outer circles, Li Jie eyed the man who had almost killed him. It had been a grim and bloody fight, and if not for the weaponry concealed within the foreigner's green suit, the outcome would have been different. Yet in a strange way, he respected the tall, fair headed man. He was a warrior. A leader. A fighter. And one to be feared.

Fei Hung, along with Li Lin Wei, the village leader who had first met Commodore Ahuja after the landing of the Third Fleet, sat in places of prominence alongside the senior military personnel. This was as much their table as anyone else's and the survivors of the original New World Colony were granted representation.

At length, the Commodore opened the meeting.

"With deference to Li Lin Wei," she began, "it is obvious I have assumed command of the colony. We are in the aftermath of war and until the community is stabilized, we need military leadership. There will come a time when I yield command but until then, I want to acknowledge your own leadership, Mr. Li."

The man bowed humbly.

"And now for matters at hand. I have three objectives that I seek input on . . .

"How to establish communications with Earth now that we no longer have external access to the *Zhinu Phoenix*.

"What to do with the prisoners in the Detention Center.

"And how to understand the treachery of Nirani."

In this way, the meeting began. Much was said concerning the difficulties associated with interstellar communication and that Earth was beyond their reach, but there was no wisdom offered that could potentially help them. A hand shot up from the second row of the gallery. It was Lakshay Varma.

"Varma, do you have something to add?" the Commodore asked. "God knows we need it."

"Please, sir. If I may, sir. Ma'am, I'm sorry. I don't think we need the *Phoenix*. Not for communication, at least, sir. Ma'am. Sorry, sir. Ma'am!"

"Explain."

"Earth communicates with us directly from the Space Control Center in Xianggang. But they could do that from five or six facilities if they wished."

"What's your point?" demanded Ahuja. "We know that."

"My point is, ma'am, they don't communicate with us via the Tiangong Space Station. We don't need the *Phoenix*. All we need is a communications center powerful enough to beam directly from Zhinu."

Puzzled looks from the whole room were directed at the young man. If he was intimidated by it, none of them would have known.

"The mountain research facility, ma'am. The Gravimetric Discriminator. It would not be out of the realms of possibility to reconfigure its mainframe. Give us five months and I think we can have visual contact with Xianggang. Three if we just want audio. And two if we want text."

Ahuja looked at the chief technicians around the table. "Can it be done?" she asked.

As Lakshay had been addressing the audience, three of them had already started making notes and examining files on their electronic notepads. They had seen where he was headed.

Presently, after a brief conference within their ranks, one of them said, "Varma speaks ambitiously, Commodore. But much of the physical apparatus that establishes the Discriminator could be used to open communications with Earth. His timelines are questionable, perhaps, but his suggestion holds merit. We think he's onto something. It's worth pursuing."

"Good!" The Commodore looked pleased. "Varma, if we pull this off, we have a debt of gratitude to you."

Lakshay beamed and looked proudly towards Fei Hung. She seemed as pleased and proud as him.

They moved onto the second item on the agenda; what to do with the prisoners. A heated and tense debate followed. Many called for the public trial and execution of the SDS. They were responsible for brutal and heinous crimes. Well over a hundred villagers and soldiers of the

Third Fleet had died in the liberation of Gui Difang and countless others had been murdered in the decades following the tragic accident of 2347. Fei Hung herself was animated in the discussion. She wanted blood.

Others argued against the death penalty; it was an inhuman penalty that had been outlawed on Earth hundreds of years earlier. To execute the soldiers of the SDS was to return to a barbaric past.

Yet again others, notably those from amongst the military, defended the soldiers. They were following orders. They had come from a dire future that no one could understand. And without such intimate knowledge, no one was in a place to judge. Soldiers of the SDS had signed up for a suicide mission. The desperation that fueled that decision could not be lightly dismissed or judged.

Still others argued from pure pragmatics. They could not afford to have so many people in detention. Townships needed to be rebuilt. Crops had to be sown. Livestock had to be rounded up. There was simply too much to do. Despite the injustice of having guilty people walk free, the community needed all hands on deck.

Throughout it all, the Oberst and his officers remained silent.

"What do you have to say for you and those under your command?" the Commodore asked him.

"I have nothing to say in defense of my actions that I have not already said to you in private, Commodore. Earth is dead. All our colonies are dead. Heldentat is dead. It is of little importance what you decide. All is lost.

"We came from the future to save the Earth. We failed. If we die, we die. We are dead anyway."

"If I may," interrupted Li Lin Wei, rising to his feet. "We have a custom on Zhinu, long held since the earliest days of our colony."

The room became quiet. Li was a respected leader, an elder in the community. He had lived through the catastrophe of 2347. And he was perhaps the oldest person in the room, something that demanded respect and honor.

"It has long been our belief that incarceration neither reforms the guilty nor makes true retribution to the innocent. It is not the way of our people here on Zhinu." He held Fei Hung with his eyes, eyes that spoke of passion and sorrow and hope and healing. "If I was the leader, Commodore, and I respect that I am not and agree entirely with your taking command over our crisis . . . but if I was the leader, I would have a Ceremony of Justice and Mercy."

A hushed murmur went up from those villagers who were in the gallery.

"I don't understand," Ahuja said, voicing the ignorance of the greater majority of those present in the room.

"We are too small," the old man began, "to deal with such a giant matter. The crime is too great. We cannot pretend it did not happen; that would compound the injustice against the innocent. And yet we cannot exercise a judgment of a proportion weighty enough to balance the crime. That would dehumanize us.

"Oberst, what you have done is beyond our capacity for judgment. There is no recompense that will assuage the grief and loss of my people. There is no punishment that will bring back the years taken from us. Whatever we do, we will always carry the wound and the loss. There are none of us in our whole community that is unaffected by your people's crimes. But we understand something of the need that drove you."

"What are you proposing?" the Commodore asked.

"Our whole people will come together as one. With your people also, Oberst. We will each tell our stories. Of the loved ones lost. Of the nightmares and fears. And your SDS will hear and look on the faces they have injured.

"And Oberst, your people will tell their stories. Not to justify what they have done. But to bring closure. You will tell of your crimes. The people you tortured. Those you killed. Where they lie. You will tell your stories of personal despair that led you to accept your mission.

"Commodore, we will tell our stories. And all will attend. And all will listen. And none will interject. And none will condemn.

"It will take many days, Commodore. And we will end with a Ceremony of Reconciliation. Though the pain and loss will remain, the injured will relinquish their demand for justice and will grant forgiveness to the guilty. The Ceremony will end with a symbolic meal and we will move on. Together."

The room sat in silence, considering the enormity of what the old man was suggesting.

"Is this the way of your people?" Ahuja asked.

"It is our way." Turning to Fei Hung, he held out his hand and took hers. "My daughter, it is our way."

Fei Hung wept and wept, embracing the old man as if he was the father she had lost so long ago. The strength of his arms, the compassion of his wisdom, enabled her to let go. It would not be easy. But she would be brave and face the future together with such as him.

"Yes, father," she said through a wash of tears.

Ahuja surveyed the room. No one moved. No one made a sound. It was a holy moment.

"I do not think it is appropriate to continue the meeting at this point," she said. "We will reconvene at 1400hrs to discuss the matter of Nirani. You are all dismissed."

———◄○►———

The hours rolled on. Presently, they were once more in conference to discuss the implications surrounding Nirani and to give the Commodore guidance on how she should frame her report of the AI when communications with Earth would finally be reestablished.

They all agreed that something had happened to Nirani's algorithmic parameters in the extended interface with the *Todeszerstörer*. Yenko informed them all that the Oberst had said in a previous interview that AIs in his time were unpredictable. Assuming the technology of the mid-twenty-eighth century was more advanced than their own, Yenko argued that unpredictability could not be the consequence of poor engineering, but the result of its sophistication.

"If Nirani somehow started to become self-aware," he asked Oberst Schönebeck, "as I think has probably happened, what did she read in your files that could account for her behavior?"

The Oberst thought for a while and conferred with his senior officers.

"*Unser Militärbefehle*," the female officer suggested. The others seemed to agree.

Oberst Schönebeck addressed the Commodore. "She had access to the *Todeszerstörer*. Your AI technology is advanced in your day. There was nothing she could not review, not even my own personal logs. Perhaps the most important would be our *Militärbefehle*. They are our mission orders. They contain a brief overview of the historical wars with Kjeld and the rationale for searching through our own histories to determine what we could do to alter that history and avert human contact with the Kjeldans."

"Well that's it!" declared Yenko. "The same force of argument that convinced you and the SDS to enlist in your suicide mission indoctrinated her.

"Commodore, Nirani has likely taken it upon herself to complete the mission. You heard her threats against me. She believes I am the cause of us discovering how to fold space-time before we are ready. Somehow she blew the ship up."

The Oberst interrupted. "There is a secure code, accessible only by myself and these three of my senior officers with me. If what you say is true, she set the *Todeszerstörer* to self-destruct. It was no accident caused by any of your people in their investigations."

"It explains why she refuses communication with us," the Commodore suggested. "But what is she doing up there on the *Phoenix*?"

"The mission's not over," Yenko said. "Don't you see? She thinks she killed me, so that objective is achieved. But she knows that I've been collaborating with Earth in relation to the Gravimetric Discriminator. They are already aware of Multidimensional Werner Contractions. She can't stop that. The mission is still alive."

"What will she do?" one of the Captains across the table asked. "How will she pursue her objective?"

"I don't know," Yenko confessed. "She can hardly go and wage war on Earth. Her mission is to save it."

"Kjeld!" Oberst Schönebeck said. "How much physical control does she have over your starship's construction?"

"Total," a technician said. "She has an arsenal of robots and equipment that can remake any and every part of the *Phoenix*. Given time and material, she could build another *Phoenix* altogether."

"Then that is what she is doing," the Oberst affirmed. "She is not going to wage war on Earth as Mekförsen has reasoned, Commodore. She is going to Kjeld. What she hopes to do there, I do not know. But if your ship is as large as our histories suggest it is, she has raw materials enough to construct more than a starship. She can reproduce our chronometric power sources. All she needs is time to make the necessary transformation.

"God have mercy on us. I do not believe she can destroy Kjeld. If she does not have a rational plan, she will teach them to hate Earth . . . And seek out humans across the galaxy . . ."

"There might yet be one hope for our future," the Commodore suggested. All eyes bent towards her. "We have you with us, Oberst. Zhinu is once more in silence as far as Earth is concerned. Once we reestablish communications, we can call a meeting with the leaders of Zhongguo Xin Shijie and Bhaarat Ekata. You say they are currently engaged in espionage. It would not surprise me. But they will certainly sit together around a table that offers to explain everything that pertains to Zhinu.

"And if we can do that, we can bring the force of your argument to Earth itself. All may not be lost. If we can get both governments to consider the dangers of first contact with alien species, we can most certainly change the trajectory of history."

———◄O►———

Two weeks after the destruction of the *Todeszerstörer*, the holographic form of Nirani sat at the command center of the *Zhinu Phoenix*'s flight deck. The AI had been hard at work. No longer was she the golden Zhongwen hologram; the holographic emitters had been readjusted to a dark green. Clothed now in the uniform of the SDS, she looked a female counterpart of the Oberst as she sat in command of the *Zhinu Phoenix*.

Monitors at every control station showed that the ship's AI was busily engaged with multiple systems throughout the vessel. Suddenly, her attention was captured by a monitor at the communications board. As Commodore Ahuja and the leaders of the surviving colonists were meeting together in conference to discuss ways forward for the community, Nirani had set up a covert link with Earth to monitor the Zhongwen and Bhaarateey governments' response to the new blackout from Zhinu.

She stood to her feet and walked to the communications display. The holographic woman made as if to switch and adjust various dials. Though the image of light that represented her could not interact with the instrumentation, they turned and flicked of their own accord. Nirani, the real Nirani, the Artificial Intelligence that formed the core of the sophisticated technology of the *Zhinu Phoenix*, had complete control over every system and every console.

She had captured a news broadcast relevant to the Zhinu expedition. Removing her helmet, she replayed the report in full. Her spiked hair blew in an unseen, unreal breeze.

Newsflash: Zhinu Crisis Update

A reporter sat behind a studio desk, high resolution satellite surveillance images of Zhinu on the screen behind her.

"Government attention continues to focus on the communication blackout that has once more descended on the remote stellar colony on Zhinu. Glimpses of the colony itself have only been sporadic as a thick cloud covers much of the northern hemisphere. Probe imagery has revealed that the *Zhinu Phoenix*, the vessel of the Third Fleet that departed Earth on Wu Yue 15, 2358, is alight with activity. Hopes are high that there is no threat to the off-world colony and that the cause of the communications failure is being addressed by the *Phoenix's* onboard AI.

"In other news, Macpherson Yenko, the famed Quantum Physicist from the separatist Scot Province who is part of the Third Fleet expedition on Zhinu, has been awarded in absentia the coveted Heisenberg Prize for his radical breakthrough work in what is known as Multidimensional Werner Contractions, first postulated by scientists on Zhinu half a century ago.

"For more we cut to our Chief Science Reporter, Zhang Guozhi..."

With a flick of a holographic hand, the volume was muted.

"Scheiße," Nirani swore, tapping her holographic fingers on the console as if considering her next move.

She was about to head back to the command chair when something else in the silent report caught her attention. The presenter was back on screen with an image of the Zhongwen flag behind her. Nirani turned the volume on, though there was no need; the AI was linked to every system and aware of every input.

"... leaked report from a government insider," the presenter was saying, "has revealed that the People's State Council is considering relocating dissidents from the separatist Provinces. With the future possibilities of Macpherson's formulation of Multidimensional Werner Contractions before us, there are moves within the Council to resolve the ongoing political division that plagues our borders."

Nirani had heard enough. In an apparent rage, she threw her holographic helmet at the screen and it went blank. Taking composure of herself, she walked back to the Command Chair. As she did so, she divided into eight holographic forms of herself. In each case, her hair was different. Eight separate iterations of the holographic armored woman.

Two of them remained on the Command Deck and plied themselves to the operation of the central hub of the *Zhinu Phoenix*.

Four holographic versions of Nirani appeared in the Engine Room, setting a flurry of activity into motion amongst the plethora of remote-controlled machines and robots that formed the backbone of her hardware.

A solitary form of Nirani manned the Medical Center and commenced directing five robots, busily engaging them in establishing a new laboratory.

In the Central Navigation Control Room, she sat before a wall panel that displayed star chart after star chart. She was searching for something.

―――――◄◦►―――――

Yenko walked beside the Commodore as they climbed the crater rim that looked over the desolate remains of the once prosperous and hope-filled Xin Beijing. She had taken to wearing civilian clothing these days. It had been almost a year since the detonation of the *Todeszerstörer* that crippled the New World Colony. Though the work was demanding, and everyone was gainfully employed in the reconstruction of Beijing Chongsheng, the two had found time for their relationship to develop.

"Such a waste," Mannat said. Neither of them had looked over the ruinous crater since that terrible moment of time they wished they could erase.

Yenko held her hand. There was nothing for him to say. Down there, he had almost died. He still had nightmares of cement and earthquakes and coffins.

Varma's idea of converting the Gravimetric Discriminator to make contact with Earth had proved effective, and within the timeframes he had predicted. Collaborative work was now well underway between the Zhongguo Xin Shijie and Bhaarat science establishments. The postulation of Multidimensional Werner Contractions, MDWCs as they were coming to be known, had opened up untold possibilities in the advancement of galactic colonization.

The meeting with the global leaders, one of the first communications established between Earth and Zhinu, in which Commodore Ahuja introduced them to Oberst Schönebeck, had not gone well at first. His revelation of the secret Zhongwen armaments destabilized the mutual cordiality that existed between the two world leaders. If not for the strength of the German's passionate plea, the meeting would have disintegrated.

But the Oberst argued through the historical realities of their tensions and where they would lead. The Cloaked Wars. Both leaders were familiar with the clandestine investigations they perpetrated against the other. It was a difficult meeting, but finally, Priyansh Chakrabarti, the Prime Minister of Bhaarat Ekata, and Wu Wang Shu, President of Zhongguo Xin Shijie, shook hands and agreed to the wisdom of the future.

The Peace Accords that Oberst Schönebeck's history told were signed in 2415 became a reality in 2361. A new Global Order came into being. And one that was now aware of the dangers that existed out there in the galaxy at large.

"Manu, I think it may be possible to stop Nirani." The two had been sitting on the crater rim for a long while. Little had been said. There was little to say.

Mannat studied the man beside her. He was a genius. In Schönebeck's words, a man ahead of his time. She believed it. The AI had long ago disappeared. Where the *Phoenix* was, no one could say, but it no longer orbited Zhinu.

"It's been too long," she said. "She could be anywhere, doing anything."

"I know," Yenko affirmed. "But I still think she can be stopped."

Mannat leaned over and kissed him. "Well then," she said, standing to her feet, "come on. We've got work to do."

15

Qi Yue 2, 2437

F OR FOUR DECADES, THE holographic forms of Nirani worked on a
transformational rebuild of the *Zhinu Phoenix*. Two weeks after she
had commissioned the autodestruct sequence of the *Todeszerstörer* in the
conviction that Räuber Mekförsen would be killed, and, in that way, accomplish the glorious mission to save Earth and its galactic colonies, she
had set a course away from Zhinu. She knew what she had to do, and she
did not want the prying eyes of Earth looking over her shoulder.

Though it was all but a mathematical certainty that Mekförsen had
died in the world-shattering blast she had caused, she could not assume
that he had not already done enough to set the historical trajectory of
science in motion. He may well be dead, but Nirani had learned that he
had been credited nonetheless as a key figure in the science of Multidimensional Werner Contractions.

The success of the mission was now in Nirani's hands. Since that
time forty years earlier, her green holographic form sat at multiple control stations throughout the *Zhinu Phoenix*, overseeing and directing the
radical rebuild of the ship. The Centrifugal Gravity Rotators, so necessary
for housing the thousands of cryostatic chambers of the Third Fleet, had
been dismantled, the hardware and sophisticated machinery reassembled
elsewhere and for other purpose.

Pulsating red light filled the Engine Room. At its heart, a new engine, totally unlike the one that had once powered the *Zhinu Phoenix*, emanated a power far beyond its predecessor. Whole sections of the central spine of the ship were reconfigured, housing power sources and engines that could only be guessed at.

On the Flight Deck, every chair was filled by the green battle-ready image of Nirani.

In four languages—German, Zhongwen, Bhaarateey, and English—she gave her commands that sounded throughout the entire vessel on every intercom.

"Spatial Navigation: set a course for Kjeld.

"Chronometric Navigation: set your target for t minus three hundred and fifty years.

"Tactical Station: prepare to arm all weaponry on my mark.

"Biological Laboratories: prepare for war."

—The End—

Glossary

Main Characters

Arushi Jain—Zhinu colleague of Mahika Khatri, responsible for the destruction of Xin Beijing

Fei Hung—Angel of Death from Gui Difang

Huang Li Jie—Commander, member of Delta Squadron

Jörn Schönebeck—Oberst of the SDS, soldiers of Heldentat

Lakshay Varma—Bhaarateey technician

Li Lin Wei—village leader

Liu Wang Yong—Captain of Chi One Squadron

Macpherson Yenko—Scottish Theoretical Quantum Physicist

Mahika Khatri—Zhinu scientist, responsible for the destruction of Xin Beijing

Mannat 'Manu' Ahuja—Commodore of the Third Fleet

Priyansh Chakrabarti—Prime Minister of Bhaarat Ekata

Wu Wang Shu—President of Zhongguo Xin Shijie

Yang Zhi Ruo—Captain of Delta Squadron

Yu Yan Macpherson—Zhinu villager, later to become Huang Yu Yan, wife of Huang Li Jie

Zhou Li Qiang—the Director of the Astronomical Union in Xianggang

Zhongwen (Chinese) Names and Phrases

Note: by the mid-twenty-fourth century, intonations and forms of the Chinese language had simplified

Bai chi—idiot

Ban pingzi cu—person with limited professional expertise (literally: half-empty bottle of vinegar)

Beijing Chongsheng—Beijing Reborn

Beijing shijian—Beijing time

Bi zui—shut up

Chusheng—animal

Daxue—university

Deguo—Germany

Deyu—German

Diu lian—a disgrace (literally: discarded face)

Huoyan xieshen—cruel person (literally: evil spirit)

Gali ren—Indian (derogatory, sounds like curry; curry people)

Gui Difang—Home of Evil Spirits

Gui sunzi—bastard (literally: turtle grandson)

Ma dao cheng gong—may you immediately meet with success

Qi Yue—the month of July

Qu si—go die

San Yue—the month of March

Wang ba—son of a bitch

Wu Yue—the month of May

Xianggang—Hong Kong

Xiao tu zaizi—little brat (literally: little rabbit kitten)

Xin Beijing—New Beijing

Xin Shijie—New World

Yang guizi—foreign devil

Zazhong—half breed

Zhinu—Chinese name for the star Vega

Zhongguo—China

Zhongguo Xin Shijie—China New World

Zhongwen—Chinese

Bhaarateey (Indian) Names and Phrases

Bhaarat—India

Bhaarat Ekata—India Unity

Jarman—German

Tatti—shit

Ullu ke pathe—idiot (literally: son of an owl)

Abbreviations

AI—Artificial Intelligence

CAV—Combat Artillery Vehicle

CME—Coronal Mass Ejection

DDS—Direct Digital Synthesis (commonly used for generating test signals)

FAV—Fast Action Vehicle

FM—Frequency Modulated

GPS—Global Positioning System

LRV—Light Reconnaissance Vehicle

MDWC—Multidimensional Werner Contraction

NDA—Non-Disclosure Agreement

PGPD—Power Grid Profile Data

SDS—Schild der Schwachen, i.e. Shield of the Weak

XS—Xin Shijian, New (World) Time